MW01136423

FLYING HIGH

DIARY OF A FLIGHT ATTENDANT

BY

RUBY JEANS JACKSON

1663 Liberty Drive, Suite 200
Bloomington, Indiana 47403
(800) 839-8640
www.AuthorHouse.com

This book is a work of fiction. People, places, events, and situations are the product of the author's imagination. Any resemblance to actual persons, living or dead, or historical events, is purely coincidental.

First published by AuthorHouse 01/10/05

ISBN: 1-4208-9343-2(sc)
ISBN: 1-4208-9342-4 (dj)

Library of Congress Control Number: 2005909237

Printed in the United States of America
Bloomington, Indiana

This book is printed on acid-free paper.

To my mother, Liza Jeans Porter (1932 -2004) and my beloved

Grandmother, Bessie Scott Jeans (1898 - 1987)

They were strong, smart and beautiful. I strive to be just like them.

They raised me good.

No matter how high I fly, I'll always be looking

up to you

Acknowledgments

First, I would like to thank God for blessing me with the greatest job in the world and giving me the ability to write about it. To my mother, Liza Porter, my biggest inspiration; she died before the book was completed. Thanks to my copy editor, April Robinson, for being there, whenever I needed help, and for believing in me. Also, Rachel Foster, for reading the first draft and encouraging me to continue. A special thanks to my flight attendant friends: Julia Cox Martin, Bettie Boyd-Tealer, Frankie Myrick, Terry Taylor and others, who did not want their names mentioned, for helping me keep it real; and last, but not least, to all flight attendants who still dare to remember the good ol' days.

Prologue

September 3, 2003

The passenger door closed, and the aircraft pushed back from the gate. I picked up the interphone to start the public-address announcements:

"Good afternoon, ladies and gentlemen, welcome aboard Elite World Airlines, Flight 101 to Paris. My name is Amanda Callaway Mitchell, your onboard-leader........."

I stopped abruptly when I realized that what I said into the microphone was not the same thing coming out over the PA system. Candia Fisher, the first-class flight attendant, came hurrying from the forward galley.

"Amanda, we're going to Paris, not Rio de Janeiro," she whispered to me.

Usually it's nothing to worry about, just an honest mistake flight attendants sometimes make, but today, it was different.

"I'm sure I said Paris," I said, confused.

I looked out into the cabin. The passengers were all looking at me, waiting for me to make the correction, so they could relax again.

My eye was caught by a very old man sitting right in front of me in seat 1C. He was staring at me, it seemed, with piercing, sad eyes that unnerved me. I backed into the corner between the passenger door and the first-class coat closet. I needed to calm down and pull myself together, out of the view of passengers.

I had been at the boarding door during the entire boarding process, I knew that. And, of course, I had greeted each passenger.

"I do not remember that old man boarding," I muttered to myself.

I peeped around the corner to get a better look at him, but he had moved. His seat was empty.

"Where did he go?" I asked Candia, who was still watching me, worriedly. "He had to come by me to get to the lavatory. Besides, he should not be walking around the cabin while the aircraft's taxiing. He needed to be in his seat with his seatbelt fastened."

"Amanda, are you all right?" asked Maggie, another crewmember who had joined us.

"What happened to the old man in seat 1C?" I wanted to know.

They stared at the empty seat, then back at me, then at each other.

"There was no old man in that seat. That's the only empty seat on the entire airplane." Candia kept her voice low.

"Are you sure?" I asked, louder than I intended.

"Amanda, what's wrong?" Maggie said.

"Amanda, are you all right?" asked Candia.

I had to read their lips: I could no longer hear them over the loud ringing in my ears. My heart was pounding, and I could hardly breathe. I was frightened and started to hyperventilate. I cannot be having a nervous breakdown, not here in front of my crew and all these passengers. The old man has put a spell on me!

I slid to the floor and put my hand over my ears to block out the sound, but the ringing got louder and louder, closer and closer. Now all I could hear was a telephone ringing and ringing and ringing...

One

I woke up in a cold sweat, with the phone ringing next to my bed. I couldn't shake the image of the old man. He had been in my dreams before, always sitting, never standing, sometimes happy, and other times very sad. He was old enough to be my great-grandfather, but I felt I knew him. What a crazy nightmare!

I was disoriented, and my mind couldn't decide if I was in London, Munich, or Madrid. It was too early for our wake-up call; maybe Crew Operation was calling to say our flight was cancelled. The phone continued to ring. Realizing I was at home in my own bed, I relaxed a little.

I picked up the receiver automatically. Before I could get my wits about me and say hello, someone screamed my name. "Amanda! Amanda! Are you awake? Amanda! Are you all right?"

"I'm fine," I said when I found my voice.

"What took you so long to answer the damn phone?"

"I was having an awful dream," I responded.

"Ooh, excuse me, I thought you and Bob were having a good fuck. You're breathing hard," the voice giggled. "Too bad it was only a dream."

I recognized the thick, husky voice right away: Dominique Van Stinchcomb.

"Your head is always in the gutter." I regained myself quickly.

Dominique was Dutch, spoke several other languages, and had a distinct accent; no one talked quite as she did. We'd been friends for thirty years, with so many ups and downs, and I knew her voice very well. Today, it was lively and energized, hardly pausing to breathe. In my experience, this meant only one thing: she had met a man, and the sex was good, though not necessarily in that order.

"I'm awake," I said, still groggy. I had to remind myself it was only dream, a nightmare.

"What time is it? I swapped trips. I have to fly to *Rio* tonight."

"I know, I checked your schedule because I needed to talk to you before you left. Girl! I flew with an old friend of yours." Her husky voice took on a provocative tone, and I knew I was right.

The clock on my nightstand said nine o'clock. My husband and daughter were gone; they usually left at eight thirty. I had been sleeping so hard, I didn't hear them leave.

"Calm down, Dominique, breathe, before you have a heart attack." I propped myself up on the pillow and forgot about the dream. "Now, tell me who you flew with, and are you sure he's a friend of mine?"

"Captain Franco Bordeaux!" she squealed, almost as if she was having an orgasm. I had to jerk the phone away from my ear; I was wide awake after that.

"Captain Franco!" I echoed. I was surprised because I had not seen him in years. He had fucked hundreds of flight attendants, and no one ever heard a single complaint. We called him the "Cockpit Stud," or "The Wilt Chamberlain of Big E World Airlines." He and I had met years ago. As a matter of fact, I bought his old house when he moved from New Orleans to Atlanta in '78 or '79. For months, different kinds of half-dressed Hoochie Mommas were ringing my doorbell, looking for Captain Franco. When I told them, "He doesn't live here anymore," some left very disappointed, and others didn't believe me and came back three or four times before they concluded that he had, indeed, moved.

If my memory served me correctly, he married a Las Vegas stripper about ten years ago. Rumor had it that Captain Franco had met his match when he married her, and that he flew long layovers so he could rest.

Dominique was still talking a mile a minute. "Girl, he flirted with me on the flight over to Amsterdam. You know, I didn't pay him any attention at first, because we all know his reputation. On the layover, the whole crew went to dinner, and he insisted on sitting next to me. We all had too much to drink, and he started playing with my feet under the table. Then he put his hand on my thigh. By the end of dinner, he had worked his hand all the way up my thigh and under my panties." It sounded like something Captain Franco would do, and she was giggling like a teenager. "I was getting turned on, so I didn't try to stop him. Instead, I reached under the table and felt his thing, and he was hard as a rock. We couldn't wait." Her voice was rising.

She hesitated.

"What did you do?" She was waiting for me to ask.

"While the crew was dividing up the bill and the co-pilot was downing the last ounce of wine, Franco excused himself to go to the restroom. He discreetly punched my shoulder to tell me to follow. So a minute later, I followed him. He was waiting outside the door. We both went into the men's room, and he locked the door. He pulled out a pack of Viagra and broke one in half. He took one half and offered me the other half. He said that by the time we got back to the hotel, it would have kicked in. I took it, because I've taken it before, and it worked wonders. You should try it, but I didn't need it."

She was still giggling like a school girl. "Then he started fondling me and squeezing my breast. The next thing I knew, he had my blouse open and bra unsnapped, and his tongue was all over me. He removed my panties, lifted me up onto the counter, put his hands on my knees, and opened my legs. He looked at me and said, 'This is only a sample of what you'll get later.' He got down on his knees, and he liked what he saw, because I had just got it waxed in Buenos Aires. I only left a little hair shaped like a heart, right on top. He put his head down there and touched nerves I didn't know I had. He put two fingers up my vagina and toyed with my clitoris with his teeth, and my juices started to flow. I thought I had died and gone to Heaven." She stopped to breathe.

Flight attendants did not mince words.

"The bastard I was married to didn't do that. He said if I could get it up, I could have it. Most of the time, I couldn't get it up, and when I did, I didn't want it anymore. You remember what an ass he was." She finally stopped long enough for me to get a word in.

"Yessss, I remember your wealthy ex-husband, let's not go there." I changed the subject. "I'm glad you enjoyed yourself."

I knew if she got started on her ex-husband, we would be on the phone all day.

"Wait! There's more. When we got back to the hotel, I didn't want the crew to know, so he pretended to go to the hotel bar, and I went up in the elevator with the rest of the crew. About ten minutes later, he tapped on my door. As soon as I opened the door, we were all over each other and the rest is history. I'm telling you, the man knows how to fuck."

She let out another giggle, and I remembered my best friend, Sarah Ferguson, using those exact words to describe her brief affair with then-Second-Officer Franco Bordeaux, many years ago.

Dominique was still talking. "It had been a long time since I had any action. I needed it. He was like an animal. I had a one-night stand with him years ago when I was young and stupid, but he has gotten better with age. Lordie, Lordie, he really knows how to take care of business down there. I get chills just thinking about it. None of that 'sixty-eight-plus-one' pilot bullshit." I knew she was reflecting on the past, because I had not heard that term in years.

"Is he still married to that stripper?" I asked.

"I don't know," she said. "He wasn't wearing a wedding band. There wasn't much time for talking. After we finished, I was exhausted. I'm not a young thing anymore. I went straight to sleep, and when I woke up, he was gone. He left me a note and called one hour before pick-up to make sure I was up. That was so sweet of him," she said, almost not believing it herself.

I believed it, because flight attendants talk, and in the thirty years most of us knew Franco, no one has ever called him a dog. He was not a "wham-bam, thank-you-ma'am" type. Every flight attendant who slept with him said he could lay pipe. And they all grinned and called him a stud or Casanova. They also said that, if they had the opportunity, they would sleep with him again.

One of the comments that was made was that he was the only pilot who knew how to use his tongue. He also liked to use toys and exotic oils.

"Franco and I made plans to go out together next week, without the crew. Maybe we'll have time to talk." Dominique giggled. "Besides, I don't care if he's married or not. He has my number in more ways than one. I would be happy just being the other woman and meeting every week or so."

She got defensive. "There was a young reserve on the flight who gave him all kinds of play, yet he chose me. I didn't throw myself at him."

"I know you didn't." I assured her.

"I'll call you next week and keep you informed. I have a copy of your schedule. I put a check in your box for Robbi's birthday," she said.

I thanked her.

"Have a good trip," she said and hung up.

It was good that she was happy. Her first husband broke her spirit and left her with no self-esteem. We were all happy when she divorced him. She was still a very attractive, rich woman, and today, she sounded like her old self again.

I hung up. Next to the phone was a note from my husband. It said:

You were sleeping so hard we didn't want to wake you.

Have a safe flight and we'll see you when you return.

Love,

Bob/Robbi

I got up and looked out the window. It was a beautiful day; the type of day that lets you know that God was alive and real, because only He could make a day so beautiful. Since I flew at night and slept-in on my days off, I was hardly ever up this early. But today, I had a list of things to do before leaving for the airport. Cleaning my son's room was at the top of the list, because he was coming home in two days for his sister's birthday party. Getting the good tablecloths washed and ironed was also top priority, because I needed to cover the picnic tables out by the pool. And I needed to get the punchbowl down from the attic. The balloons and party favorites were ordered, and the invitations had gone out two weeks ago. Forty teenagers were coming, and I was not sure of the number of adults attending.

"Um, I could bring back a few bottles of Spanish wine from Rio." I told myself out loud.

Our neighbor down the street was preparing the food. She had been a caterer before she retired, so I didn't have to worry about that.

I worked like a madwoman. The telephone rang several times, but I let the recorder answer, because I didn't have time to chitchat.

Four hours later, the only thing left to do was order the cake, and that I could do on my way to the airport. I had left myself just enough time to shower and put on my uniform.

Around two o'clock, I wrote my husband and daughter a note, picked up my suitcase, and left for the airport.

"Too bad I have to go to work on such a beautiful day," I thought, as I drove through the city.

'I didn't have an inkling that something tragic was going to happen today. There was no premonition. My grandmother always said she would have an uneasy feeling when something bad was going to happen; she could feel it in the pit of her stomach, she said. I didn't inherit that instinct from my grandmother, and no black cat crossed the road in front of me, either. There was no warning that this would be the day my number would be called, and that my time left on earth might be limited to this day. Nothing would ever be the same again.'

Two

Allow me to introduce myself: I'm Amanda Louise Callaway Mitchell, and I'm fifty-two years old. I had been a flight attendant for Elite World Airlines, known as Big E, for thirty-one years, and still I loved my job; I had no intention of retiring any time soon.

I had been married for twenty-two years to Robert "Bob" Mitchell, former NFL player and Hall-of-Famer, who now owned and ran a bail-bondsman business downtown, next to the courthouse. We lived in Sarasota, Florida, with our two children: twenty-one-year-old Malcolm Alex, who was attending college in Tallahassee; and our daughter, Robertette, or "Robbi," who would turn sixteen in four days.

My commute to work took me to Atlanta, Georgia, my job's home base. Flight attendants commuted to their home base from all over the world. That was one of the perks of our job.

This particular day was supposed to be just like so many: Commuting to Atlanta to work a flight from there to Rio de Janeiro; layover for thirty-six hours; then work back. It was an easy trip: I'd done it so many times, I could do it with my eyes closed.

Robbi's sixteenth birthday party was scheduled for the day I would return home. I stopped on my way to the airport to order her birthday cake and still arrived at the airport early.

My commuter flight from Sarasota to Atlanta departed on time.

Several flight attendants commuted from there and we usually booked the crew-jump seat ahead of time, because the flight was always full, and that was the only way we could get to work; but today it had empty seats. It was my lucky day.

After takeoff, and after the captain turned off the "fasten seatbelt" sign, I moved to a window seat. The captain's voice came over the PA: *"Ladies and gentleman, our flying time today is one hour and five minutes. It's a beautiful day for flying. We aren't expecting any delays, and will be arriving in Atlanta ahead of schedule. Now sit back, relax, and enjoy the flight. Thank you for choosing Elite World Airlines."*

Looking out the window, I agreed: It was a beautiful day, indeed; not a cloud in the sky. You could see for miles in all directions. Taking the captain's advice, I sat back and relaxed.

'It never occurred to me this would be my last commute from Sarasota to Atlanta; that this would be my last day as a flight attendant for Big E World Airlines, or for any other airline; or that I would never wear a flight attendant uniform or wings again. If only I had known. I would have done things totally different. There were options: I could have called in sick; but I felt great. Managed Time Out, or MTO, was another option, but that was reserved for emergencies. In addition, we all were allowed Authorized Leave Days, or ALD; we didn't need a reason to use those days. But there hadn't been a clue that I wouldn't be

coming home after this trip, or that I wouldn't be attending my daughter's sweet-sixteen birthday party. There would be no party and the cake I ordered would never be picked up. I could not imagine things could go so terribly wrong on such a beautiful day.'

I took out my copy of the latest issue of *The In-Flight Bulletin*, which was mandatory reading for all pilots and flight attendants. As usual, this quarterly report included incidents involving crew members on layover, along with a lot of other crap.

I read about the first incident, involving a co-pilot on layover who washed his underwear at a hotel in Little Rock and hung them over a lamp in his room to dry. He then left the room to have dinner with the crew. When they returned, the hotel was being evacuated, and fire trucks were everywhere. His underwear had caught fire, and his entire room was damaged. Thanks to the sprinkler system, the fire was confined to his room. I shook my head; how stupid can a pilot be? I'm sure his mother taught him better than that.

The second incident: Airline crews had been kicked out of the hotel in London. Apparently, flight attendants were using layover time to dye their hair. They were damaging so many towels, pillowcases, and sheets, the hotel was seeking to recover some of the costs of damages from the airline.

For a variety of reasons, we were being kicked out of the best hotels across the United States, and around the world.

From the plush old hotel in downtown Charleston, South Carolina, Big E flight attendants were stealing sheets, pillowcases, comforters, and even crystal ice buckets with matching glasses! How they got all this stuff home was a mystery to me, but we all knew flight attendants were very resourceful. The hotel said the loss was in the five-thousand-dollars-per-month range. I blamed this on the young, new breed of flight attendants. Big E crews had stayed at this hotel for years, and there were never reports of stolen items. Of course, I could not say for sure who the culprits were. In the late eighties and early nineties, Big E merged with a smaller airline and purchased another. The merger was with a popular, west-coast airline that hired its flight attendants right off the street. None of them had the college education that was required for the original Big E flight attendants. The purchased one was an old U.S. Airline with senior citizens for flight attendants. Because of its financial situation, that airline had not hired flight crews in twenty years.

All I could say was that all this really started after Big E acquired those two airlines. In the good old days, we were never kicked out of hotels. In fact, we had a good relationship with hotel staffs. Usually, when the company moved us, hotels would beg for the crews to stay. Now, every month, we were being thrown out of hotels because flight attendants and pilots wrote bad checks or forgot to pay their room-service bills. As a matter of fact, one store, on Virginia Ave in Atlanta, that catered to airline employees went out of business after many years, because of flight attendants' pillage. Most senior flight attendants were afraid to go shopping with the junior girls, because they changed the prices on tags and shoplifted.

The bulletins went on and on: two pilots were robbed and beat-up while walking on the beach in Rio at night. We all knew, or should have known, better than to walk on the beach at night in Rio because of the homeless street children. It was obvious those pilots were trying to pick up prostitutes.

I put the bulletin away and looked out the window. The sounds of the aircraft engines always made me sleepy when I flew as a passenger. I dozed off, and we were making our initial approach into Atlanta when I woke up.

Just as the captain promised, our flight arrived in Atlanta ahead of schedule. I looked at my watch and had exactly three hours before my sign-in for Rio de Janeiro.

I started my weekly routine.

I went to the food court on the International Concourse for a bite to eat. With plenty of time, I decided to go to The Atlanta Petit Cafe. Flight attendants knew to stay away from this place if we were ever in a hurry. The food was delicious, but the service was lousy. The young folks behind the counter were unprofessional and moved at a snail's pace. Their appearance and attitude always made my day. You never knew what to expect! The young ladies' hairstyles were immaculate; from beehive styles that would make bees envious; to braids from micro to cornrows; colors from beet red to platinum blonde and sometimes green; and waves so deep they induced seasickness. They had names such as *Boquisha, Tashanka,* and *Le Juana'nique.*

"Can I help you, ma'am?" A young man's voice brought me back to reality. His name tag read, *Quientavious.* I couldn't imagine where his mother got his name.

"Whatcha want, ma'am?" he asked again, a little impatient.

"A cheeseburger and a salad, please," I responded. He was new, I was sure I hadn't seen him before; I would have remembered his dreadlocks and mouth full of gold teeth. He wasn't destined to work here long, because he was downright rude and his use of the English language left a lot of blank spaces.

When he asked me what kind of *sal'let* I wanted with my burger, I knew he had just arrived in Atlanta from rural South Georgia, and "customer service" was a foreign concept for him. I wondered who trained these young people, or if they were put to work right off the street. As he bagged my order, he was carrying on a personal conversation with the pretty cashier ten feet away. He handed me the bag, never missing a beat in the conversation. I paid for the order and headed for the flight attendant's lounge.

I was stopped several times by passengers.

"Miss, Miss, can you tell me where the Crown Room is located?" a tall man with a British accent wanted to know. I knew it was not in the direction I was going so I pointed in the opposite direction, toward the information counter. I knew he would ask the same question of the next uniformed person he saw.

"Excuse me, where is the nearest restroom?" This time it was a lady with a small girl squeezing her legs together. I looked around and said, "It's right behind you, ma'am."

"Oh, thank you." She chirped, hurrying into the restroom, dragging the child behind her.

I picked-up my pace to give the impression I was in a hurry, until I had to stop to maneuver my way around a crowd at gate E10, I noticed the flight was going to Frankfurt, Germany, but before I could move, someone tapped me on the shoulder.

"Do you work here?"

I turned and was face-to-face with a dark-skinned man; his looks and accent told me he was from India. I opened my mouth to say no, but he cut me off.

"Can you tell me what time the six-ten flight is leaving for Frankfurt?"

I looked at the screen behind the gate agent and in big bold letters it read:

DESTINATION - FRANKFURT, GERMANY

DEPART - 6:10

ON TIME

"Sir, the six-ten flight to Frankfurt departs at six-ten," I said.

"Oh! Thank you, thank you. I have to make my connection to New Delhi."

"You're very welcome," I said and smiled.

"Are you a flight attendant?" His voice was calmer now.

I turned away, rolled my eyes, and looked at my wings.

"Yes, I am," I said.

"Well, I am just visiting my mother in New Delhi for two weeks, I live in New Orleans. My name is Anish Patel, I own two Motel Eight's and a gas station in Metairie, Louisiana, close to the airport. Let me give you my card... you can call me if you ever have a layover in New Orleans. I'll take you to dinner."

I knew where this conversation was going, so while he was fumbling in his pocket for his cards, I excused myself and walked faster toward the lounge. When someone bumped against me, I said, "Excuse me," without looking up. My mind was on Mr. Patel. I had flown the Frankfurt flight many times, and I was very familiar with the passenger lists. I am willing to bet Mr. Patel had ordered a special meal. Sometimes we had fifty Hindu and twenty vegetarians meals on that Frankfurt flight. It reminded me of the New York-to-Fort Lauderdale flights on which half the passengers, on a full L-1011 aircraft, ordered kosher meals, and the other half swore they also ordered them. It was total chaos. Just the memory of those flights sent chills down my spine. Flight attendants disliked special meals, because they were time consuming. We have to match each special meal with the passenger who ordered it, and that takes time away from other passengers.

I was glad to reach the door leading to the flight attendant's lounge without further interruptions.

Three

The flight attendant's lounge was crowded at this time of day because of the European trip's sign-in time. I checked my mailbox, my Duty Free check had arrived, along with a new revision for our workbook. There were birthday cards addressed to Robbi and junk mail that I took directly to the trash, just as I would do at home. I greeted a few girls with whom I had flown; offering a casual, "Hello"; "where are you going today?" "How are the kids?" This is what flight attendants called small talk. I looked around the lounge and saw several gay guys huddled in a group, giggling and strutting their stuff. Some of these guys were fun to be around, and some were overbearing. Most females looked at them as a waste, because half of these guys were good-looking, and there were many single female flight attendants looking for men.

Collette Parker Coleman-Young was coming in my direction. I had not seen her in years. We used to be best friends, and did everything together. After a major argument, we went our separate ways. Today, I barely recognized her, because her face looked different. Facelifts and menopause were the main topics for women in our seniority group. Collette's face was tight, and she didn't have a wrinkle. Maybe the divorce had something to do with it. Someone had told me she had gotten a divorce from her third husband. I didn't get all the details. However, Collette was about to change that now.

"Amanda! Amanda!" she called out when she got closer to me.

"Girl, it's so good to see you; you're looking good. What is Bob doing to you?" She gave me a big hug, but didn't release me. I realized there really was something different about her.

"Amanda, I've missed you, and we aren't getting any younger. What if something happened to one of us, and we hadn't straightened things out between us? I love you. Good friends are hard to find. Can we be like old times?" When she finally let me go, there were tears in her eyes.

"Oh, Collette, cut it out. I love you, too. You know we will probably live to be a hundred and end up together at Clipped Wings or some other flight attendant's retirement home. Let's just pick-up where we left off and fly together soon. Now, you look great. How have you been?"

"Just fine," she lied.

"And what are you doing to keep yourself so young?" I pretended not to notice her face job.

"Well, a little Botox injection here and there. Remind me to give you the name of my doctor," she said.

"At five hundred dollars a shot? No, thank you," I answered.

"Amanda, for a lady with money, you've always been cheap. I bet you are still shopping at JCPenney's."

She didn't wait for an answer, but got straight to the point. "I know you heard about my divorce."

I knew she was going to tell me every detail. That's the kind of person she is. So we sat down at an empty table, and I sharpened my ears. I also started eating my cheeseburger before it got cold; this could take some time. She started talking.

It seemed that Collette and her husband, Mason Young, had been having sexual problems for over a year. He could not get it up, yet he refused to see a doctor or go to counseling. One day, he moved out of their bedroom and into the guest room.

"He cut me off completely, although I was doing all the work," Collette complained. "I couldn't entice him with sexy nighties, expensive perfume, whip cream, nothing. You know me, I tried everything."

"Oh, I know you well," I thought to myself.

One day she was cleaning the guest room and "just happened" to start snooping through his belongings.

"You'll never guess what I found," she said.

"What!" I asked, curious.

"Viagra, in a small overnight bag, together with two pairs of cheap underwear."

This comment let me know right off that the underwear was not Collette's. God help us all if she ever had to wear anything cheap.

"And you know all hell broke loose," she said.

She found out he had been sleeping with his secretary for over a year.

"There were hotel receipts in the bag. He had even taken the bitch on a cruise while I was on a ten-day Barcelona trip. I found a receipt where he sent her flowers. The bastard has not sent me flowers since we were dating." I could hear the anger building in her voice.

It was just like old times, almost thirty years ago, when we were young and stupid. Collette's first husband, Roscoe Parker, was staying out all night, sleeping with another woman. Collette was no angel back then, and I had a sneaking suspicion the same held true today. Her second husband, Marcus Coleman, a high-school teacher, ran off with one of his students, just fifteen months into their marriage. The student was four months pregnant. Collette was angry, especially because she had been trying to get pregnant. She wanted to start a family.

"I kicked his ass to the curb so fast, it would make your head spin, and got a restraining order against him. Then I called his secretary's husband and asked him did he know his wife was fucking my husband?" Collette was still talking.

The secretary's husband knew about the affair. He said this was not the first time: His wife broke up another family three years ago, and he had forgiven her. She was a sick woman and a gold-digger. He told Collette his wife would sleep with anyone she thought had money. Even though he was more than willing to give her whatever she needed, and despite her infidelities, he stayed with her because he loved her.

"Some love!" Collette sneered.

I watched Collette's face as she talked. She really had not changed after all these years.

She grew up in the projects of Chicago. She knew little about her parents and was raised by several foster families. She was still looking for a father and the family she never had. I had hoped she had finally found that family when she married Mason Young fifteen years ago. Collette was a survivor, and I was always sure she would eventually come out on top. But I could see this had hurt her deeply, although she was trying hard to hide it.

"I'm sorry, Collette, I don't know what to say. Is there anything I can do?" I asked, feel compassion for her.

"Amanda, you have not changed a bit. You can't save the whole goddamn world! How can everyone else change, and you remain the same? I guess that's what makes you special. Well, old friend, don't feel sorry for me, let me show you some pictures of my new man."

She reached into her bag and pulled out several pictures. The first picture was of her and a very tall, good-looking hunk dressed in black leather, standing next to a motorcycle. The next one was of him and Collette. She had on some tight black leather pants and a black, studded-leather jacket. There was also a picture of her sitting behind him on a motorcycle.

"I'm going to buy me a motorcycle. I'm ready for a new life with no restrictions," she announced.

"*You always lived your life that way. So what's new?*" I thought, as I smiled at her.

She held the last picture to her chest, as though debating whether or not to show it to me. When she sprang it on me, I could see why. It was a picture of him in Collette's bedroom, standing next to her bed in red boxer shorts bulging in the front. I had to admit, the brother looked good. It was a very sexy picture.

Collette was smiling from ear to ear, because she knew I would like the picture; that was why she saved it for last.

A supervisor and a few other flight attendants stopped by the table to look at the pictures and chat with us. They all knew about the motorcycle hunk. Collette must have been passing these pictures around the lounge for months. I was the only one hearing the story for the first time.

Janice Tollicella, the white, big-chested Brussels coordinator, stopped by our table, looked at the pictures, and smirked with disapproval. We all looked at her as though she was crazy. What in the hell was she smirking at? Only three years ago, she had been in jail! The story was told that, one rainy afternoon, somebody called her at home to inform her that she saw Janice's husband going into a Holiday Inn with a bleached blonde.

Janice went to the hotel and immediately spotted her husband's car parked out front. He hadn't tried to hide. The fool even signed in under his own name. So it wasn't hard for Janice to find his room number. She pounded on the door for ten minutes, screaming and cussing so loud that the hotel manager called the police. Her husband finally opened the door, and by the time the police arrived, Janice had beaten him and the woman with a Louis Vuitton umbrella she was carrying.

The police placed Janice under arrest for disturbing the peace, and for assault with a deadly weapon, the umbrella. She spent twenty-four hours in jail while flight attendants scraped up enough money to get her out. So her disapproval now sounded, to me, like the pot calling the kettle black.

Collette didn't like Janice, because they had it out on a flight not long ago. So she gathered her pictures in a rush and said, "It's time for my briefing. I'll finish telling you about Mason some other time. Oh! Before I forget, Roscoe Parker died two weeks ago. His mother called me. I hadn't spoken to the woman in years, but I'll tell you all about it when we fly together. Call me, we'll get together next week for lunch, it will be like old times." She hugged me and rushed off.

I knew I would eventually get the whole truth, if not from Collette, then from other flight attendants, because we didn't keep secrets well. I was sorry to hear about Roscoe, Collette's first husband, although I hadn't seen or thought about him in twenty-five years.

Collecting the remnants of my meal and throwing them in the trash, I went to one of the lounge chairs vacated by the girls who had left for the European trips. I got back on track with my routine; laid back in the lounge chair and drifted off to sleep, thinking about Collette's situation.

I woke up forty minutes before sign-in for my Rio trip and went to the restroom to freshen up. As I was coming out, I saw Barbara Ann Washington, my old roommate, on the telephone. I went near her to get her attention. Her twenty-four-year-old son had gotten a girl pregnant, and she had delivered twin girls. Her son had been lying for nine months, saying the babies weren't his. His mother was the only one convinced he was telling the truth. We all remembered his father, Calvin "Big Daddy" Washington, lying about the exact same thing before he and Barbara Ann married. The paternity test results should have been back by now, and had the test proved her son was not the father, she would have called or e-mailed me immediately.

When Barbara Ann saw me, she quickly hung up the phone.

"Amanda, how are you?"

"Great."

"I've been meaning to call you. I put something in the mail for Robbi's sixteenth birthday," she said.

"Thank you, but you didn't have to. How are you doing?"

"Not too well; you know I'm a grandmother. I feel too young to be a grandmother." She tried to smile.

I wondered how old you had to be to be a grandmother. We were in our early fifties. I had no doubt about her being a good grandmother, once she got used to the idea, and I told her so.

"You'll be a wonderful grandmother," I assured her.

"I told Calvin Jr. he has to stand up to his responsibility, because there are just too many kids being raised without their fathers. The twins are so cute, I'll send you some pictures," she said, and suddenly changed from sad to happy.

"Amanda, Calvin and I will be celebrating our twenty-fifth wedding anniversary in September. You know he is the only man I've ever loved, and we want to renew our wedding vows. I want you to be my maid of honor again. Please say you will!"

"Of course I will, just let me know the time and date, and I will be there."

"Thank you, Amanda. You are the best friend a girl can have. I don't know what I would do without you."

"I hope you never have to find out," I said.

"Look, I want to invite everyone. You know, the last time we all got together was at Dee Dee's funeral. That was such a sad occasion. This time we can all celebrate and have some fun, it will be like old times. What do you think?" she asked, ecstatic.

"I think it's a great idea," was all I could say.

Just the mention of Dee Dee's name made me sad. She died over ten years ago. The airline gave us paid personal-leave days and full-fare tickets to attend her funeral in Pittsburgh. It was a sad day for all of us. However, it was hard to remember Dee Dee without also thinking of Helena. She died such a horrible death. Memories… The memories made me shiver. We all missed our old friends.

I gave Barbara Ann a kiss and a big hug. I really wanted to stay and talk, but I had to sign in and she was going home.

I went to the computer, signed in, and checked my schedule to see with whom I was flying. Not a single name was familiar to me.

I was having second thoughts. *"Maybe I shouldn't have swapped for this Rio trip; but I had needed the time off for Robbi's birthday party. Good thing I know my way around Rio; I don't need anyone to show me the city."*

When you fly with a new crew, you make a conscious effort to go with the flow and pray for the best. I was the third most senior person to sign up for a working position on the plane. In the airline business, seniority is everything.

I decided there was enough time to check my e-mail before briefing, and sure enough, there were several e-mails.

The first one was from Mr. Richard Maulligan, president and CEO of Elite World Airlines. It was a long e-mail. None of us were interested in what he had to say but I started to read it anyway:

"Morale is low within our company. I am asking all employees to recommit to customer service because every passenger counts. We want to be number one in customer's service."

I stopped because I had read enough. For the first time in our airline's history, the president and CEO was an outsider. Mr. Maulligan was the first head of the company who did not come up through the ranks of Big E. He came from an Internet company, and he had no experience with running a major airline, and it showed. Last year, this president and CEO cut employee's salaries and benefits while giving himself a thirteen-million-dollar raise. Now, he wondered why morale is low!

I hit "DELETE" without reading the rest of his message and went to the next.

The second e-mail was from management:

"There will be one less trash cart on your aircraft. Please do not place any catering equipment, excess supplies, or trash in the jetway at any city. It could become a fire hazard."

"Also, any visible trash or supplies in the jetway can provide a negative customer perception while boarding our flights. As a reminder, don't put any trash in the airplane lavatories."

My immediate response to these "instructions" was: Where were we suppose to put all of the trash? They never tell us that! We had been putting trash in the jetway for years, and it never caused a fire. I always wonder who in the hell were the people sending these e-mails? They were certainly not flight attendants, and they certainly had never worked a full flight.

To hell with them. I deleted it as quickly as the first.

I clicked on the next e-mail. It was from Nicole Stevenson. I knew she was having problems with her daughter, Jennifer, who was my Godchild. Jennifer had shaved her head and put rings in her nose, eyebrow, and tongue. I figured Nicole wanted to tell me before I got a call from my son. He and Jennifer attended the same university. For two years, Nicole had hidden from me the fact that Jennifer was gay. I told my son to look Jennifer up during their freshman year. I called him after classes started to ask if he had seen Jennifer.

"Mom, don't you know?" he asked.

"Know what?"

"Jennifer is gay."

"Gay! What do you mean? Don't play with me, son. This isn't funny." I tried to get a grip on what he said.

"Yes, Mom, she is pushing around campus with some rough girls that look like boys. I heard they stay in Jennifer's room and smoke 'blunts'...uh... cigars stuffed with weed...uh...marijuana, and trip out on ecstasy," he said.

I could tell by my son's voice that he wanted nothing to do with Jennifer. He was a little intimidated by her friends, and I had never heard of "blunts," but it sure didn't sound good. Kids were always coming up with new ways to get high and end up dead.

As soon as I got off the phone with my son, I called Nicole. She started to apologize right away, which meant she had already knew about Jennifer.

"I was going to tell you about Jennifer. It's just hard to find the words. I...I...I thought it was a phase she was going through, until I caught her and another girl in bed together, going at it like animals. Now, she wants to quit college and become a nun!" she said as her voice wobbled.

I could hear her sniffing. I wasn't sure if she was crying over the situation or was drunk.

"It's all my fault. I should not have been such a whore back then. God is punishing me. You know, you reap what you sow," she added.

In my thirty-one years of knowing Nicole, that was the first time I ever heard her mention God's name. So I knew she was drunk.

Now I leaned back in my chair and started to read Nicole's e-mail. She was asking me for advice and help with Jennifer.

"You promised to stand by me no matter what! You are my best friend and she is your godchild. What would you do? You know my situation, and Jennifer never had a father. Heaven knows I've done the best I could," the e-mail read.

I closed my eyes and thought about the day Nicole told Collette and me she was pregnant with Jennifer. It was not a pretty memory. She was not married, and she was a regular sky slut like so many of us. She was sleeping with two–or was it three?–men. Anyway, she didn't have the slightest idea which one was the father.

Collette had suggested Nicole get an abortion and forget about the whole thing. I told her the choice was hers, and I would stand by her no matter what she decided.

Nicole never told me who Jennifer's real father was. She mentioned something about a one-night stand. Now I wondered if she ever knew.

"Nicole, poor Nicole, you can't win for losing," I thought to myself.

I would have to get back with her when I returned from Rio. Answering her e-mail would not be easy. It required the right words, and that would take some time. I had learned that, in situations like this, you have to choose your words carefully, or they could damage a friendship. I clicked on the next e-mail.

"Oh, it's from Sarah…I mean the Rev. Sarah Ferguson!"

> *"Amanda, please come to the flight attendant prayer meeting at my house on Monday night at eight p.m. I'll pick you up. We missed you last time. Try to bring some new people. Oh! Amanda, Wendell will be released from prison today. I am on my way to meet him. He is getting out early on good behavior. Maybe we have a future together after all. I still love him. Pray for us. Have a blessed day.*
>
> *Love you,*
>
> *Sarah"*

"Wendell, Wendell, I don't know a Wendell. Do I?" I thought hard for a moment. There was something familiar about that name. Then it hit me like a ton of bricks. I must have been getting old; how could I forget Wendell

Johnson, the owner of the Lagniappe Club? I thought he was dead. Was he still in prison? Sarah hadn't mentioned his name in twenty years. What was up with this?

It was hard to believe that Sarah Ferguson was now a minister. She used to be a drug abuser, a prostitute, a chain smoker, and the most foul-mouth flight attendant you would ever meet. Now it was always, "Praise the Lord."

My grandmother said that sometimes God takes the worst person and turns him into a saint. I wondered if that was true of Sarah? How ironic: I remember being at her house, doing cocaine or smoking weed, sometimes all night. These days we held prayer meetings at her house. She was a good cook. Her hot wings were to die for; she always served them at prayer meetings, and she knew they were why most of the flight attendants came. If she served wine and beer instead of punch with those hot wings, every flight attendant in Atlanta would be there.

Last year, someone spiked the punch, and we had our best prayer meeting ever. Flight attendants started to testify about shit we knew was true, but about which they had lied for years. The meeting got a bit out of hand. Reverend Sarah yelled to the top of her voice to get our attention and get the meeting back on track. "Look, we aren't here to call each other a bunch of names. This is a prayer meeting, not a whore meeting. Praise the Lord. Now, which one of you whores put this bottle of cognac in my punch?" she asked, holding an empty Courvoisier bottle.

We all humped our shoulders like we didn't have the slightest idea where that bottle came from. For added effect, everyone looked at her glass and pretended not to know the punch was spiked. We later apologized for our behavior. We decided to "let bygones be bygones and let sleeping dogs lie," and we continued our prayer meeting. We were having a good discussion about the Bible until some young woman started analyzing things that only young, drunk people thought about: "Why does God allow bad things to happen to good people? Is there really a Heaven and Hell?"

We told her to shut the fuck up.

The meeting wasn't over until three o'clock in the morning. Some girls were too drunk to drive home, so they fell asleep on the sofa and on the floor, just like we used to do!

Sarah had really turned her life around. She was our flight attendant spokesperson. She officiated at all the funerals and weddings, and she christened our children. If we needed her, she was always there. She hardly flew anymore because of all the flight attendant crises that needed her attention. The company never knew about her past.

I stared back at the e-mail. It was hard to say no to Sarah. She was still my closest and dearest friend. I loved her like a sister, but I had to think about the prayer meetings and how Wendell would fit into her life, now. Could he be the reason why Sarah never married? Why had she, in all these years, never mentioned his name to me? I just didn't know. I decided I would call her as soon as I got back from Rio, because we needed to talk.

"Memories, memories." I looked at my watch, and suddenly my eyes were fixated on it. It was as though I were seeing it for the first time, and my mind flashed backed to the first time I actually saw this watch. My husband gave it to me a few years before we got married. We weren't even dating. It was around the time I was going with Sarah to visit Wendell in federal prison.

I ran my index finger over the crystal. Cartier must have made some damn good watches. I had the band changed a few times and the watch itself cleaned once; but other than that, it hadn't missed a beat. I couldn't remember owning another watch. From habit, I touched the diamond earrings I had worn for the past twenty-nine years. I would be lost without them.

Memories, memories, they had a way of hitting you at the most inopportune times. These earrings are my connection to my first love, the love of my life. I could still see his smiling face after all these years. Here I was, a happily married woman with two lovely children, and still my heart skipped a beat every time I thought about him. It's always, "*What if this had not happened? What if that...?*" I was about to get teary eyed, and I had to catch on to reality.

"I can't sit here and reminisce all night. It's almost time for my briefing." I told myself.

I didn't have time to read anymore e-mails. I didn't want to be late and let some junior person sign up before me. I logged off and went directly to the briefing room.

The onboard-leader, or OBL, Carole Palmesi, was a full-figured woman, about thirty pounds overweight. She looked about sixty years old but I was sure she was much younger, because she was under my seniority. However, I was absolutely positive I had never flown with her before. We all introduced ourselves. There were three Portuguese speakers. One was a very attractive female named Maria Madonia, and two were males or maybe I should have said, "Three females." One of the guys, Juan Delgado, looked like a woman. I think all of the male Portuguese speakers were openly gay. They sat on the jump seats and talked about their partners the way the females talked about their husbands or other males talked about their wives.

A Jewish woman, Christine Goldstein, sat next to me, a French woman, Victoria Ballovan, sat in the back, and I missed the other three names. I would get them on the flight over to Rio. As we got older, we seemed to have a harder time with names.

Carole started her briefing by telling us she commuted from Portland, Oregon. She had been based in Atlanta for two months. She had never flown Rio. Instead of briefing us on what to do, she asked us how to work the service. Most of us felt she got paid to be onboard-leader, and we didn't want to do her job. However, the two male language-speakers were happy to oblige. They were the most junior on the line, yet they knew everything about the service, and they proceeded to brief Carole and the rest of us. I signed up to work 4L tonight, which meant that I would sit at the "4-left door" and work coach class, and work business class coming home. I didn't have to sell "Duty Free" products, so I signed up for the first break. Most of us hated selling Duty Free on the international flight and viewed it as a waste of time. I got the position I wanted, and that was all that mattered to me.

The cockpit crew came in, interrupting the briefing. I recognized the captain, John Bankhead, right away. I had flown with him out of the New Orleans base years ago. He was married to a flight attendant named Susan Mayos, who was a good friend of mine and a good flight attendant. He made her quit shortly after they married. They had two boys. John cheated on her with other flight attendants from day one, and didn't try to hide it. That was why this asshole made her quit. He divorced her ten years ago, and tried to have her declared insane and take the boys. All of this was to avoid paying child support for the boys and alimony. After Susan's friends told the judge what a whore he was on layovers, the judge threw the book at him. Susan got the boys and half of everything they had, in addition to alimony and child support.

He was now living with a flight attendant half his age, and Susan stayed home and enjoyed life.

Half of the pilots who married flight attendants thirty years ago were divorced and dating other flight attendants. The other half were still married and screwing around with flight attendants every chance they got. In some cases, they did two or more flight attendants.

We all knew who was screwing whom on layovers. We could tell if it went well or badly by their body language the next day. Sometimes, the flight attendant would describe in graphic detail what had gone on between them.

I turned my attention back to briefing, because the co-pilot, Jack Callico, was talking. He was over six feet tall and looked like Tom Cruise. He may have been a good candidate for our young, attractive Portuguese speaker, but Victoria Ballovan looked excited when she saw him and spoke up.

"I've flown with you before, Jack," the Frenchwoman said, her voice suggestive.

"Yes, ah, you look familiar. London...aaah...two months ago, didn't we go dancing?" He was unsure of himself and was trying not to say the wrong thing. We all concluded he did just that, because Victoria had a funny look on her face, as though she had stepped in a pile of shit.

"Yes, we went dancing all right," she said, and her words cut like a knife.

We'd all heard this before and we all knew what it meant: You sleep with a pilot on layover and he forgets your name the next trip. You couldn't blame the poor guy. There had been too many layovers and too many flight attendants willing to give it up.

It looked as though Victoria was going to cuss him out, so the captain spoke up to save his co-pilot. "The flying time tonight is nine hours and twenty minutes." He cleared his throat and followed quickly with the weather conditions en route.

The engineer had nothing to say, and the triumvirate left the briefing as quickly as they had come in.

The briefing was over. The other flight attendants gathered their paperwork and left the room while Carole and I were talking about going shopping in Rio, and Victoria was still fuming.

"Two months ago, in Paris, he tried to fuck and suck my brain out," she finally said. "Now, tonight, he can't remember my name. Well, I'll see if I can refresh his memory on layover. He has a big dick and was the best fuck I ever had." She threw her things together and stormed out of the room.

Carole and I looked at each other. She smiled and said, "I guess she found a gold mine, because we all know, for a fact, that most pilots have big egos and small dicks." We laughed, gathered our belongings, and proceeded upstairs to the airplane.

Four

It was an old McDonald-Douglas, an MD-11, our least favorite airplane. To us, it was not very dependable. It usually broke down with some kind of mechanical problem that took hours to repair. This aircraft had just arrived from Panama City, Panama. It had made an emergency landing in Panama with engine problems, then sat on the ground for three days while the passengers and crew stayed at a local hotel. The airline finally sent a team of mechanics to Panama to repair the engine so it could fly home. I sure hoped they fixed the problem. I cringed at the thought of being stuck in Rio or some other foreign country and missing my daughter's birthday party. Tonight, everything looked perfect, almost too perfect. There were no mechanics on the aircraft when we arrived. The plane was clean, and the agent said we would have an on-time departure. I guess there was always a first time for everything, because I couldn't remember the last time we had an on-time departure on this flight.

"Great! Ten hours to go before we land in Rio de Janeiro," was all that was on my mind.

I checked the emergency equipment at 4L and started setting up the galley. The caterer came onboard to check meals. He was a tall, dark, handsome black man. We all took turns flirting with him and accidentally, of course, rubbing up against him to see if we could make him get a hard on. What could I say? It was a small galley, you know. I noticed the gay guys trying to get in on the action, because they rubbed up against him just as we did, maybe even harder.

The caterer had been around a long time, and we didn't know of any flight attendant who had ever slept with him. He had never asked a flight attendant for a date, that we know of. Maybe he was happily married or gay. One can never tell these days.

The onboard leader called for boarding positions. The gay guys loved to board or stand at the door to meet, greet, and prance around. I stayed in the back cabin. It was almost a full flight, which added up to a lot of people. The MD-11 capacity is fifty passengers in business class and two hundred and fifty in coach class.

We pushed back from the gate on time. During takeoff, I sat in the back at the 4L door, facing the cockpit; Maria, the cute Portuguese speaker, sat directly in front of me, facing the tail. Juan Delgado sat at the 4R door, and Victoria Ballovan sat on the back galley jump seat. She was happy after talking to the co-pilot, because they made plans for Rio. I guessed he remembered who she was.

It was a smooth takeoff. After we reached our cruising altitude, the captain turned off the "fasten seatbelt" sign, and we set up the carts to start our beverage service. It appeared to be a quiet, older group of people, unlike the usual Rio party crowd. We didn't have many drinkers.

As we finished serving beverages and began setting up the meal carts, one of the business-class flight attendants came back and told us Captain Bankhead had called Carole, the onboard-leader, to the cockpit. He wanted us to put away all carts. We did not think much of the request. Maybe there was some clear air turbulence, because it was a beautiful day. Remember, I flew in several hours ago from Sarasota; not a cloud in the sky.

Moments later, we heard the emergency call bells. We picked-up our interphone headsets. This time it was Carole Palmesi, calling all flight attendants to the first class cabin for a briefing.

"Come as fast as you can!" was the order.

It didn't sound good, so we dropped everything and hurried to the front of the aircraft. Carole's face was completely white, and she looked every bit her age. She was trying to calm herself and speak to us in a normal voice. Her mouth was moving, but nothing was coming out. She had the flight attendants' instructions manual out, flipping to the emergency procedures page. When she did speak, her voice was trembling.

"We have an emergency," she said and stopped.

We were all staring at her in disbelief, and we could tell it was bad. We wanted her to go on, even as we wanted her to say it was a big joke.

No one was prepared for what finally came out of Carole's mouth.

She said, "We have twenty minutes to prepare for an emergency landing. We have bo-ombs..." her voice cracked when she said "bombs," but she was able to continue. "The bombs were strategically placed: one in the wingspan, near the number-three engine; and in the tail cone near the number-two engine, shortly before the aircraft left Panama. Someone with a muffed voice called the tower and said the bombs were timed to go off while the aircraft was parked at the gate in Atlanta, that it was not their intention to hurt passengers."

She did not have to tell us that the number-two engine sat on top of the tail cone, and the number-three was on the right side of the aircraft. Thank God the bombs were not in the cabin, for then we would not stand a chance.

"Because of the location of the bombs, the captain feels he will be able to land the plane, even if the bombs detonate. We have no time to dump fuel. We are going to land in Jacksonville, Florida, as soon as emergency ground crews can prepare a runway and evacuate the airport. When we come to a complete stop, evacuate, using all doors. The bombs could explode at any time, so get everyone off and away from the aircraft as quickly as you can." Her voice was more in control now, and so were we.

There was simply no time to be afraid or to panic.

"The captain will let us know five minutes before touchdown, and he will give the signal to brace. He will say, 'Brace! Brace!' I will explain everything to the passengers over the PA system. Now get moving."

We were all in shock, but we would have to deal with that later. The captain was on the PA, explaining the emergency to the passengers and asking them to follow the flight attendants' instructions. Afterward, Carole came on the PA, explaining the bracing positions, and we were in the aisles, demonstrating as she spoke. We checked seatbacks and tray tables. We made sure all carryon luggage was stored. There was no time to answer questions. We ordered passengers to remove their shoes and all sharp objects, any of which could puncture a slide.

"Leave everything!" we shouted to everyone.

"Keep your heads down on impact because of flying objects, and hold your child's head down. Put sharp objects in the seat pockets. Put your glasses in your socks," we screamed.

One lady wanted to know about her dog, and I told her to bring the dog, but leave everything else. "But for now, ma'am, please place your dog back in his cage and put it back underneath your seat," I said. A man wanted to know about his connecting flight in Rio. Another asked about luggage. I couldn't believe it. They had plenty of questions that we didn't have time to answer. Some were visibly upset, some were praying and holding hands, and some were cussing and swearing. Some were incredibly calm and tried to help us prepare the cabin. These passengers could assist us in the evacuation. Still others were in denial and continued doing whatever they were doing.

It took us five minutes to prepare the cabin. Just as we reached the back galley, the plane dropped about five hundred feet. The passengers screamed, and the crew was knocked to the floor. We were all injured in one way or another, but we shook it off, except for Juan. He hit his head on something, and when he saw a little blood, he started to cry like a baby.

"This is too much! I'm having an anxiety attack, I need a Prozac," he said, as he ran to his bag, opened up a prescription bottle and took a handful of pills. "Who's going to take care of Carlos if something happens to me?" he was still crying.

I wanted to slap him and tell him to get a grip, but I couldn't spare the time or energy. Both was of essence, so I fought the urge.

Maria whispered that Carlos was his partner. She led him to his jump seat at 4R and buckled him in while Victoria and I finished securing the galley. We were sweating and breathing hard, but amazingly calm. We had gotten over the initial shock and didn't talk, too busy working, doing whatever needed to be done. Just as we turned the last latch and gave a thumbs-up to each other, the captain came over the PA:

"Ten minutes before touchdown," he said, calmly.

I asked Victoria and Maria if they wanted to join me in a quick prayer before we sat down. Victoria refused and took her jump seat. Maria grabbed her rosary with one hand and me with the other. She was shaking like a leaf. We bowed our heads, and I prayed:

"Heavenly Father, please hear our prayer. Have mercy on us tonight. Please don't leave us. Be with us and keep all of us safe. These and other blessings we ask in your name. Amen."

Maria repeated the amen, and we took our jump seats, quickly buckling up. Minutes later, there was a loud explosion on the right side of the aircraft, and the tip of the wing blew off in a ball of fire. We knew it was no longer a threat; it was real. The plane dropped and stalled in midair, followed by violent shaking and swaying, as though the captain was fighting to maintain control.

We heard a passenger yell "Fire!", and screams were coming from every zone in the cabin. We all looked out the window, but couldn't see the fire anymore. A man was running down the right aisle screaming, "We are all going to die. We are all going to die. We are all going to hell!"

The aircraft made a vicious flip to the right, and the screaming man's head was slammed against the overhead bin. Blood flew everywhere, and he was knocked out. A passenger grabbed him by his belt and threw him into a seat. I hoped someone would remember to carry him off the aircraft.

After seeing that, passengers who had wanted to get up and move froze and decided it was best to stay seated. An announcement came over the PA in

English, and then in Portuguese. *"Ladies and gentleman, please remain seated with your seatbelts fastened."* I don't know who made the announcement.

Thick, black smoke was slowly entering the cabin through the air vents and I soon heard coughing. The aircraft was swaying to the right, and then to the left, as though it wanted each time to flip over and take us with it. Passengers were screaming. Babies were crying. There was pandemonium.

I looked at Victoria and Maria. I guessed the fear I saw in their eyes was reflected in mine, but we had a job to do.

My heart was pounding as I sat on my hands with my palms up and waited for the captain's signal to "Brace! Brace!" Ten minutes seemed like an hour. A lady in the last row, aisle seat, was vomiting, and it poured from her mouth like water. It was spraying everywhere, but no one cared. I was sure she was not the only one throwing up, because we all felt like doing the same.

The aircraft stalled again and dropped about a thousand feet.

Overhead bins popped open, and carryon luggage fell out. Oxygen masks and light fixtures followed.

The plane took a nosedive, and we were hanging in the air, held only by our seatbelts. Everything loose in the back cabin went flying to the front, like missiles. The captain pulled the nose up, and those same missiles came flying back. We held on to our jump seats in desperation as the aircraft shook violently. Something hit me in my chest with such force that I heard the crack of my ribs, but I felt no pain. When things calmed down a little, I looked at Maria, across from me, and saw the gash in her forehead and blood streaming down her face. Our eyes met as though to say, "*We can get through this!*" I looked around the corner for Victoria and saw her slumped over in her jump seat. A steel oven and a meal cart lay at her feet; she was covered with blood and food. Soft drink cans, cups, glasses, and everything else to be found in the galley were on the floor, as well as part of the ceiling. The aircraft looked like a tornado had gone through it.

I knew Victoria was unconscious, and I made a mental note that she would be no help to us in the evacuation. She would need to be taken off the plane first. I looked at Juan, and he was acting like he was on a roller-coaster ride. He was laughing, although he was bleeding, and blood was drooling from his mouth. Obviously, the Prozac had taken over. I tried to get his attention, but then we hit a bump, and my head jerked in one direction, and my body in another.

Fixtures inside the plane were coming apart like they were put together with school glue. I knew we had to be close to impact but there was still no "Brace! Brace!" from the cockpit. I felt something running down my face. I could not tell if it was blood or tears. Smoke was filling the cabin, and it was becoming hard to breathe.

Another loud explosion came from the back of the aircraft, but it seemed millions of miles away. Instantly, I felt wet, and I realized we'd been hit with gallons of jet fuel, and everybody and everything in the back was drenched. Next, the tail cone fell off leaving a large, jagged hole in the fuselage, and the plane dropped another thousand feet. We were nearing the ground, and through burning eyes, I could see the runway lights. I also saw a small fire, and I was paralyzed with fear, and my chest caved in.

"Focus on the evacuation procedures! Land! Please! Land! Now!" I kept telling myself, waiting for the plane to hit the ground.

I had to get three flight attendants, myself, and two hundred tourists off this aircraft. I could not worry about the fifty business-class passengers. The OBL and the forward flight attendants had to take care of them.

It was hard to focus. I thought I felt heat and knew it was all over. I could not run had I wanted to. I could no longer hear the screams and cries. Either they had stopped, or the roaring of the aircraft drowned out everything else. I think most of the passengers had accepted their fate, and like me, were plotting their exit off the airplane as soon as it hit the ground. I closed my eyes, bowed my head, and prayed like I had never ever prayed. I thanked the unknown person who installed our jump seats, because it was the only thing I had to hold on to. It was my security blanket. I asked God to keep the captain strong enough to be able to maintain control of this monster aircraft, which had a mind of its own. "*See all of us through this, O Lord, we are in your hands.*"

I felt the intense heat and covered my head with my hands and braced. Now my prayers were that death would come quickly. I started to hallucinate. *An old man was sitting on a stool, staring at me with very sad eyes. His arms were reaching, beckoning to me.* It felt familiar, only I was too afraid to move *And then I was writing in my diary: "The Final Chapter."*

"Stay focused." I blinked my eyes several times but could see nothing . *"If I can't see, at least I can think."*

So I thought about my two children; my husband; my mother; my sister; my brothers; my grandmother, who died in 1987; my grandfather, who died in 1992; my girlfriends; and the love of my life; I saw them all in one split second. Then it became very quiet, and my mind began to drift... and... drift... back to when I first started this job; when we were stewardesses, and we were young and beautiful. Flying was fun, and each day was an adventure. They were the "*Good ol' days,*" but they seemed like only yesterday. Had it really been thirty-one years...?

Five

May, 1972

Two weeks before graduating from Christian College in Nashville, I received a letter from Big Elite World Airlines, offering me a position as a stewardess. I was elated that they had received my application and quickly accepted the position. When I received a roundtrip ticket to fly to Atlanta for an interview, it was a dream come true.

For as long as I could remember, I had wanted to be a stewardess for Big E World Airlines. I grew up in Shelby County, Tennessee, just twenty miles east of Memphis, where the airline had a large stewardess base. We saw Big E stewardesses all the time, shopping in the mall, or at grocery stores.

As a child, I followed them around the stores, because they wore such cute hats with their uniforms. They looked liked paper dolls, and like paper dolls back then, they were always white. I was a teenager when I saw my first black Big E stewardess. Dancing with excitement, I wanted to follow her home, so I could see where stewardesses lived and what they did when they were not on an airplane. I thought it was the neatest job, traveling all over the world, meeting interesting people, wearing cute uniforms, and getting paid for it! It didn't occur to me that stewardesses had to work. I only visualized serving Coke and 7-up and smiling. We're all allowed to be naïve when we're young.

June 1972

After my college graduation, I went home for three weeks. My family threw me a big graduation and going-away party. The whole town came, and I told everyone I was going to be a stewardess.

"Sistergirl," they called me, since that was my nickname, "you mean to tell me them white folks lettin' Colored girls work on them there airplane nowadays?" Mother Sadie Wooden, the town's midwife in the old days, wanted to know. She was ninety-something years old.

"Yes, Miss Sadie, we saw one at the mall," my sister said.

"If God wanted us to fly, He'er given us wings," Miss Sadie said, nodding off.

"Times are changing, Miss Sadie, Colored girls can be whatever they want," my granddaddy said.

My granddaddy was the only father I'd ever known, and I was happy for his approval. He always said he would rather pay to walk than to fly for free, but he wanted me to see the world instead of staying around home, working in the family funeral-home business. He gave me five hundred dollars to buy some new clothes, and he promised to buy me a car when I received my stewardess wings. Before I left, he pulled me aside and reminded me always to represent the family well, and to never forget where I came from.

I bought a few new outfits from JCPenney's and saved some of the five hundred dollars for spending money before flying to Atlanta for the initial stewardess training. This flight to Atlanta was my third time on an airplane. The first time was when I flew to Atlanta from Nashville for my first interview, and the second time was the return flight.

I checked into the Elite World Airlines Training Center for the June 26, 1972, Stewardess Class. There was a lot of paperwork to fill out. The company did not give lie-detector or drug tests back then. I admit I had never seen or used drugs at that stage of my life, and I had only been drunk once, in college.

I was assigned to a room with another black girl from Anniston, Alabama, named Barbara Ann Harris. I was first to arrive, so I picked the best bed and dresser and started to unpack.

A few hours later, I heard a key in the door, and I held my breath to see what my new roommate would look like. The door opened, and one of the most beautiful women I had ever seen entered the room. She was light brown, with thick, black hair, and a perfect round face. She was probably accustomed to people being blown away by her good looks, because she didn't notice me staring. She introduced herself. "Hello, I'm Barbara Ann Harris, and you must be Amanda," she said with a heavy southern accent.

I liked her right away. "Yes, I'm Amanda Louise Callaway."

"It's a pleasure to meet you, Amanda." I could feel that she liked me.

"I'm from Tennessee, and you're from Alabama, right?" She looked a little surprised, so I said the housemother had told me, when I checked in, I would be rooming with someone from Anniston, Alabama.

She started to unpack as I sat on my bed and watched. "I don't care which bed I take, you can choose," I said, just to make conversation because I wanted the bed I had picked.

She put her suitcase on the other bed. "This one is fine," she said, and she started unpacking.

She had four large suitcases and two large garment bags. She unpacked the garment bags first. She took out beautiful designer dresses and suits and hung them on coat hangers. She had designer shoes to match each outfit. I went to my closet to get her my extra clothes hangers, then quickly closed my closet door. Compared to hers, my clothes looked liked they came from a garage sale, though I did have four new dresses from JCPenney's.

Before we graduated from training, I would find out that her boyfriend was a big-time hustler, and most of her designer clothes were stolen. That was only the beginning of the things I would learn about Miss Harris as time went along Looks could be very deceiving. There was a lot more to come.

The mandatory trainee meeting was at eight o'clock that evening. We would meet the other stewardess trainees. Barbara Ann and I started to dress early. She had on a designer's light-blue suit with matching shoes, and I had on my off-the-rack, department store dress with black pumps from the Shoe Outlet. I estimated our outfits' total worth at two hundred, thirty-five dollars. My outfit accounted for only the thirty-five.

I never had a problem with low self-esteem. I was five-foot-four, with a perfect, hourglass shape. So my thirty-five dollar outfit felt like a Couture, designed just for me.

Barbara Ann and I entered the meeting room, left our purses on seats next to each other to reserve them, and mingled. There were about twenty trainees already in the room. We introduced ourselves and generally sized each other up: like who was pretty, and who was ugly; who was sophisticated, and who was a country bumpkin. We felt the housemother and the teachers watching our every move, so we tried hard to act sociable. Stewardesses were supposed to be friendly and outgoing, and we wanted to make a good first impression. We sipped soft drinks offered at a table in the back of the room and smiled a lot.

The training director called the meeting to order at eight o'clock sharp. No one was late: There was an unwritten rule inscribed on our brains: *Stewardesses are not supposed to be late.* They had stressed that fact enough in our previous interviews.

There were thirty trainees in the June 26, 1972, class. Eight of us were black, and twenty-two were white. We were all female, because Big E wasn't hiring male stewards at that time. The training director introduced herself first. She had a harsh, manly appearance, like a lesbian. Then she introduced the house mother and our four teachers, who were line stewardesses on loan to teach initial training. Next, she asked us to introduce ourselves and tell where we were from. Twenty-five of the trainees were from the South: Seven were from Alabama, nine were from Georgia, two were from Florida, three were from Mississippi, two were from Tennessee, and one was from each of the Carolinas. Four were from Texas, and one outcast, from California, was named Jackie O'Brien. Her bleached blonde, Hollywood-tamed looks just did not fit in with the rest of us. To put it mildly, she looked like one of those ladies-of-the-evening. Everything about her looked fake. She had fake eyelashes, fake nails, and fake breasts, which were about a 40D. We were all thinking the same thing: "*Who did she screw to get here?*" It wouldn't take long to find out.

After our introduction, the director went over a breakdown of our four weeks of training. We would be tested each morning on the previous day's lesson. We had to maintain a ninety percent average throughout training. On the day we fell below ninety, we would be given a full-fare ticket home. We had to wear heels and stockings, with makeup in place, and be in class, promptly, by eight a.m. At eight a.m., the doors were locked. If you were late, you had to report to the director's office, and you had better have a good excuse.

"A makeup artist will be coming later this week to show all of you how to apply your makeup and wear your hair to best compliment your face." The director continued. "Until then, you will have to work with what you were born with; no false eyelashes or wigs." Of course, we all looked at Jackie.

We all knew we needed help in that department, not just Jackie.

"Just please don't let our makeup artist be the same one who taught you how to apply your makeup." I was thinking as I looked at the director as she spoke.

"Are there any questions?" she asked.

As we expected, Jackie raised her hand.

She said she had no natural eyebrows or eyelashes, and she had a doctor's note to testify to that.

"We will review your doctor's notes tomorrow," the director said, then continued her speech as though Jackie's question was not important.

"First thing Monday morning, each of you will be given a complete physical. You will have to pass weight check, too," she added.

Making weight check didn't look like a problem with this class. No one looked overweight.

Each of the instructors spoke. All were stewardesses on assignment to teach initial training, and each said she knew what we were going through, because they had been where we are.

The house mother was the last to speak.

"There are house rules you all must follow. Number one: No men in your room." She knew that would produce a chuckle from all of us.

"You have to sign out when you leave the building, and sign in when you return. You have a ten o'clock curfew during the week and a midnight curfew on weekends. Trainees who live in Atlanta may go home on weekends, but you have to be back in the building by midnight Sunday night. Breaking curfew is grounds for dismissal from training. You must conduct yourselves like young ladies at all times." The housemother paused. "Are there any questions?"

There were none.

At the end of the meeting, we all gathered at the back of the room, drinking Coca Cola and eating snacks. We were all determined to be there in four weeks on graduation day and be given our wings to fly.

Six

Eight o'clock on Monday morning, we packed into an employee bus and rode five miles to the airline's general offices to receive an ID card and to take a physical. We all had to meet with a psychologist to see if we were mentally fit for the job.

One by one, we filed into the psychologist's, office only to realize he was crazier than we were. He asked the white trainees if they got along with black people, and he asked us if we held any animosity toward white people. I don't have to tell you what we said. There was a picture on his wall that was obviously crooked. We couldn't decide if this was part of the psychological test, but we all noticed the picture.

He spoke with the whole group at the end of the day, and one of the trainees asked him if we were supposed to comment on the picture.

"What picture?" he asked.

He was surprised the picture was crooked, and he said that he would straighten it as soon as he got back to his office.

At the end of day one, our class was down to twenty-eight trainees. One of the black girls from Georgia had sickle-cell anemia, and one of the white girls from Alabama was three months pregnant and did not know it. They were sent home immediately.

The first two weeks went by like lighting. All twenty-eight of us were still there. We were beginning to know each other a little better. Jackie was able to wear the false eyelashes and penciled-in eyebrows. They treated her with kid gloves, and we couldn't figure out why, although, I must admit, she was really a very nice girl.

Barbara Ann and I got along perfectly. We studied together every night. Sometimes, we included Michele Crawford and Helena Meriwether, two of the black girls from Texas. We studied our butts off and only maintained a ninety-four average. We couldn't understand why most of the white girls had ninety-eight or ninety-nine averages, except for Jackie, whose average was always ninety. The white trainees went out every night and studied less than the black trainees, and believe me, they were not smarter. Then Joann from Birmingham let the cat out of the bag one day while we were having a casual conversation.

It turned out that most of the white trainees had friends who were already Big E stewardesses, and who had given them all of their old training materials. Thus, they knew what was going to be on all the tests and were able to study the actual material in advance. In contrast, all the material was new to the black trainees. Big E Airlines did not have very many black stewardesses back then, so we had no way of knowing what to expect, and so we, of course, had to study every night.

Fredricka Johnston, a pretty black trainee from North Carolina, refused to study with us. She hung out with and studied with the white trainees from Alabama. We had no problems with that. Barbara Ann and I decided there was always one black person in a group who would prefer to hang with another race and, vice-versa. It was not as though she ignored us, she simply preferred their company to ours.

At the beginning of the third week, the white trainees had Fredricka studying the wrong materials one night while they were out partying. The next morning, she flunked the test. Her average fell to eighty-nine-point-nine. The director came and got her out of class, and by lunch break, she had a full-fare ticket and was on a flight back to North Carolina. They didn't give her the opportunity to say goodbye.

Fredricka telephoned us several times when she got home, crying. She realized she screwed up by not studying with us or some of the other black trainees. She felt she was setup by those white trainees with whom she studied.

Two days later, a white trainee from Florida had an average that fell below ninety, and she was sent home, just as Fredricka had been. We didn't feel sorry for her, because she was one of those girls who had the training material. Her best friend was a Big E stewardess, so she had answers to the test questions months in advance, and she still flunked. She was one dumb chick!

One of the trainees from Georgia, Mary Thomaston, didn't add up, either. She didn't look like she had gone through the same interview and scrutiny as the rest of us had gone through. She was homely, and there was nothing attractive about her. She appeared to be afraid of blacks, and would not sit next to any of the black girls or eat at the same table with any of us.

"Mary is a racist," I remarked to Barbara Ann and Michele, and they agreed. When you were raised in the South, you could tell by a person's body language, or how they related to you, whether or not they are prejudiced. Mary was filled with hatred and we didn't make her life any easier. We sat beside her every chance we got. We made sure to touch her hand or arm with our black skin. She knew better than to let signs of her prejudice show during training. Ironically, Mary went to church every Sunday, and to bible study on Wednesday nights.

We came to find out that Mary's father and one of the senior vice presidents of Elite World Airlines were on the same deacon board of the local United Methodist Church. My granddaddy always said the white United Methodists had a history of racism, dating back to slavery, and that KKK meetings were held in those churches. He had no proof of this, but I believed my granddaddy.

"How could you *not* be hired if you got a recommendation from the company's senior vice president?" we questioned her.

"It's like me getting a recommendation from the vice president of the United States," I said.

We found out about her family connections when one of our instructors came back from the general offices and said to Mary, in front of the whole class, "Mr. Motley asked about you. He wanted to know how you were doing in class. He told me he knew your family and that he had recommended you."

Mary had a funny look on her face, as if she had been caught with her hand in the cookie jar. Her secret was out, and she knew it.

She came to our room one night to apologize.

"I tried to get this job on my own, but I was rejected five times, Mr. Motley got me this job as a favor to my father," she confessed. "Also, my father is a racist. I was taught to hate black people. He believes y'all are bad people. He calls y'all niggers, orangutans, and monkeys." She started to cry. "I know it's wrong, please forgive me."

After the "monkey business," Barbara Ann wanted to have nothing to do with Mary. "I don't have the stomach for this, I'll be in Michele's room," she said, as she got up and left the room without looking at Mary.

Mary was still crying, but I was clueless as to why.

"You can't help what you were taught," I said, trying to comfort her. "We come into the world not knowing anything. Our parents are our teachers."

"My father said if I ever looked at a black man, he would disown me," Mary said. "He might kill me."

"But your father is a deacon in one of the biggest churches in Atlanta. A man of God!" I protested.

"Yes, but he is also a liar, an alcoholic, a wife beater, and a lousy father," she said, with a lot of anger in her voice.

"Mary, you have a lot of issues, but I can't help you." I felt sorry for her.

"Amanda, I want to keep this job and make friends. Please don't tell the other trainees," she begged.

I reassured Mary I wouldn't tell a soul. Her secret was safe with me, but I was sure they already knew. That's why she was there in our room. She was trying to cop a plea. That was her problem, and I didn't really trust this girl. So using a southern term, 'I showed her the door.'

By the end of the third week, Barbara Ann and I had brought our average up to ninety-seven. We were feeling proud, and we felt we should go out to celebrate. She was feeling horny, and her hustler boyfriend was coming to town on Saturday. He had two cousins who lived in College Park, Georgia, a town not far from the training center. They wanted to meet a couple of her friends. Of course, she picked me and our other study partner, Michele Crawford.

Many nights, after we finished studying, Barbara Ann and I would sit on our beds and talk. She talked about her boyfriend and wondered what he was doing every minute of the day. Every morning, noon, and night, when we weren't studying or in class, she was on the telephone, begging him to drive to Atlanta to see her. After three weeks of begging, he must have said yes. She was all excited about getting laid. I could not imagine loving anyone that much.

"Girl, I've been screwing this man since I was fourteen, and he was eighteen. He put me through college, and I am going to marry that Calvin one day," she told me one night.

Barbara Ann was one year older than me, and I was twenty-one. However, she had years of experience on me. I didn't start screwing until I was eighteen and in college.

I had to be careful, because I didn't want a reputation of being "green." I was already voted most trustworthy of our group. I was becoming the one all the other trainees could count on, and in whom they could confide. Maybe it was because of my religious background and Christian schooling. Little did I know that this label would follow me throughout my career with Big E World Airlines.

On Saturday afternoon, around three o'clock, Barbara Ann's boyfriend, Calvin "Big Daddy" Washington, pulled up at the training center. He was driving a long, red-and-white Lincoln Continental with a diamond in the back and a sunroof top. When he stepped out of the car, our mouths fell open. He was at least six-foot-four and weighed about two hundred and twenty pounds. He looked like he lifted weighs every day of his life. He had on navy blue pants and a matching safari button-down shirt, the kind Nelson Mandela wore. We knew he was packing a rod that could satisfy all three of us and still have some left over for five other women. Barbara Ann ran into his arms, even though she knew she had to be cool, because all the white trainees and the house mother were peeping out of their windows. She couldn't help herself.

For a minute, she forgot about us, but we knew that, eventually, she had to breathe and would remember us. We waited to be introduced to this fine specimen of a man. I hoped that, when God made him, He hadn't thrown away the mold.

Somehow, he managed gently to push Barbara Ann off of him and remind her where she was and to be cool.

"Smart guy." I was amused.

"Oh, excuse me," Barbara Ann said, clearing her throat. She looked up at his face, then smiled. "This is my roommate, Amanda. I told you about her, and my friend Michele Crawford from Houston. Amanda, Michele, this is my boyfriend, Calvin Washington," she said proudly.

Calvin smiled, removed his Stetson, and shook our hands. We both almost melted right into the cement sidewalk.

"Pleased to meet you, ladies." He has a deep Southern drawl. "Forget about Calvin, just call me "Big Daddy." That's what everyone else calls me," he said and smiled again. He had straight, white teeth, slightly stained from cigarette smoking, and his voice was smooth, but quite gentle for a big man.

Barbara Ann always called him Calvin, but we called him "Big Daddy" from then on.

"So you ladies want to see the town?" Big Daddy said as he opened the front-passenger door for Barbara Ann, and the back door for us. Michele and I slid in. He closed the doors and went around to the driver's side to get in. We could see Big Daddy was used to having an effect on women, and we had not disappointed him.

Michele and I smiled at each other. We both were thinking that, if Big Daddy's cousins looked anything like him, we were giving it up tonight. We were in love. Big Daddy had set the standard for how we would view men for the rest of our career.

We rode around Atlanta for about three hours. Big Daddy showed us downtown, Auburn Avenue, The Rev. Martin Luther King's home, and Ebenezer Baptist Church. Coming back to Southwest Atlanta, we went by Spelman College, Morehouse and Clark Atlanta University. Barbara Ann sat close to Big Daddy in the front seat and kissed and snuggled him, every chance she got. We knew she wanted to be with him all by herself, and we couldn't blame her. However, she was cool and allowed him to show us around town without complaining.

We stopped at Paschel Restaurant to eat, and Big Daddy paid for everything.

When we left there, we headed for his cousins' apartment in College Park. We arrived at the apartment around seven-thirty, and the cousins were expecting us.

Disappointed, we saw right away that Big Daddy's cousins didn't look like they were related to him. Since we were already there, we went along with the program. They had bought Morgan David wine and potato chips.

Charles, cousin number one, was my date. He was short and overweight. Shawn, cousin number two, Michele's date, was a little taller, slimmer, and a little better looking.

Barbara Ann and Big Daddy went immediately to the back bedroom while Charles served us wine in plastic glasses.

Shawn and Michele sat on the sofa while Charles and I sat on the floor, next to the stereo, going through the albums. Things was going well. The wine and the music were good, and we began to loosen up.

Barbara Ann and Big Daddy were getting it on by now. We heard moaning and growling and the bed squeaking. Charles and I smiled at each other, and he turned up the music to drown out the sound.

I looked toward the sofa and noticed Shawn rolling a joint. I had never smoked weed before, and I was not sure about Michele. She didn't look surprised, and she was drinking the Morgan David like water.

Charles asked me about the training, and I turned my attention away from Michele for a while.

I became aware of the aroma of marijuana as the smoke drifted through the room and reached my nose. Michele was smoking like a pro, and Shawn was already rolling another joint. He lit it and handed it to Charles, who offered it to me first, and when I shook my head no, he brought it to his mouth and inhaled deeply.

As the evening went on, Shawn and Michele were getting cozy, and she was giggling. Charles and I were having a good time, although we had made no physical contact. I was feeling groovy, probably from the second-hand smoke, but still kept my eye on the clock on top of the stereo, because I didn't want us to be late for curfew. I could see Charles was digging me, but he didn't want to be pushy and scare me off.

"Maybe we can see each other again," he kept saying.

"Sure," I said, but I really wasn't sure. I started thinking, *"I don't have a steady boyfriend. Why? I'm not bad looking. People always say I'm cute, like a Barbie Doll dipped in chocolate, with a beautiful smile. My flawless dark skin and small features were complimented by my hairstyle, a short curly Afro."* I decided I was just moving through life, one day at a time, trying to find myself.

The evening went by quickly. Michele and Shawn had moved past talking and were necking. I didn't know Michele was so loose.

At eleven-forty, I asked, "Michele, shouldn't we be getting ready to go?"

Michele was two sheets to the wind and was in a happy mood. I knew she was too sensible to break curfew.

"What time is it?" she asked.

"Eleven-forty."

"Okay, yes," she said, groggily. I could tell she was ready to give Shawn some.

"We're having a good time; we hate to leave," I said to the guys. "But we must."

Charles offered to drive us back to the training center in his car.

Barbara Ann could come with Big Daddy.

I knocked on the bedroom door.

"Barbara Ann, It's eleven-forty. We are going back to the training center. Charles will drive us. We'll see you there, okay," I said, and I could smell the distinct odor of marijuana coming from under the door.

"Okay, I'll see you guys there," she said from inside.

Shawn and Michele were already in the backseat of the car when Charles and I came out. Michele's blouse was open, and Shawn had his mouth all over her tits. She was still giggling.

I ignored them. Charles opened the front door for me. I heard them necking on the whole drive to the training center. I also smelled the joint they were smoking.

Charles had an old car designed for three to sit in the front. I scooted over close so he would not feel left out of the action. He put his right arm around my shoulders and pulled me closer to him and drove with his left hand. I could tell he was enjoying the moment. It felt good, but I was glad the night was over, because I was getting turned on and wet between my thighs. I was an old-fashioned girl. I had never slept with a guy on a first date, and I wasn't about to start now.

Charles parked the car in one of the parking spaces at the side of the building and turned the ignition off. We necked a bit, and I let him run his hand up my thigh. Just when he reach my wet spot, I checked my watch, and it was seven minutes from curfew. I pulled away and said it was time to go in. Charles pulled out a piece of paper from the glove compartment.

"May I have the phone number here? I'll call you tomorrow. Maybe, we can get together one evening next week," he said.

I wrote down the number and looked to the back seat for Michele.

She was trying to push Shawn off her so she could get out. He kept unbuttoning her blouse as she was trying to button it. We left them in the car.

"I can't wait to see you again. I really like you, Amanda," Charles kept saying as we walked to the door.

Big Daddy and Barbara Ann pulled up, and Michele and Shawn were walking slowly, arm-in-arm, as though they had been going together for years.

Another car pulled up behind Big Daddy's, and Jackie jumped out. Her date stayed in the car instead of walking her to the door. I got a glimpse of him as he quickly drove off. He was a handsome, older man who looked slightly familiar.

Several other trainees were walking toward the door from the parking lot, arm-and-arm with their boyfriends. We had all made curfew.

I forgot about Jackie until I realized she was waiting for us inside the door. It was obvious that she had been drinking and was upset about something. She followed us to our room and came in without being invited. Barbara Ann and I looked at each other, because we were tired and wanted to go to bed. Jackie propped herself up in the center of my bed and started talking. We didn't have to pull any information out of her. She was crying and talking at the same time.

She told us she was a call girl in Los Angeles when she "first met the senator." As soon as she mentioned his name, Barbara Ann and I gasped. No wonder he looked familiar and was in such a hurry to drive off. He was very popular, and from a very wealthy Democratic family in Atlanta. He was always on television; there was talk that he might run for president of the United States. He was also on the board of directors of Elite World Airlines. Everyone knew he was married with children, and that his wife was a wealthy socialite.

"He brought me to Atlanta and bought me a condo in Buckhead and a car. I got tired of sitting around the house waiting to service him, so he got me this job with Big E. I didn't even interview, I just showed up." She was crying hysterically. I went to the bathroom and got her some Kleenex. This was too juicy; she couldn't stop now.

"I'm a fake, with only a high school education," she continued. "I can hardly keep up in class, and don't know how I keep making a ninety on all the tests." Barbara Ann and I looked at each other. We had some ideas on the subject.

The senator's wife found out about the affair and ordered her husband to end it immediately, or she would file for divorce and ruin his career.

"The bastard gave me a check for ten thousand dollars." She paused and threw the check on the bed. "He told me to lay low for a while. Well, I'm glad, because I'm tired of being his whore. All he wants is for me to suck his dick. That's all I'm good for." She was crying again. "I have to masturbate just to satisfy myself. We never fuck. I'm finished with him, because I met a black man who works around the pool at my condo, and he gives me all I can handle. He's this big." She held her hand about eight inches apart. "You all know what I mean, you all get it all the time."

Barbara Ann and I disagreed, but we didn't interrupt her.

"He's the best I've ever had, and all I want to do is lay up with him. I've been with him every night this week. We meet at the Howard Johnson down the street." She started feeling on herself.

Barbara Ann and I stared in disbelief. It was time for her to go to her own room.

"Come on, Jackie, we'll walk you to your room," Barbara Ann said as we helped her up, but she had more to say.

"I have also slept with Mr. Whitmore." He was one of the senior vice-presidents of Big E. "All he wanted was oral sex, too. Do I have 'Cocksucker' written across my forehead?" Jackie asked as we walked, but mostly carried her two doors down the hall to her room.

She couldn't stand up on her own. We were surprised, well, not too surprised, to find she had a suite and no roommate.

It was starting the fourth and final week, and we were very busy.

Barbara Ann and I forgot about what Jackie told us. She was our new best friend, and we couldn't turn without her. She never studied, because she was out every night until curfew and even used some of the ten thousand dollars to buy the black boyfriend a car. And every night, she stopped by our room to give us the details.

"I hope he isn't using Jackie," I said to Barbara Ann one night.

"He probably is, you know how black men love to fool around with white women with money," Barbara Ann sympathized. "But hell, he must be working hard for her, laying pipe." We both smiled.

Charles and Shawn called the training center every night. There was no time to go out. We had uniform fittings, graduation rehearsals, and pictures to take for our new employee ID card. The best I could do was promise Charles he could come visit as soon as I got settled in a home base. However, Michele found time to go out with Shawn. She had to have a piece of the action, even though she had a boyfriend in Houston. She was docile about it the next day, so we assumed the sex was not good. However, we did not press her.

There were twenty-six trainees left in the June 26 class. We pulled numbers from one to twenty-six out of a hat to decide our positions in the class. I drew eighteen, and Michele drew nineteen. Only the person who drew number one got to choose the base she wanted. The rest of us got New Orleans.

Barbara Ann drew three and was upset, because New Orleans was a long way from Anniston and Big Daddy. She cried for two days.

The rest of us were worried about Irene Bourgerone, the New Orleans base manager. She had a reputation for being a class bitch. We heard she was so mean that she would make the new stewardesses cry. If you got on Irene's bad side, your future with Elite World Airlines would be very limited.

We graduated Saturday morning. John Whitmore, senior vice president of in-flight service spoke about the challenges of being a stewardess. His speech was interesting, but all Barbara Ann and I could think about was what Jackie had told us about him. We only wanted to walk across the stage so he could pin on our wings and hand us our certificates. It had been a long, hard four weeks, and we were ready to move on. We were ready to be *Stewardesses* or *Sky Goddesses* or *Glorified Waitresses.*

Seven

By Saturday afternoon, most of us were in New Orleans. A few girls were given permission to drive. They told us we had three days to find an apartment. However, Irene Bourgerone, the base manager, could change things if she saw fit. The airline reserved rooms for us at the Holiday Inn Airport. We had orders to check in with Irene before going to the hotel.

We did not have to find Irene. She was waiting for us at the gate when we got off the plane. She was a small woman, about five-foot-seven, and she weighed no more than one hundred pounds. She reminded me of Granny on the *Beverly Hillbillies*. Of course, she was not that old. She had a permanent frown on her forehead, and it made her look mean.

One-by-one, we filed into Irene's conference room, and she sized us up one-by-one. When we were seated, she stood at the front of the room and laid down the law: Irene's Law:

"You are on call starting right now. You can count on being on reserve and probation for six months. If you call in sick during that time, you better have a doctor's excuse or be on your deathbed. No-showing a trip is grounds for termination. You must be in full uniform when you come to work, or I will send you home, which will count as a no-show. If you color your hair, I will not tolerate dark roots. Your stockings must be the color of your legs, nails must be manicured and polished. I want your legs and underarms shaven at all times. Be sure to stay out of trouble. You all will conduct yourselves in a ladylike manner at all times. You represent Elite World Airlines, and don't you forget it, or you will answer to me. Are there any questions?"

No one raised her hand. No one dared raised her hand!

"Good, then we have an understanding. You are released to go straight to the Holiday Inn Airport. I will see if I can release any of you tomorrow to go look for an apartment. I will call you tonight to make sure you're in your room, so don't plan on sneaking out," she finally finished.

Irene left a bad taste in our mouths. All she needed was a floppy hat and a broom, because she was the closest thing to a witch we had ever seen. We were all grown women, but we were being treated like children.

We took the Holiday Inn van from the airport to check into our rooms. They were waiting for us at the hotel. We had heard the hotel staff liked to check out the new stewardesses.

Barbara Ann and I roomed together. Michele and Helena Meriwether, another black girl from Texas, were in the adjoining room. The others also paired up, two to a room.

I called my grandparents to let them know I made it to New Orleans, and Barbara Ann called Big Daddy. We were afraid to stay on the phone long, in case Irene called.

All four of us were in one room with the adjoining door open when Irene called at around ten o' clock. We were released until five o' clock the next day to find an apartment. She had called the Lewis & Clark Apartments' manager, and they had enough vacancies to accommodate all of us. Graduates from the last class lived there, and they would be happy to show us around.

When Irene hung up, we all looked at each other and screamed, "We are released until five o' clock tomorrow afternoon!" The last thing we wanted to do was sleep. Michele called the front desk to see if we could get a taxi to downtown Bourbon Street. We knew nothing about New Orleans, but we were going to find out. There was a black guy working at the front desk. We had seen him checking us out when we were registering, because we were checking him out, too.

"Where would you ladies like to go?" he asked Michele.

"Do you know where we can find a party?"

"I get off in half an hour, and I would be happy to take you ladies to the Coyote Club; it's always jamming on Saturday night," he said.

"We will be ready," she said and hung up.

We looked at each other and started laughing.

"Let's party!" we all screamed at once, and danced around the room.

We put on our best party rags and were downstairs thirty minutes later. He was waiting for us.

"My name is Ricky McBride," he said.

We all introduced ourselves as we piled into his car.

Michele sat up front; Barbara Ann, Helena and I sat in the back.

As we pulled out of the hotel parking lot, Ricky asked if any of us smoked weed. He just happened to have enough marijuana for a few joints. He handed a plastic bag to Michele, and she began to roll joints like a pro. She lit a joint and passed it to the back. Helena inhaled first and passed it to Barbara Ann, who inhaled and passed it to me.

"Come on, Amanda, don't be a party-pooper," she said.

I took the joint, inhaled, and almost choked to death. Helena hit me on the back several times so I could catch my breath.

"Take another hit, slowly; it will feel better this time," Barbara Ann suggested.

She was right, the second hit was not bad. That was the first time I smoked marijuana.

We stopped by Ricky's apartment so he could change. We were feeling pretty good. He had a half-bottle of Ripple wine in his refrigerator. We finished it off while he showered and changed. Ricky was tall and not bad looking. We told Michele to go for it, because he seemed rather interested in her. We each would find our own at the club.

Needless to say, I found out more about my colleagues that night than the four weeks of training had ever revealed.

First, Michele was wild and man-crazy. After a few drinks, she was all over Ricky. She ended up spending the night at his apartment.

Barbara Ann liked drugs and drinking, but she was not going to give any ass to anyone but Big Daddy. She would tease a guy, but that was as far as it would go.

Helena was easily influenced and very insecure. She was older and should have been the leader, yet she was the follower. She hooked up with the first man who asked her to dance. Against our better judgment, he drove her back to the hotel and spent the night in her room, since her roommate, Michele, was spending the night with Ricky.

Barbara Ann and I danced with a lot of guys. I did not find a single one to whom I was even tempted to give my number.

Ricky dropped Barbara Ann and me off at the hotel at around five in the morning. Helena and her friend were already in the room, going at it. She had locked the door connecting our rooms, and we had to listen to, "Oh baby! Oh baby! Do it!" for the rest of the night.

"I wish she would shut the fuck up. She's making me wish Big Daddy was here," Barbara Ann complained.

The noise didn't bother me. I was tired and went right to sleep.

The next day, Michele and Helena talked nonstop.

"Ricky has the cutest ass; his penis crooks to the right, like a fishing hook. It was a whole new experience, I couldn't get enough. Just thinking about it gives me chills," she said.

Helena's friend told her, after the fact, that he was married. He didn't give her his number, and he said he had to call her because his wife was jealous and didn't trust him. We wondered why.

"Don't look so down and out, Helena. You win some, and you lose some. You were doing all that whooping and hollering last night, the man must have laid one on you. So you got a good fuck out of the deal," Barbara Ann said.

We all laughed, but Helena didn't think it was funny.

Eight

We signed a one-year lease on a two-bedroom apartment at the Lewis & Clark Apartments. It was in a new section of the apartment complex, and had never been lived in.

Again, Barbara Ann and I were roommates. Helena and Michele rented the two-bedroom apartment nearest to us, upstairs and across the hall.

We put in two phone lines: One for Big E World Airlines and Irene, and the other line was for our personal calls. Collette Parker; Dondenisa, or Dee Dee, Randolph and Nicole Stevenson were black stewardesses from the previous class Irene had called. They were given strict orders to show us around. Nicole Stevenson was called out for a three-day trip early that morning.

Irene's first choice had been Sarah Ferguson, the most senior black stewardess in the base and Irene's favorite. She was the one expected to keep us in line, but Sarah was out of town, so Irene chose Collette and Dee Dee to introduce us to the apartment manager.

"Damn, Irene is in everyone's business, I can't stand the bitch," Michele muttered.

"Easy! You don't want to cross Irene," Dee Dee cautioned. "She is meaner than a snake. She has already gotten a black girl from our class fired."

"Why, what did she do?" Michele asked.

"Nothing, she was pretty and wouldn't kiss Irene's ass. Look, girl, Irene doesn't need a reason to have you fired," Collette said and changed the subject. "Okay, ladies, forget about Irene for now. We are smarter than she will ever be. The New Orleans Saints are having a party in the Club House this Saturday night. Most of the Saints live right here in Lewis & Clark."

"But we'll be on call," I said. "We have to move in first."

"We are always on call. You all will be moved in by then, and the last flight we could be called for is a Dallas Turn-A-Round, one-day-trip, that leaves at eleven thirty at night. After eleven thirty, we'll take turns answering the phone. If scheduling calls, just pretend you are the person and write down the rotation."

I could see these girls had a system in place, so all we had to do was follow it.

We moved in on Tuesday, our phone had been put in that morning, and our rental furniture arrived in the afternoon, all thanks to Irene. On Wednesday, we went shopping to buy some necessary supplies. Before we could get excited about the Saints' party, I got a call for a three-day trip. It laid over in Knoxville and Augusta. Michele and Barbara Ann were sent on a three-day trip to Monroe and Cincinnati. On Friday, Collette and Dee Dee left on two-day trips and got back too late for the party. But, ah well, there would be many more Saints parties.

We still had not met Sarah Ferguson. We had heard so much about her. Her boyfriend owned the Lagniappe Club, a very upscale nightclub in the Ninth Ward. She spent most of her off-days at his house. She was a "Hot Momma" who knew lots of guys to hook us up with, and we were ready!

Nine

Our first six months of probation were uneventful. Irene was on our butts, twenty-four-seven. We worked every day we were on call. With only two days off during the week, nothing was happening, and we were too tired to do anything but sleep. Our weekends were spent stuck on a layover in Small Town USA with nothing to do but shop and sleep. Very seldom were we given the good layovers, like Los Angeles or San Francisco. Irene saved those trips for her picks.

Big Daddy drove down to visit Barbara Ann twice, and each time she had to beg him to come. They spent all their time in the bed, making love and smoking weed. He brought us a supply of weed both times he came.

Also during the first six months, Charles and Shawn, Big Daddy's cousins, drove to New Orleans to visit Michele and me. We had learned our way around the city. My grandfather had given me a 1972 Toyota Corolla, and Michele bought a Volkswagen Bug. We took the guys to Bourbon Street and went into some of those XXX peepshow arcades, which were "hot" and all new to me. For a quarter, you could watch any sex act you wanted for five minutes. There were no arcades like that in Nashville!

We ate red beans and rice at a local restaurant and went to the Al Hurt Club for hurricane drinks and jazz. New Orleans was a great city for just hanging out. We stopped by a grocery store on the way back to the apartment to pick up a bottle of Remy Martin Cognac, which had become our new drink of choice. In Tennessee, you couldn't buy liquor at a grocery store. There were lots of things we could do in New Orleans that we never knew about before!

At the apartment, Shawn rolled a few joints, and we smoked, although we were already stoned. Shawn and Michele were all over each other, picking up where they'd left off in Atlanta. They went upstairs to Michele's apartment and could barely wait until they were through the door.

As soon as they left my apartment, Charles started kissing me, and before I knew it, he had unbuttoned my blouse. I didn't have on a bra, and when he saw my bare breast, he couldn't control himself.

He was a very gentle lover and liked lots of foreplay, and so did I, but marijuana had a way of making me horny. I was wet and wanted to get right to it. Instead, he wanted to play in my wetness, then he wanted to lick it dry. I had to pull him up. When we finally got around to intercourse, he came in two minutes. I was just getting warmed up. That must have been his way, and it was not hard to figure out. He wanted more oral sex, and I wanted more old-fashioned sex; certainly, more than two minutes worth. He was good with his tongue, and I had some good orgasms, but we did it four times in three days and every time it was two minutes. He apologized.

I knew Charles and I were not going to make it. I said I would try to come to Atlanta to see him, although I had no interest in seeing him again.

After they left, Michele and I decided to compare notes, and she immediately announced that Shawn was history. When I told her about Charles, we laughed, because Shawn was just the opposite: He did not care for foreplay, and she did. He wanted to stick his penis right in. It was "long, but too skinny." He kept a hard-on and could do it three times a day. He didn't like doing oral sex, but he enjoyed receiving it from her. As we compared notes, Michele confessed she enjoyed sex, but she had never had an orgasm! I told her I had never *not* had one. She wanted to know what she could do to have an orgasm.

"Why in the hell are you asking me? Do I look like I know anything about sex?" I said.

I asked her about Ricky with the crooked penis.

"I was close and thought I was going to have one. It didn't happen, and he came. That's the story of my life, which is why I have so many men. I'm trying to have an orgasm. I've had small dicks, large dicks, fat dicks, skinny dicks, and you-name-it dicks, and I've never had an orgasm. The man who gives me an orgasm, I will marry!" She made it a declaration.

I could only hope she didn't have to screw every man in New Orleans! Michele had so many men, we couldn't see how she kept them all apart. We were getting tired of lying for her. We would say she was on a trip when she was really upstairs with another man. Men wouldn't stop calling our apartment, looking for her.

She sounded depressed, and I didn't know what to say, but I had to say something. "Why don't you ask Barbara Ann? She has been screwing since she was fourteen, and she is always horny. Surely she knows."

"I don't want Barbara Ann and the other girls to know. They may think something is wrong with me."

"Why would they think that?" I argued. "I don't think anything is wrong with you."

"You are understanding and sympathetic. I know you wouldn't hurt a fly." Then came her brainstorm. "Oh, I have an idea. *You* ask Barbara Ann, but don't mention my name. Say you know of someone who has never had an orgasm. Pick her brain and tell me what she says. Please, Amanda, pretty pleaseee?" She was desperate.

"Okay, but I don't know why I let you talk me into this shit," I said.

I really didn't mind, because we all wanted to know the details about Big Daddy. As much time as they spent in her bedroom when he was in town, I had hoped he had it going on.

The only problem was, Barbara Ann was never around anymore. We had not seen her for three weeks. She would come in from her trip, take the next flight to Birmingham, rent a car, and drive to Anniston. That was her weekly routine. I never got to ask her about Big Daddy.

Ten

During our second six months of flying, we were finally off standby and able to hold lines, which means we took the same trip every week. With a set schedule, we had a social life.

One Friday night, we decided to have a pajama party. Barbara Ann was home, for a change, and about seven of us were lounging around our apartment, watching a black movie. It was the first time most of us had a weekend off together since we started flying. Those of us not watching the movie played cards. We loved bid-wiz. Dee Dee made a pitcher of her famous strawberry daiquiri.

Sarah Ferguson was suppose to bring over some of her famous spaghetti. However, she was delayed because of something to do with her boyfriend, nightclub owner Wendell Johnson. I had never met Sarah, but I had heard about her spaghetti and her boyfriend.

So we were all just chilling out when the phone rang. It was for Barbara Ann. When she hung-up, she looked sick. Someone asked her what was wrong.

"I have to go in the back and call Calvin," she said.

When she came out, she was happy again.

"What's going on?" Collette asked.

"My homegirl called and said some country bitch is going around town, claiming she is pregnant with Calvin's baby," Barbara Ann told us.

"And what did Big Daddy say?" Collette asked.

"He said he didn't even know the bitch," Barbara Ann said, smiling. "Case closed."

"And you believe him?" Dee Dee asked from the kitchen.

"Of course, I believe him, he has never lied to me before. Why shouldn't I believe him?"

"Because men lie, that's why. They will say whatever they think you want to hear to get in your drawers and get their nuts cracked. They don't give a damn about you," Michele chuckled.

"You should know; you fuck every man you meet. You have never had a real man," Barbara Ann shot back.

"How in the world do you know so much when the only man you've ever fucked is Big Daddy. At least, I can say I've fucked more than one man," Michele said, and stuck out her tongue.

"Barbara Ann, Michele is not saying Big Daddy is lying, maybe it's just a misunderstanding," I said. I wanted to get control of the situation before it got out of hand.

"Shut up, Amanda; you always want to sugarcoat shit. I'm saying, I'll bet all the tea in China, the nigger is lying. Sometimes a girl needs to hear the truth," Collette was screaming, and I knew the daiquiris were beginning to do the talking.

"All I want to say is, I wouldn't put it past a man to lie about something like this," Dee Dee broke in.

"If Big Daddy cared anything about Barbara Ann, he never would have fucked the country bitch. I would drop him if I was you, Barbara Ann," floozy Helena said. She had never dropped a man in her life.

"Helena, please, go back to watching the television," Dee Dee said.

"Y'all think I'm crazy, don't you?" Now Helena was getting upset.

"Helena, this isn't about you. It's about Barbara Ann and Big Daddy. Now, go sit down," Dee Dee challenged Helena.

"You don't tell me what to do. You ain't all that, Dee Dee." Helena was near tears.

A loud knock at the door was in the proverbial "nick of time."

Dee Dee opened the door, and it was Sarah Ferguson. She was carrying two big containers of food and wearing a full-length mink coat.

"What are you whores screaming about? I could hear you all the way down the walkway," Sarah wanted to know.

"Oh, nothing!" Dee Dee said, and motioned to us to keep quiet.

This was the first time I had actually laid eyes on Sarah Ferguson. She made quite an impression on me. First of all, she was almost six feet tall, light-brown skinned, with long dark-brown curly hair. Looking more like a model than a stewardess, she reminded me of Jayne Kennedy.

Sarah had been flying for five years, and was among the first black stewardesses hired by Big E. Since she dated a popular nightclub owner, she was sort of a celebrity herself. She knew the "Who's Who" of New Orleans, and she socialized with famous entertainers and movie stars. We looked up to her.

"I brought the spaghetti and a salad. I also brought a treat for you all." She opened up her purse, pulled out a prescription bottle, and emptied five huge pills on the table.

"What's that?" Collette asked.

"Quaaludes," Sarah said. "Now, if you want a good high and a good fuck, try this. You can't take the whole pill. It's too strong for you wimps." She broke each pill in quarters.

We forgot all about the argument and Big Daddy.

"Look, you all, Earth, Wind, and Fire; Frankie Beverly and Maze; the Commodores; comedian Franklyn Ajaye; and a few other groups will be performing tomorrow night at the Auditorium. They are having the after-party at the Club," Sarah announced. Of course, we knew the concert was the talk of the town.

Sarah continued, "I can get you guys tickets to the concert and into the party at the club. You all know the celebrities can't party out front with the regular folks. There are rooms in the back of the club they use. I can get you back there if you want to have some fun. Are you all going to fuck?" she asked.

We were all silent for a moment, trying to make sure we heard her correctly.

"What do you think those rooms are for? People to sit down and sip tea?" Sarah winked like a sly fox. "Entertainers and athletes come all the time, and Wendell sets them up with…uh…you know.....whatever they need; girls, drugs, whatever. They pay big bucks," she added.

Collette said she would do it if Sarah hooked her up with Earth, Wind, and Fire or Mr. Cool, who was a local entertainer. Michele said she would think about it. Helena wanted to see what everyone else decided before she made her decision. Dee Dee and I said we would take our chances out front with the regular folks, and Barbara Ann said she was not going, as her mind was on Big Daddy. Nicole had to work.

She wanted to call-in sick, but we talked her out of that. Irene had spies all over the place. If one of Irene's spies saw her at the concert when she was supposed to be sick and told Irene, she would be terminated. Anyway, when we called in sick, Irene would call us every three hours to make sure we were home.

We ate spaghetti and drank wine and talked until the wee hours of the morning. Sarah's spaghetti was as delicious as everyone had said it would be. I liked Sarah Ferguson from the very beginning.

We decided to get some sleep, because we had a big night ahead of us. We all slept wherever we could find a spot. There were already three bodies in my bed, two at the head and one at the foot, so I curled up on the floor under Sarah's full-length mink coat.

Eleven

The jazz show was fabulous. All of us were dancing and singing as we left the auditorium. I was so infatuated with the young comedian, Franklyn Ajaye, that I told Dee Dee, jokingly, that I would give my right arm to meet him. He was my speed!

We went straight to the Lagniappe Club. There were so many people outside trying to get in, we were glad Sarah remembered to leave our names at the door. She was waiting for us inside. She introduced us to her boyfriend, the renowned Wendell Johnson. He was fine: I'm talking tall, dark, and handsome, with movie star looks. He could make any woman's heart skip a beat, and he had an air of importance about him. He took time to acknowledge us, but it was obvious he was all about business. People greeted him with respect. Rumor had it that Wendell took in tons of money and had law-enforcement officers and politicians on his payroll. However, Sarah had him wrapped around her little finger, and he treated her with love and respect. They made a handsome couple. They had met on a flight when Sarah first started flying.

The club's patrons knew Sarah, and she moved with ease around among them. The bouncers and guards let her come and go as she pleased.

Once we were seated at our table, Collette and Michele decided they wanted to be a part of the action in the back rooms. Helena, Dee Dee, and I stayed out front. I wanted to meet the young comedian, Franklyn Ajaye, but I was too shy to tell anyone except Dee Dee.

"You two come with me," Sarah said to Collette and Michele, "and I promise to let the rest of you see the parties in the back rooms when they get hot and heavy. Now, order whatever you want, Wendell will pick up the tab." They were gone.

Helena, Dee Dee, and I drank, danced, and had a good time. We all had hooked up with some guys by the time Sarah returned, two hours later. We dropped them and followed her through some double doors past the bouncers standing on each side. Suddenly, it looked like we were in a whole different club. The part of the club we just left had all black customers, but in here they were mostly white. I wondered how so many of these white people had entered the club. They must have come in through the back door, because I certainly didn't see them come in through the front.

The lights were turned low, but we could see what was going on. About three mirrored trays were being passed around, each with lines of a white powder on the surface. People were taking turns snorting it up their nose, through a rolled-up hundred-dollar bill. When a mirror got to us, Sarah and Helena each snorted a line, while Dee Dee and I passed. Such was my introduction to cocaine. I recognized some of the entertainers and celebrities, mostly men. Some of the women wore scanty clothing and looked like prostitutes. They were drinking, smoking, talking, and seeming to be have a good time. Helena ran into a guy who was on her flight coming into New Orleans, and she decided to stay in the room and talk to him.

Sarah turned to Dee Dee and me. "When I take you two into the next room, don't look shocked and don't stare. Especially you, Amanda! Just keep moving with me."

We nodded, and Sarah gave me a hard, long look that said, "Don't embarrass me, bitch."

I managed to reassure her by nodding my head twice. I was hoping I would find Franklyn Ajaye in one of those rooms.

I was glad she warned us, because I was not prepared for what was going on in the next room.

It was an orgy! I couldn't believe my eyes when I saw Collette buck-naked, sitting with her pussy in some man's face while some other naked woman sucked on his dick like it was a popsicle. She was stoned out of her mind, so she did not see us. My eyes swept around the dim room: Everyone in the room was nude and engaging in some form of sexual activity. There were women kissing and sucking on women; threesome; twosome; it was like a pornography movie gone wild. I spotted Michele in the corner, having sex with a guy I recognized from one of the bands. She was screaming, "*Yes*! *Yes!*" I hoped she was finally having an orgasm. I even saw two white stewardesses, Karen Schneider and Dominique Van Stinchcomb, partaking of the action. I knew they had come in through the back door. We kept walking, and I was glad Franklyn wasn't in that room. As we moved on, we noticed other doors that Sarah didn't open.

"These rooms are for private parties," was all she said.

We could only imagine what was going on behind those doors.

Sarah opened the door to the last room. It was dark, except for three colored spotlights shining on three women dancing on three different tables in the front part of the room. They had on G-strings and see-through negligees. The music was soft and low. As my eyes adjusted to the colored lights, I saw a dancer sitting on a fat white man's lap, facing him, with her long leg wrapped around his chair. She was giving him a lap dance, I guessed. Then I noticed a group of men sitting at a table in the back who appeared to be conducting business.. They were paying no attention to the dancers or the fat man. One of the men was Wendell, and the others were white. Sarah acknowledged the men, whispered something in Wendell's ear, kissed him on the cheek, and we left the room.

I was disappointed that we had not seen the young comedian, but Dee Dee and I had seen enough. We thanked Sarah and were about to leave through the back door. As I opened the door, I walked directly into someone who bumped into me!. I couldn't believe my eyes. I looked at him, and he looked at me. He was better-looking up close. I was frozen in time.

"Hello," he said.

He was with an older man, and since I hadn't moved to let them through the door, he finally said, "I'm Franklyn Ajaye, and this is my manager, Wally..."

I didn't get his manager's last name, because Dee Dee was pinching my arm so hard to get me to move-on.

"And you are?" Franklyn finally asked.

"Oh, I'm Amanda...Amanda Callaway."

"Well, helloooo, Amanda!" He said it slow and easy. "Surely you're not leaving so soon. The night is still young."

"I was…I mean my friend and I were going…to get something to eat." I lied. I didn't want to say we were going home.

"I haven't eaten since this morning. You mind if I join you?"

I couldn't believe he was asking.

"Well…" I hesitated and looked at Dee Dee, who quickly said, "I'll see you tomorrow."

I looked at Franklyn and said, "I know of a nice little restaurant not far from here."

He told his manager to meet him back at the hotel.

We went to a restaurant called Casa de Toulez. We both ordered crayfish étouffée and gumbo. We drank Coke, because he didn't drink liquor, and I had drunk enough at the club. I had the best time, because we hit it off right away. He was so funny and personable. It was as though we had known each other forever. We talked about everything and solved all the problems of the world. The restaurant closed at two a.m., and they had to kick us out.

I took him to the Rain Forest, a new nightclub downtown. It was crowded, but the bouncers recognized Franklyn and let us in. We danced until four o'clock. He was a good dancer.

I dropped him off at his hotel around five o'clock, because he had to catch a seven fifteen flight back to Los Angeles. He invited me to visit him, gave me his home number and said I could call him anytime. He was on the road a lot, but he had a roommate who was always home.

I gave him my number, and he promised to call as soon as he got home.

I arrived back at my apartment half an hour later.

Collette and Michele came home around noon. They were still stoned. They both lied and said they didn't do anything but dance and snort a little cocaine. Dee Dee and I didn't say anything. I was still on cloud nine about Franklyn.

We didn't see Helena until three days later. We were about to report her missing, but as usual, she showed up with some man.

It was years later before we told Collette and Michele we saw them that night and knew they had lied. It was a good thing Sarah was our witness.

Twelve

I sat by the phone all day on Monday and all day on Tuesday, but there was no call. I went on a three-day trip and left instructions with Barbara Ann to take a message if Franklyn called.

"What else would I do, tell him you don't live here?" she joked.

When I returned, there was still no call.

"You have his number, call him," Dee Dee said after a week. "Maybe he gave you a wrong number."

It never occurred to me to call him. I was not in the habit of calling guys. I took out the piece of paper and stared at the number he had written down for me. I put it away.

It took me three weeks to get up enough nerve to call. My heart was pounding; I didn't know why I was so nervous. I dialed the number. After the second ring, I was about to hang up, when someone picked-up and said, "Hello."

"May I speak to Franklyn, please?" I tried to sound normal.

"You just missed him, he left this morning. He's on the road and won't be back for three weeks. I'm his roommate, can I take a message?"

"Yes, tell him Amanda...from New Orleans, called. He has my number, thank you," I said it fast and hung up.

He never called.

1974

I went back to Wendell's club many times with other people after that first night, but I never had the desire to go into the back rooms. Once was enough for me. Wendell always picked up the tab.

Every time there was a black concert in town, the after party was at the Lagniappe Club. Collette and Michele were always there. If they were scheduled to work, they would swap their trips. I would pick-up a trip to make sure I was out-of-town. After Franklyn Ajaye, I didn't want to party with entertainers.

Wendell never allowed any of Sarah's friends to get close to him. He was always cordial, yet very reserved. He never came to our Apartment, and only called once looking for Sarah. He never engaged in small talk with us.

He owned a big house on the lakefront where Sarah would cook big Thanksgiving dinners or have little get-togethers. Wendell would eat with us or make an appearance, then disappear to his office in the back of the house, never to be seen again.

Wendell's bedroom had a comfortable, round, king-sized bed. Beautiful black art was on the wall, and a mirror was on the ceiling.

In the wee hours of the morning, when we were too stoned or drunk to drive home, we would fight over who would sleep in his bed, even though the house had five other bedrooms. Sometimes there would be six of us in his bed, including Sarah. On those occasions, I guess Wendell slept in his office.

Two years after our first visit to Wendell's Lagniappe Club, it was raided by the FBI. They found drugs, weapons, and a half-million dollars in cash. We watched it all on the ten o'clock news. We saw Wendell led away in handcuffs, along with several of New Orleans's high-ranking officials. Good thing Sarah was on a five-day Caracas trip, or she might have been caught up in the scandal. The FBI confiscated Wendell's house and all of his property. They came and picked up the sports Mercedes Sarah drove. We had all known Wendell was a drug dealer; however, we had never discussed it. During the times we were in his company, we never saw him use drugs. The only thing I saw him drink was club soda with lime. He was always a perfect gentleman, and he certainly didn't seem to be the man they talked about on TV.

Needless to say, Sarah was distraught. The FBI investigated Sarah, because they thought she was hiding over a million dollars for Wendell.

Irene sprang into action. She could not stand having one of her stewardesses' names being dragged through the mud. She went with Sarah when she was questioned for several hours by the FBI.

"My girl was on a trip," Irene told the FBI. "She is only the girlfriend of this Wendell Johnson man."

Sarah had us in stitches imitating Irene.

They didn't have anything on Sarah, but since the car was in Wendell's name, they took it. Wendell had made sure she stayed clean.

We felt a newfound respect for Irene, and after the scandal, she would not let Sarah out of her sight.

We all gained a lot of respect for Sarah, too. She stood by her man to the bitter end, and we stood by her. We were there when she lied for him at the trial. The government lawyers portrayed him as a mobster and a cold-blooded killer. He was acquitted of the murder charge, but still convicted of racketeering, extortion, drug trafficking, prostitution, and God knew what else. He was sentenced to ninety-nine years in federal prison. Sarah visited him whenever she could, and she wrote a letter or sent a card every week. I went with her to the prison many times to visit Wendell. It was hard on Sarah, seeing her man behind bars.

Sarah and I spent a lot of time together. We found out we were sorority sisters and shared a special bond. She taught me how to cook macaroni and cheese and fried chicken. My spaghetti never tasted quite like hers, no matter how hard I tried.

Thirteen

Dee Dee started dating a dentist, he was a very gentle man, very soft spoken and dressed immaculately. I really liked the guy and I double dated with them several times when I could find a date. I wasn't dating anyone special. Everyone said I was too nice and picky, but I didn't feel like changing my ways. I was really happy with myself.

With Dee Dee happy, Helena started driving us crazy. She came in from a trip one afternoon and got us all excited. She had met her dream man on a flight. His name was Marvin Something-or-other—she hadn't bothered to get the man's last name—and he was an attorney in Detroit. He was coming to New Orleans to see her next weekend, and she wanted us to meet him. What she "conveniently forgot" to tell us was that she had slept with the man in her hotel room in Detroit just after meeting him on the flight.

It didn't surprise us that her friend never came to New Orleans. Helena had to fly to Detroit to see him, and she always stayed in a hotel. We tried to tell her it made no sense.

"If the man lives in Detroit, why can't you stay at his house? Why do you have to stay in a hotel? Why do you only have his office number? Are you a moron?" Dee Dee asked her one day.

Helena just did not get it, so we had to take charge of the situation. Collette called his work number and asked to speak to Marvin. She told the receptionist that she was his cousin, that she was stuck at the Detroit airport, and that she needed to get in touch with him right away so he could pick her up. The receptionist sounded young, and she gave Collette his home number.

Collette called the number, and a woman answered the phone.

Collette asked to speak to Marvin Shoemaker—Helena had finally gotten his last name—about a new loan for which he had applied. The lady said she was Marvin's wife, and they had not applied for a loan. Collette kept chatting and found out the wife was six months pregnant.

Helena was listening on the extension, and still her pea-brain refused to believe it. She continued to see Marvin! We left her alone after that. When Marvin called it quits after four months, Helena was surprised and upset. She went into a shell and became even more insecure. She didn't think she was attractive and wanted to get a nose job. Everyday, there was something new irking her. She stayed in bed for three days and wouldn't eat or talk to anyone until she found another man.

Helena's next boyfriend told her that her boobs were too small, so she saved up enough money, went to LA, and got a boob job. We begged her not to do it. The guy broke up with her two months afterwards, saying her new boobs were too hard.

Then, some man at a spa said she was too fat, so from then on, she was always on a diet, although she was five-foot-eight and weighed only one hundred pounds. She was borderline bulimia, as we discovered when Dee Dee caught her in the bathroom, vomiting up her dinner. We could never get through to Helena.

We were relieved when she moved to the French Quarter and starting living with a local artist she met at a nightclub. We didn't hear from her for four months, until she called us from the hospital.

"I'm dying, I need help," she wailed.

She wouldn't tell us the problem on the phone. We thought she had been raped, so Dee Dee, Collette, and I dropped everything and rushed to the hospital. Everyone else was on a trip.

It wasn't life-or-death, but it was serious.

She needed surgery because of an ectopic pregnancy and tumors in her fallopian tubes. Her problem was so bad that the doctor had to remove both her tubes. This meant she would never be able to have children!

"I won't be able to have children!" she yelled.

She was hysterical, and it was hard to calm her down.

"It's either this now or a complete hysterectomy later, no in between," Collette told her.

That was the truth; the doctor had explained it all to us. I couldn't help wishing Collette had said it with a little more compassion.

"You can always adopt, Helena," I said.

She finally agreed to the surgery, and we sat there almost all night, until she woke up, and the doctor assured us she was out of the woods. We took turns staying with her at the hospital for three days. She was such a big baby! She was unable to get in touch with her artist friend, and we refused to go to their apartment to look for him; no matter how much she cried and begged.

Dee Dee and I came back on the fourth day after the surgery to take her home, because her boyfriend, Jindel Chapman, was not answering the phone. When we pulled up to the French Quarter apartment, we had to park on the street because Helena's car and another car were parked in the driveway. Jindel didn't have a car, and he always used hers.

Helena went ballistic when she saw the other car. "What's that bitch's car doing in my driveway?" she yelled.

"Calm down, whose car?" Dee Dee asked.

"Jindel's old girlfriend," Helena said, still raging.

"Listen, Helena, we don't want any mess. Let's just go home. You can stay at our place," I said, knowing Barbara Ann was in Alabama.

"No! That bitch better not be here."

Helena started to get out of the car by herself, but a sharp pain hit her, and she sat back down. We let her lean on us as we helped her out of the car and up the stairs.

She rang the doorbell and banged on the door.

"Jindel, I know you're in there with that whore! Open this goddamn door," Helena yelled.

We heard some scrambling behind the door.

Helena banged on the door again, only a little harder. We had to hold her up.

Jindel cracked open the door.

"Baby, I thought you were in the hospital. Why didn't you call me to pick you up?" he said.

"Jindel, open this goddamn door. I did call your ass."

The door opened, and Jindel was standing there with nothing on but his pants. A small, attractive Creole woman, with an attitude, was standing in the bedroom door, zipping up her pants.

"Bitch, what are you doing in my house?" Helena asked, almost in tears.

"I was invited," the woman said, looking at Jindel. We all looked at Jindel, except for Helena. She was focused on the woman.

Jindel said nothing. There was nothing to say. He had been caught, dead to rights.

I looked around. The house was a mess, and it smelled like marijuana smoke. There were drug paraphernalia on the kitchen counter, and the sink was filled with dirty dishes. I saw a big cockroach crawling over the dishes.

"Baby, it's not what you're thinking...uhh...I can explain...we were just talking. I thought you were coming home tomorrow..." Jindel stopped mid sentence.

He sounded stupid. I wanted to slap the shit out of him myself. He should have sat down, shut his mouth, and let the chips fall where they may.

We looked at Helena, waiting for her to cuss him out and take a swing at him. We always watched out for each other, and right now, we had her back.

Instead, she said to the woman, "Get out of my apartment, bitch, and don't ever come back."

The woman grabbed her purse and car keys and went past us like a whirlwind, but still with attitude.

We eased Helena down on the sofa; my arm was getting tired.

"We'll get your things, and you can come with us. You don't have to stay here with this niggah," Dee Dee said, emphasizing "niggah."

Helena made herself comfortable on the sofa, so we knew her Answer, and we decided she was the biggest fool we had ever seen. Dee Dee and I gave Jindel dirty looks as we left.

"You better be happy you're dealing with Helena, because if it was me, you would be dead by now," Dee Dee said.

"If you hurt Helena, we'll be looking for your sorry ass. There is not a place on this Earth you can hide," I warned, and I was proud of myself.

It didn't matter, because two months later, Helena was back at the Lewis & Clark. This time, Jindel had moved the same girlfriend in while Helena was on a three-day trip. She went back into her insecure state. It was hard to feel sorry for her. Most of this shit she brought onto herself.

Fourteen

July, 1975

Sarah called one morning from her apartment and hit us with a bombshell: Dee Dee's boyfriend, who was a popular dentist in New Orleans, was identified as one of eight bodies found in the ruins of a gay bar. The French Quarter bar, called Les Boys, had caught fire around three o'clock one Saturday morning. Dee Dee was in Pittsburgh for the weekend, visiting her family.

"I'm calling everybody, we'll be at your apartment in one hour with the newspaper." Sarah hung up.

We all read the article, and it was him. They picked me to be the one to call Dee Dee while they listened in on the extension. It was one of the hardest things I ever had to do. I knew Dee Dee wanted to marry this man, or maybe he wasn't all man. I called, and Dee Dee's mother answered the telephone.

"Hello, Mrs. Randolph, this is Amanda in New Orleans, how are you today?" I asked.

"Just fine, sweetie, how are you?"

"I'm fine, thank you. May I speak with Dee Dee, please?"

"Of course, hold on." We could hear her calling Dee Dee.

"Hello, Amanda, what's up?" she asked as soon as she picked up the phone.

"Dee Dee, there has been an accident. You need to come home right away." I tried to sound normal.

"What's wrong? Who! Barbara Ann? Sarah? Is everyone okay?"

"We're all fine, it's. . .Winston, Dee Dee. He..." I couldn't finish.

I put the phone down, and I could hear Dee Dee screaming. "What's wrong with Winston? Amanda!"

Sarah took over. "Dee Dee, calm down, there has been an accident and Winston was...uh...killed...I mean died. You can take the four o'clock flight out of Pittsburgh. We will meet you at the gate. Everything will be all right." Sarah didn't say anything about the fire in the gay bar.

While Dee Dee was on her way home, Sarah, Barbara Ann, Collette, Michele, and I tried to figure things out. Helena was on a cruise with some man she had met at a health food store.

"Did any of you ever see any indication that Winston was gay?" Sarah asked, lighting a cigarette.

We all looked at each other and shook our heads.

"I can see him fooling Dee Dee, she was in love. But how in the hell did he fool all of us? I think we all need a drink. I have heard of men leading secret lives but this son of a bitch deserves an Oscar. Oh! I mean, bless his soul," Sarah said, catching herself. Down South, we respected the dead.

Barbara Ann fixed a pitcher of Bloody Mary, using some left over Bloody Mary mix and the vodka miniatures we had taken from the airplanes. I didn't drink any Bloody Mary because I knew I had to drive to the airport to pick up Dee Dee in a few hours. I wanted my head clear.

So they sipped Bloody Marys and pieced together what they knew about Dr. Winston Sylvester Cardeau.

"I know Dee Dee met him on a flight from Vegas ten months ago. He had been to a medical convention, I think she said. He didn't do anything for me, he was a little too thin," Michele said.

"Michele, you mean you finally met a man you wouldn't jump in bed with?" Barbara Ann asked, and everyone laughed. The cocktails were taking effect.

"You know Dee Dee is very private and tells you only what she wants you to know. Like someone else in this room," Collette said, cutting her eyes at me.

I pretended not to hear that, because Dee Dee had confided in me about Winston, but I couldn't tell them. I really liked Winston, and I was sorry he was dead. My mind was going over things Dee Dee had told me about him. It was about six months ago when Dee Dee first mentioned to me that Winston had a problem getting an erection.

Some nights, she had to put on several different nightgowns before she got the right one that turned him on. Usually, it was the boxer shorts and T-shirt that did the trick. He always liked to do it from the back, doggie style, and could not come in the missionary position. He shaved under his arms, and he used cocoa butter every night to keep his skin smooth. I told her I didn't think I could put up with that shit every night. It hadn't meant much when she first told me all that; I thought he was just weird when it came to sex. Now I realized, maybe he was gay.

I was sitting on the sofa, and the four of them were sitting at the table. I looked at each one of them, and my mind drifted to some other place and time. I was half-asleep and half-awake...We had become a group of six, Sarah, Collette, Michele, Barbara Ann, Dee Dee, and me. We had acquired the nickname, the "Sexy Six." When you saw one of us, at least one of the other five was not far behind. Helena and Nicole were never considered a steady part of our group. Helena was more like a hanger-on when it was to her advantage. For instance, when she was involved with a man, she didn't have time for friends, and we understood not to count on her for much. As for Nicole Stevenson, Dee Dee's old roommate, she had transferred to Boston without telling anyone, not even Dee Dee.

The rest of us would bid for the same trips each month, so at least two or three of us would be flying together. In public, we stuck together and defended each other to the bitter end. But in private, we cursed, disagreed, and fought like cats and dogs; especially if we felt one of us was in the wrong. We had friends independently of the group, but when someone in the group needed us, we would drop everything and go. We always had each other's backs, and when one of us had a problem, we all had a problem.

Sarah, our leader, was sitting at the head of the table. As a native New Yorker, she was beautiful, confident, and could take control of any situation. Her parents were both successful medical doctors with their own private practice. Her father graduated from Morehouse, and her mother was a Spelman College graduate. They sent Sarah to Spelman to get the "*Black Experience.*" College was how she came to be down South. After two years at Spelman, she applied for a job as a stewardess with Big E World Airlines. Her parents were crushed, at first, because they wanted her to be a doctor and take over their practice. They managed to get over the hurt, because Sarah was their only child and they didn't want to alienate her.

Hired by Big E in 1967, she took a lot of abuse from racist passengers and crewmembers. As a native New Yorker and from a wealthy family, she attended private schools and had been shielded from the universal racism, discrimination, and prejudices of the South. She couldn't rent an apartment near the airport, because, at that time, they refused to rent to black people. Irene made arrangements for her to live with a black lady who cleaned the airplanes. Later, Irene had a white stewardess rent an apartment at Lewis & Clark and put Sarah down on the application as her roommate. She had orders not to mention that Sarah was black. When Sarah moved in, the apartment manager called Irene and said he had reservations about renting to a black. Irene told him if they refused to let Sarah live there, none of her girls would live there, and she would contact the company lawyers about filing a discrimination lawsuit. That's why Irene and Sarah were tight. Irene had taken care of Sarah during those difficult times.

Once, Dee Dee and I went to New York with Sarah to attend a surprise birthday party for her mother. Her family was what blacks down South called "Black *Bourgeoisie*." The party was in their lavish home. They served gourmet foods, such as shrimp cocktails and caviar, and waiters offered the food on trays. There were as many whites at the party as blacks. Blacks and whites didn't party together down south, and I wasn't used to black people spending that kind of money on a party. My grandfather spent money on the civil rights movement and helping the poor, so that was all new to me. The only whites who sat at our table were local politicians who wanted to curb a boycott, or sympathetic white people who wanted to help. Everything back then had to do with race relations, and my grandfather was the local black leader, looked up to by the people in my community.

At the party, I was very uncomfortable, and I could tell Dee Dee was, too, because her family lived in the inner-city.

Bringing my thoughts back to the group anxiously waiting for Dee Dee, they were laughing and talking, and they had forgotten about me. I turned my attention to Collette, who was sitting at the other end of the table.

She was our ghetto, five-foot-eight hoochie mama. She was dark-skinned and a bit heavy around the hips. She owned several wigs, wore false eyelashes, fake nails, and always wore too much makeup. Growing up in the mean housing projects in Chicago made her streetwise and self-sufficient, and she would always take care of Collette first and anyone else second. Her mother was an alcoholic who was living on the streets when Collette was born. She never knew her father. She moved from living with relatives, to foster homes, to group homes. As a result of her life experience, it was hard for her to trust people. She managed to graduate from high school and, with the help of a guardian counselor, was able to attend Morgan State University with a federal grant. We knew that, in her heart, she wanted to open up and trust us, but she couldn't. Maybe in time she would.

Also sitting at the table was Michele, from Houston. She was homely, but cute, and she had a figure with legs to kill for. Her large features and long, straight, black hair made her look more Native American than black. Her father was a postman, and her mother was a housewife. She graduated from Southern Methodist University in Dallas with honors, so we called her the brains of the group. Her only problem: the girl was man-crazy. We got tired of all her men coming and going. It was as though she ran a whorehouse, with herself as the only whore, and she liked it that way.

Across from Michele was Barbara Ann, our Southern Belle Princess, who had been taking care of by Big Daddy since she was fourteen. However, her part in the relationship didn't include cooking. She couldn't boil water. I did all the cooking and cleaning around the apartment. She was the only one of us with no college degree. She had been spoiled rotten by Big Daddy since he became "her man." She wore or carried designer everything: Gucci, Louis Vuitton, Armani, Calvin Klein; you name it.

Then there was me, Amanda Louise Callaway, the peacemaker. I was raised in Shelby County, Tennessee, twenty miles east of Memphis, in a small town where everybody knew everybody. I was raised by my grandparents, Alex and Bessie Louise Callaway. My grandfather owned two funeral homes, a casket-manufacturing company, and an insurance company. He was one of the wealthiest black men in Tennessee, and was known throughout the Mid-South. They had eleven children, and all of them worked in the family businesses at one time or another.

My mother was the youngest, and my grandparents' pride and joy. She ran away with my father, a gravedigger, when she was fifteen, and she had four children by the time she was twenty-one. My father, who was drunk every time I saw him, never married my mother, so we never had his name. The only home we had ever known was the Callaway Estates, which was a big, ten-bedroom house on sixty acres. The property has been in my family since slavery.

My father was killed by his girlfriend when I was six years old. She claimed he tried to break into her house one night when he was drunk, and she was with another man. She feared for her life, so she shot him, five times! Nobody blamed her, because everybody knew the kind of man my father was, especially when he was drunk. She never spent a day in jail. As a matter of fact, she was at my father's funeral, whooping and howling.

The most vivid memory I have of my father was of him lying in his casket at my grandfather's funeral home. During the funeral, my mother, my two brothers, my sister, and I sat in the front pew dressed in our Sunday best. Just before the services started, we heard a scream. We all looked back and saw a woman dressed in black, coming up the aisle, screaming my father's name. There was a small boy with her who looked to be my age, and looked very much like us. All five of us had our father's curly hair, dark, smooth skin, and small features. It did not take us long to figure out what everyone else in the church already knew: This was daddy's other woman. Everyone knew she would be there, and that was probably why the church was packed!

Mother sat frozen, her head down. We could see this woman had more self-assurance than Mother. The minister waited for them to be seated before he started the services. They sat at the other end of the front pew, as if it was reserved for them. The little boy and I stared at each other throughout the entire service.

After the funeral, Mother slid into a depression, and our grandparents took over raising us. My mother married three years later and moved out to live with her new husband. My brothers, sister, and I continued to live with our grandparents. We called them "Mommy" and "Daddy," and we called our mother by her first name. She was more like a sister than a mother.

Years later, when we would run into the lady-who-killed-our-father, she would always say, "Y'all knows, I'm sorry I killed y'all's father. Y'all good people. I ain't got nothing 'ginst y'all. I hate what I done, God knows, I do." People say she had lost her mind and was never the same.

My grandmother would try to console her, because we all knew her folks, and they were good people.

Unlike Sarah's parents, my grandfather had been actively involved in the fight for civil rights and in voter registration. All of the big names of the movement had stayed and eaten at our home. In 1965, a cross burned on our lawn, and my grandfather was threatened.

During my high school years, I worked in the funeral home. At first, my job was collecting burial insurance, keeping records, and planning "Homegoing Services." By my senior year, I was so good at planning funerals that the bereaved families started asking for me to plan their loved ones' funerals. I learned that with black folks, a funeral didn't have to be expensive, it only had to *look* expensive.

It all started when one of our well-known black bigwigs, a gambler and hustler, was shot and killed by enraged customers. His family wanted to put him away really nicely, but they could not come up with the money. I called the casket company and asked them to paint a gold trim around one of the cheap caskets.

The casket turned out better than I though it would. The "deceased" looked like a million dollars lying in it. The family was so pleased that they wanted the funeral to last forever. While they were crying and carrying on at the gravesite, I kept hoping the grave attendants would lower the coffin into the ground quickly before the gold started to tarnish.

Afterwards, I had so many requests for that casket, I got a bonus from my grandfather. People were ordering it from as far away as Jackson, Mississippi.

For the deceased mothers' and grandmothers' Homegoings, I had the company spray paint the caskets pale pink or blue. The funeral home had an account at Sears and JCPenney's Department Stores, where my grandmother bought our clothes. I would purchase nice suits and dresses for the deceased. The bereaved family thought the clothes came from Goldsmiths, the expensive store.

I was so good at what I did, I could have stayed at home after graduation and started my own funeral-planning business; but my grandparents believed in education. My great-grandfather had donated so much money to Christian College that all his descendants had to do was show up. There was a building on campus named after him, Callaway Hall.

Sarah and Dee Dee went home with me once to plan my former pastor's wife funeral. She had requested my services before she died. "I want to help you and see how it's done. I might need your services…someday." Sarah was being sarcastic.

Well, they were no help: They said the Callaway house reminded them of a haunted house, because it was old and all the furnishings were old.

"Of course it's old: The house and the furniture have been in my family for three generations," I told them. "My great-grandfather died right there, where you two are standing."

They both jumped from the spot at the same time.

"I was just kidding; but my great-grandparents did die in the back bedroom," I said, laughing.

"That's not funny, Amanda," Dee Dee said.

They wouldn't sleep in the guest room, because they said it was creepy, and they heard noises. They slept in my old bedroom with me. The bed wasn't big enough for the three of us, but they didn't care.

Neither one wanted to have anything to do with planning a funeral. When it was time to pick out the casket, they went across the street to the local bar for drinks. They were afraid to go to the funeral and didn't want to ride in a funeral car. However, they had no choice, because they were afraid to stay behind at the Callaway House by themselves.

On the plane back to New Orleans, they told me they were never going home with me again. "So do not ask," they said.

"I hope I don't have nightmares about dead folks. And, Amanda, you have my permission to do my funeral, just don't tell me anything about it," were Sarah's comments. She sounded relieved to be going home.

The only thing they enjoyed about the visit was my grandmother's home cooking...

Suddenly, I woke up to someone shaking me and shouting my name. "Amanda! Wake up, are you all right? Are you all right? Amanda!"

I opened my eyes and saw Sarah, Collette, Michele, and Barbara Ann, all standing over me. Before I could brace myself, Sarah threw a cup of ice-cold water in my face. Collette broke an ammonia swab under my nose.

"Are you crazy? Y'all trying to kill me?" I screamed, wiping my face.

"You are the one who's crazy! You were having a bad dream or something, your eyes were wide open. You scared us half to death. I'm sorry. Go wash your face, it's time to go to the airport and get Dee Dee," Sarah said.

I was still a little shaky as I walked to the bathroom. I hadn't realized I'd fallen asleep.

Sarah and I met Dee Dee at the gate when she arrived, and we knew she had been drinking. She had already called Winston's mother. She wanted us to drive her straight to Winston's mother's house.

If we had any doubt that Winston was gay, it was quashed when we arrived at Mrs. Cardeau's house. There were more gay men there comforting

Mrs. Cardeau than I had ever seen in my life. They looked at Dee Dee like she was the queer one. Winston's mother told Dee Dee that Winston never meant to hurt her. "He was confused about his sexuality," she said.

"You should have told me, Mrs. Cardeau," Dee Dee said in tears.

"I wanted to, but it wasn't my place. Winston wanted to tell you. He had to think about his business and his image. He died too soon, he just didn't have enough time to work things out. That's all, honey," Mrs. Cardeau said, trying to comfort Dee Dee. "I loved my son so much, and now he's gone."

Mrs. Cardeau started to cry, and some flaming guy came over to comfort her and give us a mean look.

"Can't you see she is already upset, maybe you all should leave!" he insisted, popping his finger at us and pointing to the door.

If Mrs. Cardeau had not been there, Sarah would have cussed this flaming cross-dresser out. Instead, she was forced to be nice.

"Come on, Dee Dee," she said, and looked at me for backup.

"Yes, Dee Dee, maybe we should go," I said.

We drove Dee Dee back to her apartment and gave her two motion-sickness pills, taken from an airplane, and had her wash them down with vodka. She was sleeping in ten minutes.

Dee Dee was so angry and felt so betrayed that she didn't want to go to the funeral. She couldn't bear to see all those gay men and cross-dressers crying over her man and wondering how many he had slept with. We all felt her pain. If Winston wasn't already dead, we would have killed him for doing this to our friend.

It took Dee Dee several months to get over Winston. She started finding something wrong with every man with whom she went out, and She would dump them without giving them a chance. She was becoming very secretive, and every other weekend, she was off to Chicago. Naturally, we thought she had found some hunk in the Windy City, and didn't want to share him with us. But we always tried to be there for her. Finally, one day she admitted to Sarah and me that she did have someone in Chicago but it was not a man, it was a woman!

"I have been hurt enough by men, and I decided to give a woman a chance, and I found myself. Yes, I am a lesbian now. You all don't have to be my friend if you don't want to. But don't try to change my mind," Dee Dee warned.

Even Sarah was at a loss for words.

"Don't be silly, you will always be our friend," I told her. "We love you, and you are still Dee Dee." And I meant every word.

"That's right...that's right," was all Sarah could add.

Dee Dee started staying more and more at my apartment with me, because her roommate, Nicole Stevenson, left without a word. Barbara Ann, my roommate, was more and more determined to spend as much time as possible in Anniston with Big Daddy. The girls hit the nail on the head, about Big Daddy that night at our apartment when I first met Sarah. The paternity test proved that Big Daddy was the father of the "country bitch's" baby girl. Barbara Ann still had a hard time believing it, but she had too much time and emotion invested in Big Daddy to end the relationship.

She finally got her transfer to Atlanta and would be leaving on the thirtieth of the month.

She and Big Daddy had gotten an apartment, and they were going to live together in Anniston, because he wasn't ready to commit to marriage yet.

She would have to commute to Atlanta to work.

I would have to find a new roommate.

Fifteen

Two months after Barbara Ann moved out, I had a new roommate, Caroline Webber. She had been based in Atlanta and was a year senior to us. On her first day in my apartment, she explained why she transferred from Atlanta to New Orleans. She came home from a trip one night, she said, and found her boyfriend in bed with her stewardess roommate. They were getting it on, big time, and making so much noise that they didn't hear the bedroom door open.

Caroline went berserk. She took a broom and started beating both of them while they were in the heat of passion. Her boyfriend ran out of the apartment in his birthday suit. Fortunately for him, he lived in the same complex. Her roommate managed to grab a housecoat before she, too, fled.

Caroline tore up the apartment and cut up her roommate's clothes.

She told everybody in the Atlanta base about the incident. The stewardesses who knew her boyfriend assured her that he was no good anyway. They were glad Caroline found out for herself, but were sorry it involved the other stewardess, who everyone liked.

Caroline reacted as expected: A woman scorned. She put sugar in her boyfriend's gas tank and spray painted the word "Motherfucker" on the side of his car. She started leaving nasty notes in the other girl's mailbox and broke the windshield out of her car while it was parked in Big E's employee parking lot. The airline would have put her on probation, but it was unable to prove she had done it.

The other stewardess and the boyfriend started living together, and that turned out to be too much for Caroline. She admitted that she really cared little for the guy and had been planning to break up with him, but she had a hard time dealing with him dumping her first. Her supervisor recommended that she transfer to another base and start over, before she did something that would get her fired. She was a beautiful woman, and a change of venue would do her good.

Irene had the rap sheet on Caroline before she arrived in New Orleans. She told Caroline, as soon as she arrived, that she would never tolerate what happened in Atlanta, not here in New Orleans.

"Young lady, you had better get your act together. We run a respectable base here. One wrong move and you will be fired."

Caroline disliked Irene from the get-go, and every time they met, they clashed.

We had learned how to get along with Irene. There were certain things we knew she would not tolerate. A wrinkled uniform; old, beat-up shoes; and messy, bleached hair were her main pet peeves. She didn't have to worry about black stewardesses bleaching their hair red or blonde: Many of us wore Afros, and we were too proud to walk around with our hair bleached blonde. We were not allowed to wear braids until black stewardesses sued and won in 1978.

We tried very hard to stay out of Irene's way and be on our best behavior when she was around. Caroline learned fast and flew trips that signed in late and got back early. Irene only worked from nine to five on weekdays, but her spies worked on weekends and nights and reported directly to her.

It didn't take Caroline long to hook up with a Creole guy, named Joseph "Joe" Guillory, who worked as a cook at a popular seafood restaurant. He fell head-over-heels in love with Caroline and was always at the apartment, cooking gumbo, red beans and rice and my favorite, crawfish étouffée.

You learn fast about Creole men in New Orleans. First, most of them usually lived at home with their mothers, who took care of their every need. More importantly, the Creole mother wanted her son to date only Creole girls. If you were not high-yellow with straight hair, you were not good enough for her son. You could be a doctor, a lawyer, or an Indian chief, and the Creole girl could be a cocktail waitress with a tenth-grade education; a Creole mother would prefer that her son date the Creole girl. That was just the way they were. They worshiped their sons. It was crazy, but Joe's mother was no exception. Caroline was brown-skinned, but not light enough for Joe's mother, and her hair was a long way from being straight. So Caroline dated Joe for the fun of it, because we all knew there was no future in their relationship, and Joe's mother would eventually win. His mother would call the apartment several times a day, looking for Joe. Very annoying!

"Have him bring me [this or that] when he comes home this evening," she would say.

"Yes, ma'am." We couldn't bring ourselves to be mean to the lady. We knew she didn't need anything. She just didn't want Joe spending the night with Caroline.

Sixteen

Sarah was drinking and using drugs on a regular basis since Wendell was sent to prison. She preferred dating around, with one-night stands here and there. Whenever a guy tried to get close, she dropped him like a hot potato. She was a strong woman, stronger than any of us, so we decided to let her live her life for now, but we kept a close eye on her.

My life was moving slowly. I dated a few guys, but there was nothing special. My friends thought I was too picky, and my clothes were too plain and, especially, too cheap. I refused to shop at expensive stores like they did and I saved my money. I still shopped at JCPenney's. Furthermore, I didn't dress sexily enough and didn't jump into bed with every man I met. Their opinions never bothered me, as old habits were hard to break.

I went over to Clearview Mall one afternoon to buy a toaster oven and a few other things that were on sale. On my way out, I happened to notice a fine, tall, dark, good-looking brother parked two spaces over from me. He was about to get into his car, but he stopped when he saw me struggling with my packages.

"Can I help you with that box?" he asked pointing at my toaster oven.

"Thank you," I said and smiled up at him, because he was at least six feet four.

"My pleasure to help a beautiful lady in distress," he said and smiled. I was in love. He had the most beautiful smile I had ever seen. Every tooth in his mouth was white and straight.

"Where do you live?" he asked, after putting all the packages into my car.

"At the Lewis & Clark Apartments," I said.

He looked surprised. "I live there and I've never seen you."

"I've lived there for two and a half years, and I've never seen you." I tried to add a little mystery to my voice and flirt a little.

"What building and apartment do you live in?" he asked.

"Building one-0-one, apartment ten."

"And your name?" he asked without looking at me, like he was shy.

"Amanda Callaway," I replied, "and yours?"

"Malcolm Brown. Look, I know a shortcut back to the complex. If you follow me, I'll show you."

"Sure," I said, because I only knew one way, the long way.

"I'll pull my car around, and you can follow me," he said, heading toward his car.

I got in my car and watched in my rearview mirror as he crossed the parking lot to his car. He was wearing tight pants and a polo shirt. I could see every muscle in his behind, and there was a lot of muscle to see.

He pulled out and blew his horn. I backed out and followed him. He was driving a funny-looking foreign car I had never seen before. It was maroon, with a white top.

I followed. I would have followed him to the moon.

He parked in the parking lot of building one-0-one. I parked beside him. He got out and helped me carry my packages to my apartment door.

"Would you like to come in?" I asked.

As soon as I opened the door, I realized Joe Guillory was in the kitchen, cooking something that smelled delicious.

He was staring at Malcolm like he had seen a ghost.

"Joe, this is Malcolm; Malcolm, this is Joe, my roommate's boyfriend," I said, because I didn't want Malcolm to think for one second that Joe was my friend.

"I know. Pleased to meet you." Joe wiped his hand on a towel and shook Malcolm's hand with pleasure. Joe was rolling his eyes and looking at me funny, but I wasn't picking up on what he was trying to tell me.

"I have to leave. If you aren't busy maybe I could stop by later this evening. I live in building one twenty-nine," Malcolm said.

"That will be great. We'll be home," Joe answered for me.

I looked at Joe like he was crazy. This was not his home.

"Sure , that will be fine," I said to Malcolm, trying not to act as excited as Joe.

We made eye contact, and Malcolm gave me that million-dollar smile again. I almost melted.

"See you later," he said and winked at me.

I nodded and closed the door.

When I turned back around into the kitchen, Joe had his arms folded and was looking at me, the ecstasy clear on his face.

"Don't you know who that is? Where did you meet him?" Joe demanded, almost screaming. He didn't give me a chance to answer.

"No, who is he?" I asked. I didn't have a clue.

"Malcolm Brown, the Saints' million-dollar, all-star running back; probably the best running back in the entire football league. He made a thirty-yard touchdown in the last game of the season. It was spectacular! Too bad the Saints lost, because he's good. You didn't see the game?" Joe was talking fast. He was more excited about meeting Malcolm than I was.

"Damn, I should have gotten his autograph," Joe said, slapping his leg.

"Well, he said he would be back this evening."

My knowledge of professional football was little to none. I had never been to a Saints game or any other professional football game. The weather down south was too cold.

I didn't know a single football player by name or face, and I couldn't name more than four NFL teams.

"Joe, do you think he will be back this evening?" I needed hope. After Franklyn Ajaye, I was gun-shy.

"He said he would, and maybe he will, you can never tell about those guys, they can have any woman they want." Joe replied. That wasn't very reassuring.

"Are you saying I'm not his type?" I asked deflated.

"No, no, I'm not saying that. I just don't want you to get your hopes up." Joe got defensive. "Amanda, I like you, and I don't want you to get hurt. This guy is good-looking, rich, and you are about the only person in New Orleans who does not know who he is."

"Thanks a lot, Joe," I said, and braced for the disappointment.

Joe gave me the lowdown on Malcolm Brown: Heisman Trophy winner and first-round draft pick from Southwestern State University. He was traded to the Saints last year from St. Louis.

"How old is he?" I asked.

"Twenty-seven, twenty-eight at the most," he said.

I decided that was old enough for me.

Caroline came in from the store. Joe told her about Malcolm, and she was excited about meeting him. She was a big football fan.

Around six o'clock that evening, I showered, washed my hair, and put on a new pantsuit I had just bought in LA. It was the sexiest outfit I had in my closet. If he came back, I wanted to be ready. Deep in my heart, I did not believe I would ever see Mr. Fine Malcolm Brown again.

"Well, it will be his loss," I thought, trying to protect myself.

Collette stopped by to borrow fifty dollars to buy a sweater to go with a new outfit. She had a hot date on her layover in San Francisco with some new guy named Johnny Lee Jones. Dee Dee had already told me that Collette had a drug problem, and not to loan her any money.

She thought Collette was prostituting in San Francisco, and this evening, she looked like she was high on something. However, she had never asked me for a loan before, and I knew if I mentioned drugs, she would only deny it. So I loaned her the money and told her we needed to talk.

"We will, as soon as I get back. We will go to lunch. I promise you, Amanda." She was already out the door.

"I'm going to hold you to that," I yelled after her, but I doubt she heard me.

She left in such a hurry. She did not want me asking any questions. She was hanging with a new crowd of people. Drug users, I guessed.

"I will get to the bottom of this, as soon as we have lunch," I told myself as I closed the door.

The phone rang, and it was the gate agent I met a year ago. We had gone out and had slept together a few times, but it was nothing to write home about. He wanted me to come over to his place. He had a new porno movie he wanted me to see. He liked to watch them while we screwed. He was a nice guy, but I had a date. I told him no. I lied and said I had an early sign-in and needed to get to bed early.

Again the phone rang. Rozlyn Taylor was calling from Las Vegas, excited and talking fast. "Amanda, girl, guess who I met today?"

"Who?" I asked. I knew it had to be someone big.

"You will never guess, not in a million years."

"Who! Who! Just tell me." Now she had me excited.

"Elvis Presley!" she screamed into the phone. I had to jerk the phone away from my ear to keep her from bursting my eardrum.

"Elvis Presley!" I was shocked and never would have guessed, not in a million years.

We had entertainers on our flights all the time, but Elvis had his own airplane that he bought from Big E World Airlines. We all knew this bit of trivia.

She described the big event: "Me, Joan and Bea were getting out of the hotel van. As soon as we were in the hotel lobby, this big, bodyguard-looking man approached us and said Mr. Presley wanted to see us.

"'Presley, as in Elvis?' we asked.

"'The one and only,' he said.

"The bell captain confirmed that Elvis and his entourage had the top floor, so we left our luggage with him and followed the bodyguard to the elevator. He had the special key you need to get to the penthouse. Then we walked down a small hall and the guard knocked on the penthouse door, and

Elvis said, 'Come in.' His bodyguard opened the door, and there was Elvis sitting in a big chair, looking out a bay window. We realized this is how he knew we were staying at the hotel. He had seen us getting out of the hotel van." Rozlyn was now out of breath.

"What did he say? How did he look?" I was speaking fast to get a word in edgewise.

"He looked like Elvis, a little overweight. He said he loved Big E stewardesses. He used to fly Big E Airlines all the time before he bought one of our DC-9 planes. He told me that people had been spreading rumors that he hated blacks. 'I love black folks,' he said. He grew up with blacks, and he loves black music. He said some of his best friends were black musicians." Rozlyn was still excited.

"What did you say?" I asked her.

"Girl, I didn't say a thing, I only wished I had brought my camera. He invited us to his show tonight."

"Are y'all going?"

"Do birds fly? What do you think? We are going to the mall in a few minutes and buying something sexy. Look, I've got to go, I'll tell you all about it when I get back."

"I want to hear every detail," I said.

"Okay, bye."

I hung up the phone and started telling Joe and Caroline about Rozlyn's call. For the first time since morning, I had forgotten about Malcolm Brown. We started singing Elvis's songs.

"I like 'Hound Dog,'" Caroline cried, and she started to sing.

I grabbed the broom and started imitating Elvis.

We sang everything from "Blue Suede Shoes," to "Return to Sender," to "Love Me Tender." I grew up twenty miles from Memphis, with Elvis Presley and the blues.

We were laughing so hard, singing Elvis's old songs we almost missed the knock at the door.

I went to the door and peeped out through the peep hole, and there he was, looking like my Prince Charming. I stepped back and checked my pantsuit and hair before opening the door.

He had showered and changed clothes. He now had on a light-blue dress shirt and black slacks. I felt honored that he dressed up for me.

"Hi," I said trying to act cool, when my heart was beating a thousand times a minute.

"Hello again," he said, softly.

"Come in." I opened the door wider.

He walked in past me, and I could smell his cologne. It almost hypnotized me. I never saw a man look as good as he looked; never in my whole life!

Joe and Caroline were standing at attention.

"Malcolm, this is my roommate, Caroline Webber. Caroline, Malcolm," I said.

"Hello, pleased to meet you." He shook Caroline's hand and shook Joe's hand again.

I thought Caroline was going to faint or kiss his feet. Joe had to hold her up. Caroline would have dropped Joe in a heartbeat if Malcolm had looked twice at her. But it was obvious that he had eyes only for me.

"Would you like something to eat or drink? Joe cooked some Jambalaya," I asked.

"No thanks, but would you like to go out to dinner?" he asked me.

"Sure...uh...let me get my purse." I was shocked, I hadn't expected a dinner date. I thought we would sit around the apartment and watch TV.

We went to one of his favorite restaurants, called the Three Sisters. It was a Ma-and-Pa place off the main drag. I could tell he had been there many times, because they treated him like a son. They brought out his favorite dishes, all of which were delicious.

On the way home, we stopped by the liquor store to buy a bottle of champagne. There, he signed a few autographs, and his fans wanted to talk football.

"Who do you think will make it to the Super Bowl next year?"

"What about the Saints?"

Malcolm only smiled and signed a shirt, a cap or whatever they handed him. Somehow we were able to get in and out of the store pretty quickly. He had the neatest car.

"Would you like to drive?" he asked me.

"Sure," I said, and he let me drive back to the complex. It was a Citroen, a big car for me, but the smoothest one I had ever driven.

We went back to his apartment. While the champagne chilled, he made a fruit-and-cheese tray and took it into the bathroom; yes, the bathroom!

He was in there a long time.

"Can I help you?" I asked several times.

The answer was always the same.

"No, just relax, I have everything under control."

When he came out, he handed me a joint and turned on some soft music. I sat on the sofa and felt good. Marijuana was the only drug Malcolm said he used. "I don't do cocaine or pills. I have to take care of my body."

That was fine with me, because I didn't like snorting cocaine.

He had lit some candles in the bathroom and had run a bubble bath. I knew I had a rule about not sleeping with a man on the first date, but tonight, I had to break my rule. This guy was just too good to pass up.

He finally invited me into his bathroom. The candles made beautiful silhouettes on the wall and had a nice fragrance. The tub was full of bubbles and rose petals! It was so cozy! I was really impressed that he would do all this for me. Most guys just wanted to jump into bed.

Malcolm got in the tub first, leaving only a little room for me. I took off my clothes and squeezed in. He poured us a glass of champagne and offered a toast. "To a wonderful evening," he said, and we clicked glasses.

I laid back in the tub and relaxed. I hoped he felt as good as I did.

He talked a little about himself. He was an only child, raised by his mother. He hardly knew his father, who had died young of a rare heart defect and hadn't contributed much to his son's life when he was still alive. His mother sacrificed for him, working two jobs so he could stay in school and play football. She came to all his high school games and to many of his college games. "Mom cried when I won the Heisman Trophy. I was more happy for her than for myself."

When he got his first bonus, after signing with St. Louis, the first thing he did was buy his mother a new house and a car. He bought stuff for her before he bought anything for himself. Over the years, he set up an account for her to make sure she wouldn't have to worry about anything again. His mother came first.

"She has never asked me for anything. But I pay her before I pay myself," he said.

I talked as little as possible about myself, only telling him that I was from Tennessee and had graduated from Christian College in Nashville. I wanted him to know I was educated, though I chose not to tell him about my background. Over the years, I had learned that some black people didn't like middle class blacks, and I didn't want him to think I was spoiled. I changed the subject.

"Do I remind you of your mother?" I said.

"No, my mother is six feet tall and weighs two hundred pounds; maybe the same color and Southern accent, I love it. My mother was from Tennessee." Then, he said, "I first noticed you in JCPenney's."

"I didn't see you." I was shocked.

"I know, you were too busy looking at toaster ovens," Malcolm said. "I was paying a bill for my mother. As a matter of fact, I saw you when you went into the mall. I knew where you parked, and I waited for you to come out."

He was full of surprises.

"You were stalking me!" I said jokingly.

"When I saw you coming out of the mall with those JCPenney's bags, you reminded me of my mother." He was trying to make fun of me, so I threw some water in his face.

"For real! JCPenney's is her favorite store. It's the only place she wants to shop." He was laughing. "Do all Tennessee women like to shop at JCPenney's?"

I had just met this guy, and I felt as though I had known him all my life. It wasn't the champagne or the marijuana, either.

"Turn around and let me wash your back." He gestured for me to turn.

I maneuvered my body around the small tub until my back was to him. He washed my back and slowly moved the soft, soapy towel along my shoulders, my arms, and around my breasts. For the first time, I felt ashamed of my 34A bust.

"I guess you are used to women with bigger breasts than I have?"

What a stupid thing to say! How could I have asked something so childish? I wanted to apologize.

"I don't like anything on a woman that is not natural," he said as he moved his finger around my nipple. "Nice," he murmured.

Then he moved his hand around my stomach and kissed the back of my neck. It felt so good that I forgot all about sounding stupid. I felt myself getting wet as he moved his hand in that direction. I tried to distract him.

"What kind of women do you like, Malcolm?"

"A small-framed woman, and I'll tell you why tomorrow," he said.

I was happy to hear him say tomorrow, because that meant he wasn't taking me home tonight.

"Why?" I wanted to know.

"Long story, I'll tell you tomorrow," he promised.

Now his hand was closing in on my wet spot, and he was massaging it.

I laid back against him and enjoyed the feeling. I felt like I had died and gone to Heaven. His hand moved, and I think he was surprised about the degree of wetness. He gently moved his index finger into my vagina.

"Have I struck gold? Why are you so wet?" He groaned as he took his finger from inside me and put it in his mouth. "And I like the way you taste."

He had found my secret, and I knew he liked it, because I felt his hardness against my back. It felt like a lead pipe. I wanted to turn around and touch it, lick it, then get on it and ride. This man had me hot. I had to count to ten.

"Relax," I told myself. *"He is in control of the situation, and don't act too anxious."*

"Are you ready to get out?" he asked.

"Sure."

We had been in the tub for over two hours. It felt more like two minutes. I took another sip of champagne and tried to compose myself.

He lifted himself out of the water directly over me, and I looked up at a black god. He had a full erection and it was about ten inches long. He had the most beautiful penis I had ever seen in my life. It complimented his six-foot-four frame. I was mesmerized, just looking at it. I couldn't help myself; I reached for it to make sure it was real. It was hard as a rock, and I moved to wrap my tongue around it. I was careful not to choke, but this was the first time I really enjoyed giving oral sex. I was just getting started. He groaned to let me know I was doing a good job, yet he pushed me away.

"Easy, later," he mumbled.

I didn't want to stop, but he gently pushed me off him. He lifted me off my knees, out of the water, then handed me a large towel. I wrapped up in the big, soft towel.

"*Everything about this man is big,*" I was thinking.

I needed some ice water to cool me down; though, to be truthful, cooled down was the last thing I wanted to be. I wanted this Malcolm, and I didn't want to wait. Sometimes a girl's got to have it, and this was my time.

Malcolm told me to jump on his back, and he gave a ride to the bedroom.

Once in the bed, he kissed me from the top of my head to the bottom of my feet. He paid special attention to my wet spot, and that drove me crazy. I tried to climb on top because I was ready. He pushed me away again.

"Amanda, wait a minute. Look, I need to ask you something," he said.

"Oh, my Lord, he wants kinky sex," I thought. *"I knew this was too good to be true."*

"Sure, anything," I said, kissing his neck and trying to get back on top.

"Are you on the birth-control pill? Because...if not...I have condoms in the drawer," he wanted to know.

I was happy; no kinky sex after all.

"I'm on the pill. If you don't believe me, I'll show you." I waited, he did not say anything.

I jumped out of his bed, grabbed the comforter to cover my naked behind, found my purse, and showed him my birth-control pills. They were in the rotary type box. I showed him where I had taken my pill for today while he was in the bathroom.

"See? Saturday." I pointed to the day.

"I just needed to know, I don't want any surprises nine months from now," he smiled, but I could see he was happy.

I put the pills on the nightstand and picked up where I had left off. I was still hot, and I had no intention of being denied.

Malcolm was much more relaxed, and as soon as he entered me, I was ready to come, begging to come.

"Not yet," he said, and he pulled completely out of me. He started the kissing process all over again. My body was screaming for more.

I never knew sex could be so good. When he entered me for the third time, I tightened my vaginal muscles and held him there; I had read about that in a magazine. He screamed, and we both came at the same time, with every muscle in our bodies. It was the orgasm of orgasms. All he could say was, "Oh baby! Oh, baby!"

Now we both laid limp, unable to, and not wanting to, move. I wished I could package this secret and give it to every woman, especially Michele. With that thought, I fell asleep in his arms with a smile on my face.

I woke up several hours later to hands slowly moving up and down my body and tender kisses on my neck and back.

I stretched and said, "Ooh, what a night!"

"Would you like a repeat, my lady?" he asked.

I did not answer. Just the thought of it made me wet. I rolled over and got on top of him. He already had an erection. Soon, I was in Heaven again. He held on as long as he could, and when I was ready to explode, he let out his, "Oh baby, Oh baby!" and we exploded together again.

We lay in bed talking and snuggling for about an hour. There was something special about this man, and I wanted to find out what it was.

I didn't know if we would be together again, and I needed to take what he had given me into my next relationship.

"What's up with all this?" I asked.

"All what?"

"You know, bubble bath, sex, and seducing me." Hell, I didn't know how to ask the question, but somehow he got the message, and his answer surprised me.

"First, my job is to please you. I'll get mine. Mine is easy, but some women are so damn hard to please." Before I could agree, he continued, in a serious tone. "I told you last night I would tell you the kind of woman I like. Well, I like an uncomplicated woman with a spirit of her own. She's got to have her own career and not get caught up in mine. I don't want phony bullshit." He then smiled and pinched my butt.

"I enjoy pleasing a woman, especially when she shows me her wet spot," he joked.

I raised my fist to punch him out, and he caught it in midair. Quick reflexes!

"I like black women, because they are who I can relate to and cherish, because of my mother. She can be short or tall, as long as she has a small frame and slight build. Sex is only a part of it. Having sex is something a man wants to enjoy. We work hard enough on our jobs." I wondered where I fit in. Before I could ask, he said, "Now, you're perfect. You have what a man dreams about, what men kill for."

"What could that be?" I was puzzled. "Don't tell me, let me guess, my good looks. No! What is it?" I asked after he shook his head.

"You really don't know, do you?" he asked.

I nodded my head.

"You are a good-looking woman, no doubt about that. But don't get the big head when I tell you this." He sounded serious, so I promised. "You have a tight pussy. That is all a man wants. You can be ugly, fat, or skinny. It's just that simple. You can have any man you want."

That was food for thought, but I didn't want any man. I wanted this man. However, I knew better than to say that on our first real date.

We got up and took a shower together. Malcolm washed me all Over, and I had to stand on my toes to wash most of him, but I washed the important parts. I had lost all track of time. I was without a change of clothes, so he loaned me one of his shirts and a toothbrush. He finished dressing, and went into the kitchen and started cooking. I heard the phone ring, which was the first time it had rung since I'd been there. *"He must lead a clean life,"* I pondered.

When I came out of the bathroom, he was off the phone, and something smelled good. I looked at the clock, and it was eleven-thirty Sunday morning. My next trip was not until Monday afternoon.

"How are you?" he asked from the kitchen.

"Great, but a little tired from all the action last night...and...this morning." I laughed, for I was in a good mood.

"Oh, I see, you poor baby. Maybe this will perk you up," he said as he came from the kitchen and handed me a glass of mimosa.

"Do you have enough energy to set the table, Baby Doll?" He gave me a peck on the cheek.

"I think I can manage," I said and started to do so. My mind started to drift, and I reminded myself. "*Sooner or later this is going to end. This man has had his fun with me and when I leave on my trip tomorrow he'll have another woman in here doing the same things to her; champagne, bubble bath, candles and all. So don't get your hopes up, Sistergirl. Joe warned me.*

"Hey! Hey! You are suppose to be setting the table." I heard his voice as I snapped back to reality.

"You left me for a minute; what were you thinking about?" Malcolm asked.

"Oh, nothing." I couldn't tell him.

"You are not a good liar. You want me to tell you what you were thinking?"

"You can't possibly know what I was thinking," I said, but I wasn't sure. This guy was smart.

I went to him and put my arm around his waist and held on tightly, not knowing why or how he would respond. Some men act differently when they've gotten what they want.

He had a plate of hot food in each hand. He walked with me holding on and placed the food on the table. Then he put his arms around me.

"Look, I'm older than you. I've been around and have had a lot more experience. Don't put the cart before the horse. Don't doom our relationship before it begins. Give me a chance. I may surprise you, or I may disappoint you. I'm willing to take a chance. Contrary to what people think, I don't think with my penis. What we did last night, I don't do with just any woman. You can have sex and that's all it is: sex. But to make love to a woman takes time. Your head, as well as your body, has to be there. Making love to a woman you really care about is the most wonderful thing in the world." He hesitated. "I would like to spend today relaxing with you. Tomorrow is a new day. Now, your eggs are getting cold."

He popped me on my butt so I would get moving. He pulled my chair out, and I sat down. I thought he was going to sit down, too, but instead, he went to the bedroom and brought back a small gift box and gave it to me.

I was shocked and started to tear into it.

"No, don't open it until after we eat. It's just a little something."

I set it next to my plate. He said a short blessing, and we ate and drank mimosas. The food was delicious. He was a better cook than I was.

When we finished eating, he gathered the dishes.

"You can open the gift now," he said. He knew I was anxious to do just that.

I opened the box, and a black velvet jewelry box was inside. I flipped open the top to find a pair of diamond earrings staring back at me. My mouth flew open. Each earring looked close to a carat.

"Oh! My God," I whispered. "They are beautiful."

I ran to him and gave him a big hug and kiss.

I took off my old, faux-pearl earrings and put my new diamonds on. I ran to the bathroom to see how they looked. I was so happy.

"*Wait a minute, Amanda, why me?*" I thought, as I came to my senses. "*Don't be no fool. This is a very expensive gift for the first date. Maybe he really likes me, or maybe it's a payment for last night. He had a good time and doesn't want to send me home empty-handed."* I must have been in there a long time, because when I came out, he was standing at the bathroom door with his arms folded.

"Well, I didn't realize the earrings would make you so happy. I must confess, I didn't buy them. They came in a gift basket I received last year when I first arrived in New Orleans. I was going to give them to my mother, but had forgotten all about them until I saw the sparkle in your eyes last night. I want you to keep that sparkle. I thought I had lost it earlier when you were deep in thought." He sounded serious.

"What would you like to do today?" he asked

"Can we just stay here and be close, listen to some music, maybe watch a movie." Today, I didn't want to share this man with the world, and definitely not with his fans.

"I was hoping you would say that. I'm not up to going out either. You're so easy, I can't remember the last time I've been this relaxed with a woman." He smiled. "Oh! By the way, the apartment manager called me this morning. Your girlfriends...ahh...let me see...Dee Dee, Sarah, and Caroline...called him and asked for my number. They wanted to know if you were with me. They told him that you were out all night and they hadn't heard from you. They were worried. They thought I had kidnapped you, and if they don't hear from you by the end of the day, they are calling the...'blank-blank'...police." I laughed, because I knew that was Sarah. "I told him to call them back and tell them that you were with me, and not to worry, but they probably want to hear it from you."

"I completely forgot, I usually call them and let them know where I am. I don't usually stay out all night. I better call my apartment."

I dialed my number.

"Hello!" Joe picked up on the first ring.

"Joe."

Before I could say anything else, he said, "Your friends have been worried about you, they've been up all night drinking. Caroline called Dee Dee, and Dee Dee called Sarah. Malcolm's phone number is unlisted, and the stupid apartment manager wouldn't give it to them. With Malcolm being a star and everything, I'm sure women are always trying to get his number. I told them you were fine. Dee Dee went on a trip, Sarah went home, and Caroline went to the store. They left me here just in case you called."

Caroline was always going to the store, picking up items Joe needed for his dishes.

"Tell them I'm fine, and I will see them tomorrow," I said.

"Okay, are you really having a good time? What are y'all doing?" Joe was teasing me, but I wasn't buying it.

"Goodbye, Joe." And I hung up the phone.

I went over and snuggled on the sofa with Malcolm. I was feeling horny again.

"Did you really enjoy last night?" I asked.

"The question is, did *you* enjoy it?" Malcolm asked.

"You can't answer a question with a question, but *Yes! Yes! Yes*!" I screamed.

"Then, that's what really matters. I do love your wet spot." He laughed and I felt a little embarrassed. Then he became serious. "It's hard to find a woman you can connect with. Some women think all a man wants is sex, like you never want to just talk and relax. When you do get around to sex, they bring all the demons from their past into the bedroom. Some have childhood issues they've failed to deal with. When you fuck them, you're fucking every bad experience they ever had. Because of their past, they can't have an orgasm." I thought of Michele. Malcolm kept talking. "Yet, the man is supposed to make it happen for them. I've found some women simply are not capable of caring. They want to be with a man because of who he is. I get propositions every time I go out. They don't care about me, they just want me to fuck them. Then they go tell their friends, and the friends want me to fuck them, too. So it gets to be a twosome or a threesome. That life is all right when you're young, but I'm getting too old for that wild life, and I don't enjoy it anymore. I've always been a one-woman man." He got it all off his chest.

However, I found that hard to believe, but I didn't say so.

I hadn't forgotten he was one of New Orleans's most famous citizens, and an eligible bachelor. For today, he was all mines. I didn't want to think about tomorrow. I kissed his neck, and suddenly we were at it again. Yes, we made love, Sunday afternoon, evening, and night. We did it on the sofa, and on the floor. He cooked again, and we did it in the kitchen. He was an all-around lover, and I matched his drive, tit-for-tat. There was no kinky stuff, just good, hard sex. He gave more than he received. I learned more about lovemaking that one weekend than I had in all my twenty-four years. He was a good teacher. I was the student.

I sure didn't want to go to work on Monday, and that was mostly because I hated to leave Malcolm. This weekend was the best two days I had spent with a man in my life. He was a star, but he was not stuck on himself. He made me feel like a queen, and I wasn't thinking about how long it would last. I was just thankful for the past two days. He had given me the best days of my life.

He dropped me off at my apartment and kissed me. "It's been wonderful," was all he had to say.

He did not say: "I'll see you when you get in from your trip." He didn't give me his telephone number, and I was afraid to ask. I just wanted to remember the two special days.

When I walked into the apartment, Caroline, Joe, Dee Dee, and Helena were all standing in the living room with a thousand questions.

"You could have called us while you were whoring around. We were worried sick," Dee Dee said.

"I'm sorry, I just forgot. I was having a wonderful time." They knew I meant it. "The best time of my life." I kept smiling.

I didn't have time to talk. I had to get ready for my trip. They almost followed me into the bathroom with questions. I told them I would give them the whole scoop when I returned from my trip.

"I have to shower, iron my uniform, and go to work. Damn, can't a girl have a few secrets?" I was not ready to share my weekend with anyone. It had been too special.

I was the A-Line, the stewardess-in-charge, on this trip. I was in the first-class galley of the Boeing 727, cutting up lemons and limes, when the captain came onboard.

"Good morning," I said

The captain chose not to open his mouth. He didn't even acknowledge I had spoken to him. He noticed there were three white stewardesses in the back galley, and he headed in that direction. Being from the South, I was used to this type of treatment from white people, even in my airline profession, so his actions didn't upset me. The co-pilot came onboard and greeted me. I knew him because he lived at the Lewis & Clark Apartments. He was dating a stewardess who was a friend of mine.

"Hello, Brian! What's up with the captain? I spoke to him, and he didn't acknowledge me," I said.

Brian had a strange look on his face. He came closer to the galley, but stood in the aisle so he could see the captain before he returned to the cockpit.

"Amanda, don't you know who he is?" Brian asked, his voice low.

"Should I?" I was puzzled.

"That's Miles Gilbertson!"

I dropped a whole cup of lemons on the floor. My blood started to boil. I slipped the galley knife into my apron pocket.

Miles Gilbertson was one of the most racist, redneck captains at Big E World Airlines. He simply hated black people and felt we should still be picking cotton and scrubbing floors. He had been quoted as saying he "would never fly with a nigger, a woman, or a Jew in the cockpit," and "hiring niggers and gays was the worst thing Big E had ever done. The only good nigger was a dead nigger."

"Don't worry, Gilbertson is an asshole, but he stays in the cockpit when a black or gay steward is working first class. Don't say anything to him, and everything will be fine." Brian tried to be reassuring.

I had heard so many stories about Captain Gilbertson, from Roswell, Georgia. He was, so the story goes, always small for his age, and black kids would beat him up. His family was very poor, and he resented having to stand in line with black folks to receive government-relief food. His sister married a black man, and he disowned her. Regardless of this past, there was no excuse for racist remarks such as, "I've never met a smart nigger," or "all niggers are stupid."

Stories circulated that some black stewardess would challenge Gilbertson, and he would order her off his aircraft. Of course, the stewardess would get her bags and get off, because, on the airplane, the captain was in charge and always had the last word. It seemed that old Gilbertson knew the right buttons to push to get black stewardesses steaming. *"Maybe that's how he got his hard on."*

At first, Big E didn't have many black women, so the airline put up with Gilbertson's racist ways and allowed him to put black stewardesses off his planes. The stewardesses would call Irene, who would authorize full-fare tickets for them to get home. They would also get full pay for the trip.

Irene always went to bat for her stewardesses. She could talk about or treat us like dogs, but no one else was allowed to say a word against her girls. Irene was a lot of things, but she was no racist.

With Irene's help, and as Big E hired more black stewardesses, the airline ordered Gilbertson to stop putting her black stewardesses off the aircraft, or he would be fired. His reaction to this company order was to board the aircraft, go into the cockpit and close the door if a black stewardess was A-Line on his aircraft.

Black stewardesses had a way of getting back at Gilbertson. They would spit in his coffee and stir it up, or they would stick their finger in his Coke and give it to a white stewardess, who hated him as much as we did, to take to the cockpit, and she was ordered to leave the door open so we could see Gilbertson take a sip of the drank. Somehow, word got back to Gilbertson, and he stopped ordering any drinks from us. He would send the co-pilot out to fix his drink.

Now I waited for Gilbertson to come from the back to the cockpit. If I could provoke him into making a racist remark, I could get my bag and run off the airplane, crying to Irene. I would get a day off with pay, and I could be back in Malcolm's bed tonight.

Gilbertson was not going for it. When he got even with the galley, I said. "Would you like a cup of coffee, Captain?"

He still didn't acknowledge me. He went straight into the cockpit and slammed the door.

On the third leg of the flight, Gilbertson sent Brian, the co-pilot, out to get him a Coke.

"Amanda, this Coke is for Miles, do you want to stick you finger in it?" he asked.

I thought he was kidding. When I realized he was not, I licked my index finger and swirled it around in the Coke.

"Miles is a control freak," Brian said on his way back into the cockpit. "I can't touch a button without his permission. He never asks you to do something; he orders you to do it."

I could tell he was having a miserable trip.

Starting with the satisfaction from the Coke incident, I had a wonderful trip. I couldn't keep my mind off Malcolm, wondering what he was doing. Gilbertson was the least of my worries. One of the other girls wanted to swap positions with me so I could get away from Miles, but I refused. I made sure I was the first person he saw when he came out of the cockpit. I wanted to be the thorn in his side.

At the end of the trip, I walked to the parking lot with the co-pilot.

"I like the way you handle Miles" he told me, "and I'm glad you girls didn't go to dinner with us last night," Brian said sadly.

"Why?" I asked.

"Miles got drunk and almost got into a fight with a black waiter. We were asked to leave the restaurant. All the pilots are tired of his racist attitude. We all have to work together; it just makes for a better trip. Miles is an old alcoholic. He needs help."

It didn't surprise me to hear that Gilbertson was an alcoholic. It seemed that a lot of our older pilots were Vietnam veterans and alcoholics. On layovers, you could always find them at the hotel bar or a favorite bar near the hotel, where the owner would give them discounts on mixed drinks. I'd never met a pilot who wasn't a heavy drinker.

There was a pilot from Boston, named Cedric Mahoney, who had an apartment five doors down from us at the Lewis & Clark Apartment Complex. He drove an old car and dressed like a homeless person. We had no idea he was a Big E captain until we saw him in uniform one day. He had been suspended for two months for beating his wife, who was one of our stewardesses. He was in the middle of a bitter divorce, and when he was not flying, he was drunk. Other than that, Cedric was always friendly.

One day, I was going to the store and found that my car battery was dead. Stupid Amanda had left the lights on. I was parked next to Cedric's car, and I decided to go to his apartment to see if he was home and would give me a boost. I knocked on his door, but it was already ajar, and as I knocked, the door opened. I heard some strange noises and peeped around the door. The first thing I saw was a stewardess's uniform draped over a chair. Then I saw Cedric. He had some young, redheaded stewardess on the table. He was standing at the end of the table in only his captain's shirt; stripes and all. He had the woman's legs over his shoulders, and he was working hard, pumping and grinding. His eyes were closed, and sweat was running down his face. She wasn't making a sound and was just lying there. I thought that was funny.

Fortunately, they were too busy to notice me, so I backed out and closed the door. I waited about half an hour, because I figured that was as long as Cedric could go without having a heart attack.

I was right. Thirty minutes later, I knocked on his door. He answered the door in his bathrobe. I heard the water running, so I assumed the redhead was in the shower. I told him why I was there, and he got dressed and came out.

All the while he was hooking up the booster cables, he complained about his soon-to-be ex-wife. He was depressed over how much alimony and child support he would have to pay.

"My ex-wife has turned my family and friends against me and wants to get me fired from my job," he complained.

I was thinking: *"Can't you just focus on the good fucking you just gave some young stewardess? She wouldn't be in your apartment or on your table if she didn't care something about you."*

I guess I was wrong, because I saw the young redheaded woman, in full uniform, come from the complex, get in her car and leave without saying a word to Cedric. He pretended not to see her and continued to hook up the cables. I guessed the wild sex wasn't that good.

Two weeks later, I came home from a trip, and there was yellow crime-scene tape blocking off Cedric's apartment from the rest of the complex. He hadn't shown up for work and didn't answer his phone. The chief pilot came out to check on him and found him dead of a gunshot wound to the head, an apparent suicide. They found two notes, one to his ex-wife, and the other to his children. They also found an envelope with his divorce papers. He killed himself the same day he received his final divorce decree. It was a waste, because he forgot to change his beneficiary. Big E had no choice but to give all of his insurance and pension to his ex-wife.

Seventeen

When I returned from my trip, all my girlfriends were in my business. They had been waiting for my return so they could get the story of my weekend with Malcolm. They wanted every detail.

"What did you all do?"

"I know you fucked."

"Amanda, don't tell me you spent two days with that fine man without giving him some. Did you? Because if you didn't, you're a bigger fool than I thought you were."

I told them enough to satisfy their curiosity.

"Yes, we fucked…Yes, he's good, as good as he looks…It's none of your business about his anatomy…No, he didn't ask me out again, and he didn't give me his phone number. Now are y'all satisfied?" I said.

"Amanda, you're holding out on us," Michele said. "You sly fox."

"You little bitch," Dee Dee said, laughing.

"Just because you all tell all of your business, don't think I'll tell all of mine. Now, may I please get some sleep." I yawned to prove my point.

I know they were all thinking I was too square for a man like Malcolm, and he would dump me after the first date. Thank God, they were wrong!

Malcolm came by later that evening, and we went out to eat at another one of his favorite places. We went back to his apartment for a repeat of our first date, only it was better, because I kind of knew what to expect.

He acted like he was glad to see me. He was a wonderful man, and every day was like our first date. He never mistreated or disrespected me in any way. He always introduced me as his girlfriend or his lady.

After six months of dating, Malcolm bought a house in East New Orleans.

I spent most of my time with him in his new home. I decorated it, as though it was my home, but I only kept a few of my clothes and personal items there. I didn't have a ring on my finger, so I kept my apartment with Caroline, even though I was never there.

Malcolm made it quite clear, several times, that he was not ready to get married. He sat me down one night in his new home and laid down the law.

"Amanda, marriage is not in my immediate future. I only want to marry once in my life, when I'm older and more stable. I want to be out of football. I can't marry when I'm not ready, because it will end in divorce. Then I would have to share everything I've worked so hard for." He hesitated, collecting his thoughts.

"You know I love kids, I work with kids every summer, and I want kids someday. However, I want to be there for my kids. My father was not there for me. I probably would have been a much better football player if I had a father to show me the way. Now, I'm telling you again: I'm trusting you to stay on the pill. I don't want any kids out of wedlock. That's why I don't run around with different women. Some of these guys have babies by several different women. I don't want that kind of chaos in my life." Finally, he asked, "Do you understand?"

I had never seemed him so emotional. I sat with my head down. I didn't like what he was saying. Nevertheless, it was coming from his heart, and that I truly appreciated.

"Look, baby, this doesn't mean I don't love you, because I do. I want to be with you. But I can only promise you today. Tomorrow will take care of itself. If it was meant to be for us, it will be. Now, what do you say, are you going to stay in my corner, or are you going to leave?"

He was watching me and waiting for my answer. I thought I saw a tear in his eye. I walked to him, put my arms around his waist, and held on. At least, I knew where I stood with him.

"Let's not have this conversation again. It takes a lot out of a man to expose himself like this to a woman," he said, as he kissed my forehead and gave me that million-dollar smile that melted my heart.

I agreed never to have the conversation again; however, every six months or so, we went over the same scenario. All I wanted was a ring. I felt I deserved a ring. We didn't have to get married right away, just give me a ring. *"Maybe for my birthday, my twenty-fifth. I'll keep my fingers crossed."*

I had to work on by birthday, but I got in at ten thirty in the morning. I called Malcolm from the airport to let him know I was on my way to his place.

As soon as I pulled into the driveway, he came out and got in my car. "Drive to Metairie and I'll tell you where to go." He directed me to pull into a BMW dealership. We went inside, and the salesman brought around a brand-new, maroon BMW-2002. I took it for a test ride while Malcolm did the paperwork. When the salesman and I arrived back at the dealership, I signed on the dotted line. They took my Toyota Corolla and handed me the keys to the new BMW.

Malcolm kissed me on the cheek. "Happy birthday, baby," he said.

We drove to Chez Marie, an expensive New Orleans boutique. Malcolm drank champagne and watched as I tried on several expensive dresses. I picked the two he liked best, and he paid the saleslady. I was so happy, I could hardly wait until we got home. I was feeling on him and wanted to go down on him right there, in my new BMW.

After a wild afternoon in bed, we got up and dressed to go out. I put on one of my new dresses, and he put on an Armani suit. He had made a reservation for dinner for two at the Blue Room.

That night we made love again to the sound of Barry White, and I fell asleep in Malcolm's arms. It was a wonderful birthday. I was very happy, but deep down within, something was missing. I would gladly give back the BMW, the designer clothes, and the expensive dinner at the Blue Room for a ring. It was the only thing I would ever ask of Malcolm.

Eighteen

1976

Once, during the off-season, Malcolm went home to St. Louis for a month to take care of some business. I decided to stay at my own apartment to catch up on what was going on with my girlfriends. I talked to them often, but that was not like being there.

Things were changing fast. A lot of new, young, black stewardesses were in the New Orleans base and lived at Lewis & Clark Apartments.

Collette and Michele were deeper into drugs. I hadn't realized how bad things had gotten until I flew with them that month on our most popular rotation. The flight left New Orleans at seven a.m., stopped in Dallas, and arrived in San Francisco at eleven thirty a.m. Collette's boyfriend, Johnny Lee Jones, was now her pimp. He was also pimping Jackie O'Brien, the California blonde from our class, and another stewardess name Karen Bushwagner, a regular at the Lagniappe Club back rooms. Karen was from a very wealthy, Jewish family. We never understood why she turned to prostitution.

Collette told me all of this on the flight that morning.

"I don't believe you, Collette!" I was shocked.

"Amanda, you have been living out in East New Orleans in a mansion in la-la land. Well, this is the real world. Come by my room after we check in, and I'll show you my sex toys," she said.

As soon as we checked in, I left my bags in my room and went directly to Collette's room. I didn't even take off my uniform.

I propped myself up on the bed and waited while she unzipped a side pocket of her suitcase. She pulled out a black, silk, see-through negligee with a slit in the crotch, plastic handcuffs, a small vibrator, and a bottle of expensive perfume. I was shocked, and evidently it showed on my face.

"Amanda, you're a wimp. Miss Goodie-Two-Shoes. You don't have the stomach for this. I'll never understand how you keep your fine man happy." She continued, "Johnny books us a room at this nice rooming house in Nob Hill. I got this regular white guy who comes every Thursday. He is the president and CEO of a Fortune 500 Company." When she told me the name of the company, I was bowled over.

She was still talking. "First, I go in and shower and put on this." She held up the silk, see-through negligee. "Then I spray on his favorite perfume. This shit costs three hundred dollars an ounce. He gave it to me to wear." She sprayed a little bit on my wrist, and it did smell nice.

"When he comes through the door, sees my black ass, and smells this perfume, he's ready to go. He automatically gets a hard-on. I delay the action. We do a little Coke, drink a little champagne, and talk dirty."

"Talk dirty! What do you say?" I had to admit I was getting a little hot.

"Oh, I ask him if he missed my black pussy. Does he get a hard-on thinking about it and masturbating? Shit like that." She paused. "I may sit with my legs open and play in my pussy, whatever. I'm telling you, girl, he's ready. So I tell him to take off his clothes, one piece at a time. Then I handcuff him to the bed. His little dick be sticking straight up. It's only this big." She held up her thumb. "Now, Amanda, you know a little dick does nothing for me, but I work with the little thing. He starts moaning and groaning, but I won't let him come just yet. I turn him over and lick his ass."

I gagged and thought I would throw up. "You're a lying bitch!" I shouted.

"I knew you were a wimp," she sneered. "I don't know why I'm telling you all this shit, but that's the difference between a two-hundred-dollar job and a five-hundred-dollar job."

"I'm sorry," I said, "I'm just a little shocked. Go on."

She hesitated, but continued; she was enjoying herself. "I sit on his face and let him smell it. Then I let him nibble on it, slowly at first. I'm telling you, girl, no one can eat pussy like a white man. He sticks his tongue so far up in me it ain't funny. It's bigger and longer than his dick."

We both laughed so hard that tears ran down our cheeks. Collette could be dramatic when she wanted.

"We were going to use this today," she said, pulling out a can of whip cream from the first-class ice cream dessert cart. I didn't have to ask her what it was for. I've used some many times, myself.

"Look, Amanda, you can make five hundred dollars tonight if you want to. I'll have Johnny set you up. These rich, white men love black women. Something about black pussy really turns them on."

I shook my head, but Collette kept talking. "They'll love you, because you're Southern and sweet."

"No, thank you."

"Okay, have it your way."

The telephone rang. It was Karen Bushwagner, inviting us to come by her room for a surprise. Collette hung up the phone, saying, "That Karen is a stone whore. I did a threesome with her last month, and she licked up semen, like it was syrup, and swallowed it. She even let the guy screw her in the ass. Now, that's where I draw the line. I won't do that," she said, and she made a face to show her distaste for that sexual act.

Collette put her toys into her small bag, and we went down a flight of stairs to Karen's room and knocked. Jackie opened the door, and I could tell she was as high as a kite. They had towels stuffed under the door and burning incense to eliminate the smell of marijuana. Catherine Becker, a good friend of Karen's, was sitting on the side of the bed. Karen was sitting in the middle of the bed, with a round, plastic bottle in her hands. It had one tube sticking out of the top, two tubes out of the side, and a little water in the bottom. She had a joint sticking in one of the side tubes, and she was smoking out of the top tube. This was the "surprise," and I swear I had never seen anything like it. I couldn't figure out what the water was for.

She took a hit and passed it to Collette, who inhaled deeply and passed it to me. I hesitated, but Collette had already called me a wimp, so I took a hit and my head started to spin. I sat in the nearest chair and tried to act cool, as if the hit hadn't affected me. They passed the pipe around again. After my second hit I was feeling mellow.

Karen had us all laughing about an incident on her last flight. Some crazy woman in D-zone went into the lavatory with a man she had just met on the flight. The seatbelt light came on, so Karen knocked on the lavatory door and told the couple they had to come out. They refused. Karen took a knife and opened the door and froze in shock. The lady was sitting on the toilet, and the man was standing with his back to the door and his pants down around his ankles. The lady was giving him a blowjob. The man reached back, slammed, and locked the door. Karen let them have their way. The seatbelt sign was off when they came out, but the lady had left her panties on the lavatory floor.

By this time, Collette was rolling on the floor. We were having a good time when I noticed Catherine playing with Karen's toes. She started running her hand up Karen's thigh, and soon they were kissing. When I saw that, it broke my high.

"Feel free to join the fun." Karen looked up at me. "Don't be shy, I have some toys in that little bag on the dresser."

"No, thank you, I have to leave, I'm waiting for a phone call from Malcolm." I was already at the door.

Collette and Jackie said they had to leave, too.

Karen and Catherine were in their own world. I doubt they heard us. We left them on the bed and closed the door behind us.

By the third trip that month, I realized that their actions were the norm, instead of an isolated incident. During another flight from Dallas to San Francisco, I went down to the galley of the L-1011 aircraft. Karen was drunk as a skunk. She and Catherine were necking and grinding.

I tried not to act surprised.

"You two are at it again," I said, raising my eyebrows.

I got what I came for and left.

When we finished our first-class service, I told Collette what I had seen.

"Amanda, get hip. That's why they buddy-bidded. This has been going on for years. Yeah, Catherine is married to a pharmacist, you know. However, she and Karen were roommates before she got married. Last month, Karen was so drunk, we had to pretend she was sick to get her off the plane," Collette said.

"I have one more trip to fly with these fools, and I will be through with this shit," I thought.

Wouldn't you know the last trip was even worse? Our pick-up was six o'clock, but at two o'clock in the morning, a knock on my door woke me from a deep sleep. It was Collette, just getting in. I could tell she was high and excited about something. She was grinning from ear to ear.

She held out her arm and showed me a beautiful diamond bracelet. She pointed to her ears, and I saw huge diamond earrings to match.

"George gave me all this. What do you think?" She pranced around, as if it was two o'clock in the afternoon.

Collette had already told me her john was a wealthy businessman who lived in Sausalito with his wife and two children. He had a penthouse in New York, and Collette had met him there several times. She also met him in hotels when he was on business trips.

"Oh, let me show you something else." She went to my bed and started pulling things out of her bag. She threw a huge bag of marijuana on my bed.

"What in the hell are you doing with that?" I asked. I could not believe my eyes.

"I'm taking this back to New Orleans for Johnny. This is the good stuff. He gave us five hundred dollars in advance to do it," she said, as she pulled out a handful of cash to show me.

"Who is us?" I asked.

"Karen also has a bag. These white girls do it all the time. Why should I let them make all the money?" She flipped her hand.

Not only did Johnny Lee Jones have them whoring for him, now he had them transporting drugs.

"Collette, we need to talk. You need to think about what you're doing. This fucking around is fine, but transporting drugs is serious business."

"We know what we're doing and the money is great." She brushed me off.

I knew she was not saving the money. Instead, she was spending it on drugs. She had never paid me the fifty dollars I loaned her, over two years before.

I couldn't get back to sleep. The next day, I was nervous all the way back to New Orleans and couldn't even concentrate on the meal service. I didn't relax until I was in my car, on my way to my apartment.

Collette's trips were too stressful. I decided to swap and fly with Sarah on her three-day trip with layovers in Los Angles and Chicago. What a mistake that was! I had jumped from the frying pan into the fire.

Sarah and her crew had hooked up with a Madame Douveaux, who owned a brothel in Beverly Hills that catered to Hollywood stars. Sarah was one of the highest paid and most requested of her ladies. The movie stars loved her. She recited names, and I was shocked because they were some of the biggest names in Hollywood.

"What do you all do," I asked, "in the Madam's house?"

"We do drugs, mainly coke; drink fine wine and champagne; walk around half-naked; and sit on the actors' laps, massage their penises; dance and...you know...whatever turns them on...just the usual shit. They spend thousands of dollars, and we entertain them."

"How much do you get paid?"

"I get five hundred dollars a night base pay, or a thousand dollars plus tips if I fuck." She was so nonchalant, you'd think she was talking about a walk in the park.

She had gotten offers to do porno movies, and she was seriously thinking about it.

"Are you crazy?" I shouted.

"Calm down! I said I was thinking about it."

"Well, you need to forget about this shit," I said with conviction.

"But, Amanda, I could make enough money to retire in two years." She tried to plead her case, but I was not buying.

"You could be dead in two years. If some disease doesn't kill you, your parents will," I told her.

"They are the only thing that's stopping me: my parents and grandparents."

"Now you're thinking." I was happy, because I thought we got that settled. Then Sarah hit me with a bombshell.

"I have been spending a lot of time at the Playboy mansion and 'The Man' himself asked me to be a Playboy Bunny."

"Don't you dare tell me you screwed 'The Man'!" I yelled. It was disgusting. She could only smile and look away.

"They want me to pose nude for the magazine as a hot stewardess," she said, with pride.

"And what did you say?"

"I haven't given them an answer yet." She was chain-smoking as she talked on the jump seat next to me.

"When Irene sees it, you won't be a stewardess for long," I reminded her.

"I know, I know. Why do you always have to be so sensible? Collette and Helena have been telling me to do it. I know you are right."

"Damn right, I'm right. And when did you start listening to Collette and Helena?" Finally, I felt like I was getting through to her. "Sarah, you will bring shame on yourself and your family. Use your brain instead of your body."

"Thank you, Amanda, you are a true friend," she said after a while, and then gave me a big hug. I really needed to get my friends off drugs. It was driving them, and me, crazy.

Coming home on the last leg of the flight, half of the crew was so stoned, they could hardly stand up, much less work the flight. They couldn't work an emergency exit if their lives depended on it. They took turns sleeping in the galley. I kept nudging Sarah to keep her from falling asleep on the jump seat. To this day, I don't know how we got through that flight.

Thank God, the next month we lost the Los Angeles-Chicago layover. Sarah and I buddy-bidded, and I wouldn't let her out of my sight. We flew to Monroe, Louisiana, and to Macon, Georgia. Thank goodness that nothing was happening in those cities.

Nineteen

Six months later, we also lost the San Francisco trip to the Dallas base. I was so happy. It was a blessing in disguise for Collette, Jackie, and their group. Collette still flew out on her off days for her rendezvous with the Fortune 500 president and CEO. She even met him in New York, at his penthouse. She jetted across the country whenever he called.

The San Francisco layover was replaced with a Las Vegas layover. Johnny Lee Jones hooked them up with a pimp friend of his in Las Vegas. Unlike San Francisco, where they had the same special johns to service every week, in Las Vegas, they had to take whoever was around at the moment.

One evening, Karen Bushwagner got a call to service a john in room 409, at ten o'clock that evening. She got all dressed up and put a few sex toys in her bag, just in case. Promptly, at ten o'clock, she knocked on the door, and to her dismay, the captain from her trip open the door; buck naked!

As soon as he saw her, he scrambled to the bathroom and returned with a towel wrapped around himself. He apologized, saying, "he was just about to get into the shower."

Karen had to think up a quick lie, saying she was checking on him to see if he wanted to go for a late snack.

He said no and tried to get rid of her, as though he was expecting someone to show up. We laughed about this for years. The captain was married to a stewardess, and he certainly didn't want it to get out that he was trying to hire a prostitute in Las Vegas. Even worse, if Irene found out one of her girls was prostituting in Las Vegas, she would drop dead on the spot.

Two months later, Jackie agreed to service a john in her own room. Things got out of hand. He put duct tape over her mouth, choked, and beat her with a leather whip. Then she was handcuffed to the bed, raped, and burned with cigarettes. He urinated on her and left her for dead. She banged her body against the wall until the people in the next room called security. The security guards heard the banging coming from Jackie's room, and they opened the door and found her. Of course, Jackie told the police she opened the door for a man who said he needed to check the air conditioner. The police had an idea she was prostituting, but they couldn't prove it, so they had to accept her word. Jackie stayed in the hospital for two weeks, with third-degree-burns all over her body, and bruises and cuts that required thirty-two stitches. When released from the hospital, Jackie went home to California for months of rehabilitation and psychiatric care. She never flew again.

When the word got around about what had happened to Jackie, Collette and her group decided to stop prostituting. It broke our hearts to know someone could be so brutal to one of our friends.

After the Jackie incident, Collette gave up drugs and became a born-again Christian. Her changed life didn't last long, however.

Collette started dating Roscoe Parker, a no-good bum from New Orleans, who worked at a used car lot. He had three kids by two women, and he also had a bad drug problem. Collette and Roscoe had only been dating for two months when she decided they would get married. We tried to talk her out of it.

"Collette, can't you see this guy is going nowhere fast?" Dee Dee was the only one who had the nerve to tell her, but Collette wouldn't listen. Malcolm usually didn't get involved in my girlfriends' business, but this time he, too, tried to talk to Collette, all to no avail.

Two weeks later, we all put on our Sunday best and went to her new church, The Church of the Rock, for the wedding.

Collette was frantic, nothing was going right. Dee Dee was the maid of honor, and Sarah was the bridesmaid. Nicole, Michele, and a few other stewardesses were spectators. I was the wedding director, and I told everyone where to stand! I didn't have any special wedding-coordinator's training, I simply used my experience from directing funerals, and I had seen many weddings over the years. Many times, we would have to wait for a wedding party to leave the church, before we could bring the body and the funeral party into the church, and vice-versa. Many times, there would be a wedding and funeral on the same day, a Saturday.

I remember one such incident, when a friend of mine pulled me out of a funeral I was directing. She was frantic. "Amanda," she cried, "I reserved this church when Old Man Jameson was drinking himself to death behind Tony's Liquor Store. You know I need to decorate the church for my wedding. Now, you hurry his funeral along and roll Jameson's body out of here before you're the one lying in that box!"

I knew she was not kidding, so I went back into the church to hurry things along. I realized most of the people at Mr. Jameson's funeral were also her wedding guests. I knew they were not going to go home, change clothes, and come back for the wedding. They would stay at the church. So I asked them to help my friend with the decorations for her wedding.

But back in reality, if Collette's wedding was only as simple...

She had good reasons to be frantic. For starters, Roscoe was so stoned; he couldn't stand in one position. One of his brothers had to hold him up at the altar. He also didn't have a ring, and his brother had to nudge him when it was time to say, "I do!"

Collette paid for the honeymoon and got the apartment in her name, because Roscoe had no credit. Collette's wedding was the talk of the New Orleans base for a few weeks. We could only hope everything would work out, although we were sure they wouldn't.

Accepting Collette's new husband was a major challenge for us, that moved us above and beyond the call of duty.

Twenty

Things were going along well, until out of the blue, Sarah called me at Malcolm's house early one Sunday morning. Malcolm and I had just gotten to bed after a night of partying at one of the Saints' birthday celebrations.

Malcolm answered the phone. "It's your friend, Sarah," he said, handing me the phone.

"Amanda, I'm downtown at the St. Charles Hotel. This motherfucker has run off with my purse, my clothes, my car, and left me in this room with nothing. I don't care what you're doing. Just get your black ass down here and bring me some clothes and money."

She was livid.

"Sarah, what happened? What's going on?" I was half-asleep and trying to focus.

"I met this son-of-a-bitch at the Coyote Club last night. He seemed like a nice guy, and he had some good stuff. You know what I mean."

I assumed she was talking about drugs.

"We came over here to the hotel to have some fun. I had no interest in fucking the bastard. I just fell asleep, and when I woke up this morning, the bastard and all my shit were gone. How long is it going to take for you to get here?"

Although Sarah was in a bad situation, she was still in control. I guess she learned control from Wendell when she was seeing him before he lost his club and went to prison.

"As soon as I can get up and get dressed. Thirty minutes at the most," I said.

"Now, don't you dare call any of those other bitches. If you do, I'll kill you. I'm only calling you because I know I can trust you," she said, and gave me the room number before hanging up.

"*She sure as hell didn't give me time to call anyone else*," I thought as I scrambled through my closet for one of my dresses that would fit her six-foot frame. "*Someday she's gonna get herself killed.*"

Malcolm's mother had left a pair of shoes in the guest closet. I grabbed them, and I checked my cash. Malcolm drove me, because the St. Charles Hotel was not in the best part of town.

He stayed in the car while I went up to Sarah's room and knocked on the door.

"It's Amanda," I said.

Sarah opened the door, and she was wrapped only in a towel. She was still cussing.

"Can you believe that nigger?" she snarled.

"Do you know the name of this man?" I asked. It seemed like a reasonable question to me.

"Rollo, or some shit like that. I didn't get his last name. You know how these drug dealers are. That's probably not even his real name." She wasn't the least bit embarrassed, and she acted as though this type of thing happened every day.

"I was sitting at the bar, minding my own business, when he came over and offered to buy me a drink. One thing led to another, and he said he had some good coke. I should have known better." She was talking from the bathroom as she got dressed.

When she came out, my dress looked better on her than it ever looked on me, and Malcolm's mother's shoes were a perfect fit. She had put her hair in a ponytail and looked like she just stepped out of *Vogue*. We went downstairs and paid the hotel bill. Our first stop was the police station, so she could report her car and purse stolen. I went in with her, and Malcolm again stayed in the car. I didn't have the slightest idea what Sarah would tell the police, but if I didn't know the truth, I would have believed her, too.

"I was robbed at gunpoint outside of the Coyote Club last night. They took my purse and my car." She was almost in tears.

The police officer took down the report. He wrote down the make and model of her car and the license-plate number. He said there had been a lot of robberies outside that Club: "Young hoodlums looking for cash and drugs."

"I'll need your home number, if you don't mind. I will personally call you if we find out anything, Miss Ferguson. It is 'Miss,' isn't it?" the officer asked.

"Yes, officer," Sarah responded, nodding her head.

"What's a beautiful lady like you doing going to a club alone?" he asked.

The way he was coming on to Sarah, I was sure they would find her car by tomorrow. "My girlfriend," Sarah looked at me, "was at work, and I didn't want to stay home alone. Besides, I like the music at the Coyote Club. I thought it was safe." Sarah was in tears again. The officer handed her a tissue.

"He is crazy if he falls for this," I thought.

"I understand, Miss Ferguson, but it's a dangerous world out there. We will find your car, but I can't promise you we'll catch those hoodlums. I'll, I mean, we'll be in touch."

Malcolm and I drove Sarah to her apartment at Lewis & Clark and made sure she had everything she needed before we left. Malcolm had always liked Sarah. He told me one of his white teammates wanted to meet Sarah after seeing her at a game with me.

"What did you say?" I asked.

"I told him to go to hell."

"What was his response?" I was curious.

"Oh, he was pissed! He said. You black guys fuck our white women, but you don't want us to look at your women."

"What did you say?" I wanted to hear more.

"Nothing, I picked him up and sat him in the trash can. He knew better than to mess with me." Malcolm laughed, and I could see he enjoyed it.

We decided to stop and have breakfast before going back to his place. I couldn't wait to curl-up in bed with Malcolm. This had become my favorite pastime.

The officer from the police station called Sarah three days later. They found her car in Biloxi, Mississippi, stripped clean. He wanted to know if they could meet for lunch, and he would give her all the details.

They met, and Sarah went out him a few times afterward.

"He has a big dick, but he doesn't know how to use it. I don't have time to teach a grown-ass man how to fuck. He doesn't drink, smoke, or do drugs. I have no use for him. All he does is go to church," she complained to me. I knew he was history.

With her drug problem and her past history with Wendell and the nightclub scene, it wasn't in her best interest to be dating a police officer. It made no sense to ask for trouble.

Sarah's insurance company paid up, and she bought a brand-new car. All the other girls and stewardesses felt sorry for her, being robbed at gunpoint. I never told a soul the truth about that incident. I never felt the need to, because she would have done the same for me. However, I was still worried about my friend.

Sarah called me a month later. Wendell needed to talk to her about something. He said it was urgent, and she asked me if I would go with her to the federal prison to see him next week. I couldn't go, because Malcolm and I had planned a trip to Jamaica. I only hoped Wendell would talk some sense onto her. I told Sarah to tell Wendell I said hello.

I felt things were going to be fine with Sarah, because I had written Wendell a letter, which he answered, thanking me for writing and saying he "had everything under control."

Twenty-one

Malcolm and I had become an item around town. I never went to his road games, but he always brought back a gift for me. I went to two Pro Bowls in Honolulu, and that was a lot of fun, and I went to most of the home games. There was always something going on in the players' box. I wasn't Malcolm's wife, so I could not be part of the Wives' Club. I sat with the team's girlfriends, who changed every week. A player usually gave all of his lady-friends tickets to sit side-by-side in his seats in the players' box.

Several times, a wife would show up, and the lady-friends would be in the husband's seat. One player had two women pregnant at the same time, with due dates three-months apart. Both women were at the games, sitting in the players' box, cheering for their man. There were frequent fights over seats.

As soon as the game was over, there would be so many women outside the locker room, waiting for the players, it was like a zoo. Women would go up to a player and slip their telephone number and other notes into his pocket.

I was waiting for Malcolm one day, and a lady tried to proposition him when he was only a few feet from me. When I walked over and put my arms around him, she called me a bitch. He was trying to get away from the lady, but she put her hand on his crotch and said she would do anything for some of that. I was getting ready to kick her ass on the spot, but Malcolm pushed me into the car, locked the doors, and drove off. This was the first time he really became angry with me. I had to promise never to act that way again.

"Do you realize someone could get hurt, and it would be my name dragged through the mud? I told you how these women act. If you can't take it, I'll meet you out front," he yelled.

I never waited outside the locker room again. Since Malcolm chose to seldom associate, off the field, with any of his teammates, I didn't get close to the players' wives or girlfriends. Besides, I had my own friends.

As the players' representative, Malcolm was one of the most respected and dependable guys in the league. He was also one of the most stable. Players called him from all over the league for advice about football and personal matters. He counseled younger players when they first arrived in the league. Many of the younger guys called him when they got into trouble.

"I wish they would call me *before* they get in trouble. It's a shame because most of this shit is preventable," Malcolm always said.

Most of the black players would, at the least, buy their mothers a house and a new car. Malcolm encouraged them to invest the rest of their money. That is, if they had any left after buying fully loaded cars and clothes and paying child support. Some of the guys had three or four kids and had never been married.

During off-seasons, and when Malcolm wasn't busy with football camps or union business, we took some wonderful trips. Once, I talked him into going on a layover with me to Las Vegas. He signed autographs in the gatehouse and on the plane. The stewardesses and cockpit crew wanted autographs for their children. I was very proud of the way he handled himself. However, he vowed never to go on another of my flights. He didn't enjoy the attention. He wanted it to be about me.

After our first year of dating, Malcolm went home with me to meet my family. Unlike Sarah and Dee Dee, he wasn't afraid to sleep in the guest room. My entire family, and half the community, came to our house for Sunday dinner, just to meet Malcolm. It was late May, and my grandmother had gone out in the fields behind the house and picked some poke salad, because she knew it was one of my favorites.

My brothers and uncles were huge football fans and were honored to meet Malcolm. My five-year-old niece wanted to sit on his lap. I told her to sit her little butt in the chair. She did sit next to him at the dinner table, and he couldn't turn without her little butt on his heels.

After dinner, my grandfather took Malcolm for a ride. He showed him every inch of the Callaway estate. I remember hoping my grandfather would refrain from trying to entice Malcolm into becoming a member of our family. My grandfather was a good judge of character, and I could tell he liked Malcolm. I hated to admit it, but I needed all the help I could get.

On the flight back to New Orleans, Malcolm told me my family was Great, and he enjoyed meeting them, especially my grandfather.

"What did you two talk about?" I asked

"Oh, nothing." Evidently he didn't want to tell me.

"You all were gone for two hours."

"Men talk, none of your business. Now, don't be so nosey."

"So you two talked about me, didn't you?"

"Maybe! Now, let it be, Amanda," he pleaded, and I knew I had to drag it out of him.

"What did my grandfather say? Pleeease?"

"If you must know," he finally responded, because he knew I wouldn't let it rest, "he offered me five acres of land and to build us a house when we got married. He wanted us to live on the estate, and I could help run the business when I retire from football."

"Wow! My grandfather must really like you. I can't believe he tried to buy you. What did you say?" I was interested to know how he handled the situation, because my grandfather was an astute businessman.

"He didn't try to buy me, and I told him I would think about it. He's a smart old man. I respect him…what did you expect me to say?" Malcolm sounded upset. "It's hard for a black man to build a successful business, especially in the South. Your grandfather had to struggle and fight racism to get to where he is today. Now he wants to make life a little easier for his grandchildren. Nothing wrong with that."

"Don't be angry with me, that's between you and my grandfather," I said. I knew better than to press him anymore. He appeared to be deep in thought. I hoped he was thinking about us and my grandfather's offer.

Later that summer, Malcolm and I went on a ten-day, European cruise and an unforgettable trip to Tahiti. People thought we were on our honeymoon, which got us the royal treatment everywhere we went. Malcolm was so loving, I had to pinch myself to make sure I was not dreaming.

That was two year ago, and this year, we were going to Jamaica, and I was looking forward to it.

Malcolm was out, having lunch with his only friend on the Saints' team, Robert "Bob" Mitchell, and I was at the house finalizing our plans for the trip, when the phone rang.

"Honey!" It was Malcolm. "Do you mind if Bob goes to Jamaica with us?" he asked. "I told him I thought it would be all right, but I had to check with you."

"Bob always goes home during the off season. Is he still here?" I asked.

"He broke up with his girlfriend back home. He's feeling kind of low, and a trip will be good for him. He won't bother us. He'll probably meet someone when we get there."

"Sure, I'll get him a ticket and make his hotel reservation," I replied.

"Thanks, baby. I love you," he said before hanging up.

I thought Malcolm sounded very tired. He hadn't been quite the same since he came back from his month's stay in St. Louis.

I really liked Bob. He had been Malcolm's only close friend for five years. He was a Duke University graduate, and one of the smartest guys on the team. He and Malcolm were two of only a handful of guys with college degrees. I had never seen Bob with a woman, and I thought he was a loner until, one day, Malcolm told me he had a girlfriend back home in Raleigh-Durham, North Carolina. He was putting her through Duke Law School.

While visiting us one day at Malcolm's house, Bob showed me a picture of his girlfriend. She was a pretty, petite, dark–brown-skinned woman. I was surprised to see that she looked a lot like me. I noticed that Bob was watching me, as though he wanted me to make a connection, but he didn't say so. His girlfriend had never come to New Orleans, and he always went home as soon as football season was over. I felt very uneasy about the way Bob had looked at me that evening. I told myself that maybe he just missed his lady. Of course, I knew of several stewardesses who would have loved to go with him to Jamaica; no questions asked. Bob was one of the most sought-after guys on the team. Many girls had asked me to introduce them to him or set up a blind date. Bob always refused.

On the flight to Jamaica, Malcolm was not feeling well. He slept the entire flight. He was taking some new medication and was sleeping a lot lately.

Malcolm had undergo a complete physical when he was home in St. Louis for a month by his family doctor. His doctor had put him on this new medication for an old football injury. At least, that was what Malcolm told me.

While Malcolm slept, Bob and I had a long time to talk, and we got to know each other. This was the first time I had ever had a real conversation with him. He talked about his girlfriend most of the time. Her name was Mary Catherine. He was very much in love with her, and had put a lot of time and money into the relationship. He had bought her a car and a house in Durham, where they lived together. They broke up three months ago when he found out that, during the last football season, while he was in New Orleans, she moved another man into their house. The other man turned out to be a law student to whom Mary Catherine was now engaged. Bob tried to hide the fact that he was hurting. He had just bought a brand-new Cartier watch for her and had plans to surprise her with it, when he found out about the other guy. I realized Bob was very generous because, when he reimbursed me for the tickets and hotel, he gave me an extra three hundred dollars to spend in Jamaica.

I couldn't believe I was sitting between two handsome superstars, both of whom made a ton of money and could probably have any woman they wanted. Yet one was fast asleep, and the other one was crying the blues because some woman had broken his heart.

I was thinking, *"Usually, it was the other way around."* Most football players I knew were studs. Some had a different woman every night. All they did was chase pussy, even though they didn't have to chase too far. I have seen some players with three women during a single day. Most had no respect for women.

Most of the brothers treated the white women worse than they treated the sisters. Sisters wouldn't do all that kinky sex that brothers demanded from the white girls. For instance, a brother would bring a white woman to a party, dump her, and leave with another white woman. But if he brought a sister, he damn sure better leave with her, or there would be a fight. A sister would tell the brother where to get off and call him every name but a child of God.

Malcolm continued to sleep while Bob and I talked about a little bit of everything. I found we had a lot in common. We both attended Christian secondary and high schools, our families were Missionary Baptists, and we know what it was like to stay in church all day, every Sunday. We both sang in the junior choir and had been president of the local Baptist Training Union, the BTU. He lived in rural South Carolina, and I lived in rural Tennessee.

Bob was really a nice guy, and extremely smart, which was unusual for a football player.

Although we laughed and talked, I felt he was holding something back. Maybe it was something he wanted to tell me about Malcolm, or something Malcolm had told him about me. Several times I caught him staring at me, and when our eyes met, he would look away. I couldn't figure him out. He was not my type, but I could see why women fell for him. He was very handsome, with beautiful eyes.

In Jamaica, after we checked in, Malcolm and I hardly saw Bob, and each time we did see him, he was with another woman. I knew he was on the rebound. We all met one night for a limbo contest. Bob and I won, because we were the last two standing. He had to "pick me up off the floor" several times to keep me going. He knew how to have a good time. I never laughed so much in my life. Malcolm didn't feel up to competing, and he wasn't quite himself during the entire trip. He didn't drink and was very sluggish because of, he said, the new pain pills he was taking. I wanted to get a close look at his medicine bottles, but he kept them in his personal bag instead of on the bathroom counter or in the medicine cabinet. I wouldn't dare look through his bags. Besides, at the time, I didn't think he was hiding anything from me.

He was very protective and wouldn't let me out of his sight. I couldn't go to the bathroom without him asking where I was going. It was very unusual for him to act this way. Other than his watchful eye, we had a wonderful time, and I enjoyed the added attention. We made love on the balcony one night, and he told me how much he loved me and worshiped the ground I walked on.

"You stole that line from a song." I was only half kidding.

"I may have, but I mean every word." He was serious.

I felt I would be getting a ring soon. I was on cloud nine.

Twenty-two

When we returned home from Jamaica, I called Sarah several times, but she wasn't home. I had checked her schedule, and I knew she had six days off, so she must have gone home to visit her parents for a few days. I didn't think anything about it. I had a three-day trip to fly, and I would talk to her later.

After returning from my trip and still not reaching Sarah, I called Dee Dee.

"Dee Dee, where in the hell is Sarah?" I asked.

"Amanda, I don't know what's gotten into that girl. Sarah's in Las Vegas with that pilot, Franco Bordeaux." She paused for me to react. When I didn't, she continued, "Last week, they flew to Acapulco together. You need to talk to her, because you're the only one she will listen to."

I couldn't believe what Dee Dee was saying. Wendell said, in his letter from prison, that he would talk some sense into her, and I thought he had. This was out of character for Sarah. Of course, we all knew about First Officer Franco Bordeaux.

At twenty-eight, he was the sexiest second officer on the L-1011 aircraft. His father was French, and his mother was from Chile. With olive skin and black, curly hair, he was one handsome devil. He had bedded more stewardesses than any other pilot with Big E. We all knew he had the hots for Sarah, but she had never given him the time of day. "Why now? What's going on?" were questions running through my mind as Dee Dee spoke.

"When did all this happen?" I asked Dee Dee.

"About a week ago. I first heard about it from a group of junior stewardesses. Sarah and Franco were on their flight, all lovey-dovey. I saw her when she got back from Acapulco. That's when she told me she was going to Las Vegas with him."

After hearing this mess, I was ready to strangle that girl. I left four messages on Sarah's answering machine. She called me back as soon as she returned from Las Vegas.

"Hi, girlfriend! I missed you. How was Jamaica?" She sounded happy, and she knew Dee Dee had told me.

"I had a great time. Now, what's going on with you and Franco Bordeaux?" I said, getting straight to the point.

"I flew with him two weeks ago, and he kept begging me, so I gave him some." Then her voice got all romantic. "Oooh, girl! If I had known he was that good, I would have given him some sooner. He fucks like a brother. He must have some black in him. The man is well-endowed, can keep a hard-on, and he can eat some pussy." She was still excited.

"Sarah, you know his well-endowed ass has made the rounds," I reminded her.

"Yeah, yeah, I know that, I hope you don't think I'm serious about him. I just needed a good fuck, and he was there at the right time." I knew she was telling the truth. That was her personality, so I let it go.

"How did it go with Wendell?" I asked.

"It went great. He wants us to have a life together when he gets out of jail. I want that, too, but it will be a long time before he gets out. He wants to marry me, and I promised to wait for him. But can't a girl have a little fun in the meantime?" she cried.

I asked her about Acapulco and Las Vegas.

"Franco offered, and I wasn't about to turn down an all-expense-paid trip. We had fun, and I gave him all he wanted. What's wrong with that?" she asked, and I had no answer. "Would you believe those bitches working the flight wouldn't speak to me when they found out we were together? But they were all over him," she added.

"Yes, I believe it. What did you expect? They were jealous. I'm sure he has slept with most of them, and he never took them on a trip." We both laughed. At the time, we underestimated just how jealous the other women were.

It took only a week for the news of Sarah and Franco to hit the New-Orleans-base grapevine. Sarah got a call from Irene.

"Sarah Ferguson, be in my office, first thing in the morning." That was all she said, and we knew Irene's spies had been working overtime.

Irene was waiting for Sarah at eight o'clock, sharp. She had twenty letters on her desk from stewardesses and cockpit crewmembers about Sarah and Franco.

"I don't believe in interracial dating, especially at Big Elite World Airlines. It simply causes too much animosity in the workplace. You know I would do the same if you were one of my white girls dating a black pilot. I love all my girls, and I don't want to see them hurt." Irene lectured Sarah for thirty minutes, while I waited for her in the scheduler's office.

"I like you, Sarah, I have always supported you, but I cannot support you on this. Just do as I say, and don't cause me any trouble," were Irene's final words. It was a direct order, and we knew what that meant: "Obey or get the hell out of Dodge."

Sarah and I went to lunch after the meeting. She took everything Irene said with a grain of salt. She continued to see Franco, just to make the others jealous. However, Sarah was smart enough not to defy Irene openly, because she could make your life a living hell. The only thing left to do was transfer to Atlanta. She was my best friend, and I didn't want her to leave.

"I don't give a damn about Franco, I just refuse to let anyone tell me who I can and cannot fuck," Sarah said, and I knew she was right.

Sarah transferred to Atlanta the next month. Since she had lived there before in college, it was an easy adjustment.

After she left, I was lonesome, so I started buddy-bidding to fly with Dee Dee. She had a new lover in Chicago, and she was head over heels in love.

"When are we going to meet this new man of yours?" Collette kept asking, teasing her.

I said nothing, because I knew her secret.

"When the time is right," was all Dee Dee would say.

"He must be some hunk," Caroline said provocatively. But Dee Dee didn't bite.

We all noticed that Dee Dee had started dressing differently. She wore more pants and big shirts. She had her hair cut short, and she used less makeup. Caroline and Collette didn't think too much about it, because she seemed content with her boyfriend. If he liked her that way, it was fine with them.

Dee Dee and I flew together a lot. It was certainly more serene than flying with Sarah and Collette and their bunch. Dee Dee was interested in antiques, and I knew a lot about good antiques, because antiques were all around me when I was growing up. So we shopped for antiques on every layover.

We flew one trip with a layover in Phoenix. On the second day, we flew from Phoenix to Atlanta. Dee Dee was working the meal cart, and I followed close behind with the beverage cart. I heard a lady screaming behind me, nearly jumping out of her seat. We thought she was having a seizure, so we three stewardess rushed to her rescue. She was pointing to the salad on her meal tray, like it was poison. At first, we couldn't understand what she was trying to say. Then I looked closer and saw the salad move. I picked up her whole tray, held it at arm's length, and transported it to the galley. One crewmember followed me to the galley so we could take a closer look under the lights, and Dee Dee stayed to calm the lady down.

I raked through the salad with a cocktail pick, and sure enough, hiding under a piece of lettuce, there was a big fat juicy worm. We both screamed and jumped into the aisle. We covered the salad, worm and all, with plastic wrap and left it for the caterer in Atlanta. We apologized to the lady. It took almost a whole bottle of champagne to calm her. We wrote up the report and left it for the company to deal with the incident.

Two weeks later, on the same trip, except that this time it was on the leg from Atlanta to Little Rock, a lady's flowing skirt got caught in a wheel of the beverage cart. We pulled and tugged until we were finally able to free the skirt. The damage to the skirt included little holes, grease, and dirt.

When I began writing up the report, I asked the lady to give me an estimate of the cost of the skirt. I almost fainted when she said five hundred dollars, because I seen that exact skirt in JCPenney's and the Sears catalog for twenty-five dollars. We would have given her twenty-five dollars out of the liquor money or a voucher for that amount. Instead, she had to talk to someone higher up in the company than us, and we wished her luck. We never did learn the resolution of that problem.

I was spending a lot of time at my apartment because Malcolm still wasn't feeling well and was having an awful season, the worst of his career. He was even contemplating retiring. When the phone rang, it was Malcolm, telling me to come home; he had a surprise for me. When I got to his house, he picked up a gift box from the kitchen table and gave it to me. I thought it was a gift from him, maybe a ring, but when I opened it, I saw a Cartier watch, identical to the one Bob had bought for his girlfriend, Mary Catherine. I looked at Malcolm, and he motioned for me to read the note. I opened the small note and read aloud:

To: Amanda,

Just my way of saying thank you for allowing me to come on your vacation. It was nice talking to you on the plane. I had a great time in Jamaica, especially, the Limbo contest. Besides, I have no use for it anymore.

Bob Mitchell

I would have given it back, but Malcolm insisted I keep it.

"You don't want to hurt Bob's feelings, do you?" he asked. "He bought it for his girlfriend who's now with another man. I'm sure he just wanted to get rid of it."

Since Malcolm put it that way, I took my old watch off and put the Cartier on my wrist. It was beautiful, as well as expensive.

I sent him a thank-you note.

Twenty-three

1978

This was a year of change: For starters, Elite World Airlines increased their hiring of male stewards. They were a strong minority and soon began to flex their muscles. To begin with, they disliked the name "stewards," so we changed our name from "stewardesses" and "stewards" to "flight attendants." We liked our new name, and it was catching on fast with our younger passengers. However, our older ones stilled called us stewardesses or waitresses. Old habits were hard to break.

Irene was getting old, and there were rumors that she might be retiring soon. One of the characteristics of the New Orleans base was that everybody knew everybody's business. We knew who was sleeping with whom, who did drugs, and who didn't. So if there were rumors that Irene was going to retire, it meant that she probably was.

By the summer, we had a new president and CEO. He relaxed the rules so Irene's rules no longer applied, and she was forced to retire. My thoughts on that subject were that Sarah left the base six months too early.

The new base manager, Mary Robocelli, was a former stewardess and had a better understanding of our job than Irene, who had never flown.

Also, Miles Gilbertson, our old racist nemesis, was forced to retire, but for different reasons. He had gotten into a fight with a black male, and two white, gay flight attendants onboard the aircraft, but the last straw was when he got into a fight with a black comedienne who starred in a popular black television sitcom. The story was that while the comedienne was boarding the flight, she overheard Gilbertson use the word "nigger." He was the only one on the plane who had not recognized her.

"Who are you calling a nigger?" the comedienne demanded.

When Gilbertson turned to go into the cockpit without acknowledging her, she grabbed him.

"I said, who are you calling a nigger? Motherfucker!" she screamed. She had Gilbertson by the collar, holding him up off the floor with one hand. She was in his face.

"I'll kick your ass right here on this plane, little man," she said, and for the first time, in anyone's memory, Gilbertson was speechless.

Flight attendants working the flight said he was so scared, he was shaking all over, and he almost wet his uniform. When the comedienne let him down, Gilbertson fled into the cockpit and closed the door.

The television star refused to talk to Elite World Airlines, and she called the NAACP and held a press conference all within hours:

"Elite World Airlines is a racist airline with deep, Southern roots. It doesn't treat black people fairly and allows racist pilots to fly their airplanes. I was called a 'nigger' by the captain, so I had to act like a 'nigger.' I will be filing a lawsuit as soon as I get back to Los Angeles." She said this on national TV.

This time, Gilbertson was given an indefinite suspension without pay for using the "N–word," and the airline settled out of court with the comedienne.

While he was on suspension, he used a vacation pass to take a woman, posing as his wife, to Europe. First of all, it was against the airline's rules to use a travel pass while on suspension, but to have another unrelated person use the pass was grounds for termination.

There was some kind of family emergency, and Miles' wife had called Big E looking for him. His wife didn't know about the suspension. He had told her he had three weeks of training in Atlanta. The chief pilot knew that Gilbertson was supposed to be in Europe with his wife. Well, when the shit hit the fan, Miles' wife had not been on an airplane in over twelve years, because she had developed a fear of flying.

Big E checked Miles' pass records and found that, over the past twelve years, he had taken his girlfriend on twenty trips. Flight attendants who had seen the woman traveling with him, assumed she was his wife. The airline charged Gilbertson full fare for every flight he took with his girlfriend, and the total came to eighteen thousand dollars. He was forced to retire, and he lost all of his pass privileges.

Also, that spring, I got a call from Barbara Ann. She and Big Daddy were getting married after four years of living together. She was having a big wedding, and she asked me to be her Maid of Honor. Collette, Sarah, Helena, and Dee Dee were all bridesmaids. Barbara Ann was two months pregnant. We all were happy for her, and we looked forward to going to Anniston for the wedding. Barbara Ann had always kept in touch with all of us. We talked on the phone at least twice a month. She was happy, and we were happy for her.

"I had to have the slut's baby in the wedding. I really believed, at the time, that Calvin couldn't be the baby's father, but tests don't lie. That country bitch tricked him. She told him she was on birth-control pills," she confessed during one of our conversations.

I knew they were having problems. Big Daddy had been sued for child support, which Barbara Ann had been paying. But lately, Big Daddy had cleaned up his life, and there was no more hustling. He got a real job as a police officer with the Atlanta police department, which was a good move, because no one knew the streets like Big Daddy. He must have been smart, because he had never been caught.

The wedding was beautiful. The "other woman's" little girl was the flower girl. She was the splitting image of Big Daddy, no one could deny that.

Twenty-four

The fall of that year brought about the biggest change of all. The New Orleans Saints hadn't had a winning season since they had been in New Orleans, so the Saints management team decided to trade players. Malcolm was traded to Detroit, and his friend Bob Mitchell was traded to Atlanta. I was crushed. It all happened so fast. Malcolm had been my life for three and a half years.

He put his New Orleans house on the market and it sold in three weeks. I packed his personal belongings and had them shipped, along with his furniture, to his house in St. Louis.

"Why St. Louis?" I thought. "He was traded to Detroit." I used to know Malcolm, but now I was not sure how well I knew him. I knew he owned a house in St. Louis. However, I had never seen it. I had never been to St. Louis. I had met his mother, Mablelean, when she came to visit him in New Orleans about three times a year.

"Maybe I'm overreacting," I told myself, and left it at that.

I had to move back into my apartment at Lewis & Clark with Caroline. My fairytale romance was over. The distance between Malcolm and me was too much for our relationship, and there were just too many beautiful women in the Motor City. I called him every night straight for a month, left messages on his recorder, and he never returned my calls. Every Sunday, I watched the Lions play on television, and he hardly ever played. I saw him on the bench.

I would have continued to call, except that one night a woman answered his phone. I forgot my manners.

"Who are you?" I was shocked.

"I'm the woman who's living with Malcolm now, and you can forget about him and keep your skinny ass in New Orleans," she answered, as though she knew me.

"How do you know I'm skinny?" I asked.

"I've seen your picture, I know you're from Tennessee, and I recognized that southern country accent Malcolm told me about." The voice on the other end was nasty.

"Just tell Malcolm Amanda called." I really didn't want to get into a cussing match with this woman.

"Don't hold your breath, now get it through your head, it's over." And she slammed the phone down.

I held onto the phone a minute, feeling sick. This woman, whoever she was, seemed to know a lot about me, but I knew it was over, because Malcolm was a one-woman man. It was the same way when he came to New Orleans. He had put his girlfriend in St. Louis down when he started dating me. He wouldn't return her phone calls. He told me at the time that they were only friends, and "nothing serious."

"Yeah, right, that's what they all say. He's probably telling this new woman the same thing about me," I told myself as tears filled my eyes. It wasn't like we had a big fight and broke up. He never said, "I don't want to see you anymore, it's over." When I asked to go with him to Detroit, he said, "Maybe later, Amanda, we'll see."

He left for Detroit, came back once to close on his house, gave me a check for five thousand dollars to oversee the packing and shipping of his belongings, and he was gone. He refused to let me visit him in Detroit. He was too busy "getting used to his new team."

So our relationship was over, and I was devastated. Malcolm was my first real love. I had never shared such intimacy with another man. I didn't know how to start over, so I cried, day and night. I couldn't eat or sleep. I lost ten pounds in one month. I went to work, came home, and went to bed. I cannot tell you with whom I flew or where we had our layovers. Sarah called from Atlanta, and when I stopped answering my phone, she picked-up a New Orleans layover, came by the apartment, dragged me out of bed, and threw me under a cold shower. Dee Dee told her I had been in bed for three days. I couldn't remember.

"Look, Amanda, honey, I know what you're going through. I felt the same way when Wendell went to prison, but I had to keep living. You have to do the same. It will get better, I promise you." She was very sincere, and chose her words very carefully.

April 9, 1979

I came in from a trip, and as soon as I opened the door, everybody screamed: "Happy birthday! Happy birthday! Amanda!"

Was it really my birthday? I thought hard, and it was April 9. How could I have forgotten my own birthday?

I looked around the room at the balloons, streamers, and party favors. I saw Sarah, Dee Dee, Caroline, Helena, Barbara Ann, and a few other flight attendants I knew. Joe was putting candles on a birthday cake. He was the only male there, and of course, he was the cook.

The last thing I felt like was a party. When I raised my hand to object, Sarah cussed me out.

"Get your skinny ass in the shower, change, and come out here and eat. Joe has cooked your favorite, crawfish étouffée, and you are going to eat it, if I have to cram it down your throat," she yelled at me.

I knew better than to challenge her when she was talking like this, so I greeted everyone and excused myself to shower and change. I went into the bathroom, turned on the shower and let the water run so they would think I was taking a shower. I wasn't in a party mood, and I needed time to collect myself. Since I couldn't fall through the floor and disappear, I felt a need to get down on my knees and pray. I knelt in the small space between the wall and the toilet, and I prayed.

"Heavenly Father, give me strength to get through this evening...and tomorrow...and the next day. For I am weak, but you are strong...you know what I mean. Amen."

I hadn't prayed in so long, I had almost forgotten how. I got up off my knees, and I felt better. I took off my clothes and stared at my naked body in the mirror. I was shocked at how much weight I had lost.

"You are a fool, Amanda, to let a man do this to you. Where is your common sense?" I whispered aloud to my reflection in the mirror.

I had two choices, I could sit around and cry, or I could remember the good times and move on. I had learned so much from Malcolm. He had taken a country girl and turned her into a woman. He set a high standard for the man who would come after him, because he taught me not to settle for anything less than the best. I had also managed to save a lot of money during the three and a half years I was with him; enough for a down payment on a house. I didn't even have to make a payment on my car, because Malcolm had bought me a brand-new BMW-2002 that still looked new. I had made sure the car was in my name, because I remembered what had happened to Sarah's Mercedes when Wendell went to jail.

Suddenly I felt better. They say prayer changes things. A knock on the bathroom door interrupted my thoughts.

"Amanda, are you all right, or do you want me to come in and wash your ass," Sarah yelled, and I heard laughter.

"I'm fine, I'll be out in a minute," I called out.

When I came out of the bathroom Sarah handed me a glass of my favorite champagne. "This shit cost me a small fortune," she joked.

"Amanda, you know you aren't the only woman who has been dumped by the man she loves," Helena said. "I get dumped every month."

I had to laugh, because it was true. It felt good to laugh. I drank some more champagne and ate a plate of étouffée. I was surprised to find myself having a good time. I thanked all my friends for caring and being there for me.

Sarah and Barbara Ann spent the night in my room, and we talked until daybreak about men: the good, the bad, and the ugly. With their support, maybe I could live and love again. I would force myself to look for a new house, starting tomorrow. That would take my mind off Malcolm, a little. I would take it one day at a time.

I flew a two-day trip with Franco Bordeaux. He cried on my shoulder about Sarah. I wanted to tell him the cold truth: white men cannot do very much for a black woman, and she will always choose a poor brother over a rich white man, any day of the week, but I kept my thoughts to myself. He was moving to Atlanta, chasing after Sarah, and his cute little house in Metairie, Louisiana, was up for sale. I had been to his house a few times for some wild parties, and I liked the house.

"Franco, can I stop by tomorrow and take a look at your house?" I asked. "I'm looking for a house."

"Sure, Amanda. And I will give you a good deal, an offer you can't refuse. Now, will you put in a good word for me with your friend, Sarah?"

"Sure, why not?" I answered, even though I had no intention of doing that. Sarah had already told me how she felt about this man.

I went by his house the very next day, and I loved the three-bedroom, brick house. We settled on a price and closed three weeks later. The neighbors were glad to see First Officer Franco Bordeaux go. I soon found out why: Franco didn't tell all his lady friends that he was moving. For weeks after I moved in, women were camping out in my driveway, waiting for him. Women drove past the house, four and five times a day. Some were bold enough to ring the doorbell at all times, day and night.

I moved from my apartment at the Lewis & Clark that October, and by December I was settled in my new home, with all new furniture.

For Christmas, I had a housewarming party, and everyone came and used the opportunity to find out what everyone was up to.

Of course, everyone noticed how thin I was, although I had gained back some of my weight.

"You can't afford to lose anymore weight, girlfriend," everyone echoed, like I didn't know that. They all knew my problems, and now I wanted to know about them.

Joseph Guillory's Creole mother finally broke up his relationship with Caroline, and she transferred back to Atlanta after I moved. She came to the party with a doctor from Atlanta.

Sarah had bought a home in Atlanta. She had gotten bored with Franco Bordeaux and was now dating a police captain.

Dee Dee and Helena were transferring to Chicago in a few weeks. We finally got to met Dee Dee's friend. All the girls were shocked, except for Sarah and me. Danny was really Danielle. She wore blue jeans, cowboy boots, and a hunting jacket. Her hair was cut short, and one couldn't tell if she was a man or woman. Collette dragged Dee Dee into the kitchen and asked her if this really was the kind of life she wanted to lead. Sarah and I said nothing. The two of us were a little shocked that Danny...uh...Danielle didn't seem to have a feminine bone in her body.

"Dee Dee, I don't want to hurt your feelings, but when did you realize you were...uh...you know... gay...uh...lesbian?" Collette was coy, with a grin on her face.

"The same time you realized you were a whore," Sarah said, answering for Dee Dee.

"Ouch! Look who's talking. At least I didn't sleep with a French pilot who has slept with every woman in town." Collette was still grinning.

"Only because he didn't ask you," Dee Dee answered for Sarah, and we all laughed.

"I don't have to listen to this shit. You can't even ask a simple question without someone getting nasty." Collette threw her head in the air and went back into the living room, her feelings hurt. It was obvious to us she was back on drugs. Her husband, Roscoe, had already passed out on my sofa.

Our little group was drifting apart. Helena was seriously dating an older man from Dayton, and they were talking about getting married. He thought she was too fat, although she was thinner than I was. We felt she might have been bulimia again, because someone saw her in the bathroom vomiting up the food she had just eaten at the party.

Michele was dating several men from Los Angeles to Florida. When she started talking about her boyfriend, I had to ask. "Which one?" She was still drinking and doing drugs, but otherwise she was fine. She was also transferring to Atlanta.

Collette and I were the only ones left in New Orleans, so we started to hang out together more.

I had been on dates in the last few months with a few guys. There was no one special, because I kept trying to find someone like Malcolm. I didn't care what women said. Take it from me, once you have had a man with a big penis, it's hard to get used to a small one. A little one just cannot reach all the spots inside you that need to be tended to and massaged.

"I have to get over Malcolm." That was my New Year's resolution. I had to pray on it, night and day. I had to gain some more of my weight back, and I certainly couldn't afford to lose the weight I had gained back so far.

Collette's on-again, off-again marriage was back on the rocks. She was at my house most of the time.

One day she called to see if, while I was working a trip, she could use my house to entertain a man she met on her last flight. I was skeptical.

"Come on, Amanda, do me this one favor. You know what an asshole Roscoe is. I'm sure he's messing around with his first kid's mother," she begged.

"Please don't put me in the middle of your mess, Collette. You're a married woman. I thought you had given up the whore life."

"I have, but I just want to have some fun; this is legit," she lied.

"Okay, but keep my place clean." I gave up trying to reason with Collette. My grandmother was right when she said, "You can't turn a whore into a housewife."

Twenty-five

Most of the ladies from my stewardess class had been married and divorced. One white girl from Georgia, Caren Bell, had been married three times, and we called her by all her names, Caren Bell Jones Smith Kitzman. She seemed to have bad luck with men. We didn't know her first husband, but they say he left her for another woman. Her second husband was a pilot who dumped her for a brand-new stewardess. Her third husband, Samuel Kitzman, was the worst. He was a dog. They had only been married two years when Caren's neighbor asked her about her maid. When Caren told her that she didn't have a maid, the neighbor told Caren that whenever she left on a trip, a woman in a blue station wagon came to Caren's house.

"The woman goes into your house and stays all day," the neighbor said to Caren. "So my husband and I thought the woman must be a maid."

Caren made a deal with the neighbor. On Monday morning, she got dressed as if she was going to work, but she went to a friend's house. She had given the neighbor her friend's telephone number, with instructions to call her as soon as the blue station wagon showed up.

Sure enough, the neighbor called within three hours. Poor Caren came home and found her husband and a woman in her bedroom, doing a sixty-nine. He had never done that position with her and had pretended he wasn't into oral sex. They were so into it that they didn't hear her come into the house, so Caren left the room, got a camera, and took pictures of them. We were all shocked to learn that the woman was the wife of one of our male flight attendants.

Caren made Samuel pack his bags and get the fuck out. She had the house and all the furniture before they were married. All he had to pack were his clothes, and Caren had bought most of them. Of course, her neighbor was standing on the front porch, waiting to see what happened. "I thought something hanky panky was going on," she said.

Caren showed the pictures to everyone at Big E. It wasn't a pretty picture, and flight attendants like juicy gossip. The poor husband had no idea his wife was having an affair. He divorced her and got custody of their two children. He and Caren starting flying together, and soon after, each divorce was final. He and the two kids moved into Caren's house, and they all lived together as a family. Caren said that she was in no hurry for husband number four.

Twenty-Six

Summer, 1979

Reality set in. When we started this job, we thought we would be flying for only three, four, or five years at the most. Now it had become our careers. Most of us had given up on finding a rich husband. Don't get me wrong, many flight attendants married well-to-do men: doctors, lawyers, and small businessmen. But only two flight attendants from the New Orleans base had married very wealthy men.

Gloria Trousis, a cute brunette from Dallas, was one of the two. She married a famous Hollywood movie producer, Maxwell Silversteinman. She met him on a charter flight when he took his whole production crew to Mexico City to shoot a movie. After six months of dating, he gave her a five-carat diamond engagement ring, and they flew to Paris for a secret wedding. Gloria quit flying after the wedding, but she continued to keep in touch with her friends in New Orleans.

When we had LA layovers, she would have her limousine pick us up at the hotel and take us to her mansion in Malibu. She had an upstairs maid, a downstairs maid, a chef, and a butler. We would sit out by the pool, smoke weed, do a little coke, and drink margaritas. Her chef prepared nice snacks for us to sample. We enjoyed seeing how the rich and famous lived.

On one occasion, Gloria had some good cocaine. Dominique Van Stinchcomb, a lovely flight attendant from Holland and a good friend, decided she would go for a swim, because she was a world-class swimmer, but she caught a cramp as soon as she hit the water. Of course, flight attendants are trained to handle emergencies but all of us were stoned or asleep. So the gardener ran to the pool and pulled her out of the water. After spitting up a bucket of water, she was fine. The only one shaken up was the gardener. We were looking at Dominique like she had lost her mind: She had blown our high!

Later that month, Gloria again invited us to a party at the mansion. All of the famous movie stars were there, along with every drug you could name.

This time, Dominique took two Quaaludes, and as the party was getting hot and heavy, she fell off the balcony and sprained her collarbone. We thought she had broken her neck. Once again, she spoiled the party for us, because we had to leave and take her to the hospital. We couldn't have an ambulance coming to the director's house. It would have made front-page news the next day, because the "who's who" of Hollywood were there. Most of the guests were too stoned and didn't even know an accident had occurred. Dominique was a nice person, and we all liked her, but she could do some stupid shit.

Before we left, I had to find Becky Gromenfield, a young, voluptuous German reserve, who was new on our trip. I hadn't seen her since we arrived, but, of course, this was a big house, and people were wandering around everywhere. I asked around, until a guest, with a sly grin on his face, told me that he had seen her upstairs in the third bedroom on the left. I went upstairs, walked to the third door on the left, and knocked, first lightly and then harder. The door opened, and I gasped. There was our new reserve on her knees, topless, and squeezing a popular soap opera star's penis between her huge tits. I recognized him right away. She was sucking on the tip while he sat on the bed talking on the telephone.

"Excuse me, Becky, I'm sorry to interrupt your fun, but we're leaving. Dominique has been in an accident," I said.

"Oh," was all she said, and she looked at me as though to say, "*What do you want me to do about it?*" I was spoiling her fun.

"Don't leave!" The soap star said, holding his hand over the receiver, "Why don't you join us?"

If looks could kill, he would have been dead. So he returned to his phone conversation.

"I heard you, baby, someone came into the room looking for the bathroom. I miss you, too...I get a hard-on just thinking about you...What are you wearing?... Are your nipples hard?...Can I suck them?. . ." He went on and on, as he pushed Becky's head down on his penis. "Baby...oooh...keep...uhh...talking."

"Are you coming? Becky?" I was getting irritated. "I mean, coming with us."

She begged us to bring her to this party. We did, against our better judgment because she didn't know Gloria, and now she was acting like a common slut.

"I'll be home tomorrow night...Can't wait. . .I miss you too, baby. . .Gotta go." He hung up the phone.

"Don't worry about your friend, I'll put her in a taxi later," he said. He sounded as if he did this all the time, and it was no big deal.

I looked at Becky, and she made no move to leave, so I left the room. I was angry, because a senior flight attendant would never abandon her crew: These junior girls only cared about themselves.

We took Dominique to the emergency room. She was in a lot of pain. We told the doctors she fell off one of the Santa Monica piers. We were all out walking around and she slipped.

They admitted Dominique to the hospital, so we had to call the airline to report the accident. We counted to make sure we had enough flight attendants for minimum staff on the aircraft. The FAA had so many rules. We called Big E flight operations and reported that Dominique had been in an accident and was in the hospital, telling them the same lie we had told the hospital. They bought our story, and we were able to work the flight home with the minimum staff. Thank God the flight wasn't full.

After all that drama, Mr. Silversteinman told Gloria never to invite any dumb flight attendants to his house again.

Instead, she started taking us to eat at some of Los Angeles's finest restaurants. All she had to say was, "I'm Mrs. Maxwell Silversteinman," and doors opened magically. That was fine with us, because we liked eating out more than we liked parties at her house with the movie stars. They were arrogant , self-centered, and downright pompous. They would grin in your face and sleep with your husband or wife the next day.

Rumors were already circulating in the tabloids that Maxwell was sleeping with the star of his current movie. We saw her at the last party, dressed in a little top, two sizes too small, that barely covered her 44-D silicone bosom. Maxwell paid more attention to her than to Gloria.

Gloria was an outsider and didn't know who she could trust. That probably explained why she was happy when we came to town.

Six months after the party, when Gloria was four months pregnant, we lost our Los Angeles layover, but she would call us three or four times a week because she was so lonesome. She had gained forty pounds during her pregnancy. She called to say Maxwell wouldn't have sex with her anymore. "He says he doesn't like screwing a fat, pregnant woman," she cried.

He would spend weeks at his villa in the South of France, and she knew he was with another woman.

Shortly after the baby was born, Maxwell filed for divorce. Gloria had tried everything to keep him, including hiring a personal trainer to help her lose the weight, and offering to do the same kinky things to Maxwell that his girlfriends did. In the middle of the night, she would call us, crying that he had told her she was fat and ugly.

"He doesn't want me to go down on him anymore," she cried and cried. She would call me, and after we hung up, she would call Dominique, then Dee Dee, or whoever was answering their phone. We all felt so sorry for her.

One night, while we were on layover in Newark, we put our heads together and came up with a solution to Gloria's problems. We called her and told her to hire a private investigator to follow Maxwell for a few weeks with a camera. Next, we said, hire that Beverly Hills divorce attorney, Marvin Hitchingson, and "take the bastard for everything he's got." We'd show him how dumb flight attendants really were.

When she realized she couldn't save her marriage, she took our advice. She got a divorce settlement for fifty million dollars, the house in Malibu, and child support of twenty thousand a month.

She stopped calling us after that. The last we heard, she married her personal trainer and was strung out on cocaine.

Twenty-Seven

September, 1979

It had been a year since Malcolm and I had broken up. I felt as though I was finally getting over him. I had gained my weight back, and felt like my old self again.

Dominique, Michele, two other flight attendants, and I were planning a trip to Africa for a month. Three weeks into our planning, Dominique met a crown prince from some foreign country while partying at his mansion in Atlanta. He was smitten with her at first sight. I knew lots of flight attendants who partied at the prince's new mansion, and they all said the prince had a one-way mirror on the party room wall, and from the next room he would view the party and decide which women he wanted to meet. Then he'd send his servant out to invite those women into another room, which also had a one-way mirror. From that group, the prince would choose a woman with whom he'd sleep. Dominique made the cut, and after their first night, he was so infatuated with her, and he asked her to be his houseguest. We all knew Dominique had lots of experience.

Dominique called me early one morning, as she was an early riser. "Amanda! Are you awake?" She yelled into the phone

I recognized her deep voice. "I'm sleeping, call me back later," I begged her.

"No, I can't, it's important." Her voice was high-pitched and excited.

I knew I couldn't get rid of her, so I propped myself up on a pillow.

"All right! All right! It better be good," I warned her.

"Amanda, I'm sorry, but I can't go to Africa with you all," she just blurted out.

I was surprised, because it had been her idea to go to Africa. She had broken up with her longtime boyfriend, and she needed to get away, just as I did. We were in the same boat, as far as men were concerned.

"What happened?"

"You won't believe this, but I met the crown prince, and I spent the last week at his mansion in Atlanta. He invited me to be one of his mistresses. I'm taking a six-month leave. I leave tomorrow for his home." She was talking so fast that I could hardly understand her.

"Hold on! Hold on! You mean to tell me that you screwed the crown prince himself?"

"Yes, and it's not bad. All expenses paid. I have my own room and a maid at the mansion. His Highness came to me twice last night." She sounded happy.

"Wait a minute, what do you mean, came to you twice?"

"He has three other American mistresses. We all have dinner with the prince every night. We dress in saris, and if we are on our menstrual, we must wear black veils so the prince won't come to our room that night. They are different from us. They won't touch a woman when she's on her period."

"What does His Highness say when he comes into your room?" I asked, because this shit was interesting. I was wide awake now.

"Usually nothing, there is no foreplay. He comes for one thing, then he leaves."

"That's all?"

"That's all."

"Does he go to more than one room in the same night?" I wanted to get the facts.

"Oh, I'm sure he does, because he comes to my room twice in one night. He has a healthy appetite." She giggled like a teenager. "The first time, I used some of that hot peppermint cream we bought at that sex shop in Las Vegas. I gave him a blowjob like he never had before. The man...I mean His Highness...came all over me."

"When did he come back?" We were both laughing into the telephone.

"About four hours later. I think he put some coke on his penis, because after the blowjob, he flipped me over and entered me from behind, and we fucked all night."

I had heard enough.

"We, the mistresses, that is, are flying home with him on his Lear Jet tomorrow."

"I see." There was nothing else to say. "Enjoy yourself, and I'll see you in about six months."

"I plan to enjoy every minute, I have nothing to lose."

"I'm not so sure about that." I thought as I hung up the phone. But at least she was happy.

I called Michele and the other two flight attendants.

"Dominique is not going with us, because she has met some crown prince," I told each one.

They understood. *"One monkey don't stop no show."*

I had to take booster shots, get malaria pills, and send for my visa. I was looking forward to a month in remote Africa, away from civilization. We were going on a safari, with no TV, telephone, or newspapers. I had mailed my passport to the Kenyan Embassy for a visa and was anxious for them to return it.

I went to my mailbox one afternoon to check the mail, and I was so happy to receive my passport back that I almost missed a small letter stashed between my passport and a few bills. It had been forwarded to me from my old address at Lewis & Clark. I didn't realized they were still forwarding my mail. I recognized the handwriting, and I stopped dead in my tracks. I had seen it so many times before, on cards, notes left on the refrigerator, and on checks. Why was he writing me now? What did he want? My hand was shaking. I put the letter on the mantle over the fireplace and stared at it. The return address said "5134 Cumberland St., St. Louis, MO." It was his old address; the address where I had sent his furniture, the house I had never seen.

"So he's back in St. Louis and at his old house," I surmised and wondered what it was like. *"What she was like?"*

I checked my passport for the visa and looked at the bills. I wasn't ready to read the letter.

A crazy thought ran through my mind: *"Maybe he wanted to tell me he was getting married."* That was none of my business. Maybe he wanted to get back together. That thought made my heart stop. What would I say? I knew damn well what I would say.

I decided to go shopping. There was nothing I needed to buy, but the house wasn't big enough for the letter and me.

Once at the mall, I couldn't wait to get back home to read the damned letter.

"This is crazy; I must be losing my mind! What are you afraid of?" I kept asking myself.

I walked around the mall in a daze. I purchased a few things I felt I could use on my trip and drove home. The letter was still on the mantle.

"Where did you expect it to be stupid?" I scolded myself, out loud.

I ate, showered, and crawled into bed with the letter. I wanted to give it my undivided attention. I opened the letter and began reading:

Sept. 11, 1979

Dear Amanda,

I hope this letter finds you well. I called your old number and found it had been disconnected, with no forwarding number. So I decided to write and just hope this letter reaches you. It has taken me a year to find the courage to call or write you.

I'm sorry if I hurt you, but whatever you went through, multiply it by a thousand, and you will have some idea what I'm going through. I had to leave, because marriage was the next step for us, and I couldn't commit to it.

Please believe me, if I could marry someone, it would be you. I have to live with the fact that I will never marry or have children. I have missed you very much this past year. I keep looking for a little bit of you in every woman I meet. I can't find that sparkle I found in your eyes. I have looked. You are one of a kind. I know that now. I saved every message you left me. I listen to then sometimes just to hear your voice. You are the only woman I will ever love, and it hurts me that we have no future together. You may not understand now, but you will thank me one day.

Take care of yourself.

Love always,

Malcolm

I held the letter to my chest. *"So we have no future together?"*

"Fuck you, Malcolm. How can you say you love me, and at the same time, say we have no future together? I don't understand, and I will never understand." Tears were running down my cheeks, but I read on.

PS: I saw Bob Mitchell last week. He came to visit me for a few days. He asked about you. He lives in Atlanta and he wants you to call him. His number is (404) 46- ----. Tears fell on the paper as I read on. *He has been cut by the Falcons and has a job in New Orleans. He will be moving there soon. I told him to look you up. He is really a nice guy.*

"So that's how it is! He was finished with me, and he's passing me on to his friend. No thanks! Men are assholes," I screamed. "Goodbye, Malcolm." He had opened up an old wound. I was still in love with him, but I couldn't go back.

"Goodbye, Malcolm," I whispered.

I put the letter back in the envelope and put it in my secret hiding place, a shoe box on the top shelf in the back of my closet. I didn't want to see it again unless I was looking for it.

I went ahead with my plans. I called the girls about our Africa trip to make sure they got their visas and shots. I couldn't wait to leave. I needed a vacation. Maybe I would meet someone interesting.

Michele's mother became ill and had to go into the hospital, so she had to cancel at the last minute; leaving me with two women that I hardly knew.

One week later, we were on a British Airways flight to Nairobi. We stopped in London for twelve hours, and we took the grand tour of London by taxi. We paid fifty dollars to a Nigerian driver to take us sightseeing. We saw Big Ben, the Changing of the Guard, and Madame Tussaud's Wax Museum. He dropped us back at the airport around six thirty p.m. for our eight thirty flight to Nairobi. It was an all-night flight that arrived in Nairobi at ten forty-five the next morning. We were so exhausted from our tour that we slept most of the way.

Africa was a big adventure for us. We spent two days in Nairobi, then we were out on the safari, miles from civilization, just as I wished to be. There was nothing out there but wild animals. We spent four nights in the Treetop Hotel, and three nights in the Mud Hut Hotel. After that, every night was spent in a different place, miles from nowhere. We were so tired from the activities of the day. All we could do at night was eat, have a drink, and sleep.

We visited the Masai tribe and participated in a dance ceremony. They didn't wear a lot of clothes. We stopped by a school and enjoyed helping the kids practice their English.

During our brief stay in Tanzania, I had the opportunity to visit with an old medicine doctor. He was the elder of the village, and his job included taking care of the sick, delivering babies, and predicting the future. He was also a famous fortune-teller, or so the people said. Tanzanian people came from miles away to consult with him before making major decisions about anything in their lives.

There was a long line of foreign tourists waiting to have their fortune told. My friends were afraid, because they didn't want their fortune told by the medicine doctor, and they decided to tour the village instead.

The sign said "$5.00." I had nothing to lose, so I got in line. There were about a dozen people ahead of me, but the line was moving quickly. The doctor was inside a mud hut that had long strands of beads hanging at the entrance, so you couldn't see inside. A Tanzanian lady was standing at the door, collecting the money and escorting the visitors in and out. I was taking all this in when a very tall, very dark-skinned man came out of the hut. He started moving up the line as if he were looking for something or someone. He was too young to be the medicine doctor. I couldn't imagine what he was looking for.

He stopped when he got to me and looked me over from head to toe. I was shocked and afraid to say anything.

"You! Come with me!" It was an order, in accented English.

I couldn't believe he was talking to me, so I pointed to myself and raised my eyebrows for confirmation.

"You!" he said again. "Follow me!"

I followed him up to the front of the line. I looked at the people ahead of me in line. I was as confused as they were. I was just following orders.

Once inside the hut, I paused to adjust my eyes from the bright sunlight outside. The smell was old and musty, in spite of the strong incense that was burning. My eyes focused on an old man sitting on a tree stump. He was smoking a handmade pipe. Without looking up, he motioned for me to sit. He looked well over a hundred and ten years old, and from what I could see, his face had deep wrinkles. If there was such a person as Father Time, this man was he!

I sat on the stump in front of him, and he took my hands, palms up; but didn't raise his head.

He spoke in his native language, in a voice so low that I could hardly hear him.

"He said he got strong vibes as soon as you entered the line. Your heart spoke to his, and that's why he sent me for you," the translator said.

There was a pause. Then he spoke again. "He said you have a good heart, a loving family, lots of good friends, a good life. Someone loves you very deeply, he thinks of you now, today; he wants to see you, but can't. There is a message." He paused to receive the message. "Joy."

I listened, but I hadn't the slightest idea what he was talking about.

After another long pause, the doctor seemed to be in pain. He jerked and twitched, then he was very still.

"Gee, I hope he doesn't die right here in front of me," I thought, while the translator and I waited for him to speak again. Maybe he had fallen asleep.

He started murmuring words fast, and he kept his head down as though he was in a trance.

I looked at the translator to tell me what he was saying. But he seemed to be weighing whether or not to tell me. Finally, he muttered, "Pain, pain first, then happiness, long life."

I was getting tired of this mumbo-jumbo. I wanted to ask questions.

"Ask him if I will ever get married, and will I have children?"

The translator spoke to the old doctor, who mumbled, nodding positively.

"He says, yes, yes. Long marriage. He sees two, beautiful, healthy children. You will be very happy."

"Ask him who will I marry. Can he see that?" I asked. Now we were cooking.

The translator spoke again to the old man, who mumbled a long statement, paused, and mumbled again.

I looked at the translator.

"He said you already know the man you will marry. He is not a stranger to you. The one who lies heavy on your mind and heart is not the one. He is trying to send a message to you. He loves you."

That sounded interesting.

"Ask him, is he rich?" Why not? I might as well have gotten my money's worth.

He translated.

The doctor responded instantly, he didn't have to think. "Not rich, not poor. He will be kind, understanding, wonderful man, don't worry, you know him," the translator repeated.

That was enough. I knew there was a long line outside, and he had answered all my questions. I tried to pull my hand away, but he held on for a minute. I thought he had more to say. Instead, he slowly raised his head and looked into my eyes for the first time. His eyes were old and tired, but I saw something when our eyes met. It felt so familiar, but I couldn't place it. I didn't want to get too deep into this.

He uttered something, and the translator looked at me strangely, and I knew he had never heard the doctor say that word before.

"He said, move your fingers."

I moved my fingers. Then he muttered a single word.

I looked at the translator again.

"He said 'Joy.'" The translator spoke in a low voice.

I looked up at the doctor and he had a single teardrop in his eye. He let go of my hand, and as I rose to leave, he mumbled something else.

"He say no charge; it was his pleasure, and he will see you again," the translator told me sadly.

I thanked both of them and left the hut through the beaded door, then paused to adjust my eyes to the sunlight . My immediate thought was, *"This is what my grandfather calls a 'racket.'"* First, he would never see me again. Second, I knew of no one named 'Joy,' and third, the only man I already knew who would possibly marry me was Malcolm. Maybe he was right about the two children. Well, one out of four was not bad for the medicine doctor.

I left the doctor's hut and joined my group. I was no more enlightened than when I had gone into the hut. I would write Malcolm as soon as I got home. I wished I had brought his letter so I could send him a postcard from here. The medicine doctor said we would be married, at least I thought that was what he said. I was confused.

I forgot about the medicine doctor and wouldn't think about him again until years later. But even so, he would haunt me.

The next two weeks flew by. We visited Mt. Kilimanjaro, Lake Victoria, and the Historical Museum in Uganda. We were warmly received by the people, and Africa was really a beautiful country. We had our hair braided, and we dressed in African attire. You couldn't tell us from the natives, until we spoke.

We spent the last night in Nairobi before boarding our British Airways flight to London. We had a four-hour layover, then boarded our plane to New York. It was an uneventful flight. We slept most of the way and ate two meals on the flight. Twenty hours later, we were glad to be on a Big E flight from New York to New Orleans flying south. We had lost a day.

When we arrived in New Orleans, I stopped by the flight attendant's lounge, picked up my mail, spoke with my supervisor, and went straight home.

As soon as I opened the door to my house, the telephone started to ring. I caught it on the fifth ring.

"Amanda, I'm glad you're home." It was Collette.

"This is good timing, I just walked in the door."

"I told your supervisor to call me the minute you left the lounge. You need to call Sarah, and I'm on my way over." She was adamant.

"But...but...I just got in, can't it wait until tomorrow? I need to shower," I pleaded with her.

"No, it can't wait! Go ahead, shower, call Sarah, and I should be there by the time you finish. I put your mail on the kitchen table, and I watered your plants." She wouldn't give up.

"Okay, if it's that important." I gave in, I didn't feel like arguing with her.

"I replaced the phone and brought my bags in and put them in a corner. I glanced at my mail. Maybe there was a letter from Malcolm.

I looked at my answering machine and found there were fifty-two messages! He wouldn't have called, because he didn't have my number.

I took a long hot bubble bath. It felt so good. We took showers in Africa, because we were afraid to sit in the tubs.

I put on my bathrobe and went back into the kitchen. I sorted my mail and clicked on the answering machine.

"Hello, Ms. Callaway, your dry cleaning is ready for pick-up at Value Cleaners. Thank you."

I had forgotten that I had dropped off my clothes before I left.

The next message was from my cousin, who attended Christian University in Nashville, asking me to send him some spending money.

There were a few other telemarketing calls that I deleted, and then I heard Sarah's voice:

"Amanda, please call me as soon as you get in. It is very, very important. Hope you had a good trip."

I clicked off the answering machine, went into my bedroom to be comfortable, and called Sarah in Atlanta. She answered the phone on the first ring.

"Sarah, what's up?" I asked. "I got your message."

"Amanda, I'm so glad you called. You have been gone a long time and things have happened." She was talking slowly, measuring her words. I had heard that tone many times.

"I have been gone twenty-eight days, It seems like a year, but we had a great time. Never a dull moment. I have pictures and slides to show y'all," I said, but Sarah was quiet, and I knew something was wrong.

"So what happened while I was gone that's so important? Is everyone okay?" I asked, becoming concerned.

"Yes, everyone's fine. Now, are you sitting down, Amanda?" she asked, cautiously.

"I'm sitting on the bed." She was scaring me a little.

"Collette and Dee Dee are on their way over," she said.

"I talked to Collette, and she insisted on coming over. I didn't know Dee Dee was in town. Sarah! what's going on?" I was getting antsy.

"We just wanted you to hear it from us first. It's Malcolm." Her voice was low.

"Malcolm? What about Malcolm! Look, don't tell me, he got married while I was gone." I tried to sound normal, but my heart was breaking.

"No, Amanda," There was a pause. "He died," she said sadly.

"He what?" I was not sure I heard her correctly.

"I'm sorry, honey, he died two weeks ago. He had a degenerative heart condition. Did you know that?"

"No! He was healthy. How could this happen?" I was devastated.

"Only his family and the family doctor knew about it. It has been in all the papers, even the Atlanta papers. I had Collette save them for you. People said a lot of nice things about him. He was also very wealthy. I'm sorry, Amanda, I know you still loved him. He was a good man. He did lots of good work with kids and the football league."

She was talking, but I couldn't hear a word she said. I was in shock. I couldn't breathe. I put the phone down.

"Amanda! Amanda! Talk to me! Are you all right!" Sarah was screaming.

Someone was beating on the door.

"Go away, I don't want to talk with anyone." I was in pain. I couldn't move. My mind was working, but my body wouldn't move.

Collette used her key to open the door. She ran into the bedroom to me, and Dee Dee was right behind her.

"Amanda! Are you all right? Don't you freak out on us! Why didn't you open the damn door?" Collette screamed as she picked up the phone.

"Hello?...Sarah...she's all right...hah...she's all right...yes, we'll stay here all night...I'll tell her." She hung up the phone and looked at me.

"Sarah will be here tomorrow, and she'll stay with you," she said.

"He's gone and it's over," was all I could say.

"He's gone, you're right about that," Collette responded. She never had any tact.

Collette gave me two pills, and Dee Dee came with a glass of whiskey.

They took my bathrobe off, slipped a nightgown over my head, and put me to bed. They sat on the side of my bed until I had cried myself to sleep. I didn't know what they gave me, but I slept for twelve hours.

Collette and Dee Dee were there when I woke up. Sarah arrived that afternoon. I tried to read some of the articles in the paper. I couldn't bear to look at the pictures of the man I loved, because he was smiling in every picture, in every paper. I wanted to call his mother, but I had no reason to call her. Besides, I didn't have her number. I guess I could have called the funeral home. People used to call us all the time at my grandfather's funeral home when they wanted to get in touch with the bereaved family. We always took the messages and gave them to the families.

I had no choice but to accept the fact that Malcolm and I hadn't had a relationship for over a year. It was over. I had no claims on him, and there was probably another woman who had sat in the front pew at his funeral, next to his mother. Now, I had to get over him, for good.

It was not going to be easy. For the next three weeks, I went about my daily life in a daze. Sarah came down, and we went to eat at the Little Cajun Cuisine. I couldn't eat half of my food. I flew my trip and went through the motions of serving the passengers. However, I wasn't there. I was lost! My fellow flight attendants knew what I was going through, and they were very understanding. Some even offered advice from their own experiences.

Twenty-eight

One morning, I finally got up enough energy to unpack from my African trip. I had just started when the telephone jarred my nerves. It was my supervisor.

"Amanda, I have a lady on the line who says it is very important that she get in touch with you. Her name is Mablelean Brown, Malcolm's mother. Is it all right if I give her your number?"

"Sure, I mean, please, by all means, and tell her that I will wait here for her call," I told her.

"Are you sure?" It was her job to be protective.

"Yes, I'm sure it will be all right, thank you."

I hung up the phone and waited. I didn't have to wait long. Almost immediately, the phone rang. The voice on the other end of the line was warm and friendly.

"Hello, Amanda, dear, I'm Mablelean Brown, Malcolm's mother. You remember me, don't you, dear?"

"Of course I remember you, Miss Brown. I'm sorry about Malcolm,

I was in Africa at the time....of...his...d-d-death," I tried to explain. "I... wanted..."

"I know," she interrupted me. "I called Big E and got your supervisor's number, and she told me you were in Africa. I didn't leave a message, because I didn't want to give you the bad news when you were that far from home." She paused and cleared her throat. I could feel her pain right through the phone. "I'm calling you today, because we will be reading Malcolm's will next week, and his lawyer said he included you. He also entrusted me with a small box to give to you. It is marked 'personal.' Can you come to St. Louis for the reading of the will? I don't want to put you out. I know you work and have a life."

She was very kind, and I couldn't tell her that I had no life.

"I will be there," I said, without hesitation.

I needed to talk to her. I had so many questions about Malcolm that only she could answer. I needed closure, and I knew Malcolm had been very close to his mother.

I called my friends and told them I was going to St. Louis for the reading of Malcolm's will. Sarah wanted to go with me, but I told her that this was something I had to do by myself.

That following Tuesday, I was on a flight to St. Louis. Malcolm's mother met me at the gate. I had met her many times before when she came to New Orleans to visit her son. I liked her. She had been very nice to me and didn't mind that Malcolm and I were living together.

She gave me a big hug. We had a few hours before we were due at the lawyer's office, so she took me to her home and made us some tea.

She was easy to talk to; like my mother.

She spoke first. "My son loved you very much. He wanted to marry you and give me some grandchildren. But he knew he had this degenerative heart condition, and later, leukemia. He didn't want to make you a widow."

"I wish he had told me," I said.

"He was stubborn, like his father. He inherited this heart defect from his father, and doctors said he could pass it on to his children. He didn't want to take that chance. I couldn't tell him what to do. He had his mind made up. His father died when he was thirty-two. Rest assured, Amanda, he loved you deeply, and keeping this secret from you was one of the hardest things he ever had to do."

I started to cry. I couldn't hold back the tears. She put her arms around my shoulders to comfort me.

"He passed away quietly. He was never in pain. His heart was that of a ninety-year-old man. It just gave out." She shook her head, as though she still could not believe it.

"He asked for you in his final hours, but he knew you were in Africa, and he understood," she said.

"I would have come," I said through my tears.

"He knew you would," she said, and that comforted me a little.

I cried into my tea until it was time to go to the lawyer's office.

As I picked up my purse, she said, "Wait a minute, I almost forgot." She went into her bedroom and came out with a beautiful jewelry box. It was about six inches, square.

She gave it to me, saying, "Malcolm's lawyer has the key. He will give it to you today."

I took the pretty box and held it close to my heart. I didn't care what was in it; it was from Malcolm, and that was all that mattered.

At the lawyer's office, I met Malcolm's aunt and cousins. His grandparents still lived in Tennessee and were too frail to make the trip.

The lawyer went through the legalisms of the will. Malcolm had left a large estate. He had saved and managed his money well. He left two houses, two cars, prime real estate, stocks, bonds, and all of his personal belonging to his mother. His mother and grandparents were beneficiaries of his life-insurance policy. He left fifty thousand dollars to his aunt, and twenty-five thousand dollars to each of his cousins. Then it came to me. The lawyer looked at me sadly.

"Ms. Callaway," he said. "Malcolm wanted me to give you these keys." He handed me two small keys on a small chain. "Also, one hundred thousand dollars to be invested for the education of the children you will have someday; the children he wasn't able to give you." He cleared his throat. It was hard for him to continue, because he was also Malcolm's friend. "If you have a boy, he hoped you would find it in your heart to name your first son Malcolm. You are under no obligation to do this. He and I discussed that."

I started to cry all over again.

"So he did love me and wanted to marry me. He wanted me to have his children,." I said, mostly to myself.

I was so deep in thought that I almost missed the second part. He left me two hundred thousand dollars "for the pain and suffering" he put me through. The lawyer gave me the two checks. My hand was shaking as I took them. His mother and aunt didn't object, so I assumed Malcolm had already discussed it with them.

He left a donation to his church and the Boys and Girls Club of New Orleans.

When it was over, I asked his mother to stop by the cemetery and let me visit with Malcolm for a few minutes. She gladly obliged.

It was late November, and a chill was in the air. I stood at his grave and thanked him for everything he had given me. I understood the Situation, and it took a strong man to stand his ground. He taught me how to love and dream. I was ashamed that I had doubted him. All I wanted to do now was put my arms around him and hold on. I wanted to curl up next to him and share his warmth. I closed my eyes, and I could feel his warm body next to mine.

"Thank you for that million-dollar smile. It brightened my life, and I will never forget you. I'll always love you, and we'll meet again in Heaven." I prayed.

His mother and I hugged at the airport, and we promised to keep in touch.

On the flight back to New Orleans, I drank a screwdriver, and I ate the whole dinner. I never ate airplane food, because I knew how flight attendants liked to stick their fingers in the food to see if it was hot. Many times, the bread fell on the floor. But today, I was hungry. It was like I hadn't eaten in months. I felt better than I had felt in years, or since Malcolm and I had broken up. It was like a weight had been lifted from my shoulders. But soon, the stress of the day was taking its toll on me.

My stomach was suddenly upset, and I had to use the lavatory, badly. However bad, it had to wait until I got home. Out of habit, flight attendants never pooped on the airplane. We held it until we got to the hotel or home.

As soon as I got home, I went straight to the bathroom and sat for ten minutes. Then I went into the bedroom, sat in the middle of my bed, and unlocked the jewelry box. Lying on top was a letter addressed to me. It was his handwriting again, I would recognize it anywhere. He had a beautiful handwriting for a man, and I shivered just looking at it. My hand was trembling as I opened the letter. It was dated October 9, 1979, one week before he died. He died on October 16, the day I visited the medicine doctor.

My dearest Amanda,

By the time you read this letter, I will be gone to a better place, I hope. I asked my mother to call Big E to try to locate you, I just wanted to hear your voice one last time. Your supervisor told her that you were in Africa. It sounded like a wonderful trip. I only wish I was with you.

I'm sorry for all the pain I've caused you. I only did what I thought was best for you. Now you understand why we couldn't have any children , I wanted this degenerative heart disease to end with me. You are young, beautiful, and you will love again. With me, you would be a widow now. I had to accept the fact that I have no future, at least not here on Earth.

I want you to start living for both of us. Please marry and have the kids we could never have.

There has never been another woman in my life. I had the cleaning woman answer the phone the day you called. I couldn't tell you myself, because I couldn't lie to you. I knew you were the one for me the very first time I saw you in the parking lot of the Clearview Shopping Center. I stalked, you remember? If you only knew how many times I've played our first night together over and over in my mind. That was the night I fell in love for the first time, and since that day, I have been trying to find a way to keep you in my life without making the commitment you wanted. I couldn't tell you the truth, and I know that under different circumstances we would have been married years ago. Please forgive me.

If there is a life after death, I will wait for you. I feel we will meet again someday. Then, we will be together always. You are my joy. Every day with you had been a joy.

All my love,

Malcolm

I wiped at the tears that wouldn't stop and put the letter back in the envelope carefully, only to be read again later. I looked in the box. There were two little telephone answering machine cassettes. I ran to get my small, handheld tape recorder, popped one of the tapes in, and hit play.

"Hello, Malcolm, this is Amanda, please call me when you get in. I really would like to come up to see you this weekend. I miss you a lot. I love you."

"Hello, Malcolm, it's me again. Is it okay for me to come up this weekend or anytime? I really would like to see you. Just call me...please."

"Malcolm, I know you are getting my messages, but I don't understand why you won't call and tell me what I've done to piss you off!"

And the messages went on and on, there were about twenty-five in all, and I hadn't gotten to the second tape. I took that tape out and put the second one in. Most of the recording was my voice. I fast-forwarded, and I heard another voice. I reversed it and hit play.

"Hello, Malcolm, this is Sarah Ferguson, Amanda's friend. I wish you would call her. Don't keep her hanging on. She is losing weight and won't eat.

Why are you acting like a fool? I thought you were a smart man. You know she loves you. If it's over, and you don't care anything about her, or if you have another woman, just tell her, please. She can start getting on with her life. Be a man, she's a beautiful, caring person and you are an asshole."

I heard the phone click and had to laugh. Sarah never told me she called Malcolm. I ejected the tape, put the tape back in the jewelry box, and looked to see what else was in the box. I recognized the velvet drawstring sack where he kept his lucky gold coin. He would put it in his sock before every game. Now he wanted me to have it. I picked up the small sack and realized that it had more in it than just a coin. I opened it up, and there was a small ring box inside. It looked like the box my diamond earrings had come in. I opened the box and had to catch my breath.

There was a two-carat, marquise diamond engagement ring inside, the same ring we had looked at one Saturday when we were downtown, shopping, and I had dragged him into the jewelry store. It was the summer before he was traded, and we were shopping for bathing suits. We were going to Jamaica.

I slipped the ring on my finger just as I had that day in the jewelry store. It was a perfect fit.

"So he went back and bought the ring." I was choked up. *"Oh, Malcolm, why did you have a heart condition? We could have been so happy together. You would have been a magnificent father. Why do good people die and bad people live? Why do good people die so young? I am a Baptist, and I know it was God's will, and I can't question that. He took you, but he will send me someone else to love and father my children. I will have a little Malcolm. I have to be patient. After all, I'm only twenty-eight. I think I will take a little time to get to know me better."* I was talking to myself.

I put everything back in the box. I was afraid to lock it, because the keys were so small I could lose them, and I wouldn't be able to open it.

I put the box in my secret hiding place in my closet. I went to the kitchen and fixed a late snack for myself.

Suddenly, I felt empowered to take charge of my life. I felt loved and honored that someone like Malcolm had loved me to the end.

The next day, I signed up for aerobics and yoga classes. I let my hair grow out for the first time in ten years, and got myself a new look. And I started going back to church. I wasn't going to rush into a new relationship. For now, it was going to be all about "me."

I called Sarah and asked her if it would be all right if I came to Atlanta to visit her that weekend. "I'll tell you all about my trip to St. Louis. And can we go to that new nightclub you told me about, MR. B's? Also, call Caroline to see if she wants to go with us. And will you cook me some of your famous spaghetti?" I said it all in one breath.

Sarah thought I had lost my mind. However, she was happy to have her old friend back, and I was happy to be back. It felt good!

I went to the mailbox. I hadn't checked my mail for three days. There was an international letter waiting for me. The stationery looked very expensive. The return address read, "Princess Dominique Amari Al Ahmed," and the address was written in Arabic. I opened the letter, and a picture of Dominique fell out. I guessed it was her, because I could see only her eyes. She was in full Islamic dress.

I read the letter and learned that she had converted to Islam and had married the billionaire cousin of the royal family. She had met him over there.

I put the letter down in disbelief.

"How can you go from a drug abuser, a prostitute, and party girl to a blonde, Islamic princess?" I asked myself.

I was not sure, but there was one thing I was sure of: I knew Dominique Van Stinchcomb, and this was not going to work.

Twenty-nine

Spring, 1980

Six months after Malcolm's death and my return from Africa, I found three rolls of film from the trip. I decided to take them to the local drugstore to be developed. I was only going to run down to the drugstore and back home. I threw on a big shirt and shorts, didn't put on any makeup or pay special attention to my hair.

I was at the counter, filling out the deposit envelopes, when I heard someone call my name. "Amanda?" The male voice sounded indecisive, as if it wasn't sure it was me. I didn't respond, because I didn't want anyone to see me.

"Amanda Callaway?" Now the voice was directly behind me, demanding a response.

I turned around slowly: It was Robert "Bob" Mitchell, Malcolm's friend. He wore a suit and tie, as though he was going to work.

"I wasn't sure if it was you or not. How are you?" He looked genuinely surprised and happy to see me.

"I'm fine. It's good to see you. How have you been?" I asked him. He looked like a million dollars, and I looked like shit!

"I've been good, I retired from football last fall, and I have a job with Cox Cable Television. This is great, because I was going to get in touch with you. Malcolm..." He hesitated to watch my reaction and continued. "Well he asked me to get in touch with you. He said that he thought you had bought a house here."

"Yes, I did, but I'm hardly there. My grandmother is ill, and I have been going to Tennessee every weekend to help my family care for her."

"I'm sorry to hear that. Look, maybe we can help each other out.

I'm living at the Marriott while I look for a condo to buy. I don't want to rush into something, so maybe I can rent a room from you until I find a place? I only have two suitcases, and I'll pay. I'm tired of living in the hotel."

It sounded like a good idea. I needed someone to water my plants when I was away.

"Sure, why don't you come over, and I'll show you around. You don't have to pay me. Let see, I have a three-day trip tomorrow. When do you think you can come by?" I had forgotten about the way I looked.

He looked at his watch and said. "What about two o'clock this afternoon. Give me your number, and I'll call you for directions."

As I was writing my number on a piece of paper, he added, "Maybe we can talk."

"Talk?" I asked, and I looked in his face and understood that he needed to tell me something or just get something off his chest. So, although I was puzzled, I quickly said, "Sure, that will be fine."

"It good to see you, Amanda, and I'll call you before two o'clock." And he was gone.

I dropped my film in the collection box and went home. I tidied up a little bit, changed clothes, and combed my hair.

Like clockwork, Bob called at two o'clock sharp, and I gave him directions. Twenty minutes later, he arrived. He was in the same clothes.

I showed him around, and he said he would check out of the hotel and move in that afternoon.

I gave him my spare house keys.

"Do you mind watering my plants?" I asked.

"That's the least I can do. Actually, I'm pretty good with plants. I have a green thumb." He smiled and took a seat on the sofa.

"Would you like something to drink?"

"A beer, if you have it."

"I'm sorry, I don't drink beer, so I never buy it. I have Pepsi, Dr. Pepper, or orange juice," I said.

He took Pepsi. I poured him a glass, and one for myself. I handed him his glass and took a seat on the other end of the sofa.

He took a sip and measured his words.

"You know, Malcolm was my best friend. He helped me when I first came into the league. I loved him like a brother. He was a very smart guy and helped me with a lot of investments. He was a good man, a special person, who you meet once in a lifetime." He was looking at his drink, and when he finally looked at me, I said nothing. So he continued. "You remember that trip to Jamaica?"

I nodded.

"Malcolm asked me to go."

"Really? I thought it was the other way around." I was a little shocked.

"I know, he didn't want to disappoint you. He knew you were looking forward to the trip. Well, at first," he paused and took his time, "he was going to ask you to marry him."

"What?" Now I was shocked. "I had no idea!"

"Yes, I know, but I went with him to Canal Street when he bought the ring. Then he went to St. Louis to see his family doctor."

I nodded.

"Amanda, he got some devastating news. He knew he had the heart defect, but it had gotten worse, and then he was also told he had leukemia. He was dying."

"No!" I started to cry. "Why didn't he tell me? You could have told me."

"I wanted to, but he didn't want anyone to know, and I promised him. You can understand my position." His voice was unsteady. "He was very sick, and he wanted me to come, just in case something happened."

I reached for the box of tissues and blew my nose.

"But we hardly saw you in Jamaica," I said through tears.

"You never saw me. I was always in touch with Malcolm. Believe me, I was never far away." He was almost in tears. I handed him a tissue.

"I tried to encourage him to give you the ring. But he knew that he didn't have long to live, and he wanted a clean break. He wanted to spare you the pain and suffering he had to endure from that day on. He was on some strong medication. He loved you very much, and he was hurting. I saw him that September before he died. He was weak and he was still hurting. You were always on his mind. He asked me to contact you after his death and tell you the truth."

I had my head down, I could tell that he was relieved to get all this off his chest. He also wanted to say something to cheer me up.

"You know, I was his roommate on the road. Well, most of the guys would go out to topless bars and pick up women. Malcolm would stay in his room and read those financial and investment books and magazines. When we went shopping, anything he saw that was shiny and pretty and reminded him of you, he would buy it. He loved you with all his heart and soul. He told me that you satisfied his every need, both physical and emotional. I was a little jealous, because I have never known that type of love. I hope I can feel it someday, before I die." His voice had gotten very low, almost as though he didn't want me to hear that last part.

"What else did he say about me?" I wanted to hear more.

"Well, he said that you couldn't cook. As a matter of fact, he said you couldn't boil water." he smiled.

"That's a lie, I can cook. Let me see. I can cook southern fried chicken and macaroni and cheese. I just couldn't cook as good as he could." I was defensive.

He smiled and looked at me. Our eyes met, and he quickly looked away. I had seen that look before, and I knew there was more he had to tell, but I didn't want to push him.

"Well, I better be going. I need to check out and get my things together. Thank you, Amanda. I'll see you later."

He moved into my guest room that night. I left for a three-day trip the next morning, and I went directly home to Tennessee afterward.

I knew he worked from nine to five, so I came in from Tennessee, repacked my bags, checked my mail and messages, and left again.

I left him a note telling him I was on another three-day trip.

I had called Sarah, Collette, and all my friends to let them know that Bob would be staying at my house for a few weeks, or until he found a place. They had questions, but kept them to themselves for the moment; all except Collette, whose marriage was on the rocks again.

"That man is fine, and if you don't want to give him any play, I will," she told me.

She would call my house, knowing I was out of town, just to talk to Bob. She got all dressed up one evening when she knew I was away and went to my house. Bob answered the door, and of course she asked for me. He told her that I was on a trip, but she invited herself in anyway.

"What was he doing?" I asked her later.

"He was cooking something, and it smelled good," she said

"Did he ask you to stay and eat?"

"No, but I wish he had. I'm telling you, that man is fine. I couldn't live in the same house with a man that good looking and not get horny. He said some nice things about you. I think he likes you. Look, I don't care if he was Malcolm's friend, Malcolm is dead, and you are alive. I think you should give that man some play." She was serious.

I didn't care what Collette said, I didn't have enough nerve to make a play for Bob. Beside, I was not sure I wanted to.

When I got home from my three-day trip, there was a note on the refrigerator from Bob, asking me to call him at his office. I put my suitcase away and dialed the number he had left. His secretary answered the phone. "Mr. Mitchell's office, may I help you?" she asked.

"May I speak to Mr. Mitchell, please? I'm returning his call," I lied.

"Who may I say is calling?" She was being nosy.

"Amanda Callaway."

"Hold on, and I'll see if he can take your call." A minute later she put me through to his office.

"Hello, stranger." His voice was very friendly, as if he was glad to hear from me.

"Hi, I got your message, is everything all right?" I asked.

"Sure, everything's fine, I just haven't seen you. Did I run you from your own house, or maybe you're just avoiding me?"

"No, you know that my grandmother was ill. But she is doing much better now."

"Good. I'm glad to hear that. Would you like to have lunch?"

I was a little surprised, and I didn't know where he was coming from. I needed time to think. So I made something up. "I'm sorry, but I have a hair appointment for two o'clock. Can I have a raincheck?"

"Sure, anytime. Then, will you be home this evening?" he asked.

I said yes.

"I'll see you then, I'll pick up some Chinese food." We said 'bye, and he hung up.

I held the phone for a minute, thinking, "*That's strange, he didn't tell me why he wanted me to call. Maybe he'll tell me tonight. One thing for sure, I want nothing to do with a football player." Once bitten, twice shy.* I'd had my heart broken into a thousand pieces, and I wasn't going that route again. I was sure of that.

I had to run by the beauty school to see if I could get something done to my hair, since I had lied. I knew they took walk-ins.

Good thing the beauty school wasn't busy. I got a wash and set, and I was out in an hour. My hair had grown to my shoulders. It was really too much trouble and I wanted to get it cut.

Bob arrived home about six o'clock with two bags of food.

"I like your hair," was the first thing he said as he put the food on the table.

We ate and talked. He offered to have cable TV installed in my house. Since he was the installation manager at the cable company, he got free cable. He could put a rush on the order, and it would be installed right away. It sure sounded like a good idea.

He challenged me to six games of Backgammon, of which I won four. He demanded a rematch, but it was already ten o'clock, and I was ready for bed because I had an early sign-in. As I was putting the game pieces away, he asked, "what time Saturday will your trip get back?"

"Around five in the afternoon."

"I'm off Saturday, I can cook dinner for you. I'm really a good cook." He tried to sound casual, but he didn't look at me.

"Okay, that sounds like a good idea. It's a date, but only if you have the time, don't put yourself out." I said, and was off to bed.

I went on my trip and forgot about the dinner. I really hadn't thought he was serious. I figured he would buy some Popeye's Chicken or pizza.

I arrived home around six, Saturday evening. As soon as I opened the door, I smelled something good cooking, and my favorite album of Richie Haven was playing. When I walked into the kitchen, I almost dropped my bag. The table was beautifully set for two, with a linen tablecloth and napkins. There were two candles, and a bottle of champagne chilling in an ice bucket. He must have bought all this because I didn't own a matching tablecloth and napkins.

Bob was dressed in a royal-blue sweater and black dress slacks. I could see his muscles bulging through his sweater. Collette was right, he was very handsome.

"What's all this? And you shouldn't have!" I said. I wasn't sure I was up to all of this.

"And hello to you, too. I had your cable installed." He motioned for me to look behind me.

In the living room was a new thirty-six-inch color television with a cable box on top.

"Your TV was too old and too small for the cable box. It's a gift for letting me stay here."

"Thanks, but all this isn't necessary, Bob." I moved closer to the stove. The smell was making me hungry. "Excuse me, I'll put my suitcase up, shower, and slip into something more comfortable." I had heard that line in about a dozen movies and I needed a quick exit.

"Dinner will be served in thirty minutes," he called after me.

I showered and sprayed on a little perfume. I went through my closet, looking for something nice, but not revealing. I settled on a fuchsia blouse and a long, black linen skirt. I looked in the mirror.

"This is me, take it or leave it," I said to my reflection, and I went back into the kitchen.

I was surprised when he said, "you look very nice. Dinner is served, my lady." He pulled the chair out for me.

After he was seated, he poured the champagne and offered a toast.

"To a wonderful evening."

"I'll drink to that," I responded out of habit.

The food was delicious. After two glasses of champagne, I started to relax.

He talked a little about his job, and I talked a bit about the airline business. We were both determined not to mention Malcolm's name.

By the time he served the dessert, Cherries Jubilee, the champagne had taken effect. I also realized that I was drinking more than he was. Maybe it was my nerves.

"A friend of yours, Collette, I think, came by looking for you last week," he said.

"Oh, she did? What did she say?" I pretended not to know.

"Nothing much, she talked about her divorce. I guess it was bothering her. I was no help. I told her that I've never been married. I was only engaged once."

"You have to watch her. Did she flirt with you?" I smiled.

"You have a beautiful smile," he said, and my reaction was to go back into my shell, so I took a quick drink of champagne.

He tried not to notice, and he kept talking. "I don't think so, but it wouldn't have mattered because, she's not my type," he said softly.

"What's wrong with my friend? And what is your type?" I giggled. The champagne talking for me. I was feeling good and enjoying his company.

"First of all, your friend...uh, Collette, wore too much makeup and too much lipstick for me. Also, her red fingernails were too long, and was that a wig on her head?" We both laughed so hard. Collette had four wigs, and I didn't know which one she had worn.

"Some men like that type, but I don't; and second, as for my type, go look in the mirror, and the face you see is my type." I stopped laughing! I looked at him to see if I heard him right. Maybe he was drunk.

He kept talking. "You are refined and natural. There is nothing fake about you. I love your smile and that sparkle in your eye. You are like the girl next door. I felt it the first time Malcolm introduced us. Sometimes, when you weren't looking, I would try to sneak a look at you. I had to be careful, because I was ashamed. I couldn't let you or Malcolm find out my secret." He took a sip of his drink.

"I could feel there was more. I thought that I reminded you of your old girlfriend." I also needed to take a sip of my drink.

"That's true, you do look a lot like her. But it's more than that. Sometimes a man, or woman, for that matter, has an idea of what his or her ideal mate would be like. You just fit that ideal woman for me. I didn't want it to happen, it just happened. You were my best friend's girl. I would never have violated our friendship. Yet I would lie awake at night thinking about holding you. The best time I ever had with a woman was with you."

"With me! But we have never been together." I got up and carried my plate to the sink. I needed some space. Was I ready for this?

He came up behind me, and I could feel his breath on my neck. He put his arms around my waist and said, "Remember, in Jamaica, at the limbo contest? We were drinking, laughing, and having a good time. When we won, you were so excited that you threw your arms around my neck. You were jumping up and down, you didn't notice." He stopped to see if I wanted him to continue.

"Notice what?" I asked in a low voice, not sure I wanted to know the answer.

"I put my arms around you, I held you close, just for a moment, and it felt so good. I think my heart skipped a beat, like it's doing now." He kissed my neck. I closed my eyes, and I felt his body. It was hard. I didn't move, because I knew what love felt like, and this was it!

He slowly turned me around and kissed me on my mouth. It was tender at first, and then more demanding. I was surprised at how my body was responding. It had been more than a year since I had felt this good. His erection was hard as a stone, and I could feel myself getting wet. My mind was telling me to move away, but my body wouldn't listen. His hands were on my breasts. He was kissing my neck, and his head was moving in that direction. I didn't put up much resistance. I hadn't made love in so long, and I wasn't about to past up this opportunity. I needed this. I'd worry about the guilt trip tomorrow.

I would have done it right there in the kitchen, but I had stopped taking the birth-control pill more than a year ago. I had to check my bathroom for some sponges I had hidden for "emergencies."

"Excuse me a minute. I need a minute," I said, as I eased his hand from under my blouse. I wiggled under his arm, and he followed me to the bathroom, but I went in alone and closed the door. I found the sponge and inserted it. I felt a little more at ease.

I took a deep breath and opened the bathroom door; he was standing outside the door, leaning against the wall.

"Is everything all right?" he asked.

"Sure, I just haven't done it for about...three...four months, and I'm a little nervous. That's all." I wasn't about to tell him that it had been almost a year, because I was tired of looking for someone like Malcolm.

"Don't worry, I won't hurt you. I'll take it easy. If it hurts, I will stop, and we can try another position. Look, we really don't have to do it tonight if you don't want to. I'll be happy just holding you all night." He was very considerate.

However, I unbuttoned my blouse and then my bra.

"Too late to change your mind," I told myself. I pushed him down onto the bed and landed on top of him. He gently kissed each breast. Then he unzipped my skirt and slid it down my legs. He ran his hand between my legs and nibbled on my breast at the same time.

This drove me crazy. I moved my hand under his sweater and pulled it over his head. He had a beautiful body, a broad chest, and a six-pack stomach. First, I ran my hand over the hair on his chest. Then, I started kissing him on his neck and worked my way over his chest and down to his belly button. I unzipped his pants with my hands and chin. He had on blue bikini briefs. He had a very manly smell, and I liked it. He started to lift his shoulders up, but I pushed him back on the bed, and I enjoyed his manhood. He had to pull me up.

"It's my turn," he said and returned the favor.

I was in Heaven. When he finally entered me, I was on top, my favorite position. I came right away, and I came again, and then we came together. It was wonderful. Afterwards, we were both exhausted, but we held onto each other for almost five minutes. I didn't want to let go.

"Did I hurt you?" Bob asked, and kissed me on my back.

"No, you are the greatest. Did I hurt you?"

"Yes, you almost killed me. You are a tigress. I have got to get in shape." He was laughing as he pulled me to him, and, oh, it felt so good. I fell asleep with a smile on my face and in my heart.

One year later, in the spring of 1981, I became Mrs. Robert Mitchell.

Bob and I had decided on a simple wedding at the courthouse. I called all my best friends, but only Sarah, Collette, and Dee Dee were able to come. Sarah had to drop a trip in order to be there by my side, a true friend. After the wedding, Bob took us all to dinner at my favorite restaurant, the Little Cajun Cuisine. We didn't plan a honeymoon. We were happy to be married and wanted to start a family right away. I hadn't yet told Bob about the money Malcolm had left me. The last time I checked, it was close to half a million dollars.

Bob wasn't poor, he had invested his money well, and he had a good job.

Five days after our wedding, I decided to bring closure to that part of my life. After Bob left for work, I went into my closet and looked in my secret hiding place on the top shelf. I took down the beautiful jewelry box Malcolm had given me, opened it, and placed inside it all the letters, cards, jewelry, and little gifts he had given to me, except for the diamond earrings, which had never been off my ears since he gave them to me on our first date. I would be lost without them, and I also kept a strand of cultured pearls he bought for me in Honolulu during a Pro Bowl there.

From my drawer, I pulled out the picture of Malcolm that I used to keep on my nightstand, before Bob. I looked at him smiling, and my heart skipped a beat. I kissed the picture.

"You will always be my first love and my old flame. You will never be far from my heart and thoughts. I sure hope there is life after death, because I want to see you again. I will have a lot to tell you," I whispered.

I placed the picture in the jewelry box, closed it and took it to my safety deposit box at the bank.

It would be twenty years before I opened it again.

Thirty

1982

The 1980s brought a new breed of flight attendants into the airlines. Cocaine was their drug of choice. They snorted it, smoked it, and free-based it. Some were wild with no class. They slept with pilots and male flight attendants. They did drugs in the aircraft lavatory, and did lines of cocaine in the lower galley of the L-1011. They would allow passengers to have sex in the aircraft lavatory. They stole liquor, beer, wine, and liquor money from the airplane, and partied in the hotel rooms. One young flight attendant stole fifty dollars out of my wallet to buy drugs from a passenger on the airplane. Her excuse was that he wouldn't take a check, and she didn't have any cash. She was going to put it back on the trip home after she cashed a check at the hotel. Or at least, that's what she said!

We did not like flying with the "young gals," as we called them, but sometimes I couldn't avoid doing so.

The New Orleans base had an all-nighter to Los Angeles. It became a very junior trip, because the senior flight attendants didn't like the hours.

Anything was acceptable on that flight. Collette and I flew it for one month, just for the Los Angles layover, but those junior women were more than we could stand.

For starters, the coordinator was a cute little redhead who was lazy, sloppy, and lacked leadership ability. After our first trip, we added one more title to her coordinator title: "Cockpit Queen." She spent more time in the cockpit than in the cabin. She was suppose to serve coffee in first class, but she was in the cockpit. She served the cockpit crew before she served the passengers. Her crew's idea of customer service was giving the passengers their food and drinks at the same time and getting the service over with. Then they would sit in the back of the plane and talk, read, or needlepoint. They only served decaf coffee, because the regular coffee kept the passengers awake. Strangely enough, the passengers didn't seem to know the difference between regular and decaf.

Collette and I decided to work first class. That way, we could be sure our first-class passengers got good service, because they paid so much more for their tickets. The junior gals could do whatever they wanted in the tourist cabin.

On one such trip, when Collette and I finished our service and most of our passengers were asleep, we went into the galley to talk. The co-pilot was making coffee. We waited for him to leave, but he just stood around, and the first-class galley was too small for three people.

"Would you like some more coffee?" I asked him.

"No, thanks, I just had some."

I looked at Collette.

"Would you like something to eat?" she asked him.

"Oh no." Finally he realized he was in our space, and we wanted him to leave.

"I'm sorry, y'all but...uh...your coordinator is in the cockpit sitting on the captain's lap. She's going to give him a blowjob, and I decided to leave to give them some privacy. As soon as she comes out, I'll go back in and be out of y'all's hair."

We couldn't believe what he was saying. After ten years of flying, this was a first.

"I've flown with her before, and it's always the same thing. Someone needs to talk to her." Obviously he felt uncomfortable in the situation and was more than a little perturbed.

Collette and I decided to wait ten minutes. If the coordinator wasn't out by then, we were going in. She came out of the cockpit, smiling and licking her lips. The copilot smiled, shook his head and went back into the cockpit.

"Here, I know you're thirsty," Collette said as she handed the girl a glass of water.

"What's this for?" she smirked.

"Look, little slut. We know what you're doing in the cockpit, and from now on, you keep your ass out in the cabin and work. I'm sure one blowjob per flight is enough," Collette said.

"You can't tell me what to do. Besides I'm single, and he's single." She started to leave.

Collette stepped in front of her and pushed her back into the galley. I closed the curtain so they wouldn't disturb the passengers.

"If you go in that cockpit one more time, I will write you up, and the whole base will know what a whore you are," Collette threatened.

She somehow managed to squeeze around us and leave the galley. But she didn't go back into the cockpit and swapped the next two trips. That made me the coordinator. I made those young gals work the service correctly, with a complete beverage service before the meal. There was no reading or personal pastimes on the jump seat, and they served regular coffee instead of decaf, unless it was requested.

They were pissed, and we didn't care. These young flight attendants were a *trip*.

The next month, I flew with a junior gal who had little holes in her uniform dress from smoking marijuana on the way to work. The seeds would pop out, burning holes in her dress. The dumb chick didn't know you had to take the seeds out before you rolled it. During the night flight home, she was working in D-zone, the back section of the L-1011. She asked me to keep an eye on her section and be a lookout while she went into the lavatory to do cocaine with a passenger with whom she had become acquainted.

"If the coordinator comes to the back looking for me, tell her I'm in the lower galley."

"I'm going to tell her that I don't know where you are," was all I offered.

Twenty minutes later, she came out of the lavatory looking a little dazed and glassy-eyed. Her dress was rumpled.

I asked her if she was all right.

"Yes; was anyone looking for me? Did anybody ask for me?" She was paranoid.

"No one is looking for you."

She sat down and started to nod off.

I shook her. "Little bitch, don't you OD on me, I don't feel like writing up the report."

"I'm all right, that was some good stuff. Of course, once in the lavatory, he wanted to do more than drugs. I had to give him some. Is my dress wrinkled? Are you sure no one's looking for me?"

"Your dress is fine, and no one is looking for you. I have been back here the whole time, and your secret is safe with me." I wasn't surprised the passenger wanted sex. They all want to be members of the Mile High Club, and with drugs comes sex.

"Thank you, Amanda."

She relaxed a little and sat beside me in the last row. I had to nudge her several times to keep her from falling asleep.

These young women were into so much shit, but they had to learn, just as we had. They didn't live with the fear of having Irene Bourgerone, around as we had, although, come to think of it, that had never stopped us!

Before we landed in New Orleans, the same man went into the same lavatory with a female passenger. I could only hope the young flight attendant, sitting beside me in the last row, used a condom.

Several months after that trip, I was the senior flight attendant on a DC-9 trip, with a layover in Miami. Two junior gals made up the crew of three: Tina McCracken and Arial Hutcherson. They were Southern Belles, whose only reason for becoming flight attendants was to meet and marry a rich man. They spent most of their time flirting with all the male passengers in first class, of course, and I was doing all the work. On our last leg to Miami, they met a handsome Latin-looking man named Raul. He offered to pick them up at the hotel and show them Miami night life. I told them to do whatever they wanted, just be back in time for our five thirty a.m. pick-up. We had a seventeen-hour layover, and I was exhausted from doing their work and mine. I went to my hotel room and went to bed.

I got a call at two o'clock in the morning from the front desk. I was dead asleep. At first, I thought I was dreaming.

"Ms. Mitchell, this is the night manager. There are two strange-looking young women in the lobby who say they are flight attendants and members of your crew. They don't have any identification or room keys. They can't remember their room numbers, and they say they were robbed. We need you to come down to the lobby and identify them before we can give them room keys."

"What are their names?" I asked the night manager.

"Tina McCracken and Arial Hutcherson."

"May I speak to one of them?" I asked. I didn't want to get out of bed for nothing.

"Hold on."

"Amanda!...This is Tina, Arial and I...we...were...robbed, please...come get us!" She was weeping so hard that I could hardly understand her.

I jumped out of bed, threw my raincoat on over my nightgown and the hood over my head, grabbed my key, and ran downstairs.

What I saw shocked me, and I could see why the manager was suspicious. There were my two young flight attendants, shaking and obviously high on drugs. Their clothes were dirty and half torn-off. One had what looked liked semen in her hair and on her clothes.

When they saw me, they ran to me and wouldn't let me go. They were crying and slurring their words. I didn't understand a word they said.

I got their keys and took them to my room, because they were afraid to be left alone. They smelled like they had been sleeping with wild dogs. They took turns in the shower while I made coffee in the little coffee pot in the room. I was glad, for the first time, that in our flight attendant's contract, we demanded a coffee pot and coffee in each hotel room.

They told me what they could remember.

From what I could pull out of them, this is what happened: Raul picked them up at the hotel and took them to his house. They did cocaine and drank wine with him. He slipped some LSD or some other drug into their drinks. They passed out and woke up with two old men having sex with them. They kicked the old men off. It wasn't hard, because they truly were senior citizens. They wanted to know where Raul was. The old men said that they paid Raul two hundred dollars each to have sex with them, and they wanted their money's worth. Of course, Raul was nowhere to be found, so they grabbed their clothes and ran from the house. Dressing in the bushes, they had no idea where they were or how far they were from the hotel. They walked and ran until they came to a main street and flagged down the first police car they saw. There were two policemen in the car, to which they related what happened. But they couldn't remember where the house was and they didn't know Raul's last name.

The officers didn't believe their story and thought they were prostitutes. The officers then told them to get into their car, and they would drive them to the Hotel. Instead, they took the girls to a secluded area. One officer got in the back seat with Tina and made Arial get in front. Both men unzipped their pants and demanded oral sex. When they refused, the officers pushed the girls' heads into their laps and told them to "get to work," or they would be booked for prostitution.

They felt they had no choice. The officer in the back with Tina wanted more than oral sex. She had to get on her hands and knees, and he sodomized her. He kept saying, "Come on, bitch! Give it to me! You know you like it, you do this all the time." Poor Tina was crying. He came in her hair, her face, and he made her swallow his semen.

The cops dropped them off about a block from the hotel.

I asked them if they got a badge number, a car number, a name, or anything. I wanted to prosecute those dogs.

They were totally against that and didn't want anyone to know what happened. They had no idea which part of town Raul's house was located. Their memory was still sketchy, and they were still hallucinating. The effect of the drug hadn't yet worn off.

I checked the clock. It was exactly two hours before pick-up. None of us was in any condition to work a long trip home with five legs. That meant five stops and passengers boarding and deplaning. I didn't know what to do or say. I felt sorry for them, and they kept begging me not to write any of this up. They wanted me to tell Big E that someone knocked them down and snatched their purses while they were shopping downtown.

I sat on the side of the bed near the telephone. I thought about my friend, Jackie O'Brien, who was victimized in Las Vegas. She had to lie and allow a sexual predator to go free, because she needed to protect her reputation. What about the thousands of women who were victimized every day and were afraid to come forward. I had no doubt that those two policemen would eventually be caught, but how many young women would have to be raped and sodomized by them before that happened?

"Amanda, please call," Tina begged.

I agreed, because I would probably do the same if I was in their position. So I called Big E operations and told them that two of our flight attendants had been attacked while walking back to the hotel from dinner and shopping, and that they were knocked down and had a lot of cuts and bruises, and their purses were snatched, so they had no ID or money. I said that I had been up all night, trying to calm them down. Good thing the airline had a base in Miami, and they called three reserve flight attendants to take our flight so we could deadhead home. Everyone at Big E was very sympathetic.

I was glad to get home. That trip had been very stressful for me, also. Tina never got over the experience, and she quit Big E after a few months of trying to overcome her trauma. She moved back to Mississippi and married her hometown boyfriend.

Arial needed years of counseling, but was finally able to put the matter behind her. She never went out with any man she met on an airplane.

Many flight attendants had dated and married men they met on a flight and lived happy ever after. One flight attendant married a wealthy Jewish-Cuban man she met on a flight. Their wedding was on St. John Island, and he flew her flight attendant friends there in his own airplane. We stayed in his hotel, all expenses paid. He allow us to vacation on the Island for a few days before returning.

Also, many flight attendants were married to police officers. Some police officers have done good by us. One night, a flight attendant's husband got angry with her, beat her up, and took her to a landfill dump. He had decided she was trash, and the dump was where she belonged.

He took all her clothes and left her there, naked. She had to wrap up in some old clothing and hide in the weeds until a police car came along. She flagged it down. They put her in the car; one officer gave her his shirt.

When they took Margie home, her husband was sitting in his favorite chair, watching TV. The policeman tried to arrest him. When he resisted arrest, they beat the shit out of him. We all agreed that was what he deserved. When it was time for the trial, Margie and her husband were back together, and she said that the policemen beat him for no reason.

After that, Margie came to work with black eyes and bruises, but no one felt sorry for her. It was her decision to stay with him, so she had to live with it!

It seemed like history was repeating itself: A group of young flight attendants were using drugs, dating drug dealers, and prostituting in San Francisco. They took wine, beer, and champagne off the plane. And we couldn't tell them that we had been there, done that! They were partying hard.

One young flight attendant, Rachel DeCola, was dating a drug dealer in San Francisco, and he got her hooked on heroin. She called in sick in March, and never called in well. In May, her parents called the Big E Scheduling office, looking for her, because they hadn't heard from their daughter in months. The scheduler called some of her friends. They were worried about her, too, so they told Big E about her drug-addict boyfriend; where he lived, and what kind of car he drove.

Big E did its own investigation by calling the LAPD and giving them a description of Rachel and the name and address of her so-called boyfriend.

It took the LAPD only three hours to find them sleeping in a car, stoned out of their minds. Rachel didn't even remember that she had called in sick.

The police put her in detox, and they put her boyfriend in jail for violating parole and carrying a gun. Big E sent her parents out to bring her home and put her in a rehabilitation clinic in Atlanta. She was on medical leave for six months.

Shortly after Rachel returned to work, she met an old-time Baptist preacher who wanted to marry her. We convinced her to tell the preacher about her past and not hold anything back. She was afraid at first, but when she finally confessed, I think he loved her even more for telling him the truth.

We danced and drank fruit punch at her wedding. The preacher was totally against alcohol. We all went to his church a few times because he could really preach. He started trying to get us to join, so we had to stop going.

Dominique Van Stinchcomb...uhh...I mean...Princess Dominique Amari Al Ahmed called me early one morning from Atlanta, but we couldn't bring ourselves to call her Princess. I could tell from her voice that all was not well. She and her billionaire husband, Prince Hassan Amari Al Ahmed, were back in the country. They were building a mansion in North Atlanta.

"I'll have a big party as soon as the house is completed, because I miss all of my friends," she said.

"How are things going? And how does it feel to be a princess?" I asked, all excited.

"It's okay," was all she would say, and I knew something was terribly wrong.

Dominique had to oversee the construction of the house. Prince Amari Al Ahmed was always flying around the world in his Lear Jet.

By the time the mansion was completed, Dominique's marriage was on the rocks, and the party idea was scrapped.

We visited her home, and it was like something out of *Architectural Digest.* Dominique's room looked like it belonged to a princess. She had a maid and a personal assistant. Her husband's bedroom was down the hall. She was never allowed in his room; he had to come to her. His loyal assistant and an entourage of ten men traveled with him wherever he went. He was seldom in town, and when he was, he came to Dominique's room, satisfied his sexual drive, and was on his way.

"That's all?" we asked.

"There is no foreplay and he doesn't do oral sex. Sometimes I have to go down on him just to get it hard enough. His penis is short and fat, and he only lasts two minutes." She sounded resentful.

"Do you two talk?" I asked.

"The custom is, you don't talk to your husband, and he talks very little to you. These men have absolutely no respect for women. We are property."

"Does he speak English?"

"He speaks perfect English." Dominique broke down and told us the whole story: Unlike his cousin, who she had met in Atlanta, her husband was much older.

"How much older?" we asked, because we had never met Hassan Amari Al Ahmed. We had to pull his age out of Dominique.

"Well, he told me that he was sixty-five."

"Sixty-five!" we all screamed at once.

"Yes, but I think he's older."

"How much older?"

"About ten years."

"You mean to tell us your billionaire prince husband is seventy-five years old?" Michele asked.

"How do you expect a seventy-five-year-old man to come to you every night with a hard-on?" Sarah asked.

"Well, I didn't know he was seventy-five."

"Well, you certainly knew he was old, and his dick was short and fat, and he couldn't get it up when you married him," Collette said.

"I thought I could get pregnant."

We knew she had lost her mind, thinking a seventy-five–year-old man would get her pregnant…just like that.

"You better cut your losses and get the hell out of this marriage," was our advice to her.

She took our advice and dropped her veil and "princess-hood." After three years of personal leave, she came back to work.

Prince Amari Al Ahmed sent his lawyers and his sons to Atlanta to cut the best deal they could with Dominique without starting a war. They already had papers drawn up from the billionaire's last wife, a twenty-three-year-old California blonde. It seemed the old man had a thing for blondes.

Dominique got five million dollars and the mansion. That was just a drop in the bucket for the old prince.

Dominique sold the mansion and bought a modest home in East Cobb. She was love-starved. She had an affair with First Officer Franco Bordeaux, but he was still a womanizer.

She dated a male flight attendant from Chicago. When they broke up, he said Dominique's strong sexual drive almost killed him. His back couldn't hold up to her extreme sexual demands, even though she had bought him a brand new Mercedes.

Thirty-one

1983

Nicole Stevenson, Dee Dee's old roommate from the Lewis & Clark Apartments, was back in New Orleans. She could have been the seventh person in our group if she hadn't been so weird and out-to-lunch. She would be hanging out at our apartment and partying with us for a few months; then bam, for no reason we could see, she would stop speaking to us. She transferred to Boston without telling Dee Dee she was moving, and Dee Dee was stuck with unpaid rent and bills. We heard she was in a mental institution for a while. I had no idea she had transferred back until I flew with her shortly after my marriage. Since then, Collette and I could not make a move without her.

One evening, I was home alone when Nicole showed up at my door, and she was in tears. I was surprised to see her, because we knew her mother was sick, and that she had gone home for a few days. I pulled her into the house and comforted her as best I could until she was ready to talk. I made us some tea and sat down beside her, and she finally started to talk.

She told me that she was tired of running from her father. He had sexually molested her when she was a child, and it stopped only when she went away to college. Two days ago, while she was home visiting her sick mother, her father pretended to give her a hug and put his hand on her butt.

"Can you believe that? Right in my mother's bedroom!" she yelled. "I told him, if he ever touched me again, I would kill him, and I meant it. I hate him." She paused, "I've never had anyone to talk to before. I feel I can talk to you. I trust you. Don't tell anyone, please."

I could only nod my head. I was speechless. She needed counseling from someone experienced in dealing with these things.

"I have been messed up all my life. I tried to kill myself when I was thirteen. The reason I checked myself into that mental hospital, years ago, was because my boyfriend called me 'Sweetie' when we were having sex. That's what my father would call me when he was raping me, and I couldn't cope. I hate sex, but I keep doing it all the time, because that's the only way I know how to relate to a man."

After that day, we started spending more time together. We had lunch, went to a movie, or shopped a couple of times a week. I was glad when she started dating an old friend of mine, a gate agent in Dallas, Warren Farmer, because she and her problems were wearing me down.

Nicole met Warren on a Dallas layover. They dated for six months, and it looked like things were getting serious. As soon as he asked her to marry him, Nicole disappeared for three weeks. We found out she had called in sick for two of her trips, and no one knew where she was.

Collette called to tell me she just got a call from Nicole. "The bitch is in Nassau with some man. She wanted me to swap her next trip over two days. She is back to her old tricks again. I've had it with her. She can fool you, but she can't fool me." Collette was angry. "This disappearing act of hers has got to go. I'm telling you, she's crazy!"

Maybe Collette was right, because when Nicole finally called me, she acted like nothing happened. I asked her where she had been.

"Girl, I needed a vacation," she said, really casual.

I reminded her that Warren, her "fiancé," was looking for her, and that he called me every day.

After that, she would leave, and we would not hear from her for weeks at a time. We could only pray someone hadn't killed her.

Just as we got used to her behavior and were about to give up on her, she called. This time she had something very important to talk to me about. She wanted me to swap with another flight attendant and fly with her on her trip, so I could layover with her in Milwaukee. I didn't want to do it, until she said it was a matter of life or death. I gave in and swapped.

She called Collette and gave her the same sad story. It was a hard sell, but somehow she got Collette to swap as well.

Collette called me. "What in the hell is she up to?" Like I knew!

"I have no idea." And I didn't.

"It better be good, or she's going to wish she was dead. I only swapped because you did. Amanda, we had a good layover in Los Angeles. We are going to freeze our asses off in Milwaukee," she complained.

She was in a bad mood, and I knew it had to do with more than just Nicole. I didn't want to hear her problems, and I got off the phone as fast as I could.

"We'll see; let's give her the benefit of the doubt. I've got to go, I'll see you Monday," I said, and I hung-up.

Monday morning when we signed-in, Nicole was in a happy mood. During the flight, she and I worked the back of the DC-9. She wouldn't give me a hint about her life-or-death problem.

"Wait until we get to the hotel. We'll meet in my room, and I'll order a bottle of wine and I'll tell y'all," she hedged.

"It better be good, Nicole, because I don't have time for your shit. I have problems of my own." Collette was still in her bad mood.

A call bell broke up our meeting in the back galley; it was a first class passenger wanting another scotch and water, his fourth! We decided to cut him off after that because his words were slurring. That was too much to drink between New Orleans and Shreveport. When Collette wouldn't give him his fifth drink, he snarled, "Nigger Bitch" at her and threw what was left of this fourth drink in her face.

Call bells were ringing like crazy. Two other first class passengers had to restrain Collette until Nicole and I made our way to the front to calm her down. She managed to spit at the man before we dragged her into the cockpit. The captain came out and ordered the man to an empty seat in coach. Collette said she wanted to cuss him out, but we kept her in the cockpit.

When we landed in Shreveport, the police met the plane and escorted the man off in handcuffs. He was so drunk, he claimed not to remember what he had done. He spent the night in jail and paid a hefty fine.

That was only the first leg of our trip; we had four to go: Jackson, Memphis, Cincinnati, and Milwaukee. After that incident, the passengers were a little antsy. They weren't used to having an all-black cabin crew. When I closed the curtain between the cabins, they acted like Nicole and I were holding them hostage. They kept staring at the curtain as though they expected a white flight attendant to come though the curtain and rescue them.

On the leg to Jackson, we were the only blacks on the whole airplane. One man with a Southern drawl couldn't resist. He had to say it: "I've been flying Big E Airlines for twenty-five years, and I've never had all Colored girl...aah...ste'tresses."

"Well, there is a first time for everything," Collette said with a fake Southern drawl.

The white passengers who boarded the plane in Shreveport and deplaned in Memphis didn't speak to us when they deplaned. They said goodbye to the captain and ignored us.

From Memphis to Cincinnati, an attractive elderly lady fainted on the way to the lavatory. She had all the symptoms of a heart attack. I paged for a doctor, and Nicole retrieved the portable oxygen bottle. No doctor was onboard. The lady appeared to be very wealthy, judging from the way she was dressed and the expensive jewelry she wore. She was also traveling with her middle-aged son, who didn't lift a finger to help his mother.

With the help of another male passenger, we were able to get the lady into an empty seat. She was as white as a sheet. Nicole started the oxygen, while I started to loosen her clothing and noticed that she was wearing a full-body corset. It was two sizes too small, and so tight I couldn't get my little finger between her bare skin and the garment.

Nicole brought the first-aid kit, and I took the scissors out of the kit and started cutting away. The elastic in the garment started to pop. It was so tight it was cutting off her oxygen flow. As soon as I cut the corset off, the lady started to breathe. Her son looked disappointed. He was ready to make funeral arrangements and start spending her money. He did not want to go to the hospital with his mother when we landed in Cincinnati, and he refused to thank us for helping her.

In Cincinnati, we picked up a lot of black passengers going home. It had never occurred to me that Milwaukee had such a large black population. They were so glad to see us. Most of them had never seen a black stewardess, much less a whole crew. They made our day. We had been treated like shit all day, so it felt good to be appreciated. Collette moved most of the black passengers to empty seats in first class and gave them all the liquor and beer they could drink and take home.

By the time we got to our hotel room, we were exhausted.

Somehow, Collette and I managed to shower, put on our pajamas, slip on our raincoats, and go straight to Nicole's room. She had ordered a bottle of red wine and a pizza.

Collette and I sat quietly on the bed sipping the wine. We were tired of asking; we wanted Nicole to just get to the point.

"I'm pregnant! Now, are y'all happy?" She announced and started to cry.

I looked at Collette, and she looked at me. Collette spoke first, very deliberately: "You brought us to this cold-ass place to tell us you're pregnant? I swear, girl, you better do better than that!"

I knew there had to be more, so I waited for her to stop crying and drop her bombshell. Collette's patience was wearing thin.

"Well, I...uh...I... don't know who the father is. Y'all know I was engaged to Warren, and I spent two weeks in Lake Charles with Michael Tiberdeaux. I don't know who's the father of this child. I've already had two abortions, and I can't have another one. I just can't." By now she was sobbing. "My doctor said one more abortion, and I can forget about ever being a mother."

Collette jumped up and stood over Nicole, shaking her finger in her face.

"You have some fucking nerve, dragging us up here to tell us this shit. You are a whore. Have you ever heard of birth control?" She was screaming.

"Take it easy, Collette, try to calm down," I soothed.

I couldn't believe she had the nerve to call someone else a whore. She was the biggest whore I knew. Maybe it took one to know one. Had she forgotten that, about two years ago, she called me to pick her up at the Southside Abortion Clinic. She was unable to drive home after her procedure. She stayed at my house for three days, unable to get out of bed, and the only reason she had the abortion was because she didn't think it was her husband's baby.

"I have a fucked-up life. I should just kill myself. I can't do anything right." Nicole was still crying.

"Just shut up, Nicole, no one is going to kill herself, but you are a damn fool. If I had a stick, I would beat your ass right here in this hotel room. How do you expect us to help you when the damage is already done?" Collette was still yelling.

I felt sorry for Nicole. I knew about her childhood and how fragile she was. I didn't want this to push her over the edge, and Collette wasn't cutting her any slack.

"Shut up, Collette! Give her a break, please," I finally said.

Then Collette turned her anger on me.

"What do you know about anything, Miss Goody-Two-Shoes? You have never seen a hard time in your life. You come from a rich family, you didn't have to work your way through college or wear hand-me-down clothes. You have always been taken care of; you have never dated a no-good-man. You don't know nothing about life. You even look good in those JCPenney's clothes."

Nicole jumped up and started yelling at Collette. "You shut-up, bitch! It's always been about you. We've sat up all night listening to your problems. You're too damn selfish to think of helping anyone else. I'm sorry I asked for your help, and I'm sorry I asked you to come on this trip."

"I'm sorry, too! Amanda and I could have been in sunny Los Angeles. Instead, here we are listening to your sorry assss..."

Before Collette finished, Nicole slapped her so hard that I could feel the pain. Then she snatched the wig off Collette's head and threw it to the floor. We were both shocked: Collette was completely bald, and she was embarrassed! She lunged for Nicole, and I stepped between them, yelling for them to stop.

"Y'all are acting like idiots. Corporate security will be up here soon, if y'all don't keep it down." I grabbed Collette's wig off the floor and gave it back to her. She was happy to put it back on her head.

"Now, apologize to each other," I demanded, treating them like the little kids they were acting like.

Each hesitated for a moment, then Collette said. "I'm sorry, Nicole, I lost it for a minute. You better be glad you're pregnant, because if you weren't, I would kick your sorry ass."

She grabbed her coat, poured herself another glass of wine and left the room, still steaming.

Nicole was distraught, and she was drinking the wine as though it was water. It took me an hour to calm her down. I decided to stay in her room the rest of the night, so she wouldn't do anything crazy.

I told her that, whatever she decided, I would stand by her. She asked if I would be the child's godmother.

"It would be my pleasure," I assured her.

Finally, we were able to get some sleep.

Going home, the passengers acted the same as the bunch we had coming to Milwaukee, though this time, there weren't any incidents. Collette worked first class. She had very little to say to Nicole and me.

I was so glad to get home. It had been, by far, the worst trip of my career, and to top it all off, we got many nasty letters from the passengers. None of the letters complained about the service, in fact, some even said the service was great and the crew was professional. They complained about the all-black crew! Some letters were downright ugly:

"Big E is turning into a nigger airline," one letter said.

"Colored girls shouldn't be allowed to be the only stewardesses on the airplane. What if something happened? Who will save us?" Some lady wrote.

"You all have hired too many niggers. I will never fly Elite World again."

It went on and on. This was 1983 and you could see how "far" we had come as a nation. Racism was alive and kicking.

There were many letters from our people in Milwaukee complimenting the flight crew:

"The service was impeccable, and from now on, we will fly Elite World Airlines."

"Great flight. The crew was very professional."

Those letters went into our files, and we were given a "feather in our cap" award with two complimentary positive-space tickets, Big E's highest employee awards. The bad letters went into the trash can.

Thirty-two

Needless to say, Nicole decided to keep the baby. Throughout the pregnancy, she had two men each thinking he was the father. She was an emotional wreck. I didn't know how she was going to do it, but she swore that, when the baby came, she would be able to tell which man was the father.

Michael Tiberdeaux, a Creole, had light, damn near white, skin, with straight hair. Warren, on the other hand, was dark, with "not-so-good" hair. So Nicole's reasoning was, if the baby was light with good hair, Michael was the father. On the other hand, if he or she was dark with kinky hair, Warren was the father.

Collette, who was friends again with Nicole, and I thought it was ludicrous, but we wouldn't dare say anything. Nicole was already a basket case, and we didn't want her to snap. Collette slipped up and told one flight attendant about what happened in Milwaukee, and now the whole base knew about the baby.

When Nicole went into labor, there were ten flight attendants at the hospital, waiting to see the color of the baby's skin.

They would only let one of us go into the delivery room. Collette wanted to be the one, so Nicole would know there were no hard feelings about what had happened in Milwaukee. That was fine with me, and the rest of us went into the waiting room.

When Collette came out of the delivery room and announced that Nicole had a beautiful baby girl and her name was Jennifer, we all wanted to hear more, but Collette was not really talking!

"Who do you think is the baby's father?" someone asked.

Collette look confused and shook her head, "I can't really tell," she said. "The baby is a beautiful shade of medium brown, Nicole's color. Jennifer will be in the nursery soon, maybe y'all can tell."

An hour later, all ten of us were staring at little Jennifer through the window of the hospital nursery. The only thing we could agree on was that she looked like Nicole.

When we visited Nicole, it was obvious she couldn't tell which man was the father. She was having anxiety attacks, and who could blame her? There were two men thinking, "I am the father of a beautiful baby girl."

Past experience had always indicated that men always lied, even when saying they were not the baby's father. They would demand a blood test, even when they knew damned well they were the father.

One thing was for sure: Jennifer couldn't possibly have two daddies, and things were about to get ugly. Someone was going to be hurt.

After being home two weeks with the baby, and after an almost-meeting of the two potential fathers, Nicole broke down and asked Warren to take a paternity test.

At Nicole's request, Collette and I were there when she told him. We had known Warren for years, and maybe we could help soften the blow. He wanted to marry Nicole, so he was sure the baby was his. He went straight to the hospital for the paternity test. We prayed he was the father.

Mr. Michael Tiberdeaux was a different story. Although he was a successful lawyer in Lake Charles, he still lived at home with his mother. Mrs. Tiberdeaux, who was also damn near white, came to town with Michael to see her new granddaughter. After the first look, she declared that Jennifer was too dark to be her son's baby.

"All Tiberdeaux's babies have light skin and straight hair," she proclaimed.

She advised her son to get a blood test before he committed a dime to child support, and of course, he did what his mother said. She was sickening. My stomach churned just listening to her.

The only thing left to do was wait. Nicole was crying on the phone every day. We tried to comfort her.

"No matter which man is the father, Jennifer is happy to have a great mother," I said

"And a great godmother. You will still be her godmother, won't you?" she asked me that same question every other day.

"I would be honored," I reassured her.

"I'm sorry for all this mess. I hope Warren is the father. He is a good man, and he loves Jennifer. We will get married." She was happy. However, it was short-lived.

A week later, the paternity test results were in, and Nicole was nervous. She wanted Collette and me to be there when the results were read. Warren was in town from Dallas, and he would drive her and the baby to the doctor's office in her car.

"I'll meet you there," I said.

Collette was there when I arrived. Warren and Nicole drove up with the baby. He was in a good mood, because he was sure the baby was his.

When the nurse called Nicole's name to see Dr. Martin, we all went in the small office. The nurse frowned when see saw the whole delegation, but she brought extra chairs into the office so we could all sit. Nicole introduced Warren and Collette. He already knew me, because he was also my doctor.

The doctor had Nicole's folder in front of him. He frowned as he looked at the results.

"So Mr. Tiberdeaux isn't here?" Dr. Martin asked as he looked over his bifocals.

"That's right," we all said at the same time and held our breath.

"Please don't let him be the father," I think we were all praying.

"The test shows there is no way Mr. Tiberdeaux is the father of this baby girl," the doctor said, and we all breathed a collective sigh of relief. Our prayers had been answered. Warren was Jennifer's father. Warren started to shake Dr. Martin's hand. We had started to celebrate.

"And are you Mr. Warren Farmer?" the doctor asked, looking suspicious.

"Yes, Jennifer's father," Warren said proudly. "We are glad to have this behind us, Doc."

Dr. Martin cleared his throat nervously.

"I'm sorry, Mr. Farmer, but the test result shows there is no way you are the father of this baby girl, either." He paused. "Now, if you think the result is wrong, we can do another test," Dr. Martin said quickly, when he saw the look on our faces.

But no one heard him. We were all staring at Nicole, who sat with her head down. She was in shock.

"Is there some mistake? Or is this some kind of sick joke? Nicole?" Warren yelled at Nicole, but he got no answer. She was still staring at the floor. We could hear the disappointment in his voice.

Collette snatched the results out of the doctor's hand, read them, and threw them back on the desk. She looked at Nicole and screamed. "You slut! You bitch! You have two black men trying to do the right thing, and you pulled some shit like this." She was livid, and Dr. Martin didn't know what to say.

"I'm through with you. Amanda can make excuses for you if she wants, but I've had enough of your shit. You knew there was another man, you didn't have to put us through this. You need to be back in that institution." Collette was still screaming at Nicole.

Nicole was crying uncontrollably, still looking at the floor.

Collette snatched the door open to leave the room. The nurse and a staff member, who had been leaning on the door, eavesdropping, almost fell into the office. Dr. Martin was a bit embarrassed, but no one else seemed to care.

Warren was about to cry, he looked at Nicole and said, "Nicole?" His voice was trembling. And when he didn't get an answer, he left the room in tears.

The doctor wrote down a name of a family therapist and handed it to me.

"Have her make an appointment as soon as possible," he said. Then motioned to me to try to calm her.

"Come on, Nicole, I'll take you and Jennifer home. Everything will be all right," I said, helping Nicole gather Jennifer's things.

"This is just another day in the life of a flight attendant," I thought.

"Now, Amanda, you need to take care of yourself. Don't forget you're three months pregnant. I would like to see you next week," Dr. Martin reminded me.

"Thank you, doctor," was all I could muster up to say.

As we left the office, the staff was looking at us, trying not to laugh. They'd had their entertainment for the day.

When we got outside, Collette and Warren were already gone, and now Nicole started to talk. "I swear to you, Amanda, it was only one time. I wanted to forget about it. I met him on a flight, and he took me to dinner... and...brought me back to the hotel. That's when it happened. I had had too much to drink that night. I don't remember his name, and I don't know how to get in touch with him. It was just a one-night stand. You don't know how I've prayed every day that it wasn't him. Why do bad things always happen to me?" she wailed.

I didn't feel it was my place to judge her.

"Nicole, you have a beautiful daughter, Let's just forget about today and start from scratch," I said.

"Okay, but don't you leave me, don't stop being my friend." She sounded like a child.

"You know I'll always be your friend, no matter what," I assured her.

"Thank you, Amanda."

"You're welcome, friend." We looked at each other, and we both forced ourselves to smile.

This time, Collette refused to forgive Nicole, and she told the whole New Orleans Base about what happened at the doctor's office. Many flight attendants asked me if it was true.

"You know how Collette can exaggerate," I said, and left it at that.

Heaven knew that Nicole and the baby needed all the help they could get. She found a lady to keep little Jennifer while she worked. Since I was on maternity leave, Bob and I helped out with babysitting. Then Nicole called me one Sunday morning, sounding desperate.

"Amanda, will you and Bob do me a big favor? My babysitter is sick. Can y'all keep Jennifer while I work a two-day trip? I'll be back Monday afternoon."

It sounded like a reasonable request, and we liked keeping the baby. Nicole brought the baby to us, and we didn't see or hear from Nicole until ten days later! The baby was only four months old, and her mother hadn't left enough formula, baby food, or diapers. It was obvious that she was up to her old tricks again. When she finally showed up, I was glad Bob was at work.

"Girl, I needed a break. You just don't know how hard it is, raising a baby all by yourself. You understand, don't you? I'm sorry, please forgive me," she said, but I knew she didn't mean it.

I was so angry, I wanted to kick her ass. She was not a teenager, she was damn near thirty-two years old.

"I'm sorry, Nicole, but Bob won't let me keep Jennifer anymore. He doesn't want the responsibility. So don't ask me again." I couldn't bring myself to say anything more without getting fired up. I was dog-tired. The baby had kept us up three nights in a row, and Nicole couldn't care less that I was seven months pregnant.

Two months later, Nicole transferred to Atlanta and moved home to Lakeland, Florida, so her mother could help with Jennifer. Her father had died of a massive heart attack when she was six-months pregnant. She didn't go to his funeral, and she was finally able to explain to her mother why she hated the man. Nicole said that her mother had no idea about the sexual abuse. They became very close, and I was happy about that, because Nicole and Jennifer needed her.

We kept in touch, because Jennifer was my godchild.

On the day Nicole moved, my son, Malcolm Alex Mitchell, was born. Bob and I had discussed the name. I had told him about Malcolm's request, but it was up to him, of course. Since Malcolm was his best friend, and he missed him almost as much as I had, we agreed that the name would be appropriate. I was fully aware that I had a wonderful husband. He was as solid as a rock. He didn't hang out at bars "with the boys" or do drugs. If he wasn't at work or home, he was in the gym or playing tennis. There was never a time when I looked for him, and I couldn't find him. If he went out of town on business, he always called me. We loved and trusted each other very much.

When little Malcolm was four months old, I went back to flying. Collette had met a high school teacher in Atlanta, and they had been dating for about three months. Collette was transferring to Atlanta, and they were already talking about getting married. I tried to talk her into waiting and taking her time. I reminded her about her first husband, Roscoe Parker. When she divorced him, the judge ordered her to pay him alimony for six months, or less if he found a job. Of course he took the whole six months before finding a job.

"There is no harm in getting to know a guy well before getting married," I told her.

During Collette's last month in New Orleans, we decided to buddy-bid and fly the best trip in the base: a Los Angeles layover.

The first morning we signed in for our trip, there was a new flight attendant named Maci Bloome, who we had not seen in the New Orleans base before, and we thought we knew just about everyone there. She looked black, but she could pass for white. We couldn't tell. She didn't look Latin.

"She must have just transferred in, because she is senior to both of us," Collette whispered to me.

We decided to go with the flow, and sooner or later, she would let us know if she was a sister.

Sure enough, during the flight, after we had completed the cabin service, Maci came to the back where we were working. I was glad for the interruption, because I'd had enough of Collette talking about her new boyfriend.

"It sure is good to fly with some black girls for a change. You know, we have to stick together. I have been in the base for two months, and you all are the first sisters I've flown with," she said.

"Where did you transfer from?" I asked.

"Chicago, but I'm going to be commuting to LA, soon. My fiancé plays for the LA Rams. We plan to marry...uh...soon."

"Amanda's husband, Robert Mitchell, played for the New Orleans Saints and Atlanta. Maybe your fiancé knows him. Before that, she dated Malcolm Brown, he was a big star and a Heisman Trophy winner." Collette was telling all of my damn business.

Maci looked interested.

"I'll ask him." she smiled.

"What's your fiancé's name?" I asked. "I'll ask Bob if he knows him."

"Byron Tyson, he's been in the league thirteen years. I'm sure they know each other," she said. "He will be staying with me at the hotel. It sure is nice to meet you two."

When she went back to first class, Collette and I looked at each other.

"If he plays for the Rams, surely he has a house. Why is he staying at the hotel? Something's not right. You see she left in a hurry as soon as I told her about Bob and Malcolm?" Collette was trying to get into Maci's business, and I wasn't interested.

"Maybe, but she seems like a nice person, and I like her," I confessed, trying not to prejudge her.

"Oh, Amanda, you think everyone is nice and sweet. I'm telling you, something is rotten in Denmark."

Collette would have continued to speculate on Maci's relationship, but just then, a man came out of the lavatory leaving a smell that stank up the whole back galley. We had to leave. Some people are rotten inside!

Collette went to the front to drill Maci some more, and I went to find some lavatory deodorizer.

When we checked into the hotel in Los Angeles, Maci's fiancé wasn't there. However, he came later. We knew that, because her room was between Collette's and mine, and they screwed all night. We didn't get any sleep because of all that moaning and growling.

The next day, Maci was all excited, because Byron knew Bob. He went to the University of Maryland and played against Bob in college, as well as in the pros. He wanted to get together as soon as they got married and settled.

"Byron also knew Malcolm and attended his funeral. Byron said he was a great player and an extraordinary person. It's a shame he had to die so young.

He was the NFL union leader, and all the players liked and respected him," she said.

The last thing I wanted to do was talk about Malcolm. He still held a special place in my heart; so I changed the subject. "I'll talk with Bob. Maybe we can get together soon."

As soon as I got home, I asked my husband if he knew a player by the name of Byron Tyson.

Bob looked surprised.

"Yes, where did you meet him?" he asked.

"I didn't meet him, there is a flight attendant on our line who is engaged to him."

"Oh, is she white?" Bob questioned.

"No, well, not really, she's mixed. Her father is black, and her mother is German, I think that's what she said. You can't really tell what she is."

"That figures," he said. Bob didn't like to gossip. He dealt with facts, and he liked to get straight to the point. I waited for him to tell me everything, but I knew I would have to pull it out of him.

"And what else? Don't leave me hanging," I begged.

"First of all, I'm not a personal friend of Byron, and I'm sure he is a nice guy. But he was known throughout the league to date only white women. What I do know for a fact is," he paused, "I played against him in college, and we went to the a few Bowl games. Once, when the Saints played the Rams, he invited Malcolm, me, and a few other players to his crib after a few games. He was living with a white woman at the time. Malcolm didn't like Byron for some reason."

"The next year, when we played the Rams in LA, he invited us to a party he gave at some club. Malcolm had a dinner meeting that night, and he didn't go, so me and several of the other guys went." He stopped.

"I'm listening," I said. I wanted to know everything.

"Anyway, when we arrived, only Byron and six white women were there. His girlfriend had invited her friends, and even her mother. They were on us like we were pieces of meat. Jason Henderson asked Byron where all the sexy LA sisters were? And Byron said, and I quote; 'I don't deal with black women anymore. They have too many hang-ups, and they are so evil and vindictive. When you break up with them, they try to destroy you.' Well, 'Mo' Malone, the big linebacker from Jackson State, got right up in Byron's face and said, 'Niggah, who do you think you are, ain't your Mammy black?'

"We had to hold Mo off Byron. It was about to be a fight, so we left, dragging Mo with us, fussing and cussing. I haven't seen Byron since then, other than at games. And he was always with a white woman."

I immediately called Collette and told her what Bob said.

"I knew there was something funny about Maci and her fiancé. I'll find out more on Monday," Collette said.

"Please don't tell her what Bob said," I pleaded.

To put it bluntly: Collette had loose lips, and loose lips sink ships.

On Monday, Collette was poised to drill Maci on her relationship with Byron. Poor Maci didn't stand a chance.

"Why aren't you staying with your fiancé? He must have a big house with a swimming pool."

"Byron lives with a woman," Maci started to confess. "She thought they were going to get married, but when Byron told her that he was going to marry me, she got upset. She wanted twenty-five thousand dollars to leave. He offered her ten thousand."

"How long have they lived together?" Collette continued, while I just listened.

"Four years."

"That's a long time, maybe she deserves something, I don't know about twenty-five thousand." Collette was really prying. "That's a lot of money."

"Well, all I know is she will have to move her ass soon, because Byron and I are going to get married. It's over between them." Maci was sure of herself.

"Have you seen this woman?" Collette asked.

"No, I have never met her, but I know she's white trash," Maci said.

Collette and I looked at each other and encouraged her to continue. I tried as long as I could to stay out of it, but this was getting good.

"My friend who introduced us told me about her. She doesn't like her, and says she's a gold digger. Byron said he had given up on black women before he met me."

"Why?" I was curious, and beginning to understand why Malcolm didn't like him. I was beginning to feel the same.

"You know how some of us can be," she said sarcastically.

"No, I don't know, maybe you should tell us," I said.

"Well, petty, vengeful, stuff like that. Some black women can be so insecure."

"Is that relegated just to black women?" Now she was getting on my nerves. I didn't care for this conversation, so I was glad when a call bell rang in B-zone. It was my excuse to leave. She and Collette kept talking.

Two more call bells went off, and as soon as I reached B-zone, I saw the problem. A shirt and a pair of men's pants were hanging from the overhead bin. As I approached, several passengers were pointing to the man in 36B. I went to him, and he was wearing only his underwear, and I do not mean designer boxer shorts. I'm talking about white, one hundred percent cotton, Fruit-of-the-Loom briefs.

"I spilled Seven Up all over myself, and I just took my clothes off so they could dry before we land in LA. Is there a problem?" He sounded irritated.

"Excuse me, sir," I said.

I went for the first class flight attendants, because I didn't want them to miss this. They took a quick look, and we went back to the galley to decide how to handle the situation. Half of us said to leave him alone. It was obvious he wanted attention.

"Why feed his ego?" one flight attendant said.

The other half wanted him to put on his clothes. We all agreed that he wasn't well-endowed and there was nothing down there to look at.

The final decision was to let him stay in his underwear as long as he stayed in his seat and did not move around the cabin, because other passengers might feel uncomfortable. We took that proposition to the passenger, and he agreed. Since we didn't have a full cabin, and his clothes were not blocking anyone's view of the seatbelt sign or movie screen, we left him alone.

I returned to Collette and Maci. They were still talking about the same thing, so I went to make a fresh pot of coffee and cleaned up the galley. Less than twenty minutes later, call bells were going off again in B and C-zones. This time, the same passenger was walking around the cabin in his underwear, looking in every magazine rack. He walked past an elderly woman, who called him a "toothpick." He pulled down his briefs.

"Does this look like a toothpick?" he asked the lady.

Several crew members were in the aisle, responding to the call bells, and we couldn't believe he pulled down his underwear and exposed himself. It really wasn't much bigger than a toothpick. Before we could get to the flasher, a male passenger threw a blanket over him and tackled him to the floor. While two other flight attendants separated the two passengers, I grabbed the clothes from the overhead bin and told him to put them on.

"Now!" I screamed. "And there will be a special service agent meeting the flight when we land in Los Angeles. If you cannot keep your clothes on and stay seated, the captain will land in Phoenix and have you removed."

The flasher finally realized the seriousness of his action, returned to his seat, and didn't move for the rest of the flight. The police met the plane in Los Angeles and escorted him off. They took him straight to the hospital mental ward for evaluation. A red flag would go up by his name every time he tried to make a reservation on any Big E Airlines flights.

Collette and Maci talked through the entire incident. They weren't even aware that there had been a problem on the flight until we were in the hotel van.

After every trip, Byron met Maci at the hotel, and he had no interest in meeting us. They eloped to Las Vegas and were married in a small chapel before our last trip. Before he left, Byron had given his ex-live-in-girlfriend an ultimatum: "You have four days to get out of my house and take all your things with you."

While Maci and Byron were in Las Vegas, the girlfriend brought in some of her friends, and they destroyed his house: They made a fire in the fireplace and burned his clothes. What they didn't burn was cut up or bleached. They broke every mirror and dish in the house, and destroyed his black art. Some pieces were worth thousands of dollars. As if that weren't enough, they spray painted the walls, cut a hole in his water bed, and left the water in the bathtubs running.

A neighbor saw water running out of the front door and down the walkway and called the police.

When Maci and Byron returned, they got the shock of their lives. There was over seventy-five thousand dollars worth of damage. Byron tried to tell the police who did it. He wanted to press charges. However, when the Los Angeles police learned the culprit was a white woman that Byron had lived with for four years and dumped, they felt he got what he deserved.

"We hope you have good insurance," one officer commented.

Maci was in tears, telling us the story on our last trip. After what Byron had said about black women, how could we feel sorry for him?

That white woman had come up with ways to get his ass that no black woman had ever thought of.

"Now, who was evil and vindictive?" we wanted to ask him!

Thirty-three

1984

When little Malcolm was six months old, Bob decided it was time to own his own business. He had been talking with some ex-football players who had opened up fast-food franchises, and Bob was more than interested. A Burger King franchise sounded like a good idea to me. We had plenty of money. The money that Malcolm had willed to me had grown into quite a nest egg.

Bob started on the paperwork for ownership of a Burger king franchise. Once we were approved, we had to wait for a site.

When our son was one year old, Burger King Corporation offered us a franchise in Atlanta.

I was excited about moving to Atlanta. I would be reunited with all my old friends.

Collette had moved to Atlanta and wasted no time marrying her high school teacher, over our objections. We stayed with her and her new husband while we were in Atlanta, house hunting.

Bob and I settled on a beautiful home in an upper-middle-class neighborhood in southwest Atlanta, not far from Sarah and Collette. We sold our home in New Orleans and moved to Atlanta in August of 1984.

Flying out of the Atlanta base took some getting used to. Flight attendants in Atlanta lived in the fast lane. The New Orleans base was so small that everybody knew everybody. The Atlanta base was huge, with over three thousand Big E flight attendants, making it the largest such base in the world. As a result, you never flew with the same person twice. Also, these flight attendants were different. They were very cliquish, but the cliques were not based on race or color. Most were diverse, multi-cultural groups that didn't compete or dislike each other. All the groups got along and flew together. They partied hard and shared information. Since Sarah and Michele were part of a clique, Collette and I naturally gravitated toward it and became a part of theirs.

It took me about a year to get used to Atlanta, but Michele and Sarah were a big help. Collette was in the midst of her second divorce: She still hadn't learned. Her school teacher husband had gotten one of his students pregnant. He had been fired and almost went to jail. It turned out the student was eighteen, and had admitted to having consensual sex with her teacher. As soon as the divorce was final, Collette's ex-husband married the student and moved to California. Collette was distraught for a while, but as usual, she landed on her feet.

Bob bought another Burger King restaurant, and he was working hard. Business was good. The restaurants stayed open until two a.m. on Friday and Saturday nights, so he worked late and was hardly home. I started hanging out at Sarah's house with the other girls, smoking weed. Most of the girls used cocaine. However, cocaine was never my drug of choice. I didn't like putting it up my nose.

The parties at Sarah's were my secret, because Bob had never used drugs. We had a housekeeper to watch little Malcolm, and I was free to come and go as I pleased. I would make it home before midnight, shower, and be in bed by the time he got home. Several times, Bob came home early and asked a lot of questions. We argued for the first time in our marriage. Soon, I started lying and pretending I was going to work. I would park my car in the employee parking lot and have Sarah pick me up.

There were never any men at Sarah's house, just women coming and going. If Sarah was on a trip, there was always someone at her house. She left an extra key underneath the outside flower pot. We would cook, eat, drink wine, listen to music, play cards, smoke weed, and use cocaine, if there was any. Her house was a party place. If we were too stoned to drive home, we would spend the night. If a man was there, it was only to deliver drugs or pizza, and then he had to leave. Every now and then, one of the guys from the ramp or baggage service would stop by with some good stuff, and he would try to stay and party with us. He would beg to stay.

"I can go pick up a few of my buddies, and we can have a real party tonight," he would plead.

"No, thank you, we are doing quite well by ourselves. Now, get your ass out of here," someone would say, and we would pool our money together, pay him, and send him on his way.

Some of the women would get stoned and decide to go to a nightclub or out to eat. I never did that. I couldn't take a chance on anyone seeing me and telling my husband. Bob had become a well-respected businessman and community leader. I felt bad lying to him, and I would never do anything to jeopardize my marriage or embarrass my family. Bob stopped questioning me. He liked Sarah, and he thought she was very "level-headed."

"A good person for you to hang out with," he commented about her.

He didn't mind me spending time at her house. Like most people, he had no concept of the real Sarah.

Thirty-four

1985

In the Atlanta base, you needed someone to show you the ropes, and you had to learn fast. For example, you could go down on the ramp and buy anything you wanted, from drugs to all kinds of jewelry, clothes, cameras, watches, you name it; even a gun.

One day, Sarah and I were flying together, and she took me down on the ramp so she could buy a "dime bag" of coke for the layover.

Ramp employees kept all kinds of stuff in their lockers. If they didn't have what you wanted, they could get it.

It all started when a passenger checked his bags at the ticket counter. If it looked like he was carrying something of value, the ticket agents put some kind of mark on the bag to alert the ramp guys. If they had time, they would search the bag and steal anything of value. If they found cash, jewelry, or especially drugs, everyone got a piece of the action. Passengers never reported drugs missing from their bags. If they reported other valuables missing, it couldn't be proven that Big E employees were responsible.

One of the ramp guys told us that they got most of their drugs from passengers' luggage. He promised to bring some by Sarah's house when we returned. I told Bob I was on a three-day trip when I was really on a two-day.

When Sarah and I returned from our two-day trip, I left my car at the airport and rode home with Sarah. Sure enough, our ramp friend brought over some good Colombia marijuana and cocaine. He also wanted to stay, but we made him leave. About six flight attendants were at Sarah's house, and we partied until well after midnight. Our group could have gone on forever, until Rhonda Bulluck, a good friend, and one of the sweetest people you would ever want to meet, decided she needed to drive home. It was late, and we had been doing drugs and drinking since mid-afternoon. Rhonda lived in North Atlanta. We tried to convince her to spend the night, but she said that she had to get home to pack for a trip to Mexico. She rolled two joints to take with her. We weren't really worried, because she had driven home late many times before. Only this time she didn't make it. She fell asleep at the wheel, and her car went off the overpass bridge. Her neck was broken in two places, and she died instantly.

We got the news early that morning when we all were awakened by two police officers ringing Sarah's doorbell and pounding on the front door. We all got up very quickly: Some of us were in our nightgowns with rollers in our hair; some were still in our street clothes, and one girl who arrived late was in full uniform. We were all dazed and hungover. We tried to make sure no signs of our partying were visible, but shit was everywhere.

First, one officer asked us a lot of questions. The other officer was taking notes on a small pad.

"Do any of you know a Miss Rhonda Bulluck?" The officer asked no one in particular.

"Of course we do, she's our friend and co-worker." Sarah spoke up.

"Was she here last night?"

"Yes."

"Did any of you see her use drugs or drink alcohol while she was here... uh...last night?" The officer continued his interrogation.

"No sir, Rhonda didn't use drugs, at least not to my knowledge. I have never seen her use drugs, and she certainly didn't use drugs here last night. We held a prayer meeting." Sarah said, and we all nodded in agreement.

The officers looked around the room and saw all the beer cans, wine bottles, and butts in the ashtrays.

"So she was here last night at your...uh...prayer meeting, you say. Right?" He was being sarcastic. "Do y'all usually drink and smoke at these...uh... prayer meetings?

"That depends." Sarah responded, just as sarcastically.

"Well what time did she leave?" he asked.

"After midnight, around two o'clock, I think." Sarah answered again, and we all agreed. "Now, what is this all about, Officer? Is Rhonda in some kind of trouble?"

The officers looked at each other, and the one taking notes spoke for the first time.

"I'm sorry to inform you, ladies," he hesitated, "your friend was killed last night. We think she fell asleep at the wheel, and her car went over the bridge at Interstate 285 and 75. There were no skid marks."

We all screamed, and Collette fainted. Dominique Van Stinchcomb went into shock.

"Could there be some mistake, Officers? She was just here," Sarah asked, wanting confirmation. We were all crying and comforting each other.

Both officers shook their heads. For the first time, I think, they felt our pain.

"The reason we asked you ladies these questions is because we found marijuana in the car. Did she say she was going straight home, or did she make a stop?"

We shook our heads to say we didn't know. We were only half -listening. All we could think of was that our friend was gone, just like that!

The other officer said, "I'm sorry to bring you ladies such bad news." And they started to leave, but turned back to us and said, "Oh! By the way, we found these in her car after the accident." He reached into his shirt pocket and pulled out the two joints Rhonda had rolled and taken with her when she left.

We stared at the joints. Rhonda could never roll worth a damn, but then, neither could I.

"If any of you think of anything, I'll leave my card. Please give us a call. Again, we are sorry to bring the bad news."

When there was no answer, he put his card on the coffee table, along with the two joints, and left. Looking at the joints made me feel sick to my stomach.

Sarah turned on the morning news, and there was Rhonda's car, all smashed up. We could hardly recognize it.

The reporter said, "An Elite World Airlines flight attendant was killed early this morning when her car went off the over-pass at Interstate 285 and Interstate 75. Officers said there were no skid marks, and she could have fallen asleep at the wheel. Her name is being withheld, pending the notification of next of kin. The accident is still under investigation."

We all sat on the sofa in the living room, and Sarah made coffee. It was time for damage control. We made a pledge to say we were having our regular prayer meeting, and we never used drugs. Then Sarah called the police captain she dated on and off and told him about Rhonda. "Two officers came over to my house and said they found marijuana in her car." Sarah told him through her tears.

"Let me call the boss, and I'll be right over," he responded. We all knew the captain still had a thing for Sarah, and Rhonda had a brief affair with a high-ranking police officer, but we couldn't remember his name. He was married at the time, and they had been very secretive.

We started to clean up, acting more like robots than humans.

When Sarah's friend arrived, we all sat at the table and he told us to stick to our story, and he would take care of the rest. "Maybe we should think about cooling things down for a while. We have officers watching this house to protect you ladies. They saw Rhonda's car when it left around two o'clock this morning. We sent those officers over, I'm sorry if they gave y'all a hard time. We have to investigate to see if a crime was committed," he said.

When the article about Rhonda's accident came out in the newspaper the following day, it didn't mention drugs being found in her car. It said she had been at a prayer meeting at a co-worker's home, and apparently felt asleep at the wheel, because there were no skid marks. We were all glad Sarah's boyfriend was able to quash the real story.

Besides, it was not in the best interest of the police department to pick a fight with Big E flight attendants. We were three-thousand strong, and had screwed our way to the top of the city's political scene; from the police officers on the street, to the commander, to the city council, and to the mayor's office. We had flight attendants who had slept with state and U.S. senators, and everyone in between. They hadn't nicknamed us "Sky Sluts" for nothing, but we really did have friends in high places.

On top of all that, when a flight attendant in Atlanta got into this kind of trouble, the police first called the airline before releasing the story. It would have been bad for business if passengers found out there was even the slightest possibility that their flight crew was high on drugs.

Besides, the chief knew where we got most of our drugs.

I had a personal stake in the outcome of this matter. I was supposed to be on a three-day trip. If my husband found out I had lied, my marriage would have been on the rocks, and that was something I could never allow to happen.

Over two hundred flight attendants attended Rhonda's funeral in Selma, Alabama. We were asked to wear our uniforms. Sarah and Michele spoke on behalf of all of us while we wept. Flight attendants nearly filled the small Baptist church.

She was from a nice, country family. They reminded me of my family back home. It was hard to look Mrs. Bulluck, Rhonda's mother, in the eye. I wore dark glasses, because I didn't want those eyes to see through me.

After the funeral, Mrs. Bulluck questioned us.

"The police insinuated my Rhonda may have been using drugs, and that's why she had the accident. I know that's a lie. My baby would never use drugs. Y'all were with her, y'all spent a lot of time with her, you ladies were the last to see her alive; was she using that cocaine stuff?" She was in tears.

Sarah spoke. "Mrs. Bulluck, believe me, we did spend a lot of time with Rhonda, we loved her, and we have never seen her use any kind of drugs. I don't think she knew what cocaine looked like. She was at a prayer meeting at my house. She was very religious."

I couldn't believe how Sarah could lie so well on the church grounds. She didn't bat an eye as she spoke. But her lies made Mr. and Mrs. Bulluck very happy.

"Yes, we raised her in the church," Mr. Bulluck said proudly.

They had prepared a repast for us, with country food, such as fried chicken, collard greens, pinto beans, candied yams, and every kind of cobbler you could name. Our guilt wouldn't let us eat; we were emotionally drained.

Back home, I was a little despondent. I needed to tell my husband the truth, and he wasn't making it easy. He was so sweet, because he felt I was upset only over Rhonda's death.

"I'm sorry, baby, I've been so busy with the restaurants. Let's take some time off and go to New Orleans for a few days. Just you and me. We can leave Malcolm with Mrs. Price," he suggested one evening. Mrs. Price, our housekeeper, loved staying with Malcolm.

It sounded like a great idea. I needed to get away. If we were alone, it might be easier for me to explain things.

The trip to New Orleans turned out to be just what I needed. Bob had ordered a bottle of my favorite champagne and a dozen long-stemmed, red roses. They were in the room when we arrived. He opened the champagne and made a toast. "To us!"

Then he reached into his pocket and pulled out a small gift for me. I was so surprised and sad, because I didn't have anything for him. I could have picked up something on my layover, but I hadn't even thought about it.

I opened the box, and it was an eternal ring with diamonds all around it. It was so beautiful, I wanted to cry and scream at the same time. I jumped on him, and suddenly, I was excited. It was like the first time we made love in my old house. I was tearing his clothes off. I needed it right then and there. We made love that night, and when he awoke up the next morning, I was already down on him, doing it the way he liked it. He just couldn't resist me.

We took a shower together and I was ready to go down on him again. He pulled me up and said, "This is great, but a man can't live on love alone. We need to eat. Let's get dressed and go downstairs for Sunday brunch. If I had known all this, I would have spent some time in the gym before the trip. Oh, not that I'm complaining." He smiled and popped me on my butt.

I didn't want to go out. I wanted to stay in the hotel room with my husband for the entire three days. However, I was hungry, too.

Thirty-five

1986

Exactly two months after our New Orleans getaway, I woke up late to find that Bob and little Malcolm were gone. I stumbled out of bed, and I was so sick that I couldn't make it to the bathroom before vomiting. Then there was this funny feeling. If a woman had ever been pregnant, she knew the feeling. I ran to the calendar. I hadn't seen a period in two months. I was such a wreck when we left for New Orleans, I had forgotten my birth-control sponges. I had been careless before, and nothing had happened, so I hadn't thought much about it.

The damned marijuana had fried my brains!

"*Don't panic! Don't panic!*" I kept telling myself.

I called my doctor, and he agreed to see me right away. Dr. Duncan only confirmed what I already knew: I was two months pregnant. After the exam, he asked me to come into his office. When I was seated, he said, "Amanda, what is the problem? Why are you so stressed out?"

"I just don't know if Bob wants anymore children. I was supposed to use protection, and I got careless." Tears started to fill my eyes.

"Amanda, most men don't want anymore children. I didn't want any, but when my wife became pregnant, there was nothing I could do but accept it, that's part of being a man. Believe me, I know Bob. He's a good man, and you will be fine. It's normal for women to get emotional when they become pregnant."

I knew he meant well, but I didn't feel any better.

I couldn't help myself, I cried all the way home. Not only had I not told the truth about smoking weed at Sarah's house all the time, Bob thought I always used protection. A long time ago, he said it would be okay with him if little Malcolm was an only child.

As soon as I got home, I called Bob. I was crying so hard. "Can you come home now? We need to talk."

"Are you all right?" He was concerned.

"Yes! No! I mean yes." I was all choked up.

Bob dropped everything and drove home as fast as he could.

I met him at the door. I grabbed him, put my arms around him, and held on tightly. He had to pry my arms from around him.

"Amanda, honey, what is wrong with you?" He led me to the sofa and sat me down.

"I'm pregnant," I said, and the tears poured like rain. "I don't know what happened, I was using the sponge, but when we went to New Orleans, I...I... just forgot. I know I was careless, and it's all my fault."

I hoped he understood what I said, because I didn't want to try to say all that again.

He started to say something, then hesitated. I could see he was trying to calm himself down. He was angry with me. He got up, walked to the window, looked out for a minute, then turned to me. "You're pregnant? That's all? You weren't raped? No one is dead? You didn't kill anyone? Our son isn't missing or in the hospital? The house didn't catch on fire. Just, you're pregnant? Right?"

I stopped crying and looked at him. What was he talking about? I was confused.

He spoke again, this time his voice was a little louder.

"I almost killed myself driving home. I thought someone had broken into the house and hurt you, or Malcolm had been hurt at school, or someone in the family had died. Excuse me, but I don't understand how you being pregnant is the end of the world. It's not like we live in the poorhouse and can't afford another child."

"You are the one who said you didn't want anymore children. I mean, you did say Malcolm could be an only child. You wanted me to use birth control. And why are you yelling at me?" Everything came tumbling out at once.

He took two deep breaths, and his voice was a little softer this time. "Okay, I'm sorry, I thought something bad had happened to you or Malcolm. There are worse things in the world than you being pregnant. Maybe I said I didn't want anymore children, but if I really didn't want anymore children, I would have had a vasectomy. Amanda, I don't depend on you to determine whether or not we have anymore children. That's as much my responsibility as yours. I'm a big boy, and I understand that accidents happen. We had a wonderful time in New Orleans, and if a baby is the result of it, then it's a blessing. He or she was conceived out of love." Bob took a deep breath, as he watched my face.

I couldn't believe what I was hearing. What would make me think my husband would dump me because I was pregnant? I must have been losing my mind. I felt stupid!

I went to him and put my arms around his waist. He held me tightly.

"Thank you, and I love you," I whispered.

"So, I guess I'm going to be a father again. I've got to get used to the idea." Then he held me at arm's length. "Uh...are you sure? Have you seen Dr. Duncan? How do you feel?" he asked, all in one breath.

"I feel fine, I was a little sick this morning, and I have already seen Dr. Duncan. He said to tell you hello."

"We can talk about it some more tonight. If you're okay, I have to get back to the restaurant and do today's sales. Why don't you go over to your friend Sarah and tell her I miss talking to...uh...her." He stopped himself and started upstairs.

"Wait a minute, when did you talk to Sarah? When?" I wanted to know.

He stopped in his tracks. "Look, baby, it's not like I was checking up on you. But I did call Sarah several months ago looking for you. I knew you spent a lot of time at her house."

"What did she tell you?"

"She said you were just hanging out with the girls, and sometimes you smoked a little weed, and you didn't want me to know because I don't do drugs. She said she was always looking out for you, and I believed her." He hesitated. "I might as well tell you the whole story." He started back down the stairs.

"You know Karl Williamson?" he asked.

"Yes, the police officer. A big guy, he comes by Sarah's house a lot. He's her friend," I told him.

"Well, he's also my homeboy. He's from North Carolina, and we played football together in college. He comes by the restaurant and reports to me about what you all do at Sarah's house."

"And what did he say?" I had my head down, and felt a little ashamed I hadn't told him myself.

"Don't look so guilty. He said that you are always over there, and he's only seen you smoke a little weed, like Sarah said. He had never seen you snort cocaine. Karl said it's just a hangout for flight attendants. He knew you all by name and said there were never any men in the house. He told me he wanted to stay and just talk with y'all, but Sarah ran him away several times.

"I have driven by there and seen your car. You could have told me, I don't mind you hanging with your friends and smoking marijuana. I wouldn't want you doing coke, and I didn't want Sarah running a cathouse. I've been so busy with the restaurant, and I didn't want you waiting up for me every night. I trust you, Amanda, and I know you love me. I just felt a little insecure. I needed to know there was no other man." He was obviously relieved to have everything out in the open.

He was apologizing to *me?* I needed to be the one apologizing. He always knew. My husband was a better person than I was.

"Sarah told me she picked you up at the airport after Rhonda's accident. She knew you were on a three-day trip and would be very upset when you got the news. Oh, one more thing." He paused. "She suggested we take the trip to New Orleans. I didn't want to take the time off from the restaurants. She felt you needed to get away, and we needed to spend some time alone together." He smiled.

I felt great; a load had been lifted off my shoulders. Sarah had lied for me. She knew I couldn't tell Bob that I was at her house the night Rhonda died, when I was supposed to be on a three-day trip. I forgot about being pregnant. I felt horny.

"Are you sure that's all?" I flirted, as I took a good look at my husband for the first time in over a year. He was so handsome, still in good shape, and he still had those beautiful eyes. We both were thirty-five, and he was the best-looking thirty-five-year-old man I had ever seen in my life.

I started walking towards him, and he started to back up. I put my arms around his waist, then I started to unbutton his shirt and kiss his chest. He tried to push me off him, saying, "I know that look, and I don't have time. I've got to get back to work...umm...that feels good, can this wait until tonight... umm?"

It was too late. I had already unbuttoned his shirt and was starting to unbuckle his belt. I knew he couldn't resist. He picked me up and carried me upstairs. When we got to the bed, I said, "I want to be on top."

He obliged, and I attacked him. He didn't stand a chance.

I'm glad we had that time together, because after that, it was three months before we were able to make love again.

Thirty-six

Two days later, I went to Sarah's house to tell her the good news. As soon as I walked in the door, the smell of marijuana made me sick to my stomach. I made it to the bathroom just in time. Sarah was right behind me.

"Girl, are you all right?" That's what flight attendants are trained to say.

After I threw up everything inside of me, she got me a glass of water and a cold face towel.

"I'm pregnant, and it's all your fault. If you hadn't suggested to Bob that we go to New Orleans for a few days, this never would have happened."

"I didn't tell you to go down there and screw your brains out," she laughed. "So he told you everything?"

"Yep, he told me everything." I took a seat on the tub, and she sat on her vanity stool.

"Don't be mad, Amanda. You and Dee Dee are my best friends. Collette doesn't know how to be a friend. After all these years, she's still learning. But you're like my little sister, and you're married to a good man who loves you and knows how to love. I wanted to make sure he was okay with you spending so much time over here and smoking weed. Because if he wasn't, you would have had to carry your ass home, and I mean it." She smiled, but I knew she meant every word.

"And you knew Karl is Bob's friend?" I asked.

"Yes, Karl told me, and he didn't want you to know."

"Thank you, Sarah, I love you. Thanks for being my friend." I gave her a big hug.

"You're welcome, little bitch. We all want what you've got: a beautiful home, a man who loves you, and kids. Oh, don't forget the maid." We both had to laugh.

"I have never heard you mention a husband or kids before," I said.

"You know, Wendell is still the love of my life. He has to do twenty-eight years before he's eligible for parole. Until then, I'll quietly carry on. I'll tell you this, but you can't tell anyone. You promise?" I promised and she continued, "I'm holding some money for him. When he gets out, we will be able to live comfortably in the Bahamas."

I didn't ask for any details. I figured she would tell me when she was ready.

"I know you wrote him a letter about me when I was on the brink of despair. Whoring around was just my way of coping. He told me we had a future together, and I'm the only reason he could survive twenty-eight years in prison. Those words saved my life. Thank you, Amanda."

"You're welcome, and thank you for telling Bob I was on a three-day trip, and don't forget about those phone calls to Malcolm," I said.

"What phone calls?" She was trying to play dumb.

"They were on those tapes he left me."

"So I guess we're even," she conceded.

Sarah had turned the air conditioner on to blow the smoke out of the house, and we left the bathroom, arm-in-arm. She walked me to my car.

"Are you sure you feel all right? I can drive you home. I don't want anything to happen to you, besides, I want to be a godmother," she said.

"I'll be fine and you will be a godmother," I said, and drove off.

From that day on, I never could stand the smell of marijuana and I never used it again.

The next two months were holy hell, I couldn't keep anything down. I threw up my breakfast, lunch, and dinner. I had to stay in bed most of the time because I was too weak to go anyplace.

A couple of weeks later, Sarah came over and brought me a pot of spaghetti. I ate it, and two minutes later, it came up. Then Collette, who was between husbands, brought me some homemade soup. I really hated her cooking, but I was so hungry I ate it, and I promptly threw it up. Dee Dee brought me some frozen Chicago pizza. I put it in the freezer because I liked it too much to waste. Michele and Barbara Ann stopped by for a visit. Barbara Ann was eight months pregnant with her third child, a girl. She had gained eighty pounds. She waddled into my kitchen and started eating everything in sight.

"Don't eat my Chicago pizza," I yelled from the sofa, but it was too late. The microwave was going.

"It will just go to waste, you can't hold anything down. No use wasting good food." She waddled out of the kitchen like a duck, with her plate and her mouth both full of pizza.

I was losing weight, and the baby was not growing. Dr. Duncan was worried, so he sent me to Emory University Hospital for an amniocenteses.

He wanted to see if the baby was healthy and growing. The test would also tell the sex of the baby.

Bob and Sarah went with me to Emory. When they brought out the long needle, Bob bolted from the room, and Sarah fainted. I was left alone in the room with the doctor and nurse.

The test came back negative; the baby was healthy, and it was a girl. I was very happy. I liked the idea of having a daughter, but Bob was worried. He said he knew nothing about little girls. When I told my grandmother about having a girl, she swore that was the reason I was so sick.

"Girls are hard on the body because they take everything from you. Those two girls I had were worse than having nine boys. Now, baby, don't reach for anything above your head, you will wrap the umbilical cord around the baby's neck." She told me all this when I was pregnant with Little Malcolm. Of course, she had also told all this to the pregnant mothers of her grandchildren and great-grandchildren.

I started to feel better at the beginning of my sixth month, and by the seventh month, I was eating everything in sight. I had Sarah cook me a big pot of spaghetti every week. I even got used to Collette's homemade soup.

Well into my eighth month, Bob was inducted into Duke University's Hall of Fame. We flew to Raleigh-Durham for the weekend. They held a cocktail party before the induction banquet, and I was camped out by the appetizers, because I was hungry and too big to mingle. On top of that, my feet were swollen.

I caught a glimpse of my husband talking to a very attractive, tall woman. Her six-inch heels almost put her eye-to-eye with Bob. They were having a very intimate conversation. She was touching his hand, and I could tell she was making a play for him.

"Some old college girlfriend," I guessed.

I wiggled my body off the seat and waddled my way toward Bob.

He saw me coming and met me halfway.

"Honey, this is Mary Catherine Woodward, an old friend of mine."

"We were engaged once," she added.

Bob said nothing.

"Pleased to meet you," I said, and shook her hand.

I remembered who she was. She broke my husband's heart. He had shown me her picture once. She looked better with age.

"Mary Catherine is the Durham district attorney now," Bob said.

"Oh," I heard myself say.

I felt like a fat pig next to this woman. Where was her lawyer husband for whom she left Bob? Then I noticed she wasn't wearing a wedding ring.

"You are a very lucky woman," she said, looking at Bob instead of me.

"Thank you, but I don't need you to tell me. I already know." I said, moving closer to Bob, protecting my territory.

She dumped him, so her loss was my gain.

This woman made me feel a little jealous, until my husband made his Hall of Fame induction speech. He looked over at me, and said, proudly, "I would like to thank my beautiful wife, Amanda, for keeping me grounded and humble, and for being my best friend. As you can see, we will be welcoming our second child into the world soon, a daughter."

I wanted to run up there and throw my arms around him. What did I do in life to deserve this wonderful man? I didn't feel fat anymore. I looked at Mary Catherine, and she had her head down.

Back in our hotel room, I asked Bob about her. He said she never married the lawyer. He left her for another woman, and she never married. She had contacted him several times at work when we were living together and wanted to get back with him. But he was in love with me by then, and he didn't give it a second thought.

"What were you two talking about?" My curiosity was palpable.

"Do you really want to know?" he asked, without looking at me.

"Yes, you two looked cozy from where I was sitting," I said. I knew he didn't want to talk about it.

"She asked if I could meet her later for a drink at her place and talk," he said, very casually.

"What did you say?" I was ready to claw her eyes out.

"What do you think?" He paused. "I told her I was a married man with another baby due any day now. We have nothing to talk about over drinks. Besides, she never loved me. She wanted a big house, new car, new clothes; she was spending my money as fast as I made it."

"Why did you stay with her?" I asked, because my husband was a smart man.

"Oh, I didn't know any better back then. I thought a man was supposed to buy a woman things," he said, only half-interested.

He started to undress. I didn't move from the bed.

"She's very attractive," I said, hoping Bob hadn't noticed.

"Yes, she is, but not half as attractive as you." He looked at me. Sensing my insecurity, he added, "I would take fifty of her to make one of you." That answer surprised me.

I couldn't imagine where I would be without this man. He had his back to me. I walked over and put my arms around him; well, as far around as my stomach would allow.

"Did you mean what you said in your speech, about me keeping you grounded and humble?" I asked.

He turned to me and said, "Amanda, you came from a very wealthy family, yet you don't let that go to your head. You taught me that money isn't everything. It's what that person brings to the table mentally, spiritually, and emotionally. I hate to imagine where I would be without you." I didn't interrupt him, because I knew he still had something to say.

"I was thinking today: If Malcolm had lived, we wouldn't be together." He took a deep breath and continued, "When I went to see him before he died, he only wanted to talk about you. You were his joy. He told me you didn't know who he was when you all first met."

"True," I had to admit, but I was very uncomfortable talking about Malcolm. He would always hold a piece of my heart.

"He said you never asked him for anything, and you brought so much joy into his life, because you loved him for the person he was. Malcolm laughed when he told me how he had to sneak behind your back and buy you a car for your birthday, because you never wanted anything. I could never buy Mary Catherine enough of anything." He paused. "Amanda, do you realize that you have never asked me to buy you anything? You are a special lady. I'm lucky to have found you, and I love you very much. I would never do anything to jeopardize what we have," he said, and I think his voice wobbled a little.

"That's strange, I was just thinking the same thing," I said. "Only I'm the lucky one."

"I guess we are on the same wavelength." He put his arms around me and unzipped my dress, exposing my 38D bust. I was proud of my breasts for the first time in my life. He kissed each one and moved his tongue up my neck, nibbled on my chin and kissed my lips, softly at first, and then more demanding.

"Now, you must admit, Mary Catherine is beautiful," I said, teasing him.

"Ummm, yes she is," it was his turn to tease me. "But no woman turns me on the way my wife is turning me on right now. You think we can...you know?" he asked, kissing my neck and unsnapping my bra. Then he stopped and looked at me. "Is it too close to your due date?"

I didn't want him to stop. I wanted to make love to this man now more than ever.

"Dr. Duncan said we could."

"I'll be gentle." That was all he needed to say. I would have been surprised if he had said anything else.

Thirty-seven

September 7, 1986

When I delivered our baby girl a little before midnight, I had gained sixty pounds!

We named our daughter Roberette Louise, after both of us.

I was very happy, but I wasn't about to leave the hospital until my tubes were tied. I didn't want another pregnancy.

I had seven months to lose that weight, because for the third time, Collette was getting married. He was an insurance salesman named Mason Young. She was planning a big wedding with seven bridesmaids. We told her to use common sense. First, she didn't have the money to spend on a wedding. Second, we were too old to be bridesmaids; and third, the bridesmaids' dresses were too skimpy. We would look like prostitutes.

She was too busy to listen; she was in another world, and this was what she wanted. She borrowed more than fifteen thousand dollars from the credit union for the wedding. Her wedding dress alone set her back another five thousand.

She was inviting three hundred people, mostly flight attendants. Other than co-workers, she didn't know that many people, and she didn't have any family. Barbara Ann flat-out refused to be a bridesmaid. She hadn't lost any of the weight from her pregnancy. So that left six: Dee Dee, Michele, three of her fiancé's sisters, and me. Sarah was the Maid of Honor. Our dresses cost four hundred and fifty dollars each for a yard of cloth that barely covered our butts. If it was not for our long friendship and the fact that she was marrying a good man, we would have said, "Hell no! Just go to the justice of the peace, bitch."

On the wedding day, we somehow managed to squeeze into our dresses and walk down the aisle. Mine was held up with pins, and they were sticking me with every step because I refused to wear it as tightly as Collette wanted, and I still had baby fat.

The wedding was beautiful, but it left Collette deeply in debt.

On May 10, 1987, exactly three weeks after Collette's wedding, when Roberette was only eight months old, my beloved grandmother died at the age of eighty-nine. She had been born in 1898, the granddaughter of slaves. She caught pneumonia in March while attending the funeral of one of her sons. It was very cold for March, and we tried to convince her not to walk to the burial, but she insisted. She had taken his death very hard, and seemed never able to recover. Sarah and Dee Dee came to her funeral. They had grown to love my grandmother.

My grandfather started to go downhill after her death. They had been married for seventy-two years, and had always lived in the Callaway home.

He had sold the funeral-and-casket companies five years earlier to a big conglomerate of investors who were buying up small funeral homes. He lived independently, with only their housekeeper of twenty-five years, until his death in 1992 at the age of ninety-nine.

He left us all very wealthy, and the Callaway Estates started to change for the first time in ninety years. We kept the house unchanged, with all of its original furniture, and started filing papers to make the house a historic site, and maybe a museum. My two brothers built homes on the estate, changed the landscaping, and built a new iron fence around the grounds, marking the end of an era.

Thirty-eight

1991

The nineties ushered in a new breed of flight attendant. Our lifestyle changed, and the change began with three words: "Random Drug Testing." It all started in 1989, when the Department of Transportation, or DOT, and the Federal Aviation Administration, or FAA, required all frontline airline employees to be drug tested: All fight attendants, pilots, and direct-service employees were subject to random testing. The Big E Airline gave its employees six months to get clean or turn themselves in and get treatment at the company's expense. Some did neither and paid the price. I had given up drugs years ago when I was pregnant with my daughter, but I worried about my friends.

The FBI and the FAA raided the lockers of some Big E ramp employees and found stolen goods, drugs, guns, and one hundred to one hundred fifty thousand dollars in cash. Over fifty Big E employees were fired, including ramp workers, ticket agents, skycaps, and customer-service agents in Atlanta. Then the investigation moved to Miami, where ten ramp employees were fired. The trail took investigators into South America. The newspaper said that the drugs were boarded in the cargo bin in Colombia and transferred in Miami by ramp agents to Big E flights to Atlanta. The ramp employees created a special compartment in the aircraft cargo bins, just for drugs.

This shook our world, and we realized the airline meant business and that everybody had better shape up.

Also that year, flight attendants took on a new fight. Every time one of us had the U.S. Surgeon General on our flight, we would ask him to do something about the smoking on our aircraft. When he hadn't acted fast enough, flight attendants from each airline, went to Washington to testify before Congress. There were talks of filing a lawsuit. It was the first time flight attendants had come together as a group. It seemed the powers-that-be knew we meant business, because later that year, the FAA and DOT banned smoking on all domestic flights.

I guess there is always a turning point in one's life that brings you to your knees and makes you reevaluate every aspect of your life. Ours came in the spring of 1992, when in a thunderstorm, one of our L-1011 aircraft went down, just short of the runway in Chicago. Only a few were able to survive. Our friend, Dondenisa "Dee Dee" Randolph, was not one of the lucky ones. She died in that crash, and it sent us all into therapy. We lost a sister, a friend, a co-worker, and a mentor; all rolled into one. It could have been anyone of us, because the L-1011 was our favorite aircraft. We flew it all the time and buddy-bidded on so many of the trips. Now we vowed never to work it again.

Dee Dee was like me: both of us got along with everybody. She never prejudged any of her friends.

Before leaving for her funeral, we all got together at Sarah's house to pay tribute to her in our own special way. I was glad to see Helena Meriwether and Nicole Henderson, both of whom I hadn't seen in years. I was especially glad to see Nicole, who I hadn't seen since she and baby Jennifer left to live with her mother in Lakeland, Florida. Collette and I had known Nicole better than the others, because of the time we had spent together in New Orleans. Nicole was Dee Dee's roommate during training and at the Lewis & Clark Apartments. She had Dee Dee's strawberry daiquiri recipe, and she made us a few pitchers as we recalled our fondest memories of Dee Dee.

First, Helena mentioned how Dee Dee's fingernails were always perfect. "She spent more money on her nails than on her clothes. Oh, remember that time when she was clowning around on the back of the banana boat in Nassau, and it capsized, dumping us into the middle of the ocean? She damn near killed all of us. We were fighting for our life until a rescue boat picked us out of the water. She was upset because she had lost two fingernails! We were all laughing and cussing her out at the same time. The boat captain said he had never heard a bunch of black American women cuss like that before."

"You all remember the Thanksgiving Dee Dee cooked a sweet potato pie?" Nicole recalled. "It looked good, but when we started eating it, we all knew something was wrong. She had forgotten to put any sugar in the pie." We all laughed.

"I had forgotten all about that," Michele said, "but I do remember the time she cooked the German Chocolate Cake, and it looked delicious on the cake plate. When we cut into it, it wasn't done. It was running in the center."

"I remember that. Dee Dee threw the cake in the garbage and swore never to bake another cake," Helena added.

"Amanda, I know you remember the time Dee Dee came in from a trip and told us she had Little Stevie Wonder on her flight. She had talked with him during the entire flight, and he invited her to his show at the Blue Room. She asked if her two roommates could come, and he said yes. Dee Dee gave him the directions to our apartment, and he was going to have his limo pick us up at eight o'clock," Barbara Ann said. "May she rest in peace, but that heifer let us get dressed in our Sunday best and had us parading around the apartment like teenagers going to the prom. Eight o'clock came and nothing happened. Dee Dee made us some strawberry daiquiris, and we waited and waited. After we called Stevie Wonder everything but a child of God, Dee Dee started to laugh, and she laughed. Finally she said, 'April Fool.' She got us good. It was April first. We wanted to kill her. I hit Dee Dee with a feather pillow, it split open, and the feathers went everywhere. It took us two hours to clean up all the feathers."

That brought back a lot of memories for me. I had forgotten about that incident. We were so gullible, but that's what April Fool's Day was supposed to be about.

It went on and on until we were all drunk from the daiquiris. Then Collette couldn't leave well enough alone, and she had to bring it up:

"What was the name of the doctor in New Orleans that Dee Dee wanted to marry? You remember; he died in that gay-bar fire? That was probably the last man Dee Dee screwed. I'm sure that's why Dee Dee turned to Daniela, oops... I mean Danny." She was the only one laughing.

"Now that's not funny, Collette," I said, because I liked Danny, and Dee Dee had been very happy with her. They were a family and had planned on adopting a child.

"Some things never change, not even in death. Amanda was always defending Dee Dee, and Dee Dee was always defending Amanda. They were like two peas in a pod. Are you sure, Amanda, the two of you didn't have a thing going on? You two spent a lot of nights together in your old apartment after the doctor's death," Collette said, but no one laughed, and I was getting angry.

"What was his name? Carderoeau or Cardeau, something like that."

Collette kept talking. Everyone else was quiet.

"Collette, shut the fuck up. I've put up with your bullshit for too many years." I was steaming. "It's over, I don't care if I never see your face again, you selfish bitch."

"Well I was just kidding, Miss Goodie-Two-Shoes. You don't have to get all bent out of shape," she said in a baby voice.

"Don't call me Miss-Goodie-Two-Shoes, You have never liked me, you never liked Dee Dee, you don't like anybody, not even your own damn self." I wanted to hit her where it hurt.

Sarah broke-up our fight. "Just cool it, you two."

Collette wouldn't let it be. "What you really mean is, cool it, Collette. All of you treat me like a dog. But you never say anything bad about Miss Goodie over here. I want to be treated with respect from you all." She made it a demand.

"Who have you ever respected?" Sarah asked.

"There you go, taking her side! I was never good enough to be you rich bitches' friend. I was never a sorority sister. Even Dee Dee didn't like me." Collette started to cry.

I got my keys and started for the door. The reminiscing was over; it was time to leave for the airport. The flight departed for Pittsburgh in two hours.

We all had full-fare, emergency coach passes, and were a little drunk when we reached the gate. The gate agents knew us and decided we were distraught over the death of our friend. They put us all in first class!

Collette and Dominique Van Stinchcomb were on their second drink before we took off. I went to sleep, because I knew Dee Dee's family was picking us up at the airport, and it didn't make sense for all of us to be drunk.

It was a close-casket funeral because of the condition of the body.

I had seen a lot of those in my days in the funeral business.

I think everyone in Pittsburgh was there because of the publicity. It was harder on us than attending Rhonda's funeral in Selma, Alabama, after she drove off the overpass in Atlanta. We knew Dee Dee's parents and little brother. She was part of our "family." Sarah spoke again, and I spoke instead of Michele, because I was closer to Dee Dee, her closest friend.

Dee Dee's death had taken a toll on all of us. The fact that we could leave this world the way she did hit home, and we got serious about our lives. After the funeral, we all went home and made major decisions. I decided to fly part-time and spend more time at home with my husband and kids.

Sarah decided to give up drugs, cigarettes, cursing, and partying; and she enrolled in Emory School of Divinity. She started classes that fall. Yes, she wanted to become a minister and work with youth groups! We all were surprised, but we supported her decision. Part of that support meant attending prayer meetings at her house every Monday night. We all started bringing potluck dinners, and it was like the good old days, but without the drugs and alcohol.

Michele wanted to settle down. She had stopped looking, long ago, for sexual pleasure. "Perhaps, every woman wasn't meant to have an orgasm. God knows I've tried. Now I just want a good man who loves me, and maybe have a few kids," she told me several months ago. "In the meantime, I am going to travel and have a good time for me."

I didn't know what Collette had decided, because we had stopped speaking. She wrote me a note apologizing, saying she had been upset about Dee Dee's accident. I knew that wasn't true; she had lashed out at me many times before. She had personal issues that needed to be addressed.

I heard from Barbara Ann that Collette's marriage to Mason was going well, and I left it at that.

Of all of us, Helena was the only one who couldn't recover. Maybe, it was because she lived in Chicago and had flown the same trip many times, including with Dee Dee. Two months after the funeral, Helena transferred to Atlanta and started dating a well-known drug dealer. His friends became her friends, and she stopped calling us. She wasn't, but never had been, dependable, and she simply no-showed many of our functions, including my daughter's ballet recital, a luncheon at Michelle's house, and my husband's birthday party.

Helena was also associating with some dangerous people, and we feared for her. Because of her low self-esteem, she was always a follower. What she didn't know was that the Atlanta police drug unit had pictures of her and her boyfriend coming out of a house used by suspected drug dealers. When they found out she was a Big E flight attendant, they passed their information on to the company.

The next time Helena went to work, she was given a *random* drug test. She failed, and after twenty-two years of flying, she was terminated. She called all of us, crying and saying that the test was wrong. She swore on her grandmother's grave that she hadn't used drugs. Sarah and I picked her up and took her to Grady Hospital to see a doctor Sarah had known when he was a student at Morehouse College, and she was at Spelman. Helena was so convincing even the doctor believed the airline's drug test was wrong. He administered a drug test for her, free of charge, as a favor to Sarah. He put a rush on the test and told Helena to try to relax.

Three days later, the doctor called Sarah and the three of us went back to his office. He looked disturbed, and he asked Helena if she wanted to go over the test results in front of us. She hesitated, but the look we gave her let her know, upfront, that it was in her best interest to say yes.

"Helena, you have tested positive for cocaine, heroin, marijuana, and Quaaludes," the doctor said, and Helena started to cry.

"What in the hell have you been doing, Helena?" Sarah wanted to know. "You let some no-good motherfucker, excuse my French, drug dealer cost you your job. It's too late for crying." Sarah had forgotten, for a moment, that she was now in Divinity School.

"I've...been...drinking...g-g-green...t-t-t-tea. Deacon said it would remove all traces of the drugs within three hours," Helena confessed between sobs.

"And you believed some mess like that?" Sarah was disgusted, because Helena could be so stupid.

The doctor looked at Helena, then at Sarah and me, and gravely, he shook his head. "Your friend has a serious drug problem. She's in denial. I recommend you get her into a treatment center as soon as possible. We have one here at Grady. I will be happy to send her name over tomorrow," he said.

"Helena, why didn't you come to us? We're your friends, not those junkies you hang out with," I said, because she needed help, and she needed us now, more than ever. "I will lend you the money to get clean."

We stopped in her condo when we dropped her off. She agreed to get treatment, so we made arrangements to pick her up a ten o'clock the next morning and drive her to the center ourselves. We couldn't tell her we didn't trust her to get there on her own.

That was the last time we saw our beloved friend of twenty-two years alive.

When Sarah and I arrived at her condo the following morning, Helena was nowhere to be found. We called everyone we knew, and no one had seen her. We didn't know her boyfriend or any of her new friends. We went home and waited all day for her call.

Another day passed, and there was still no word from Helena. We decided to wait a few days before calling her mother.

The next day, Sarah called me, frantic. "Turn on the six o'clock news, hurry, hurry, Channel Twelve." I turned to it and got the tail end of the story: Something about two people being shot to death in the home of a well-known drug dealer named Deacon Skinner. Skinner was one of the victims; the other victim was an unidentified woman. Both had been bound with duct tape and shot in the head, execution-style. Drugs and drug paraphernalia were found in the house. They were not sure of the time of the murders. Skinner was last seen alive two days ago.

I was frozen.

"Do you think the woman could be Helena?" I asked, knowing the answer.

"Wasn't her boyfriend named Deacon Skinner or something like that? She was always saying 'Deacon this,' and 'Deacon that.' How many Deacons do you know?" Sarah asked, and I couldn't breathe.

"I'm going to call the medical examiner's office to see if I can get a description of the woman. I'll call you right back." As soon as she hung up, my phone rang again. This time it was Barbara Ann.

"Amanda, I've been trying to call you, but your line was busy, I tried to call Sarah, too, but her line was busy. Did you all ever find Helena? I just called her, but I didn't get an answer. Did you see the six o'clock news?" She was talking so fast that she didn't give me time to answer. "That Deacon Skinner was her boyfriend. I only met him once when they stopped by to pick up something. Amanda, are you there? Amanda! Say something!"

"I'm here, I hear you. Sarah is calling the Medical Examiner to see if it's H-H-Helena." I started to cry, because I knew in my heart it was her.

"Calm down now, let's not jump to conclusions. I'll call Calvin, oh, I hear him driving up, I'll call you right back."

As soon as I hung up with her, my phone rang again. It was Sarah. The medical examiner's office wouldn't give her the information she demanded.

"They need to notify the next of kin before releasing information to the public," she said. "So I called a friend of mine on the force, and it has been confirmed the dead woman is Helena Meriwether, black female, a Big E flight attendant who was the girlfriend of Deacon Skinner. She was helping him deal drugs to support her habit. He didn't think we knew her, because she had moved here from Chicago. The police had the full lowdown on her."

"As soon as we left Helena's condo, she must have gone straight over to Skinner's house, and that's why we couldn't find her Wednesday morning. My friend said they put the time of death at sometime, late Tuesday's night. When we were looking for her, she was already dead. What a loss. She was a beautiful person, and we could have helped her, Amanda." I could tell she was crying, too.

Barbara Ann called shortly after I hung up with Sarah to confirm it was indeed our friend Helena. Big Daddy had come home early to give her the news before she could hear it on television or from someone else. We all decided to get together tomorrow and see what we could do to assist her family, even though we didn't know them very well.

It was unbelievable, two years after we buried Dee Dee, we were going to another dear friend's funeral. This was taking a toll on us. It was déjà vu, all over again. Helena was the weakest one of us, and was always consumed by what others thought of her. Over the years, her self-image had gotten worse, instead of better. We all were going to miss her terribly. She must have died a horrible death.

Only Sarah, Barbara Ann, and I were around to attend Helena's funeral. Michele was on a ten-day-tour of West Africa, and Collette was ordered by her doctor to stay in bed after an artificial insemination procedure. The first such procedure had failed because, instead of going home and going to bed, she celebrated by going house-to-house, telling everyone she was pregnant. By the time she got home, she was hemorrhaging and had lost the baby.

Sarah, Barbara Ann, and I flew to a little town in Texas, about fifty miles south of Dallas, for the funeral. Several other flight attendants from Chicago were already there, and all of us were in a daze. I don't even remember who spoke. I really felt that my heart was broken.

There was more to come.

Two weeks later, Sarah, Michele, and I were at Helena's condo, helping her mother pack her clothes and personal belongings. Michele found a shoebox on the floor, way in the back of Helena's bedroom closet, marked, "Personal Property." She opened it and looked inside, and quietly came for Sarah and me. She didn't want to alert Helena's mother, who was a frail lady in her late eighties.

In the box was a Ziploc bag full of white powder, and three credit cards. We knew the cards were stolen, because the VISA belonged to me, the American Express was in Sarah's name, and the MasterCard belonged to Dominique Van Stinchcomb. Also in the box was a personal check from me, made out to Deacon Skinner, dated for the day she died, in the amount of five thousand dollars. She had forged my signature. It was a high-number check so she must have stolen it from the back of my checkbook. We hadn't missed the credit cards, which we figured she had stolen from our purses the Tuesday we brought her home from the doctor's office at Grady Hospital. Sarah and I had been on the phone, out on her patio, making arrangements to get her into drug treatment. She was in the kitchen, making tea, and stealing from her dear friends. She must have been desperate.

"She didn't have to steal a check from me, I would have given her the money," I told them, and I knew they would have done the same.

We heard Mrs. Meriwether coming, so we quickly hid the box under the bed and pretended we were looking at the pictures on the nightstand. There was a picture of all seven of us: Dee Dee, Barbara Ann, Sarah, Michele, Collette, Helena, and me. It had been taken years ago, when we lived in New Orleans.

"We all have this same picture," Sarah told Helena's mother.

She looked at the picture and started to cry. "I never thought I would outlive my beautiful daughter." And we all cried together.

"Helena was a good girl, she didn't deserve to die this way." We held Mrs. Meriwether tightly, then laid her down for an afternoon nap.

The horror had taken a toll on her, and I thought about my own grandmother.

When she fell asleep, Sarah called her friend at the police department, and he was sending someone from the drug squad to pick up the bag of white powder. We kept our own credit cards, and we would return Dominique's card to her.

While we were waiting for the drug squad, we decided this was a good time to ask Michele about the new man she had met in West Africa.

She was grinning from ear to ear, so we knew something was up.

"Don't y'all get too excited. We spent every day together, and I didn't sleep with him. Now, I wanted to, but for the first time, I was able to restrain myself." She was still smiling. "He's from Dakar, Senegal, and he is coming to Atlanta for a visit as soon as he can get a visa and all his paperwork together. He's a wonderful man, and I think y'all will like him."

"And when will that be, Miss Lady?" I asked, happy for her.

"A few months; I had to fill out some papers. I'll keep y'all posted."

"You better, bitch," Sarah said. "Bitch" was her pet name for all of us.

"What does he do? How did you meet him?" I was excited.

"He works for his father, who owns the tour bus company that picked us up at the airport. Mohammud drove our tour bus, and he was responsible for us."

"There are lots of buses to drive over here, if he decides to stay; hint, hint. We don't want to give you any ideas," I suggested.

"I know but for now we alternate calling each other every week," Michele was saying as the doorbell interrupted our conversation.

It was the Atlanta drug squad. We handed them the plastic bag. They tested it, and said it was pure cocaine, with a street value of two hundred thousand dollars. The drug officers thought that was what the killers were looking for.

They were right. It took the Atlanta police department six months, but they arrested two nineteen-year-old men for the murder of Helena and her friend. One confessed, saying they were looking for a bag of pure cocaine that Skinner and his girlfriend had stolen from them two nights before. They were supposed to be partners, but Skinner and his girlfriend double-crossed them.

One pleaded guilty and agreed to testify against the other young man, who was the shooter. They were both good-looking boys who should have been in college, and they certainly didn't look like "cold-blooded killers." Sarah had to read a letter on behalf of Mrs. Meriwether, who was too ill to attend the trial. Her letter said that she didn't believe in the death penalty, and that killing these young boys would not bring her lovely daughter back. She didn't have long to live, and she was looking forward to being reunited with her daughter in Heaven.

The nineteen-year-old was found guilty of first-degree murder, and the judge sentenced him to life in prison with no possibility of parole. Sarah and I cried. What a waste! We couldn't decide if we were crying for Helena or for the two young men who also lost their lives that day, all in the name of drugs.

Thirty-nine

Michele's African friend finally arrived in Atlanta. It took six months and a letter from Bob, offering him a job, to get Mohammud Hassan Ojobos to the United States.

We liked him from the very beginning. He spoke perfect English, because he was educated in Europe, and one could tell he was from a "noble" family. Bob got him into a job-training program with the City of Atlanta, and soon, he was driving the city bus. He and Michele were very happy, and Mohammud was adjusting well to this country.

Michele called me early one morning, when I was still asleep. After pulling myself out of bed to get the kids off to school, I had gone back to sleep.

"Hello," I mumbled into the receiver.

"Amanda, what are you doing?"

"Michele, I'm sleeping. I got in late last night, the weather was bad, and we had a reroute."

"Well, I was going to invite you to breakfast, but I guess it will have to wait until lunch." She was bubbling over, with joy, about something. "I have something very important to tell you!" She was almost singing the words.

"Can't you tell me over the phone?"

"No! I'll meet you at Shantrell at noon. Don't be late."

Before I could object, I heard the phone click.

I went back to sleep.

I dragged myself into Shantrell at twelve ten. I didn't care about the ten-minutes-late bit; Michele was lucky I got there at all. Shantrell was a popular, black, upscale restaurant in southwest Atlanta, and we lunched there often. It was cozy, and we knew the owner.

Michele was already there. She was sitting at our favorite table in the back. She had a big smile on her face. She had ordered a bottle of wine, and had finished her first glass.

She saw me come in and waved.

"Amanda, I'm glad you made it, sorry about the reroute."

"Thanks," I said and sat down heavily. I was still tired.

"Here, have a glass of wine, and I ordered your favorite dish: curry lamb over rice, creamed spinach, and plantains." She poured a glass of wine for me. "Amanda, you will never believe what happened to me! I had an orgasm!" It came out louder than she had intended.

The couple sitting at the table next to us looked at Michele, their eyes wide.

We didn't care. If they only knew how long it had taken Michele to achieve that goal, they would be cheering.

I was so surprised, I was just as loud as Michele. "Michele, girl, I'm so happy for you! Mohammud must have...I mean...be something special." We both laughed.

"Yes, and that, too," she said, trying to act shy, but enjoying every minute. "Now, I know what you bitches have been talking about. Now, it's my time." We were both happy.

Then she got serious.

"Amanda, you remember me telling you the first man who gave me an orgasm, I would marry?"

"Yes, I remember...oh...don't tell me...you go, girl." I gave her a high-five.

"Yes! Yes! Mohammud and I are getting married!"

We both jumped up. I hugged her, and we were jumping around. We were so high on joy that we were oblivious to the rest of the people in the Restaurant, until everyone clapped.

"Oh!" I said to them. "My friend is getting married."

"So we heard," one customer said.

Then, the man at the table next to us said loudly, "And she just had her first orgasm. Congratulations."

The whole crowd clapped again.

We were too happy to be embarrassed, so we sat down and quietly had a wonderful lunch. I promised to give her the biggest bridal shower, ever.

"I will invite everyone. Oh, how about having the wedding in our backyard?"

Then she got serious.

"Amanda, the first time I met you in training, I liked you. I nominated you for most dependable and trustworthy, and you haven't changed a bit.

You are definitely the most loyal friend a person could ever have. I'm a better person for having known you, and I love you. I would be honored to have my wedding in your backyard."

She was close to tears, because the words came from her heart.

She and Mohammud set a wedding date, and we immediately started planning the wedding.

Sarah wanted to perform the wedding, but she was not yet an ordained minister. However, she could stand beside the minister. I was the Maid of Honor. Barbara Ann, Collette, and Michele's younger sister were bridesmaids.

Collette had been acting strangely, even saying she might or might not be able to come, even after all we went through for her wedding to Mason Young, not to mention her first wedding!

"Don't put me down for anything." She was very brief when I called to tell her about our plans. We hadn't been close, and she hadn't participated in any of our functions since Dee Dee died. We gave her some room, because we felt she would come around when she was ready.

After she married Mason Young, her third husband, they bought a two hundred and fifty thousand dollar house and two new cars. Sarah had tried to talk to her, but she never would listen. She was too busy keeping up with the Joneses. Then, three years after her wedding, she and Mason filed for bankruptcy. They lost the house and cars, and who knows what else. Now, they were renting a house in the same neighborhood as the house she had bought when she moved from New Orleans. I guess she blamed us for that, because she felt we always had and she didn't. She never could get past her childhood.

Michele and Mohammud's wedding was beautiful. Mohammud had family in New York who he had never met, and they drove down for the wedding. It was June, and we were able to decorate the backyard with a gazebo and white carnations. Michele wore a lovely, white gown. After all, this *was* her first marriage. And Mohammud was handsome in his white tuxedo. He was over six feet tall, and built like a triathlon athlete. He was very much in love with our friend, and that was all that mattered to us. He endured months of harassment trying to secure a visa to come to the United States from Senegal. Since he had been here, he had been working very hard to make sure he wasn't living off his bride-to-be. He and Bob had become very good friends.

Four months after the wedding, Michele was pregnant with twins, at the ripe old age of forty-eight!

"That African man got his mojo working!" Sarah and I joked.

Forty

The nineties were taking its toll on us in many unexpected ways: We were losing a lot of our male flight attendants to AIDS. There seemed to be a funeral every month.

The gay guys had friends in every layover city. They were always going out with someone they knew. We also had a lot of lesbian flight attendants. We always knew who they were, only now they were able to come out of the closet with a new agenda.

If we thought the new flight attendants of the eighties were strange, well, there was only one word to describe these nineties women: "Clueless." There was definitely an identity crisis. The black girls were trying to be white, and the white ones were trying to be black. We tried to take some of the young women under our wings and teach them the ropes, but it was an impossible task. Even in the eighties, we were unable to bring any new flight attendants into our group, no matter how hard we tried.

These new young women were different from our group: they had no loyalty to each other, and they didn't know the meaning of true friendship.

They were jealous and suspicious of other women. They had no interest in taking advantage of the travel benefits the airline offered. We senior women tried not to fly with them, because some of us were old enough to be their mothers, and they reminded us of that on every flight. They had no respect for seniority.

These were beautiful women, but flaky, and when you talked to them, they had no substance. The nineties African-American women or men never had the black experience. They didn't care or want to know anything about their history or culture. The struggles of the civil rights movement were of no concern to them now. We couldn't talk to them so we chose to stay as far away from them as we could.

1996

Sarah graduated from Emory School of Divinity with a doctorate in religion. We were all very proud of her, and we all attended her graduation. Bob and the kids went with me.

Collette came with her husband. None of her artificial inseminations worked, and she was contemplating adoption. As a matter of fact, we were all in our late forties now, and too old for the work and responsibilities of caring for a newborn.

Michele and Mohammud came with my godchildren, Balyndu and Malyntu. They were still acting like newlyweds.

Barbara Ann and her family arrived late and missed the ceremony.

I was having a small dinner party for Sarah at my house, following the graduation ceremony. Sarah's parents had both retired, and were in town to see her graduate. We wanted it to be special, so we had hired a caterer to have everything ready when we returned from the ceremony. It was a gift from Bob and me. I invited a few of the young flight attendants so they could mingle with us and learn what we were about.

One young, shapely woman, Leshanda Walls, came half-dressed, looking like a floozy. She spent the entire evening flirting with my husband. She tried to corner him in the kitchen. It got so embarrassing that Bob had to ask her to leave.

"How immature and stupid can you be?" I thought, sadly.

It reminded me of something my mother warned me about: "If you show a bitch how good you have it at home, she'll want to fill your shoes."

Our group had been together for almost twenty-five years, and we had never fucked with each other's men. We had never been accused of looking at our friends' men or husbands. That was an unspoken rule we lived by. That young floozy's behavior was completely unacceptable.

After the party, we decided we just couldn't stand to fly with them young "thangs." The only way we could get away from them was to fly internationally. Big E had started flying new routes to Bangkok, Seoul, and Taiwan. They were very senior trips: No one with less than twenty years of seniority could hold the lines.

Sarah, Michele, and I flew together, and it was so much fun. It was like old times. We went on tours and sightseeing excursions. Then we shopped until we dropped. You could count on flight attendants to find the bargain in every city into which they flew.

One of the interesting parts of flying to Asia was the young language-of-destination, or LOD speakers. Big E hired a lot of young, Asian flight attendants, because none of us spoke the native languages.

These Asian women set feminism back fifty years. We had been through women's liberation. We had our men washing dishes and changing diapers.

But these women didn't care a thing about women's liberation or women's rights. They did everything for their men, and they went after our American men with a passion. They couldn't care less if he was white or black, handsome or ugly; as long as he had enough money to set them up in the United States, or at least make them comfortable in their own country.

They believed that the way to a man's heart was through his genitals. They set their eyes on our pilots, and in no time, had them eating out of their hands or pussy. We started calling it the "Ancient Chinese Secret," and we wanted in on it. We repeatedly asked Asian flight attendants to tell us their secret. They were good at playing dumb and pretending they hadn't the slightest idea what we were talking about. It was as though they had taken an oath among themselves not to divulge the truth. That oath really worked; none of the Asian women would tell us their secrets.

Juanta Hu, a young Chinese flight attendant, had started dating one of our married captains. She used her free-travel allotment every other week to fly to a layover with him. She had no shame, and she would ride to the hotel with the crew. We all knew the captain was married with small kids, and we got tired of seeing her as a passenger on our flights. We even considered sending the captain's wife a note and inviting her on a layover to be with her husband.

On one such flight, we treated passenger Juanta badly, hoping she would get the message. She never got her choice of meals, and had to ask twice for something to drink.

One of Juanta's friends told us that Juanta brought a sack of sex toys and an aphrodisiac oil in her bag. She was obviously determined to take the captain away from his wife. We were determined, now, more than ever, to get our hands on the oil.

We decided to change our tactics. On the next flight, we made sure Juanta got her choice of meals, and we gave her as much alcohol as she could drink. We tried to get her drunk enough to fall asleep so we could get a peek into her bag. As soon as we noticed she was in a deep sleep, we sneaked her bag from the overhead compartment, took it into the galley. Every flight attendant who wasn't on break was there. The bag was locked, and we couldn't break the lock without making a lot of noise. We put the bag back in the overhead bin. If Juanta Hu thought we treated her badly before, she had seen nothing yet.

We could understand why they wanted our men, because the Asian men on our flights were mean, and treated women like shit. On one trip, Sarah was taller than any Asian man on the airplane, yet they figuratively were trying to look down at her. Besides that, they smelled of garlic, the whole plane smelled of garlic, and we smelled of garlic when we got home.

Nevertheless, we intended to continue flying Asia, because we were in hot pursuit of the "Ancient Chinese Secret."

Our co-pilot, Andrew Whitaker, started dating a young, local woman in Taiwan. He put her and her family up in a small house. Every week, as soon as we landed, he couldn't wait to get to the hotel, shower, and go to her house. We wouldn't see him again until thirty-six hours later, at the airport. He would be exhausted. This went on for about three months, until we decided to put our heads together.

"Maybe Andy can give us some insight into these Asian women," one of our cabin-crewmembers remarked one day.

She was only joking, but it sounded like a good idea to all of us. We volunteered Reverend Sarah to ask him.

"What is that lady doing to you?" Sarah asked him on our next trip. "We all want to know." We were all standing behind Sarah, nodding our heads.

"Can you tell us, Andy, pleeeze? We want to know about the 'Ancient Chinese Secret.'"

We had him cornered. He was a nice guy, and he had known most of us for a long time. He knew exactly what we wanted to know. I think we were all shocked when he reluctantly nodded his head.

"All right, but I can't tell y'all on the aircraft. Come by my room when we get in, and I'll tell y'all everything I know," he promised.

We could hardly wait. When we arrived at the hotel, every attendant on the flight, excluding the language speakers, were crowded into Andy's small hotel room.

Andy sat in a chair and made himself comfortable, and we all crowded around him. No one wanted to miss a word.

He broke it down for us. Please remember that the vast majority of Asian woman we saw every week were hard working, oppressed, and were, at different levels, trying to achieve their rights. They were no different from the vast majority of their women counterparts in the rest of the world. Andy wasn't describing the general population of Asian women, only the small group that worked underground as prostitutes.

He told us that American men liked Asian women, because most don't care about being sexually satisfied.

"They will do anything, and I mean anything. All they care about is the money. In some cases, these girls are young. I think a small group of families put their daughter out to prostitute, and this is what they are trained to do, from day one: how to please a man. Oral sex is their specialty, because they know American men like it. They can make your penis stand at attention. They have a massage oil; it's hot and cold at the same time. I don't think they sell it in the States. If they did, it would probably be illegal," he smiled.

"How does it taste?" one flight attendant asked.

"It tastes and smells like cherries or berries, or something like that. Anyway, they use this stuff to service every inch of a man's body. You can have whatever you want: oral sex, anal sex, or around-the-world."

"Around the world? What's that?" Sarah asked.

If Sarah didn't know, you could believe none of us knew.

He was a little embarrassed. But he tried to explain. "They use their tongue and go all over your ass. And I mean, every inch. No place is off-limits. It's catching on at home, especially in California." He hesitated, but we encouraged him to continue.

"They will sit on you and ride you until you explode in ecstasy, or you can get on top, and they just open their legs. I don't know what they use for birth control, because they will let you come in them, on them, or wherever you want. They put this sweet stuff on their pussy, and you can bury your face in it for days."

We were hanging on every word.

"They sometime use homemade ice cream and let you eat it out of their... you know...down there. They are small women, so their pussy is small and tight. There is never any conversation. They don't speak any English. It's just raw sex, for as long as you want it, or as long as you can last. It's easy to get addicted. When I'm home, I can't wait to get back to it. It affects your mind, as well as your body. A lot of men come here, just for the sex."

"Too bad these Asian men are not as good at sex as their women," Sarah said. "Then we could all come here. I'm 'hot!' I could use some 'Ancient Chinese Secret' now; praise the Lord!" We all said Amen to that.

Forty-one

After the 1996 Olympics in Atlanta, Elite World Airline Airlines cut the Asian flights down to one destination: Seoul, Korea, three times a week. Sarah, Michele, and I were too junior to hold the Seoul trip, because of seniority years. So, we were back to flying across the Atlantic. We flew to England, France, Italy, Germany, Spain, and South America. "Everything goes" on layovers to these countries": Hot tubs, all-night room parties, and at the end, you couldn't remember who slept with whom. The only problem was that my group was too old for the parties, so we watched the younger flight attendants make fools of themselves, and remembered when it was us.

Sarah was our first flight-attendant-ordained-minister. We were already calling her Reverend Sarah Ferguson. She was also associate pastor of the New Wright Baptist Church of Atlanta and we all joined.

The airlines started asking Reverend Sarah to counsel some of our comrades going through trauma; whether they be marital problems, domestic abuses, on-the-job injuries, illnesses, or whatever. She was always on special assignment.

Within a year, Sarah was so busy that we hardly saw her anymore. Michele, Barbara Ann, and I were busy with our kids, while Sarah was busy with marriages, funerals, christening flight attendants' babies, or whatever.

The only time we saw each other was at church and community service meetings. Reverend Sarah had us working the rape-crisis hotline, or volunteering at the food bank and the Boys and Girls Clubs. We hosted fundraisers for the mayor and city councilmen. We also built several Habitat for Humanity houses.

It was strange how our lives changed: We, of all people, were giving Big E flight attendants a good name! We were respected and accepted in all social circles in the community. Michele, Barbara Ann, and I became active members of Links, Jack-and Jill, and The National Council of Negro Women. Our kids went to the best schools, and I was president of the PTA.

The young flight attendants were the ones in trouble now. Because of the drug testing, which that tested for marijuana, cocaine and opium; methamphetamine, PCP, and ecstasy were their drugs of choice. On layovers, they would come out of their hotel rooms half-naked, with their bodies pierced and tattooed. There was certainly a generation gap. Senior flight attendants didn't want to be seen with them.

They failed to pay their rent, were evicted from their apartments, and their cars were repossessed. They took care of no-good men with baby-momma drama.

They had no support system in place as we did.

Barbara Ann, Michele, Sarah, and I tried to have lunch together every month. Sarah would be so stressed out, trying to communicate with these young flight attendants, that she needed a break.

The young girls slept with married pilots, because they felt they were young and prettier than the wives, and they also reasoned that they were less likely to catch a venereal disease. It was embarrassing to us to see how the young flight attendants threw themselves at the pilots. It was too easy to forget that we hadn't been embarrassed when we were doing much of the same, years and years ago.

Forty-two

1998

My husband sold his Burger King restaurants, and we moved to Sarasota, Florida, and bought an interest in a bail bondmen business. It was less stressful than the Burger Kings!

I hated to leave, but it was a good business move for Bob. I commuted to Atlanta to work.

Also in late 1998, there was a power struggle at the top of Elite World Airlines. The board of directors fired the then-president and CEO and replaced him with Richard Maulligan, a man who had never run an airline. Mr. Maulligan was from upstate New York, and he had never lived down South. No one realized, at the time, what a mistake it was.

Big E World Airlines was the most profitable and respected airline in the world, with deep, southern roots. It was built on southern hospitality and values, and was the envy of the airline industry. Big E had always enjoyed a family-like atmosphere, and the employees worked together for the good of the company. When Big E was running in the black, the employees were rewarded with profit-sharing checks. Every Big E president and CEO before Mr. Maulligan had an open-door policy, and was accessible for any employee.

Mr. Maulligan's personality was too cold for Southerners. He never mingled with low-level employees, and instead, distanced himself from both the workers and the community.

When he introduced his "Visions For Elite World Airline," every employee knew our company was in trouble. He wanted to fix everything, whether or not it was broken.

He spent millions of dollars to paint the outside of all the airplanes, with a funky-colored tail. Employees hated the new colors, and they felt the money could have been better spent modifying the inside of the airplanes. The galleys were outdated, and the ovens were inoperable. The lavatories smelled and needed overhauling, the carpets and seats were dirty and worn, and our passengers wanted more leg room.

Next, Mr. Maulligan's vision included making the company number one in customer service. If he had read any business publication, he would have known Big E had been number one in customer service for ten years running.

He created a program called the Big E Ambassador Program. Again, if he had read the history of Elite World Airlines, he would have known that its employees were already the company's best ambassadors.

Since Mr. Maulligan was not a Southerner, he didn't understand the Southern values on which Big E was built. His credibility with Big E's employees was wearing thin. To make things worse, he paid three million dollars to a public relations company to teach him and his new vice presidents how to speak to the employees. It was another waste of money.

By giving a cold shoulder to the powers-that-be in Atlanta, Big E began to lose its customer base in the airline's hometown, for the first time in history. Big E was now spending millions of dollars on campaign advertisements to restore its creditably in its own hometown.

I could go on and on about one the most despised president and CEO in the airline's history, but you get the picture.

Forty-three

2000

Two thousand was one of the most challenging years of my career, regarding race relations. Political issues tore at the very soul of what had taken thirty years to build, and our world was split along racial lines.

It started with the 2000 presidential election. Flight attendants, pilots, and passengers had strong opinions about the campaign. Even the crews were divided as I had never seen before.

Emotions were already fragile from the O. J. Simpson trial, and from the President-Clinton-Monica-Lewinsky affair. Then the Bush-Gore election took it to the next level.

Most flight attendants were pro-choice because of our lifestyles. I was willing to bet my house that at least two of every five flight attendants had had at least one abortion. Now, those same flight attendants snuck their teenage daughters into abortion clinics, even as they claimed to be for family values and were loudly anti-abortion.

Karen Bushwagner-Bauer tried amnesia on a very early flight.

"I think President Clinton is the most immoral man on Earth," Karen said on a morning flight to Rome. She thought Sarah and I were in the back galley and couldn't hear her.

I almost choked on my Starbuck's coffee.

Sarah had to nudge me to keep me from going off on her. She was now married to a wealthy heart surgeon who was a staunch racist and anti-abortionist. Her husband would have divorced her on the spot if he knew about her past, or about the fact that she had black friends.

Karen was about to say something else, but stopped when she realized we were no longer in the back galley, and only a few feet away. She changed the subject. Karen knew better than to push it, because it would devastate her if her husband and new friends knew she had been a drug abuser, a lesbian, and a prostitute. We have old pictures of her stoned out of her mind. Had she forgotten? It was Sarah who let her in the back door of the Lagniappe Club where she often participated in orgies, nude table dancing, and God knew what else. I saw her myself on my first trip to the Lagniappe Club. We knew she had two abortions, because Sarah drove her to the clinic. The first time, she was pregnant by a black married football player. Abortion was nothing to be ashamed of back in the seventies and eighties; drug abuse and unprotected sex went hand in hand. She also had an affair with Franco Bordeaux and another pilot while she was married to her first husband.

Now she was Miss High Society, and only a small circle of her old friends knew she was a fake. She was too ashamed to speak to Sarah and me for the rest of the trip, because she was living a lie, and it was beginning to wear on her. At fifty-three years of age, she looked sixty.

In our business, we now had a bunch of hypocrites like Karen. They preached one thing and did another. One-night stands and adultery were a way of life for many pilots and flight attendants. I had never known a pilot to turn down a piece of ass, whether they be Republican, Democrat, good ol' boy, or racist.

Nowadays, Big E Airlines taught tolerance and diversity.

Sixty percent of our male flight attendants were gay. We had a large group of lesbians, so our company could not help but be tolerant. We had every nationality among the flight attendant group, and our customers were from all races, religions, creeds, and colors.

During the O.J. Simpson trial, most whites thought he was guilty from day one. Black flight attendants refused to discuss the trial with the rest of the crew. But we discussed it among ourselves, because we could not bear to tell a white person that O.J. was guilty. When the trial was over, they acted as though they had lost a war, while blacks celebrated.

Next came the President-Clinton-Monica-Lewinsky affair.

In general, black people voted for President Clinton and thought he was a good president. It was no different among black flight attendants. But it was the Bush-Gore election debacle in Florida that came down to black vs. white. Racism was raising its ugly head again.

There were fights on the airplane among flight crews, and supervisors had to meet the flight to mediate the situations. Passengers would get into fistfights over the issues, and the police had to meet the flights and arrest many passengers.

The company issued a memo to its employees, prohibiting the discussion of politics on the airplane or while on duty. Even that failed to curtail the discussions and the fights.

As an ultimatum, the next memo said altercations between flight crews over politics would result in termination. No one wanted to lose their jobs.

We stopped talking politics, but it segregated us. On layovers, black crewmembers went in one direction, and white crews went in another. That way, we could discuss whatever we wanted without precipitating confrontations.

Some of the young co-pilots had the white-boy Syndrome: Republican and right-wing beliefs. Some of our young black pilots, who were less than five percent of Big E pilots, had attended all-white schools, married women of another race, and had never lived the black experience.

In other words, some black pilots are downright sorry. Black flight attendants never discussed black issues with black pilots. We didn't hang out together on layovers, but we were cordial to each other at all times.

Forty-four

2001

September 11, 2001 changed our lives forever. It was very stressful, being stuck in a foreign country for ten days, unable to get home, especially when we were watching New York burn on CNN. A lot of flight attendants suffered from post-traumatic stress disorder, and some had nervous breakdowns. Some became afraid to get on an airplane, and others were afraid to leave the country. Many of our friends retired, including Michele. She had gotten married and had children late in life, and she now wanted to spend more time at home with her family. Mohammud had borrowed money from his father in Africa and started a charter bus service here that became quite successful. Sarah, Barbara Ann, and I talked about retiring, but decided against it. We loved our jobs. Collette couldn't afford to retire.

By 2002, many airlines were in trouble. Terrorism, as well as greed among executives, had brought many an airline to its knees.

Big E employees had lost all confidence in our president and CEO, Richard Maulligan. He seemed to be out for himself. Morale was at an all-time low among the employees as a result of layoffs, and the wage and benefit concessions they were force to accept.

Mr. Maulligan had a hard time explaining or justifying his twenty-million-dollar raise at a time when the airline was losing millions of dollars a day. It was obvious he didn't give a damn about Big E or its employees; he was out to pad his own pockets before leaving the company. It angered employees even more when he spent five millions dollars on a research firm, owned by his brother-in-law, to develop a survey to find out how employees felt about management. Flight attendants sent Mr. Maulligan two thousand e-mails telling him how the money could have been better spent. While he was sitting in his fancy office, counting his millions, we were out in the field, making do on the bare minimum.

So many times, our airplanes pushed back from the gate, short of meals, and with only half the supplies needed to work a full flight. Our airplanes were dirty; our lavatories stunk, while some were inoperable; and all the new in-flight video equipment worked only half of the time.

We were seasoned flight attendants. Once we were on the aircraft, keeping our passengers safe and comfortable was our top priority.

We would jump through hoops to make sure that happened. Yet, most of the time, we lacked the tools and support we needed from management to give our customers great service.

Just last month, on an international flight, we had no power in the back galley. We had to transport two hundred entrees from the back galley to the front to be cooked, and back to the rear to be served. Our coach passengers had to wait two hours for their food.

We explained the situation to them, and they were very understanding. We served complimentary champagne and wine to them with their meals and they were happy.

To top it all off, upon landing in Atlanta, a water hose broke under the coffeemakers and dumped ten gallons of water onto the back galley floor. During deplaning, instead of saying goodbye to our wonderful passengers, flight attendants were in the galley, mopping up water with blankets and pillows because, we didn't have enough paper towels on the aircraft.

As I looked at flight attendants close to my seniority, fifty percent were overweight. We were less attentive to the way we looked in our new uniforms, which we hated; they were rejects that Mr. Maulligan got at a discount from one of the large hotel chains. Most of us just wanted to be comfortable. With all the cutbacks, there was no one around to do uniform check. If Irene Bourgerone, our old supervisor, was around she would have had a fit.

2003

This year brought more of the same: lay-offs, pay cuts, and bankruptcy in the airline business. Crewmembers had tightened their belts and stopped indulging on layovers. Close to fifteen hundred Big E flight attendants had retired, and another five thousand had been laid off. We had one less flight attendant on each airplane, so that we worked harder, and for longer hours, but with less pay. It was hard for today's employees to find anything good to say about Elite World Airlines. Our wonderful job had become a grind. Most flight attendants hated to come to work and listen to people in management, who have never been a flight attendant, tell us how to do our job.

We suffered from chronic back and shoulder pain, from lifting passengers' bags into the overhead compartments, and carpal tunnel syndrome, from years of carrying trays and opening soft drink cans. A large number of flight attendants suffered from breast cancer. We had not figured that one out yet.

Stress and anxiety were building as flight attendants tried to find new ways to cope. Our simple use of over-the-counter sleep aids and pain medicines had become more powerful prescription drugs, washed down with alcohol, to sleep. Then, we used stimulants and jet lag medication to stay awake. Flight attendants used powerful prescription drugs for stress and anxiety, and some had many side effects. We didn't know if we were coming or going. Unlike the seventies and eighties when we were footloose and fancy-free, many were now single moms with mortgages to pay.

I was glad Bob and I had downsized. We had sold our big house in Atlanta and moved to Florida in the nick of time.

Being a flight attendant was now hard work. Where did all the fun go? In addition to irate passengers, now we had to worry about terrorists, bombs, and, more importantly, our lives. We were spending more time at Sarah's prayer meetings, only this time, we were really praying, instead of just saying the words. I tried to go to church every Sunday.

Now, I wished I could find a way to talk to everyone who planned to fly! First I'd tell our prima donnas and senior citizens: "Please check any bag you cannot lift into the overhead compartment. If you bring a bag onboard that is too big to fit underneath the seat, and you cannot lift it into the overhead compartment, your flight attendant will check it at the door. Because of back problems, flight attendants will no longer be required to lift your bags."

Secondly, to our irate and belligerent passengers: "I implore you to leave your problems at home. If you cuss out, threaten, or interfere with the duties of a flight attendant, you will be removed from the aircraft, arrested, fined, and detained. Please do not smoke in the aircraft lavatory, that's asking for trouble."

As my beloved grandmother used to say: "A word to the wise should be sufficient."

Forty-five

August 29, 2003

On our flight to London last week, the aircraft made an emergency landing in Bangor, Maine, because an "Iranian-looking" man went into the lavatory with his briefcase and refused to come out. He would only speak to us in Arabic through the closed door. After being in there for almost an hour, flight attendants, and a business class passenger tried to force the door open, but he had it jammed from the inside. Anyone who locked himself in a stinky aircraft lavatory, for almost an hour, was up to no good. The captain made an emergency landing in Bangor, and the authorities came onboard, and broke the door open; and the man was still sitting on the commode with his pants down around his knees. He said, in perfect English, "I'm just constipated." The captain decided to leave him in Bangor.

I decided to swap my next London trip, because my daughter was having her sweet-sixteen birthday party that weekend. A Rio trip gave me more time off. I didn't care if I never flew London again, because too many incidents were happening on the London flights. Flight attendants were still talking about a passenger who tried to open one of the airplane doors during the flight, causing the captain to make an emergency landing in Charlotte, North Carolina. Police escorted that passenger off the plane.

What happened to the good ol' days, when flying was fun? Oh, how we longed for those days.

Forty-six

September 7, 2003

"Open your eyes, Amanda! I said, open your eyes!" a voice in my head kept repeating.

I recognized the voice; it was on the tip of my tongue, but I couldn't put a name to it. When I opened my eyes, it took some time before my eyes adjusted to the dimly lit room.

It was a hospital room. Tubes were attached to my mouth and nose. I could hear the breathing noise. I was on a respirator.

"Why am I not breathing on my own?"

I saw the IV hanging next to my bed. I heard the heart monitor. It was close by, although I couldn't see it. My daughter was sitting next to me, with her head on the bed. She was asleep, because I could hear her lightly snoring. My eyes scanned the room. My husband was asleep in a big chair. My mother was sitting in a chair, reading her bible under a dim lamp; and sitting on the other side of the lamp was my son. He was reading a magazine called *The Source.* The sidewall lights were also dim.

"What am I doing here, in the hospital?" I couldn't remember.

"Think back," the voice coached me softly.

I tried to think. I couldn't remember a thing. My mind was blank.

"Try harder, Amanda," the voice was very kind and loving.

This time my memory came back. I didn't want to remember. It was terrifying. I saw the fire. It was hot. I wanted to run, but I was too weak, dazed, and I couldn't move. There was smoke that was making it hard to breathe. Suddenly, the aircraft hit the runway like a super bomb, and with such force that the airplane broke in half. My jump seat, with me still buckled in, was jetting through the air, as though it was shot from a cannon. I landed fifty feet away, in front of a fire truck. I felt every bone in my body break. A fireman grabbed me out of my jump seat and rolled me on the ground. He wrapped me in a blanket, picked me up in his arms, as if I was a rag doll, and ran with me, as fast as he could. Several high-power flood lights lit up the area, and from under his armpit, I saw the aircraft. The slides were inflated, and the passengers were sliding down, two at a time, running from the aircraft as fast as they could, like a stampeding herd of cattle; all two hundred and fifty of them. They were helping each other. Some were carrying others on their backs, and some had children in their arms. Someone's voice was on a megaphone or loud speaker, yelling for them to run away from the airplane. It was chaotic and orderly at the same time. When the last person was off the aircraft, I focused on the 4-left door, where my jump seat was, and I saw *Him.*

"I heard your prayers," He whispered and smiled at me. "Thank you for inviting me, I will never leave you."

He was at least seventy-five feet away, but it was as if He was whispering in my ear. At that moment, the tail of the aircraft went up in a big ball of fire. I saw luggage, seat cushions, and debris flying in the air. The fireman carrying me dived, with me, into a ditch and covered me with his body, and the lights went out.

"Move your fingers." The voice was so endearing.

I tried. My heart longed to put a name to the voice and follow its instructions, but my body parts refused to move.

"Move your fingers, Amanda."

I tried, and this time, my fingers moved.

As soon as I moved my fingers, my daughter jumped up. I hadn't known she was holding my hand.

"Mommy! Mommy!" she screamed.

In a flash, they were all at my bedside.

"Daddy! Daddy! Mommy moved her hand!" My daughter was jumping up and down.

"Okay, okay, calm down," My husband said and turned to my son, "Malcolm, call the nurse."

My son pushed a button on the nightstand.

"Daddy! Mommy moved her hand, I swear she did. Daddy, ask her to move her hand!" Robbi screamed.

"Stop screaming, Robbi. Now, move over," my husband said.

"*Stop swearing in here, young lady*," I said to her without a sound.

My husband sat down and took my hand.

"Amanda, sweetheart, move your hand," he said, calmly. "Take your time."

I had no feeling in my hand or any other part of my body. I tried to move, but I couldn't.

They waited.

My mother was looking at me and praising the Lord. Malcolm leaned over his dad's shoulder.

"Hi, Mom," he said.

"Are you in pain?" my husband asked.

Before he realized I couldn't answer, the nurse came in and asked them to step aside. She took my vital signs, and I could tell she wasn't happy with the results. She had her back to my family, and she was careful to hide her face from them. She called for the doctor and asked my family to leave the room. The doctor rushed in as my family was leaving. As they dragged her from the room, I heard my daughter screaming, "Mommy! Mommy!"

I looked at the doctor. I had never seen him before. He was very handsome. His olive skin and dark features implied he was from the Middle East, probably Tunisia or Egypt. The touch of gray in his black hair would put him in his late thirties. His name tag read "Dr. Paslinski."

"*What kind of name is that?*" I didn't feel like guessing anymore.

He took a small flashlight from his jacket pocket and shined it in my eyes.

"Mrs. Mitchell, blink twice if you can hear me."

I tried to blink, but couldn't. I called on the voice I heard before.

"Make me blink," I demanded.

The voice was silent.

The doctor took a sharp object out of his pocket.

"Mrs. Mitchell," he said with a slight accent. "Blink twice if you feel this." He stuck my finger.

I felt nothing.

I stared at Dr. Paslinski.

"Her daughter said she moved her hand," the nurse told him.

"It could have been a reflex," was all the doctor said while listening to my heart with his stethoscope.

He didn't look very happy, either.

"Her vital signs are dropping," the nurse whispered.

"I know," the doctor said, more to himself than the nurse.

Another nurse came into the room with a wash pan, full of water, in her hand. Dr. Paslinski squeezed out a face towel and patted it over my forehead. I did feel the towel. It was cold, and it felt good. I must have been burning up with fever. I looked into his eyes, and they were very sad and disappointed and tired. I could tell he was a kind and sensitive doctor. I felt sad for him, because he had done all he could do. It was out of his hands.

"Give her something for pain, and I'll go tell the family." He said it so softly, so I had to strain to hear him. He sounded choked up. He rearranged the covers under my chin and carefully moved a bit of hair from my face. Then, he turned to leave the room, and my eyes followed him.

He walked quietly with his head down. Talking to my family was the last thing he wanted to do.

"What is he going to tell them?" I wondered.

The nurse avoided my eyes and did as she was told. She added a syringe full of something to my IV.

"*What's going on? I'm not in pain."* But my words never reached my lips.

The nurse left, and my family came back in. They had somber expressions on their faces. Bob sat down, and I saw a single tear in his eye.

"Where had I seen that before?" I ordered my mind to take me there, to that place and that moment, and instantly I saw the old African medicine doctor. I hadn't thought of him since I left his hut, so many years ago.

I looked at my husband again. He had his eyes closed. I think he was praying.

My children stood beside Bob. My mother, sister, and two brothers were behind them. Mother was still reading her bible. I saw Sarah holding the hand of a very handsome, gray-haired man. I took a closer look. It was Wendell Johnson. I was glad he was out of prison. Collette, Michele, and Barbara Ann were there. Dominique was standing by the door. They all smiled at me, but tears filled their eyes.

I looked at each one of them. I hoped they could see how much I loved them.

My attention returned to my husband. He still had his head down, and was still praying. I loved him so very much. He was a wonderful man; as solid as a rock. Our two kids were beautiful. They were both leaning heavily on his shoulders. He was strong, and could carry that load. Robbi had her hand under the covers on my bed. She must have been holding my hand. I just couldn't feel it.

I wanted to stay with them, but I was so tired. I needed a nap. I closed my eyes, and there was my whole life. It was all so simple. There was nothing complicated about life. God gave us the ability to reason: to choose right from wrong, good from evil; and more importantly, to use common sense. Every day of my life had been planned for me. This was no accident. There were no accidents with God. Every road I took in life led me to this day and this moment.

A bright light interrupted my thoughts. It was the most beautiful light I had ever seen. It was so warm and soothing, and it healed my broken body. I turned my head to see where the light was coming from, but it was so bright that I had to squint my eyes. Then, in the light, I saw my grandmother and grandfather; my beloved uncles...and...oh, yes...my father! He wasn't drunk, and he looked so young and innocent. He reminded me of my son: There was Dee Dee and Helena, looking so beautiful; they looked like angels: Next to them was the old African medicine man, only this time he was standing tall, about six foot four. His clothes were clean and starched, and he didn't look tired. He was the man in my dreams, and he was the man on the plane when we pushed back from the gate. I had seen him just before the crash, and now I remembered the last thing he said to me before I left his hut in Africa: "We will meet again."

But that had been so long ago, and I hadn't believed him. Suddenly, before my eyes, he began to change, becoming a tall, dark, and handsome man. I narrowed my eyes to see more clearly. He smiled at me, and my heart stopped and filled with joy; I hadn't forgotten that million-dollar smile, but now I could put a name to the voice. He was my first love.

He and the rest of my love ones stretched out their arms, beckoning me to come.

"But I can't move, I'm in a hospital bed. My legs and arms are in casts, and there are tubes up my nose," I tried to tell them.

Miraculously, the cast and tubes were gone.

"*That's strange! What's going on?*" I looked at my hands, and they looked new. I looked at my feet, and they did, too. So I started to run. Slowly at first, then as fast as I could. But my daughter's voice stopped me dead in my tracks!

"Mommy! Mommy! I love you! Don't leave me! Mommy! It's my birthday," I heard her screaming.

I tried to tell them I couldn't come, but the light was gone, and I heard my daughter crying. She gripped my hand convulsively.

I squeezed her hand, and she caught her breath, then.

"Mommy! Mommy! Mommy?" She was screaming over and over!

I turned my head to the right, and I saw my daughter and husband. They were smiling. Again, I heard the heart monitor and noisy respirator.

I looked at my son.

"Welcome back, Mom. You gave us a scare." I had never seen him so happy.

My mother was holding her bible to her chest. She and my sister were so happy, they were shouting, jumping up and down.

"Thank you, Jesus. Thank you, Lord," they cried again and again.

Everyone in the room was cheering and crying. I tried to laugh, because they were such a funny sight. It was like Sunday morning in a Sanctified Church. He was in the room, as well, because I felt His presence.

The doctor and nurse must have been waiting outside the door to console my family, but when they heard the cheering, they rushed in.

When they looked at me, Dr. Paslinski ordered everyone out of the room. The nurse took my blood pressure and pulse. I looked at her, and she was as white as the bed sheets.

"Her vitals signs are normal!" she told the doctor in stunned disbelief.

He removed the stereoscope from his ears slowly.

"I know. Nurse Hartman, I think you can turn off that respirator, she's breathing on her own." His voice was a dazed whisper.

"*Thank goodness, I'm tired of that noise.*"

He removed my tubes.

"What happened?" Nurse Hartman asked the doctor, she tried to regain her composure.

"I don't know, but do you believe in God?"

She nodded.

"Well, I think we have just witnessed a miracle."

"Don't you two know He delivers miracles everyday?" I thought.

The doctor took out his light and shined it in my eyes.

"Mrs. Mitchell, if you can hear me, blink your eyes twice."

I was careful to blink only twice.

He stuck a sharp pin into my finger.

"Ouch! That hurts!" So I blinked twice in a hurry.

As he was looking down my throat, I tugged on his jacket with my right hand.

Now I needed to ask some questions. I only knew the date, September 7, because of Robbi's birthday.

When I got his attention, I made a movement with my finger that I wanted to write.

Nurse Hartman handed me a pen and pad.

I scribble: "The crew? The passengers? Me?"

"The crew and passengers all survived, except for one passenger who died of a heart attack. He was ninety years old. The captain and the crew have been by to see you, as well as the fireman who pulled you from your jump seat. You were the only one in critical condition, because you were the only one ejected from the plane. The jump seat saved your life. It absorbed the impact when you hit the ground. Both you arms and legs are broken. You have a broken pelvis, a collapsed lung, and internal injuries. You have been in and out of consciousness for four days. We almost lost you." I had to smile at that.

"Your throat is sore from the trauma, but your voice will start to return in a few days." He paused. "You need rest and about a year of rehabilitation, because of your broken pelvis, but other than that, you will be fine. You may never fly again, but you will have plenty of time to relax and recuperate, and maybe, write a book," he said jokingly. "Nurse Hartman will give you something to help you sleep, I'll tell your family and friends you are resting. You are a popular lady. There are thirty flight attendants waiting in the visitors' lounge to see you. They have been holding prayer meetings and drinking coffee. We'll all be here when you wake up." He pulled the covers up to my chin and patted me on the shoulder. This, time he was smiling.

"I wanted to tell him to get some rest, and I know about those prayer meetings and Styrofoam coffee cups. Believe me, those thirty flight attendants waiting to see me, are drinking a little bit of everything out of those Styrofoam cups; except coffee." The thought made me smile, because those flight attendants had the doctors and nurses fooled.

Maybe, it was time for me to retire. Some junior flight attendant would be glad to hear that. It had been the greatest job. I had traveled the world and lived the life people only dreamed of, and enjoyed almost every minute. I had a wonderful family and good friends. I had no regrets. I would do it all again in a heartbeat. There was lots of work to be done, but in a different arena. I couldn't wait to get started. I drifted off to sleep with a smile on my face and happiness in my heart. It was *Joy*!

"God is good. God is great." What a joyful day it was.

Made in the USA
Las Vegas, NV
21 February 2022